WHITE OUT

WHITE OUT

Robert Marcum

BOOKCRAFT

SALT LAKE CITY, UTAH

Library of Congress Cataloging-in-Publication Data

Marcum, Robert.

  White out / Robert D. Marcum.

  p.cm.

ISBN 1-57345-652-7 (hb)

  1. Hunting guides--Wyoming--Fiction. 2. Sheriffs--Wyoming--Fiction. 3. Terrorism--Fiction. 4. Wyoming--Fiction. I. Title.

PS3563.A6368 W48 2000

813'.54--dc21   00-020933

Printed in the United States of America   18961-6644

10   9   8   7   6   5   4   3   2   1

To all those at Deseret Book and

Bookcraft, especially Sheri Dew and Cory Maxwell,

who have believed in me from the beginning.

Editors, designers, typesetters, et al, thanks for making

me look good. To those responsible for marketing,

sales, and advertising, thanks for enticing others to

look my way. And to Ron Millett, thanks for putting

so much talent under the same roof.

A C K N O W L E D G M E N T S

I wish to thank all those who have continued to write or telephone, to inquire about another book or to make kind remarks about those already written. It is gratifying to any author to have readers take such an interest in his work.

I also wish to thank the members of the Teton County Sheriff's Office for their willingness to let me interview them about their work. As is the case with all novelists, I have taken some license in depicting their very real world, but I hope their professionalism and dedication to law enforcement still come through.

Special thanks also to Leland Christensen, Howard Turner, and others for their descriptions of the backcountry in which White Out takes place. I have tried to portray the primitive beauty and wild character of the Thorofare, but anyone who is familiar with that area will quickly recognize my manipulation of the facts in order to tell the story. Such is the luxury enjoyed by writers of fiction, and I hope real cowboys and outfitters will forgive my inaccuracies in depicting their country and their way of life.

Lastly, I trust that my love for "the Hole" can be felt in these pages. Having enjoyed the grandeur of that rare place since I was a child, I am grateful to those who continue to work to preserve its pristine beauty. It is a task well worth their dedication and effort.

1

THE WILDERNESS NORTH AND EAST OF JACKSON, WYOMING

Over the years Raif Qanun had formed strong opinions about hunters from the big city. Some were rude know-it-alls, who had little understanding of the wilderness they hunted or the animals they were hunting. These ignorant clients often challenged their guide, insisting they had a better idea of how to get what they were after. They drank enough alcohol to wash out a beaver dam and most couldn't hit a moving target if it crossed the trail twenty feet in front of them. That kind of hunter seldom got an animal, unless Raif lassoed and tied it to tree, then painted a target on its forehead just below the antlers. Such hunters went away disappointed, usually angry, and never came back. For Raif it was no loss.

Others had good knowledge, mostly from books and maps out of their local library and from weekend hunting excursions to places closer to home. They wanted to know the rules, trusted that the guide would get them a shot if they cooperated, and followed instructions accordingly. They were up before dawn, used alcohol sparingly if at all, and, usually, went home satisfied—with a trophy waiting in line at the taxidermist and a freezer full of meat. They were often repeat customers.

Robert Stevens was on the high side of this group and Raif enjoyed guiding him. Over a dozen campfires spread over two fall hunts in the previous two years, Raif had learned that a young Bob Stevens had made a good income as a top-level manager for a large national printing company with headquarters in Minnesota. He had worked his way up from an assistant press operator to president, where he had served for six years before the patriarch/chairman of the board had died, leaving the business to his family. They had immediately sold it to an international conglomerate.

Bob hadn't let them do it without a fight. He knew the old man hadn't wanted to sell; it even said so in his will. But in the end, he had lost a bitter fight with a half dozen greedy kids and their spouses; and when the dust cleared, the judge had ruled in the family's favor, ruling that the old man hadn't known what he was doing when he made out the will. A day after the judgment was handed down, Bob had been fired.

Luckily there had been a golden parachute clause in his contract that gave Bob approximately ten percent of the sale price. He left the skirmish a wealthy man, but he was also angry.

Against his wife's wishes, Bob had used his new-found wealth to start a new company in the same community, hiring the best people he could away from his old company's new owners, then going after the accounts they had successfully served for many years. Bob had thought his contacts would all jump at the chance to thumb their noses at the new conglomerate, once they knew he was set up to become the competition. He was wrong.

He had struggled to survive during the first five years, incurring some significant debt, building a new building, and buying the latest in computerized presses and other equipment. To entice his former employees to come over to his company, he had to pay them the same wage they had been used to making—no easy thing for a struggling new entity. But, through hard work and by diversifying and going after new business, Bob's company had not only survived but eventually prospered. The number of accounts grew, work doubled, then tripled, and old clients began giving them business as well. At ten years they had succeeded. In another five years Bob had purchased half a dozen subsidiary companies and had been honored by *Fortune 500* magazine as one of the fastest growing and best managed young companies in America. Financially, Bob Stevens had it made.

But success was costly. He had lost his family. Forced to practically live at the factory in order to get things going again, he had seen his already failing marriage fall completely apart. Citing his neglect and irreconcilable differences, his wife, Madeleine, had taken a good deal of his money and their children and moved to New York.

She had never remarried, but his children, Andrew and Terri, had become virtual strangers to Bob. Andrew, the eldest, refused to have anything to do with his father. Before Bob had decided to go out on his own, his sixteen-year-old son had been a spoiled rich kid, but in the lean years during Bob's struggle to get his business going, the boy suddenly found himself unable to live after the manner of his rich friends and lost them along with his favored status. As near as Raif could tell, Andrew had been blaming his father ever since for a growing string of successive failures.

Terri Stevens, younger than her brother, had followed a different course. She had responded to the hard times by working to earn the money to put herself through college and law school and was making a career for herself now as an attorney based in New York. Along the way she had renewed the relationship with her father, and the two had become good friends.

Raif liked Bob Stevens. He was a "Class A" hunter in

Raif's book, and he loved the wilderness nearly as much as Raif did. So Raif welcomed a call from Stevens indicating he would like to come for another hunt. Trouble was, this time he wanted to bring his daughter.

It wasn't that Raif had anything against women hunters. He found most easy enough to get along with. You didn't get too many spoiled, city women on a hunt where clean linen was nonexistent and the john was found in a thicket. As a lot, women who hunted proved to be as tough as the men they accompanied. It was just that Raif Qanun wasn't comfortable around members of the opposite sex. Never had been. Their temperment, interests, habits, and their expectations often left him feeling uncertain how to relate to them. Yackity women were especially tedious to him, and some women seemed never to stop talking.

Simply put, women made him sweat, and that made him uncomfortable. An uncommon feeling for Raif because few things made him uncomfortable, even fewer made him sweat, the way Terri Stevens did!

Raif took his binoculars from the case hanging from his saddle horn and lifted them to his eyes. As though he sensed his rider's purpose, the gray, an Arabian Quarter Horse cross of considerable quality, stood so still he seemed to hold his breath. They were on a ridge above Enos Creek, and Raif scanned the meadow then the brushwood and for-est in the valley leading to Enos Lake itself. A small herd of elk grazed in the fall grass. Raif counted nine cows then moved his glasses left, looking for the bulls. One. Old. A large rack, but not a trophy. Two broken points, probably from fights with younger bulls. The animal looked too old and tough to be good meat, and unless some hunter got des-perate, this one might live through another season.

He scanned the meadow but found no other bulls. He handed the binoculars to Bob Stevens who looked things over, then shook his head. "Nothing we want," he said, matter-of-factly.

"Let me see," the young woman said, reaching for the binoculars. She was seated on Raif's best Quarter Horse, a bay by the name of Storm's End. She put the glasses to her eyes and stared at the herd below. "What's wrong with the big one?" She asked, her voice sounding a bit tired.

"Bad rack, and he's too old for good meat. Be like trying to eat leather," Stevens said.

"And we can't kill the others," she said. "They're cows?"

"You're catching on," Stevens answered his daughter with a smile.

Raif knew that Terri Stevens was twenty-seven, a graduate of some law school in the East, and was working for a prestigious firm as a criminal defense attorney in New York. She had proved her mettle in a recent case where she had successfully defended an accused murderer. It was a well-publicized case, one of the few national cases Raif had followed. It appeared to him as though the evidence of the man's guilt was conclusive and overwhelming, but Terri Stevens had succeeded in creating sufficient doubt to cause the jury to return a verdict of not guilty. In the midst of a public clamor, the man had walked. A week later he was caught in the act of another murder. This time there had been no doubt—same M.O., same area of the city, and another dead teenage girl.

Raif wondered how Ms. Stevens felt about getting a man like that off, then learning he had taken another life, but he hadn't broached the subject with her. Attorneys generally left him with a bad taste in his mouth. An inordinately large number of them had migrated to Jackson because of the ambience of the town and area. But there wasn't enough work to go around, and they were constantly underfoot, making police work more difficult by filing their endless actions—trying at all costs to get their clients off, make a name for themselves, and collect their excessive fees. Too many of them were cocky young bucks who, in

Raif's opinion, cared less about justice than about paying for their condos, cars, and other toys.

Raif had been surprised, but in the short time he had known her, Terri Stevens hadn't seemed like that type. Nevertheless, in the national arena, she had shown herself to be a hard-nosed attorney, willing to rip to shreds anyone who opposed her, right or wrong. That made Raif a little gun shy of her.

He hadn't met many women who could survive in a man's world, but the ones he did know, he admired, usually from a distance. His mother was like Terri, woman soft, but man hard at the same time. *Determined*, his father called it. Downright forceful is what it was, unwilling to let anyone, male or female, get in the way of what she thought needed doing. That was Terri Stevens, all right. In detail.

Terri's high cheekbones reminded Raif of Indian stock, but her light brown hair and blue eyes showed a fair amount of European heritage as well. When he first saw her step off the plane at the airport, he thought she might be using her makeup to cover some sort of imperfection, but over the last two days she had given the stuff up, and he'd had to revise his thinking. Her olive skin tanned up well, and her eyes were set off nicely by her naturally long lashes. He decided, too, that her smallish nose and well-formed mouth needed no "touchin' up" to be admired.

He glanced at Terri out of the corner of his eye. He wasn't all that good at gauging such things, and he wondered at about five-feet-six-inches, how much she weighed. She was well-proportioned, with an athletic way of moving, and in the little time they had spent together during this hunt, she had shown herself to be fit and energetic. It was apparent she kept in shape, probably, Raif assumed, as a member of some expensive health club where she drank carrot juice, used a treadmill two hours a day, and lifted weights to keep toned. He supposed that was why riding, a challenge for most men, had been easy for her. If she had been apprehensive about being around horses, she'd hid it well—no small thing when when you're on a horse that will take as much leeway as you'll allow and outweighs you by several hundred pounds. From the moment her shapely backside hit the saddle, Terri had taken nothing from Storm and had let the spirited Quarter Horse know who was boss.

Raif had decided that Storm had been just another challenge for Terri, and it was obvious that Terri Stevens thrived on challenges—on beating the odds. Maybe, he thought, that is why she had defended a murderer, even if the scumbag did have guilt stamped all over his sadistic face.

Terri's knowledge of weapons, or better said, the lack of it, had been the bigger concern for Raif, but then it was always his biggest concern with any hunter. Guns weren't toys. There was no calling back a bullet, even if set off by accident. Every year somebody had to be flown out of these mountains by chopper because of carelessness with rifles designed to bring down a lot bigger game than man. Some of those flights carried men dead as dead could get, and there was nothing short of a resurrection that would change things. All because they didn't respect their weapons and what they could do.

Raif had to admit though, that in the hours of preparation at the Triangle X Ranch, Terri had proven an able, smart student. She handled the rifle with confidence but care, and she quickly learned to shoot straight. She might not kill an elk at three hundred yards, but unlike some hunters, she could make about any normal shot at less distance than that.

He supposed some of her savvy came from living in a sort of wilderness of her own—one made up of glass towers and concrete trails. He knew she carried a weapon there, a small revolver. Her reason was simple. Here she might be the hunter, but in the jungle of New York City she could be the hunted, and her handgun was a defense against predators almost as dangerous as a grizzly gone crazy, maybe more so. Actually, having read *The New York Times* on occasion, Raif wondered why she didn't carry a bigger weapon.

Terri saw something on the far right side of her field of vision and adjusted the binoculars slightly in that direction. "What about that one?" She lowered the binoculars and pointed at the ridge that bordered the farside of the meadow. Raif squinted and saw the animal, his head down as he labored up a steep trail and out of the valley. He took the binoculars for a closer look. The bull stopped to catch its breath and turned its head in their direction. He seemed to be looking right at them. Though only a five-point rack, it was one of the best Raif had seen that year. Probably a four- or five-year-old with good enough meat.

"You have a good eye, Miss Stevens. He's what we're after," Raif said.

"How far away?" Bob Stevens asked.

"Six, seven hundred yards. Too far for a shot." The bull seemed to sense some danger and trotted stiffly across the top of the narrow ridge, his big rack of antlers held in a belligerent pose above his proud head. Then he disappeared over the far side. Raif felt the tingle of seeing something so majestic in the wild. It was that tingle that made being in these hills such an irresistable lure for him.

"Any chance of catching up, cutting him off?" There was an excitement in Terri's voice that startled her. The call of the wild? Thrill of the hunt? Her father had tried to explain it on the flight from Chicago to Salt Lake City, and they had talked more of it the first night at the Triangle X Ranch. She had not understood. She had no desire to kill such a beautiful animal, she had told him. Hunter's fever would never catch hold of her.

And yet here it was, at high pitch, and she was just as vulnerable to the excitement as anyone could be.

Raif lowered the binoculars, thinking. Then he said, "He's headed into a valley that opens into the northeast end of Enos Lake. The other end of the valley is steep, covered with heavy timber and brushwood. Looks impossible to cross over that end, but there is a way, a trail even few guides know about."

"You're thinking he's headed that way?" Bob Stevens questioned.

Raif nodded. "That one was wary, smart. I think he knew we were here, so he isn't going to leave himself out in the open."

"But how could he know? He is just. . . ." Terri started to ask.

"Instinct, daughter," Bob Stevens responded. "Similar to what you feel when you sense some young buck staring at you in one of those crowded affairs you attend to raise money for some idiot congressman."

Bob and Terri Stevens were always jabbing at each other, usually in fun, unless the subject was Terri's mother. Then the air turned to ice, and Raif dismissed himself if the subject lingered. It was something he figured they had to work out without him being around to hinder the process. They seemed to have done pretty well. The only icy chill in the air over the last two days had come from the weather.

"Tough country, maybe we should stay clear," Stevens said.

"We can cut him off before he gets into the worst of it," Raif said evenly and without emotion. It was their decision, but they needed to know it could be done.

Stevens seemed to be hesitating. It surprised Raif until he reminded himself of Terri's inexperience.

"Terri isn't. . . ."

"I can handle it, Dad." She looked at Raif, waiting.

"That country is rough, daughter. Real rough."

"Your call, Bob," Raif said. He could see Terri wasn't happy about his circumventing her, but Bob paid the bills; it was his hunt and his responsibility. She'd just have to understand that.

Bob looked at his daughter whose eyes told him to quit treating her like a child. "You had better get moving then," Bob said.

Raif had two packhorses. He handed the lead rope to Bob. "I'll take care of her, you bring the packs along. Too many grizzlies to leave them alone, and we'll never catch that bull if I have to drag them with us," he said.

Bob nodded, wrapping the rope around his gloved hand. "Understood. Get her there. I'll follow your trail."

Raif wouldn't have trusted his animals to any other easterner. They would likely have ended up at the bottom of some ravine or lost in the wilderness because of poor handling. But he knew Bob Stevens could manage the two packhorses without incident. He had done it before.

Raif turned to Terri and asked, "You sure you wanna do this?"

She seemed flushed, a little frightened, and excited all at the same time. Raif had seen the look before. He remembered the feelings of his own first hunt—but he wanted her in it, head as well as adrenaline—because you decided a lot of things when deciding to kill something.

She nodded her head. "Yes."

"It's a slim chance, but we might get a shot at him on the next ridge over. We'll have to move fast but carefully, skirt the area, keep from scaring him another direction. It's heavy timber, steep climbs, but nothing we can't handle."

She licked dry lips, but her face was hard set in the shade of her gray felt Stetson.

"Let your mount have rein. He'll follow my Arabian. And remember what I told you back at the ranch when you were first gettin' used to riding him. Don't fight him, or he'll throw you." He turned his gray Arabian and was moving at a gallop before she could answer. Her glance at her father revealed fear mingled with an excitement she didn't completely understand.

"Just stay close to Raif. He's the best." He slapped his

rein ends on the Quarter Horse's haunches, and it launched itself after the gray, nostrils flaring with the fever of catching up. She ducked the limbs of trees, keeping low, letting the gelding take its own way, partly because that's what Raif had told her to do and partly because she simply didn't have a choice or the skills to do anything else.

Raif pushed his gray through thick timber, man and horse picking their way over fallen logs and around thick sections of trees at a speed and movement that reminded Terri of taxis at rush hour. Suddenly Raif veered left and headed down an incline that made Terri involuntarily hold her breath. There was no way she'd make it! She pulled back on the reins, trying to slow him, but the big Quarter Horse just shook its head and kept running. As he plunged down the slope, the gelding's head lunged forward, demanding slack in the reins and leaving only the tips in Terri's hands as they veered after the gray.

Suddenly, Terri lost her balance and grabbed the horn, then the gelding's mane, as the powerful animal bounded and slid down the hill. Pushing against the saddle horn, Terri exerted all her strength to shove herself back in the saddle. She knew that if she fell now, she'd either be trampled by the gelding's hind legs or begin an unstoppable roll to the bottom of the narrow ravine, ending up bruised and bleeding in the jumble of dead and fallen trees below her.

Then the trail flattened out. Raif, now only fifty feet ahead, apparently unsatisfied with the ease of it, spurred his Arabian to the left, away from the trail and up an incline steep enough to make the gray stretch its stride to the very limits. Terri's instincts all screamed to get off, but it was too late. The bay gelding planted its hooves in the soft ground, and grunting with the effort, bounded in great leaps up the steep incline, while Terri grimly held on.

She had gone once to a rodeo in Madison Square Garden and had marveled at the skill of the bareback bronc riders. Lying almost horizontally on their backs, they had somehow been able to cling to their perch as the horse bucked and kicked its way wildly across the arena. She had gone away shaking her head in disbelief, unable to imagine how anyone could stay balanced during such a ride, let alone keep their free hand flailing the air while they raked the horse with their spurs. She'd also wondered why anyone in their right mind would subject themselves to such punishment.

Now, here she was in much the same position. The difference was that the gelding was lurching up a mountain at a fifty percent incline and she was lying on *her* back, dangling precariously not only over the horse's rump but the thin air of a deep canyon. She clung to the saddle horn, both gloved hands gripping it tightly, the reins caught between rigid fingers, and her lips churning out a prayer.

The gelding nearly pitched Terri from the saddle as it bolted the last ten yards up the slope and over the crest of the hill, onto solid, relatively flat ground. Regaining a solid seat in the saddle, she adjusted her iron grip on the reins as the bay raced to catch up with Raif and the gray Arabian. She found that after the mountainside, running on the fairly level ridge was a piece of cake. They rode in that fashion for half a mile before Raif spotted the trail he wanted and turned the Arabian downhill again. Terri had lost all sense of direction by now and only hoped they'd be where they were going soon or she *was* going to get off, regardless of whether the horse stopped to allow it or not!

After crossing the saddleback and climbing a third ridge through thin timber, her gelding came into the open, broached the top of the ridge, and found flat ground. Terri saw the gray standing fifty feet ahead next to some trees, reins hanging to the ground. Raif had dismounted and was standing near the edge of a deep ravine using the binoculars. She pulled on the reins of the bay, more as show than purpose. The gelding had already made up his mind to stop and quickly did so, nearly throwing Terri over its head and then bouncing her hard in the saddle. The strenous ride and the tension she had been under left Terri feeling weak and limp. Sliding from the saddle, she clung for a moment to the horn for fear she'd collapse onto the hard ground beneath her feet. Placing her head against the heaving sides of the horse, she tried to catch her breath and will some strength into her trembling arms and legs.

"Dear God, thank you," she whispered, grateful for life and no broken bones. Inhaling deeply, she turned and took a shaky step toward Raif. Raif Qanun would never know she hadn't handled everything in stride. It just wasn't in her nature.

"Did we miss him?" she asked, amazed that she was able to feign composure while her heart was thumping so hard against the inside of her rib cage.

Keeping his eyes on the far ridge, Raif handed her the binoculars and pointed where she should look. Terri took the instrument, willing her arms to hold them to her eyes. She was shaking and had difficulty holding the glasses steady. "I don't see him," she said.

"You won't, not yet. We made good time. If he didn't go toward the lake, he'll come through those woods on that far ridge. See the opening, the space where the wind has broken off the trees?"

Terri peered through the binoculars. A stand of trees resembling jagged-topped telephone poles came into view. "Yes, I see it."

"He'll have to pass through there. That's when you'll get your shot."

She lowered the binoculars. "From here?"

Raif had already started back to the horses. She judged the distance. Two hundred yards. Little chance. She had practiced at the Triangle X firing range. At one hundred yards she had hit the target six out of a dozen times. At two hundred, she had only hit it twice. And they were LARGE targets. She turned to go back to the horses to set things straight, but Raif was already back with her rifle.

"I can't. We have to get closer," she said, adamantly.

Raif shook his head in the negative. "The wind is at our backs. He'll catch our scent. We may be too close now. This is it. If you get him, you get him. If you don't—"

"Plenty of other chances," she finished for him. She had heard it more than once over the last few days.

He gave a smile she had seldom seen. "Nope. We'll be outa here tomorrow morning. But . . . there's always next year."

She glanced at him a bit surprised. She felt he had pretty well ignored her the entire trip; she had the impression he didn't much like women or at least her. Being ignored by him had been a bit of a slam to her ego. Now he was talking about a return engagement?

She grabbed the rifle from Raif, and he gave her a surprised sidelong glance. "Sorry. Just nervous," she said, flashing a repentant smile.

Looking across the canyon she tried to focus on the wind-shorn trees Raif had pointed out. She had been given two previous shots, both at shorter range, and had missed both times. Apparently Raif had a short memory, or untold confidence in the principle of averages.

Still feeling the effects of her wild ride, she couldn't remember her rifle feeling that heavy. Palming the bolt she struggled for a moment to inject a shell into the chamber and regretted her clumsiness. It was a .338 with a 6X scope and shortened stock, purchased in Jackson the afternoon of her arrival. Her father and Raif had helped her sight it in and get comfortable with it. No small thing for a woman who had never carried a weapon that couldn't fit in the palm of one's hand.

"Lie down. Get comfortable. Sight in on one of those dead trees."

Terri did as she was told, placing herself prone on the

brittle, snow crusted, wild grass. She could smell dirt and pine needles under her, the mold of a rotting log a few inches to her right, and her own nervous sweat. Ignoring them, she looked through her scope, concentrating on the crosshairs. She adjusted the scope's focus slightly and sharpened the sight on one of the larger trees where she found an easily identifiable knot about five feet from the bottom.

Raif knelt beside her. "How does it look?"

"Close. Like the tree is going to plug the end of my gun."

Raif scanned the trees along the ridge and side of the mountain. The elk should be coming. If it came this direction at all.

"Rest a minute," Raif said. She rested the rifle barrel on a fallen tree trunk in front of her and wiggled her body a bit to get more comfortable on the hard ground. After a few seconds Raif told her to find the same tree, same spot, if she could and that she needed to do it in seconds. Anxious, Terri lifted the rifle, scanned, and found a tree. Wrong one. Too big. Looked again. Found another. That was it. Found the knot. Put the crosshairs in the center of it. "Got it."

"Not bad. Relax." He knew it would be different if the animal did come. Getting a scope lens the size of a half dollar on a moving target was never easy, then adjusting for distance, windage, and angle would make the shot even more difficult. Finally, there was the decision to kill. For some that was the most difficult of all.

She got to her knees and propped the rifle against the dead tree trunk, squinting at the place she had just seen in the scope. It looked so far away—too far to pick out which tree she had sighted in on. She only shook her head, wondering how on earth she'd ever pull it off.

Seating himself on a fallen tree trunk, Raif absent-mindedly cleared a thin layer of snow for her about a foot and a half to the right of him. Terri appreciated the gesture and took the offered spot. For a full minute they said nothing, and Terri wondered why it didn't bother her. Silence always made her uncomfortable when she was around men. It was her opinion that most men used silence as a subtle weapon in the power struggle that went on in the workplace. There, she refused to let it happen. Here, she felt no need, no threat. But then, why should there be? The environment was completely different; Raif was no macho attorney trying to put the little lady with a business suit in her place. There was no competition between them at all. At least not that kind of competition.

They were seated in the shadow of several large trees, but their view of the valley and mountains in front of them was open and expansive. She had been awed by the panoramas they had seen over the last few days—the late fall sunsets that dazzled with a thousand colors; the mountains, so wild and empty, and yet so beautiful. She had never breathed air so clean and fresh nor felt such mind-clearing silence in which to think.

"It's beautiful," she said, almost to herself.

Raif nodded, seeing what she saw, but also seeing something else. His eyes were focused on the distant gray sky to the south, his nostrils attuned to the smell of coming snow and cold. All of nature's signs said that winter would come early and stay late this year, and from the look and feel he was getting, it would begin in earnest today.

He had felt beginnings of it four days ago while they were coming in, even though it had been a cloudless fall day that didn't even warrant a jacket. Because of it, he had decided not to take them as deeply into the backcountry as he otherwise might. When the first snow, though less than two inches, had hit last night, he decided it was time to pack it in and go home.

"I hate to leave," Terri said.

Raif nodded again. "Beautiful, but deadly. Storms have been known to dump four feet of snow up here in a single twenty-four-hour period. We could call in a chopper to get us out, but the animals would be stuck. Better if we don't take chances."

Terri only nodded as she continued to look at the scene before her. There were still a few gold, yellow, and red leaves hanging on some of the trees and scrub brush. It looked so quiet and tranquil, she found it hard to believe they could be threatened by a storm of the proportions Raif had described.

As the thought passed through her mind, a breeze blew up the valley that gave her a chill, causing a shudder down her backbone. It was as though mother nature were bearing testimony; warning them to beware of making careless judgments in her domain.

In the distance, to the west, a large mountain dominated the landscape. A bank of heavy, dark clouds was building up behind it.

"What mountain is that?" she asked, pointing.

"Soda Mountain." His eyes were glued to the ridge in front of them.

She watched him. She had never met a man quite so intense or focused. He wore his light brown hair cut short, though she had hardly seen it. Raif wore his dark gray, well-shaped Stetson continually. It suited him. She had decided that some men could wear a hat—others couldn't. Her dad wore a similar hat, but it was too new and fit his head somewhat unnaturally. Raif's hat, on the other hand, sat his head easily, complementing the shape of his tanned face and head. His eyes were a nearly sky blue, clear and alert, with a natural glint she had found intriguing. When he was focused they seemed to see right through what he was looking at. Though he appeared thin, there was a lean muscularity about him that held a power unlike most men she knew. She had seen it in the effortless way he handled cantankerous horses and threw hundred pound pack boxes in place every morning and removed them again every night.

In the four days they had been together, she had taken increasing comfort in his ability to take charge of a situation and come to admire his skills as an outdoorsman.

Terri guessed Raif's height to be six feet, maybe a little less, but his lean body made him look taller. Another thing she had noticed about him was that he wasted no movement and no words. Her mother would have thought of him as hard and uncommunicative, while she imagined Ted, the master of the cliché, would describe Raif as "the strong, silent type."

Ted Hancock. Ted's proposal of marriage hadn't been unexpected, nor unwelcome, but when it occurred she found herself confused and unsure. It represented a glitch in her otherwise well-organized and fully planned life—a complication that for some reason made her feel penned in. His offer of marriage had been beautifully orchestrated— dinner at a fabulous restaurant, a carriage ride, and a formal proposal made on bended knee while she sat on a bench under a full moon in Central Park. Even so, it hadn't exactly overwhelmed her. Not feeling the emotion she had imagined such an experience would bring, she hadn't immediately responded. That was the major reason she had agreed to come on this hunt. She needed to get away, to think.

Not that marrying Ted would be a hard thing. They would settle down under the comfortable umbrella of two substantial incomes. And Ted was handsome, personable, a successful broker for the Dean Witter brokerage firm. Sharing many of the same friends, they would be compatible socially, and their goals were similar. They also belonged to the same church. Ted was a member of the New York, New York Stake high council, a polished speaker, and a man of impeccable reputation. In Church circles, Ted had no shortage of female admirers, and when he had begun dating Terri, she had felt the scorn of more than a few young women in the stake. Yes, considering his many

attributes, it was difficult to fault Ted Hancock as a potential marriage partner, but still . . .

She had come to these mountains to think about it but
was tired of thinking about it! Even an abundance of clear
mountain air and gallons of cold spring water hadn't helped
her decide, and prayer hadn't led her any closer to knowing
what to do. At least, not yet. But then she hadn't expected
that kind of answer—just some sort of comfort! Anything
that would help settle her unsettled feelings.

She supposed that part of the problem was her newness
to things that had to do with with prayer and spiritual
promptings. Though she had been born into the Church,
her activity had really begun only two years before. Her
mother wasn't a member, and her father had been only
active enough to get his children blessed, allow them some
experience with Primary, then have them baptized. After
that Terri and Andrew had pretty much been on their own
when it came to any church involvement, and both had
elected to leave it alone, preferring to spend weekends at
their parents' country club, playing golf or tennis or loung-
ing by the pool.

During college she had slipped farther away, if that were
possible, and when her career took off, religion was a long
way from being even a remote part of her life. Then she had
met Ted.

It was part of the reason she felt . . . what . . . obligated?
No, she liked Ted. A lot. He had brought her back, had
shown her what she had been missing all her life, helped
her see the reason she had never really felt completely
whole. Ted had been her guide in a religious world, which,
had he not been there, would have been difficult to break
into. Because of his tutoring Terri had found a world full of
contentment she had never dreamed possible. She owed
him a great debt.

And maybe that was the problem.

The wind was picking up, the sky getting darker. Terri

pulled her collar up and stamped her feet lightly against the cold.

She had asked Ben Munson, Raif's boss at the guide service, about Raif. Ben told her that Raif was thirty-one and had never married. She wondered why, but hadn't asked Ben or anyone else, not even her father. She wondered if Raif had avoided getting married because of some hang-ups. He was pleasant enough, but not entirely easy to read. Maybe he just hadn't gotten around to it. She understood that. Getting married hadn't been a high priority for her, either. But the gospel had changed more than what she did on weekends; it had changed her entire perspective on life. Getting married seemed more important to her now— at least theoretically.

Her father had told her that Raif was an investigator for the Teton County Sheriff's Office, had started out as a patrolman when he was twenty-two, then became an investigator at twenty-eight. He had never been to college. Maybe that was what intrigued her about him. He was just the opposite of the mostly Ivy League types with whom she had dealt. With the exception of Ted, Terri hadn't found one yet who wasn't stiff, rigid, and caught up completely in their world of high finance or high fees. Like mass-produced automatons, they were running a frantic race, scooping up all the money and prestige they could before turning thirty, playing the game and walking over the top of anyone who got in their way. Big egos and big problems, for any relationship, especially one that included living under the same roof.

"Your last name. The spelling is a little unusual."

He smiled. "My father's people came from the Middle East. It's the Arabic form of a Persian name," he said.

"And your first name. Is it also Arabic?"

Raif nodded, "A short version of Raifim." He paused, then said, "My father's ancestors, at least some of them, came to this country in the early 1900s."

"You don't look Persian, or Arabic. Aren't they dark skinned, or—"

"Not all of them, but the Qanuns aren't my biological parents. They gave me a home when my birth mother turned me over to the state because of her alcoholism. My biological father had deserted us." He shrugged. "I was a baby when they got me. The Qanuns are the only parents I've known, and I've always felt like their own flesh."

"The area they used to call Persia is huge, isn't it? Is there a particular nationality the Qanuns claim?"

"My mother has some Arabian blood, and her family are American Islamic, but several generations back, an Irishman married into the family. Unfortunately, it didn't work out, but children were born to the union and the mix is there. Dad is Persian. Most people today would call him Iranian."

"Where did your parents meet?"

"Dad's father was a horse breeder, and his father before him, in Persia. When Great-grandfather immigrated, he brought his trade and the best purebred stock he could find. Most people call them Arabians, but they are raised in many areas. From that stock our family has bred and cross-bred horses. Show horses of great beauty mostly, but some very good thoroughbreds as well. Racing stock. My mother's family did the same in Kentucky. She was the only child and worked side-by-side with her father, breeding, training, and taking care of the animals. They met when Dad delivered a horse to her father's paddock, then stayed to help the animal make the transition between trainers. They hit it off, and, after traditional ceremonies had taken place, she returned home with him."

"Was Jackson home then?"

He shook his head. "Tennessee. They came to Jackson in 1966. Dad brought the whole operation here after his father and mother died."

"Why Jackson?"

"Same reason a lot of folks move here. They came this way on vacation, fell in love with it, and ended up moving here."

"It doesn't seem like the right place to raise thorough-breds. The long winters. . . ."

"We have an indoor training arena, but Dad doesn't raise thoroughbreds much anymore. Now we cross Arabians with Quarter Horses that have Morgan blood in them. The gray is one of those. Gives him both quickness and endurance as well as strength. A lot of Dad's stock ends up in rodeo arenas as roping horses or on the Quarter Horse racing circuit. Dad also trains horses from around the world for a variety of purposes, from jumping to saddle riding. He makes an above average income doing what he loves. Best of all worlds."

Terri had noticed the gray was a breed apart from the others. He never seemed to get winded, and when it came to climbing and a long day on the trail, he was head and shoulders above her Storm. They were about even in the woods, both agile, with uncanny instinct, but the gray was something special.

"Did your parents have any other children?" she asked.

"Three. A son and two daughters. One sister lives in Laramie, the other on a small ranch over by Pocatello, in Idaho."

"And your brother?"

"He's dead." There was a long pause. "Husayn, we called him 'Hussa,' felt the need to return to his roots in Persia, Iran. He left more than twelve years ago."

"At the end of the Khomeini era."

Raif nodded while still focusing on the mountain, searching, waiting for any motion that might give away the presence of the elk. "Hussa got caught up in the religion and politics of Persia. First it was history, then modern day issues in Iran, where Persia had once ruled the world. Then he started wearing the traditional clothes, the *kavuk*—the head turban—even the *busht*—a sleeveless garment like a long shirt. He was a senior in High School at the time, and his new look got us both into a lot of fights.

"After that he began demanding that we all live the traditional way—that we do it with exactness, and that we defend the Iranian position because they were our people. He went nuts. It was a tough time for everyone in the family, but any opposition just made him more and more rebellious and militant. Then, one day Dad came home to find his two-place horse trailer missing, along with one of his finest stallions. Hussa had stolen them. By the time we found them, Hussa was gone. He had sold the stallion for twenty thousand dollars, a tenth of its worth, and had bought a plane ticket to Iran." He paused.

"We never heard from him again. Nothing. No letters, no calls. It was like he had dropped off the face of the earth. Mom and Dad wrote letter after letter—to the government, to anyone who might help them find out what had happened to him or who could say if he even arrived there. There was no response for five years, then a letter came saying they had no record of a Husayn Qanun but chances were good that if he had gone to that country, he might have joined the Army under some other name and been killed in the war with Iraq." Raif paused. "I figure he never got past Customs. Americans were targets in those days. He either landed in jail and died there, or he was executed, probably as a spy. If the Iranian government knew anything about it, they weren't about to admit it."

"That must have been horrible for your parents." She knew it sounded trite even though she meant it.

"Nearly killed them. I suppose it would have been easier if there had been a body, a burial—some sort of closure. But there wasn't and never will be."

There was a cold edge to his voice, and Terri could tell it had been rough for Raif as well. "Were you close?"

"There wasn't that much difference in our ages. We did

a lot together. Used to come up here every fall with Dad or a good friend who knows these hills like he owns 'em. Hunt, camp, ride. We knew every trail like the lines in the palm of our hands." He paused. "Yeah, we were close."

"Your father and mother blame themselves, I suppose."

"Some, but it wasn't their fault. We found letters from a man Hussa had corresponded with. An Iranian and distant cousin of my father, who Hussa had written to. The letters were fiery and appealed to Hussa's pride and youthfulness, declaring Khomeini the embodiment of Mohammad and a man every true Muslim must follow if he hopes to gain entrance into paradise. I have never seen my father so angry!"

Raif hesitated, getting control, before going on. It was apparent to Terri that Raif's father wasn't the only one who had been angered.

"My parents profess Islam. They are dedicated to its precepts and to many of its spiritual leaders. But men such as Khomeini and those who run the present Iranian regime, who use religion to gain power, take lives, and to control people . . . well, if hell exists, it will be full of such men."

They sat in silence, watching the ridge. Still nothing. It seemed clear to Terri that the animal had gone another way.

"Why did you decide to be a cowboy?" she asked, changing the subject and smiling.

He glanced over at her, returned the smile, then focused on the ridge again. "There are no real cowboys anymore, just a lot of pickup drivin' wanna-be's." He shrugged. "Me, I love the wilderness, horses, and saddle leather. They just sorta come together out here." He removed his hat and stared at it. "This is just functional gear that goes with it all I suppose; so are spurs, sidearms, durable boots, and bandanas for catching sweat." He put the hat back in place. "A cowboy punches cows. Only thing I punch is rude easterners."

Terri laughed.

Raif smiled. "Present company excluded."

Suddenly he sat up straighter and motioned with his hand to be quiet. He was focused on the distant ridge and the stand of trees with jagged tops.

"The bull is getting close, get ready," he said.

She looked, didn't see anything. Listened, heard only the wind in the trees. "How—?"

"Trust me. Get ready."

Laying prone, the rifle in her hands, Terri was as ready as any amateur could be.

"He's in the trees, about a hundred feet from the top of the ridge." Raif spoke so quietly his voice was barely audible to Terri. There was a long pause that seemed like forever.

"He isn't moving. I think he senses our presence," Raif said.

"What do we—?"

"He'll either go back or he'll . . . wait! There! He's coming out," he whispered.

She looked in the direction Raif seemed to be staring. Nothing.

"Below the outcrop of boulders. Down the side of the ridge. See the path that goes below them? At the head of the path . . . in the trees."

Terri saw the outcrop, but no path. But then a path to Raif Qanun was not necessarily a path to anyone else. Their harrowing ride to this spot was evidence of that! She squinted again. There was a difference. Yes, a path of sorts, a depression here and there that seemed to make a line across the side of the slope. She let her eyes follow it back toward the trees. She didn't see the bull at first. He was in the shadows. Then the branches of a tree seemed to move. His rack! He was standing, sniffing the air, peering out into the light of day. She adjusted her rifle on its resting place on the rotting log in front of her and squinted through the scope. She remembered the painful lesson she had learned while sighting in her gun—not to put her eye against the scope while firing. Slowly she moved the weapon . . .

searching . . . searching. There he was! She could see him now, his head nearly filling the scope!

In spite of her intention to feel otherwise, she felt a surge of excitement so sharp it felt almost like fear. Her heart was suddenly racing, and in spite of the cold, her hands were sweating. This wasn't her. Hunting. Killing. She had never killed anything in her life. Even spiders were pardoned their intrusions, removed with a hankie, and sent on their way out of doors. Why was this different for her?

She placed the center of the crosshairs on a spot just behind the animal's foreleg. He seemed leery, nervous. She was sweating, and the salty liquid ran down her forehead and into the open eye at the scope. She blinked it away.

"Now or never, Terri. He's made a decision," Raif said evenly.

Terri concentrated, thinking of what she had been told. Hold still, take a deep breath, squeeze the trigger. She did. Nothing happened.

"Safety." Raif said evenly, with patience.

She took her eye away from the scope to find the safety! Flipped it down.

"He's out of trees," Raif said. "Now or never, Terri."

Terri fumbled to get the rifle back in place, find the bull in her sight. He *was* moving! Quickly! His strong legs were churning up the snow and soil as he climbed the steep slope. She couldn't keep the rifle on him! There . . . His rack! Lower! His head and shoulders!

She fired! The gun recoiled against her shoulder, bruising it. She didn't notice. She got to her knees, looking down. The elk was jumping, leaping, down the mountainside! She had missed! She raised the gun again, tried to get him in the scope! Couldn't! A blur of brown movement . . .

Something moved the barrel. She looked to find Raif's hand on it, pushing it down.

"What are you doing!" she shouted.

"You got him. Look."

She scanned the ravine, saw the elk. It was rolling now, head over hoof. Rolling down into the ravine, into the trees. Then it stopped, its large frame coming to rest against a low stand of brushwood in the shadow of some pine trees. It didn't move.

"Nice shot, Terri. A good two hundred yards and a moving target," Raif said, genuinely pleased. He turned and moved to the horses, where he removed the saddlebags from the gray Arabian before returning to find Terri still staring at the carcass in the valley below. Raif could tell she didn't know how she felt. This was the reason it always had to be the hunter's choice.

He waited. It was a long moment before she spoke.

"I wish I hadn't done it."

"Then don't do it again." He said it matter-of-factly.

She looked at him. "Is the answer that easy for you?"

He shrugged. "For me, yes, it's that easy." He waited, knowing she'd speak her mind when she worked it through a little farther.

"It's like killing the family dog."

"You don't eat the family dog. At least most people don't."

"I don't eat wild game, either."

"Because you eat filet mignon. Either way, something dies to feed you—even if you're a vegetarian. If it helps, think of the cow you just saved by getting yourself a year's supply of elk meat, which, by the way, is a lot tastier than beef."

Raif flipped his saddlebags over his shoulder, then took her .338. "C'mon, we've got work to do. When you kill your own meat, the corner butcher doesn't drag it off the mountain for you, skin it, and wrap it in cellophane."

He started down the side of the ravine. She followed.

The slope was steep and filled with loose shale—hazardous stuff that could topple a man and send him reeling for a hundred yards and break his neck.

With that thought he slipped, nearly fell, got his feet under him, then reached back to take her hand to help her past the same loose shale. At first she ignored his hand, but, slipping herself, she grabbed onto it.

It was tough going, and they were sweating. Raif stopped to give Terri a breather while scanning the ridge line behind them, looking for Bob and the packhorses. Nothing. Stevens should have arrived by now. It wasn't that far.

They started again, but separate. It took them nearly ten minutes to get within twenty feet of the bull elk. At that point Raif motioned for Terri to hold up while he cautiously approached the animal, to make sure he was dead. One shake of that huge rack could leave a man bloodied. Certain there was no life left, he signaled she could come ahead, then laid her rifle down, removed the saddlebags from his shoulder, and began unlacing the ties on the storm flaps. Inside were all the instruments he would need for gutting the animal and preparing the carcass for removal. He thought about taking a photo, then changed his mind. At this point he didn't think she was much interested in having a portrait to hang over her fireplace. In a way, that pleased him. Although trophies were important for some people, they never had been for him.

He removed the scabbard that held his skinning knife from the saddlebags, then a whetstone. Sitting on the ground, Raif ran the knife back and forth across the stone.

"The rack can be sold. The Chinese grind it into dust and use it as a potion for all kinds of disorders including impotence. The hide will make moccasin slippers, belts, even hats. We use it for making leather straps for pack-saddles and a dozen other things around the ranch. Some are sold to make boots of soft, pliable, and very comfortable leather. The only parts that are of no value are the guts, the hooves, and the skull. But the Indians used to make use of those, too." He put the whetstone away. "Those who make the boots and moccasins make a decent living while giving us something really comfortable and durable to wear. The antlers might actually have healing properties, even if they're only psychological. There's enough meat here to feed a family of four for nearly a year. The—"

"I get the point," Terri said, irritated. "But most of today's hunters don't take the time to sell the hide, nor the antlers, and prefer beef to elk. The meat probably just gets old and is thrown out. They're more interested in the trophy."

"I can't help their bad taste in food, and I don't determine what they do with an animal once they shoot it, but we usually buy the hide from them if they don't want it. Same for the meat. We sell them or use them."

"And they mount the head and rack on their cherry wood paneling as a conversation piece. I've seen Dad's. I know," she said stiffly.

"Yeah, everybody gets something," he said evenly. He walked toward the bull. "Even if it's only a good story."

There were a few minutes of silent tension between them as he prepared for gutting the animal and packing it out of the steep ravine—a part of the job he wasn't looking forward to. Each quarter was going to weigh a good two hundred pounds, and it wouldn't be easy carting it to the top of the hill. But there was no other choice. He wasn't about to bring the pack animals down through that loose shale. They'd lose their footing for sure. Each packhorse carried over a hundred pounds of provisions, feed oats, blankets, and equipment.

He took a deep breath. "I'm glad it all bothers you, Terri. I've seen too many who act like idiots around a kill. Dancing, celebrating, treating the carcass with disrespect. It's true enough that some of them would leave the meat behind to rot if it weren't against the law. I disagree with those kind, and men in my business do everything they can to see that things are done properly and that nothing goes to waste. But just because some people don't have the respect for life they should, that doesn't make hunting wrong or evil."

He started rolling his shirt sleeves up, the large skinning knife in one hand. "I'm going to gut this one. If you don't like killing them, you'll for sure like this even less. You might want to find something else to occupy you for about half an hour."

She gave a tired smile. "Thanks. I need to visit Mother Nature. I'll. . . ." she pointed at the woods. "I'll just go and do that now." She turned and disappeared in the trees and tall brushwood.

Raif cut the cape properly and removed the elk's head, then sliced open the animal's underbelly and gutted it. As he began quartering the animal, Terri appeared from the shadows. Her face was pale, and she stared at him with wide eyes and her mouth hanging open. It was a look of shock he had often seen on the faces of survivors at the scene of a highway accident.

He straightened from his work, blood smeared on his arms and hands. He pulled the cloth he had stuck in his back pocket and attempted to wipe himself off as he stepped toward her.

"What's wrong? You look like you've just buried the family pet," he said, half smiling.

She turned, pointing down the hill, unable to utter a word. The look on her face alarmed him, and he thrust the knife point into a fallen log and picked up the rifle.

She grabbed his arm, hanging on. The only thing he could think of was a grizzly bear. They were out in force this time of year, feeding before going into hibernation.

"Was it a grizzly?" he asked.

She shook her head, adamantly. "There . . . there is a body . . . remains. . . ." She shuddered. "It's horrible, Raif. It's . . . torn to pieces."

He had seen what a grizzly could do to a man and was glad he had recommended the .338 to Terri. It was one of the few weapons that could bring down a grizzly with one well-placed shot. He quickly removed the bullets in the clip and chamber and replaced them with five from his pocket, kept there for just such emergencies. He hunted elk with bullets loaded with .185 grains, for grizzly he'd need .250s. Injecting a shell into the chamber, he put the safety on but kept the rifle ready. "All right. Show me."

She started down the hill into the thick trees, then around a stand of fallen logs and brushwood. He saw the first sign of bear as he and Terri came into a small clearing, and flipped the safety off again. The tracks were large, but he had seen bigger. From the look of the paw print, this one was probably five, six years old. Big enough to kill a man with a single stroke of his claws, and the tracks had been recently made.

He stopped, listened, and let the slight breeze fill his nostrils. You could smell a bear if it was close. Nothing. He waited, letting the breeze swirl around him, making sure. Then the faint smell of death brushed under his nose.

Moving forward, cautiously, with Terri holding lightly onto his arm, they approached a large boulder resting in the middle of the ravine. It was surrounded by thick under-growth. Terri held back.

"Around there," she said, motioning. "The body . . . it's on the other side."

Raif took a couple of more steps toward the rock then was stopped suddenly both by what he saw and what he smelled.

There wasn't much left of the man, but his short butch haircut was still attached to a portion of his skull. Raif noticed a hole in the forehead and stooped to get a better look.

A bullet hole.

He stooped further to take a closer look at the back of the skull. The bone was blown away, leaving a much larger, jagged hole where the bullet had exited.

Raif stood, scanning the ground around him with his eyes, widening his search as he moved around the clearing. Nothing. No clothes, no personal items. Strange. But then, most of the lower half of the body was missing as well. Possibly the clothes had been ripped off when those were used as food by the bear, but if so that hadn't been done here.

"What do we do?" Terri asked. Her voice was weak, strained.

He took her arm. "Come on." They walked quickly back toward the remains of the bull elk.

"What happened to him Raif?" Terri asked.

"A grizzly ate the remains, but that guy was dead by then. A bullet hole through the head."

Terri's mouth dropped open, and she turned one more shade paler.

"My guess is he was either left just so a griz' could finish him off, or buried and the animal dug him up and hauled him here."

She looked at him with disbelieving eyes. "You're serious?"

"It isn't the first time hunters have killed one another and left the scene in a hurry."

"I mean about the grizzly, digging up. . . ." She looked back the way they had come.

"The remains? A shallow grave is no protection against a predator, Terri. They can smell death miles away, and a foot of earth is nothing to them."

"What are you going to do?" She asked feebly.

"Use my two-way radio and contact the sheriff."

Terri had forgotten he carried the radio, even though he talked to the forest rangers at Moose every night he could get through. Raif had told her it was standard equipment nowadays. People got into trouble, and getting help quickly, without having to ride for a day or two to get it, often meant the difference between living or dying.

"How fast can the sheriff get out here? We're not exactly next door."

"Depends," Raif said.

"On?"

"Whether or not there is a chopper available or if they have to come by horseback."

"Surely choppers. . . ."

"We usually have quick access to three. One belongs to a private contractor who caters to tourists and guides who want to lift people in and out of the high country, but right now he's working out of Old Faithful. Some kind of scientific project on geothermal energy headed by the University of Wyoming."

"The other two?"

"The first belongs to the Forest Service and is only here a few months each summer. It's already in Cheyenne and would be hard-pressed to get here before morning, if it's available at all. We'll see. The other is housed in the Park, but went down last week in an electrical storm. It wasn't real bad, no one was hurt, but they thought it would take a month to get it operating again."

They reached the elk carcass. Terri skirted the animal's remains, holding her mouth to keep from heaving. Raif stepped over the pile of guts and quickly found his two-way radio in the saddlebags. He extended the antennae, turned it on, then spoke. There was a lot of static. He tried again. Same result.

"The signal isn't getting out of this ravine." He shoved it back in the saddlebag and removed his camera. He checked the film window. Still had twenty left on a roll of thirty-six. He started back toward the corpse. "I'll try again when we get out of the ravine. If your dad shows up on top of the hill there, get him down here, but without the pack animals. I'll be back in a second."

"But—"

"The rifle. Keep it close." He disappeared into the trees.

Terri was angry. How could he just walk off like that, leaving her alone when there was a grizzly chopping people into small pieces and eating them for lunch!

She moved quickly and picked up the rifle, then scrambled up the hill a dozen yards. Picking out a large boulder she sat against it and looked warily at the forest around her. She figured that if a grizzly came out from any side she'd have enough time to get off at least two shots. At this range it would be hard to miss. It wasn't a comforting thought.

It was a long ten minutes before Raif came out of the forest again, camera in hand. He walked directly to his saddlebags, his mind so focused on something it was several moments before he noticed that Terri wasn't sitting where he had left her. His sudden panic almost made her laugh. Then he spotted her. The look of relief that registered on his face was quickly masked with one of businesslike disinterest. He pulled his knife out of the log where he had left it and began working again on the elk.

"Shouldn't you hunt that bear, kill it? No one is safe—"

"He's no different than us, Terri. He hunts for food. Anyone who comes in here had better have a healthy respect for that or they'll end up in pieces just like that guy." He sliced through the elk's thick hide and cut the front quarter away from the rest of the carcass. As he worked, he glanced up at Terri. "The bear didn't break any laws, but whoever killed that man did. It's them we'll be after." He started gathering up his gear. "Grizzlies are animals, a particularly mean kind if you rile them, and they are subject only to the laws of nature because they can't choose otherwise. Man is different." He looked at the ridge above them. "Where the devil is your father?"

Terri had forgotten. She automatically looked to where Raif's eyes were scanning the ridge.

"Maybe he got lost, or had to come the long way around. You didn't exactly take a trail he'd be wanting to take the packhorses over."

Raif's slight smile left his lips as fast as it had come. "Yeah, just the same, he should be here.

"We didn't used to have as many problems with grizzly as we do now. Weren't many around. Then naturalists, environmentalists, and others decided to work on reintroducing them. This is wilderness, not a petting zoo. You put grizzlies in here, you'd better expect the danger that comes when they look at you like you're tonight's supper."

While Terri continued to watch, Raif finished quartering the elk.

"You think this is a case of murder?" she asked.

"Maybe. Sometimes hunters get drunk . . . fool around with guns. . . . It could have been accidental."

"With intent to escape prosecution," she added.

"Yeah. That makes it manslaughter at best." Raif cleaned his knife as best he could on snow and grass, sheathed it, then cleaned his hands in the same way before putting everything back in his saddlebags.

"That'll do for now. Let's get back to the horses. I can wash up and try to call the sheriff on the two-way. Then I'll come back down here and string up this meat."

"String it up?"

"If you leave meat out, you string it up a tree, at least ten feet above the ground. If predators come after it, its outa reach."

"So they eat what they can reach, which is us," she said. "Makes perfect sense."

They began climbing through the loose shale, scrambling back up the steep slope. Raif glanced at his watch. Getting late. The skies had clouded over, and from the look and feel of it, they'd have a lot of snow before morning.

When they reached their horses, both were relieved to find Bob sitting atop his mount.

Raif smiled. "I was beginning to worry—" Then he

noticed the look of warning in Bob's eyes, but before he could react, three men came out of the trees.

Their rifles were leveled at his midsection.

2

Raif stared at the men with cold eyes. "I'd point that gun some other way if I were you."

"Keep your mouth shut, Mister." The speaker had a mean, cold look about him. He was about six feet tall and nearly half that wide and reminded Raif of a stone wall. The brim of his battered Stetson sagged with grease and dirt, and a flat, boxer's nose spread out under it, covering much of his face. Though the eyes were in shadow, Raif knew they'd have an empty, lifeless look to them. He'd seen killers before.

The man had his finger on the trigger of a beat-up Remington rifle and looked as though he were itching to pull it. Raif decided to keep his mouth shut.

The thug ordered Bob to get off his mount and stand next to Terri. When Bob had dismounted, the stone wall stepped forward, took Terri's rifle from Raif, and eyed it with the lust of a thief who knew value when he saw it. He grinned, showing tobacco-stained teeth, then turned and shoved the weapon between the folds of the pack on one of his poorly loaded pack animals.

Terri was irate. "Hey! That's my. . . ." Raif grabbed her arm, preventing her from making a big mistake. The man's cold stare at her made Raif's stomach muscles tighten. He had been right in his estimation of this one. He was a killer. Pure and simple.

Raif pulled Terri back. "Easy," he said as calmly as he could.

The thug seemed pleased with the effect his bravado was having, even emboldened. He stepped forward and removed Raif's holster and six-shooter, while jamming his Remington under Raif's chin. "Smart, Mister. You just stay cool, and you and your friends might live to see mornin'." He turned to the pack animal and stuffed Raif's side arm and holster in one of the canvas pack bags while a second man removed Bob's weapons and did the same. The thug then went to Raif's Arabian and removed the .338 rifle from its scabbard, whistling at what he saw. The weapon was one of a kind, with a cherry wood stock Raif had made himself.

"You use only the very best, boy," the thug said, a wicked grin on his face. He walked to his own Morgan and stuffed the .338 in his scabbard, then tossed his old gun to one of his friends. His intent to keep Raif's easily identifiable weapon spoke volumes about his plans for his captives' future.

Raif tried to keep calm. "There are the remains of a man in the ravine. You wouldn't know anything about him would you?" he asked.

The thug turned to stare at Raif, but didn't say anything. Instead he spat a mouthful of tobacco juice, then went to Raif's pack animals and began looking through the bags. As he found something of value, he tossed it to the shorter of his two friends, who then stuffed it in one of their own greasy bags. It was then that Raif noticed the short one wasn't a man at all. Her hair was cut short and was mostly stuffed under a red and black wool hunting hat with earflaps. Her features were plain and rough, the face of a hardened woman who had likely absorbed a lifetime of abuse and disappointment. She wore several layers of thick, loose, and dirty clothing of odd colors and sizes, providing an impenetrable disguise for whatever womanly form she

might have possessed. From what Raif could see, it
appeared the form would be a solid mass with little delin-
eation between sections.

The second man stood with his legs apart, his rifle
trained on them. He was glaring at Raif, rubbing his index
finger on the trigger of his friend's rifle. Raif knew this one.
Knew him well.

"This is a step down, even for you, Crenshold," Raif said
to him. "But then you always did like playin' with gutter
rats."

Crenshold's finger gripped the trigger. Flat-nose turned
from his stealing and glared at Crenshold, waiting for a
response.

"He's a deputy for Teton County," Crenshold said.

The thug turned to Raif.

"Crenshold has spent as much time in the Teton
County Jail as he has in his own home," Raif quipped.

Crenshold stiffened, his finger now resting firmly on the
trigger.

The reaction brought a smile to the thick lips under the
thug's flat nose. "From the look on Burt's face, I guess you
had something to do with that," he said to Raif.

"His guardian angel," Raif said, gazing with disgust at
Crenshold. Flat-nose looked over at his friend, then back at
Raif.

The woman snickered, and Crenshold's finger tightened on the trigger. "Let me kill him, Benny. This—"

The one called Benny turned on Crenshold, doing it so
quickly his friend was startled. Something inaudible passed
between them, then Benny went back to rifling through
Raif's packs. Raif and Crenshold had both seen something
in Benny's eyes, and they both knew that, in time,
Crenshold would get what he had asked for.

Raif now knew who that flat-nosed thug was. Benjamin
Golding. A notice had come through the sheriff's office just
before Raif had left for the hunt. Golding was wanted for

questioning in a kidnapping during a convenience store robbery in which a cashier had disappeared.

Raif remembered that Benny's rap sheet had been a long one and included hard time for nearly beating a cop to death. Then, when he had been out of the penitentiary for less than a month, he and his brother had gotten into a fight over the last can of beer in their mother's fridge, and Benny had put his older brother in the hospital. The charges had been dropped when the brother disappeared and wasn't available to file any charges.

That was more than a month ago, and Raif didn't figure the body in the ravine was Benny's brother—too fresh.

It had to be the store clerk, brought up here to bury so as to leave no evidence. But that didn't mean the brother wasn't dead, just buried in a different spot. Golding looked to be a man who didn't like being crossed or sassed. His brother had done both.

"It's a long ride from Cody, Benny," Raif said.

Benny turned around, half a smile on his hard face but made no comment. Instead he tossed a box of Raif's specially loaded .338 shells to the woman, then went around the packhorse and opened another bag.

Raif felt the chill in the air and shivered, even though he was sweating under his coat. There was no reason now to think they'd be left alive.

The wilderness was the perfect place for killing and getting away with it, and Benny knew it. There were at least half a dozen unsolved murders on the books just over the last twenty years, the latest taking place as recently as last year. A cantankerous old hunter had come into these same woods with two men and was never heard of again. The two friends said he simply walked off one night, so they packed up and came out. Both flunked lie detector tests, but there was no body and no evidence of foul play. There wasn't even a proven motive, so they had walked, and until somebody dug up the old man's remains or one of the suspects turned on the other, they'd remain free. Raif figured Benny knew that and would take advantage of it. He had nothing to lose.

Raif looked at the woman again. Maggie Lerner. The wanted notice said Benny Golding had a girlfriend and that two other men had fled with them. Counting the clerk, who was probably the dead man in the ravine, that made five—three here, one dead. They were short one man.

"Why'd you kill the clerk?" Raif asked.

Golding had found Bob's camera—a Sony camcorder with half a dozen extra batteries. He walked to his own pack animal and shoved everything in a bag before turning to Raif.

"They'll put you on death row this time, Golding."

Benny tossed a length of Raif's leather tie-down straps to Crenshold. "Tie him up, Burt. Tight." All smiles, Crenshold handed his rifle to Maggie. She took a step forward and shoved the barrel against Raif's chest.

"Just in case you get any ideas," she said.

Raif knew what would come. They'd take them to an isolated spot, then kill and bury them, probably a little deeper than they had the piece of grizzly bait lying in the ravine. Raif looked at Bob and Terri, telling them with his eyes what they already knew. Bob's jaw was set, determined, his body tense. Terri looked mad and had the same set to her jaw as her dad. They'd be ready when he needed them.

Crenshold finished with the straps, knotting them tightly enough to already begin shutting off circulation. As Golding jerked Bob's arms behind him and began tying him, Crenshold stepped in front of Terri. Close. Too close. He took one of her arms and shoved it behind her as he pressed his body against hers. She turned her face away as he grabbed the other arm and forced it behind her as well. Raif felt a wave of fury, but with Maggie's rifle barrel making a dent in his chest, he could do nothing but grind his teeth. Crenshold grinned wickedly at Terri, then spun her around and began lashing her hands together. While doing so, he put his mouth close to her ear and murmured something. She reacted instantly, turning her head to spit at him. As soon as she did so, he brought his hand to her throat and lifted her onto her toes. Shoving his face forward into hers, he sneered at her, "Well, little Missy, I was givin' you a chance to be nice, but maybe I need to teach you a few manners."

Terri didn't blink, but returned his gaze, her jaw set. After glaring at her for a few moments, Crenshold shoved her backwards toward her horse. Terri stumbled but regained her balance, then stood looking at him defiantly. Cursing her, Crenshold wrapped his arms around her waist and lifted her up, flinging her into the saddle and nearly tossing her over the horse's back. He steadied her with a firm grip on her thigh, but Terri kept her eyes straight forward, even as Crenshold slid his hand up her leg.

Benny Golding was directing Bob toward his mount with a firm hand when Bob broke loose and drove his shoulder into Crenshold's back. Both men went down, but with his hands tied behind him, Bob didn't have a chance. Swearing, Crenshold got to his feet, and as the older man was struggling to get up, kicked him hard in the rib cage. Bob went down again, then as he tried to get up, Crenshold slammed a fist into Bob's face, dazing him and dropping him to his knees. Then Crenshold drew his pistol and hit the defenseless man in the side of the head with it. Bob hit the ground, face first, and lay there without moving.

Maggie had turned to watch the fracas, and with her attention diverted, Raif pushed against the barrel of her rifle, throwing her off balance. He sidestepped her and threw himself at Crenshold, who went down with Raif on top of him. Crenshold threw him off easily, and getting to his feet, leveled a steel-toed shoe at Raif's midsection. Only hardened stomach muscles prevented any real damage, but

Crenshold was ready to deliver a second blow when Golding spoke.

"Let it alone, Crenshold!" Crenshold's leg was already in motion, and when Raif, who had gotten to his knees, threw himself backward, away from the blow, Crenshold caught nothing but cold air, throwing him onto his back. Raif scrambled to his feet and crouched facing him, ready as he could be if Crenshold wanted more. Picking himself up, Crenshold unleashed a stream of vulgarities, cursing Raif and his parentage, then moved forward, his fists cocked. It was then that Benny fired his gun.

Startled by the report, Crenshold came to a stop, his eyes riveted on the spot an inch from his toes where Golding had placed the bullet. He looked at his boss with hate-filled eyes that showed the craze burning inside him.

Golding snarled at him. "Harder to pack 'em around dead. You can finish what he started later on." He spat another mouthful of juice into the snow, then looked at Bob still lying on the ground, but coming around. "Get him up on his horse. I'll take care of the deputy." He walked to Raif, grabbed his arms and shoved him toward the gray.

"That was real stupid, Deputy. Now Crenshold will make you suffer before I kill you," he said.

Crenshold hesitated, then stood, jerked Bob up and practically carried him to his mount. Raif could see Bob was hurt, disoriented, and unable to help Crenshold get him up. Angered by it, Crenshold slammed another fist to his rib cage and Bob went down to his knees, his head hanging forward.

"No!" Terri screamed, trying to jump from the saddle. Maggie grabbed her leg, keeping her aboard.

Golding demanded that Raif get down on the ground, and Raif responded immediately knowing Crenshold was about to lose total control and would likely kill Bob if Golding didn't stop him. One eye and the gun on Raif, Golding went to Crenshold and pulled him away from his victim, threatening to kill him if he didn't do as he was told. Crenshold got control again, and the two of them hoisted Bob on his horse. Raif could see it was all his client could do to stay there.

"Steady him, Crenshold. Deputy, get up!" Golding demanded.

Raif did as he was told. Benny pushed him toward the gray, then helped Raif into the saddle. As Raif's backside hit leather, Bob lifted a foot and kicked Crenshold in the mouth, knocking him backward and bloodying his lip. When Golding turned toward the new commotion, Raif siezed his chance. Driving his heels into the gray's flanks, he shouted and the gelding sprang forward, knocking Golding away and down and sending the gun flying out of his hand. Raif bent low over the saddle horn and hung on with his heels as the gray broke into a gallop. He and his horse were to the tree line before Maggie could get clear of Terri's agitated horse and fire. The shot went wide, and the big gelding was in the trees before she could inject and fire another round.

With his hands tied behind his back, Raif prayed for the strength to hang on as the Arabian worked the trees in his dash for safety. He knew they'd come after him. They had to. If he got away, he would bring help, get them. Golding couldn't let that happen. Raif hung on, afraid to turn and look, afraid he'd lose his tenuous grip, and the gray would throw him. Their only chance was his ability to turn the tables. It was a slim chance, but a chance.

The gray was well-trained as a cutter and worked his way deftly around trees and through deadfall. Suddenly they were in the open, and Raif leaned forward in the saddle and urged the gray to give all he could. They bolted across the meadow, jumping half a dozen fallen trees. Raif lowered his head, laid his Stetson alongside the gray's neck, and urged him even more. The horse responded, breaking into an even harder gallop. Concentrating on keeping his balance,

Raif tried to figure out what his next move would be. He needed to free his hands and then somehow deal with an armed enemy who would surely kill him at first chance, then return and finish the others.

As he neared the far edge of the meadow, Raif used his heels to direct the gray left. He knew of a trail down the side of a deep ravine filled with thick trees. As he reached the head of the trail, he called on his mount to slow then glanced over his shoulder. Golding and Crenshold were just emerging from the forest on the far side of the long meadow he and the gray had already traversed. They were coming on quickly, driving their Morgans forward. A thousand yards separated them. He had a good lead. Now, what to do with it?

The Arabian was working his way down the trail at a jarring trot. Raif kept his head low, dodging low-hanging branches while trying to think ahead. He knew that the trail crossed Box Creek at the bottom then split in two directions. The upper trail was narrow and led through heavy timber and scrub brush. That was his best chance. Reaching the creek, he called the gray to a halt, then twisted himself in the saddle, straining to reach deep inside the left pocket of his unlatched saddlebags with his still strapped hands. He was searching for the small Buck knife he carried there. He just hoped Golding hadn't found it.

Raif sorted through the contents—an extra shirt, underwear, a flashlight, whetstone! Where was it! In the distance he could hear Golding and his lackey advancing. They were shouting at each other and at their horses. He had maybe two or three minutes. Where was that knife! He took a deep breath, twisted even harder to his left, trying to keep his balance as he searched deeper. There it was! Smooth bone handle, cold against his numb hands. He gripped it between his fingers, but it dropped free and back into the bag. The lack of circulation made his fingers near useless stubs, and he swore at his clumsiness. He strained his muscles, searched, found it again, then used his stomach muscles to lift himself back into an upright position in the saddle.

Gripping the knife in the palm of his left hand he pressed his right heel gently into the gray's right flank, directing him up the left side of the forked trail at a quick gait. The voices were getting closer. He nearly lost the knife as he tried to grasp it in one hand and open it with the fingers of the other. He gripped it more firmly, then tried again, feeling the thin edge of metal between his fingers. Using a thumb nail in the slot, he pried at the blade, but couldn't pull it all the way open. His tied hands kept getting in the way.

He cursed as he tried to reposition it. The enemy was at the stream now, maybe fifty yards behind him, their view blocked by the thick trees, but their bickering cutting through the air.

Raif cut himself on the blade but forced it open, then called a quiet "whoa" to the gray. Swinging his right leg over the saddle horn, he let himself down and placed his back against a sturdy aspen. Leaning against the knife, he succeeded in embedding the blade, the sharpened edge facing down. Then he began rocking back and forth, sawing at the leather thong while watching the trail in front of him. He was a sitting duck if they came through the trees now. . . . He felt the knife cut into his thumb, then through the strap. He was free!

Raif grabbed the saddle horn and was quickly aboard, turning the animal downhill just as Golding came out of the trees, ducking a low branch. Raif drove his heels into the gray's flanks and the horse responded immediately. They bolted down the hill and were upon Golding in five strides. Without slowing, the Arabian rammed into the Morgan. The impact knocked the smaller horse back in screaming protest, and Raif drove the Arabian forward. Golding's shocked face filled with fear as his horse reared backward, stumbled, then fell over on its back, its hooves flailing wildly. Golding had grabbed for the mane, but only succeeded in pulling the horse over onto him, crushing his leg. The screams of both animal and man filled the air as Raif turned his attention to his remaining enemy.

Crenshold, panic already written on his face, tried to get his Morgan under control as he watched Golding and his mount go down in a flurry of flesh and noise. Raif was on him in an instant, grabbing Crenshold's Morgan by the reins and jerking up and toward its rider. The horse reared, dumping Crenshold onto the trail. He was holding his rifle but let go of it as he reached instinctively back with his hands to break his fall. The gun clattered off a boulder and went flying into the trees. Raif reined in the gray and quickly dismounted while Crenshold scrambled backward, trying to draw a revolver, but Raif put an end to his retreat by kicking him hard under the chin.

"How does it feel, Burt?" Raif said to the crumpled, unmoving form.

Golding's Morgan scrambled to its feet, its master's broken leg still attached to the saddle via the stirrup. Golding screamed with pain as the horse panicked and bolted up the trail. Golding lurched left and right, then caught in some deadfall, jerking his leg free so violently that even Raif cringed with pain. The Morgan fled up the trail as if its hindquarters were afire, and Raif watched it disappear in the trees, before bending down and picking up his own rifle, which Golding had lost hold of in his fall. The stock was scratched but the action was still good. Flipping off the safety, he stepped to where Golding was writhing in pain and placed the end of the barrel against the man's temple. Golding stopped moving but not groaning. He was obviously in agony.

"Roll over on your stomach," Raif ordered. Golding clutched at his injured leg with his hands but did as he was told. "Now put your hands behind you." Again Golding obeyed. Raif placed a knee in the middle of Golding's back and rested most of his weight onto his spine. Then he searched the man's pockets, removing a new Army issue .45 side arm. He checked the clip to determine it was loaded, then shoved it into his own belt. Golding's leg was giving him too much pain for Raif to have to worry about him going anywhere, and Crenshold was still out cold, but Raif kept an eye on them anyway as he searched for something with which to bind them.

Raif retrieved his knife from the tree where it had been embedded and approached Crenshold's winded Morgan, which was standing quietly nearby. Raif cut the leather tie-down strings off the saddle and used them to tie the two men up. He then rolled Golding over onto his back, and stuffed a dirty rag he had found in Golding's pocket into the protesting man's mouth, jamming it in so hard, the man gagged. Then he felt the leg, quickly finding the break when Golding screamed. Compound fracture. Golding wasn't going anywhere on foot.

Benny was screaming expletives through the gag, and it nearly choked him.

"Sorry, Benny, can't understand a word you're sayin'." Raif jerked him by his belt, turning him on his side to search the front and back pockets. He pulled out his wallet then jerked Golding again, rolling him back onto his stomach. He noted without feeling sorry for his prisoner that the pain had turned Goldings face a chalky white.

"You look like death warmed over, Benny. You need to take better care of yourself." He opened the wallet and found a couple of hundred dollars in loose bills. Possibly some of the loot from the convenience store robbery. The only other item was an expired driver's license.

He stood, shoving the wallet into his pocket, before checking Crenshold. He rolled the unconscious man over onto his stomach and tied his hands behind his back, then dragged him over to a tree and propped him up against the trunk. Searching Crenshold's pockets he found another Army issue .45—this one a little older. Guns like it turned up in pawn shops all over. Former military guys needing cash. Glad to have another firearm, he put it in his pocket. Approaching his own mount, he removed his lariat from the thong tie of his saddle and wrapped it around the tree and Crenshold half a dozen times, then jerked it tight. He made one last loop just under the man's chin and tied it off. The hard rope's stiff braid would dig into Crenshold's throat—a deterrent against even slight movement.

Picking up his rifle, Raif went to the gray and shoved the .338 into the scabbard, then mounted before removing Golding's .45 from his belt. He slipped the slide and injected a cartridge into the chamber before putting the safety on and shoving it back in his belt. For the first time, he examined the cuts on his hands. They stung some but weren't bleeding badly enough to take time to bandage. He turned back down the trail where he scooped up the reins of Crenshold's Morgan and headed back the way they had come. When he reached the top of the ravine, he urged the gray into a lope, and the second horse had to work to keep up. It was time to pay Maggie a visit.

* * *

When Raif had bolted, Crenshold had gone for his weapon, but had been knocked to the ground by Terri's mount as she drove her heels into its flanks. Maggie, grabbing onto the saddle, used her masculine-like strength to stop Terri's horse and drag Terri to the ground. Grabbing her by her coat collar and cursing, Maggie had dragged Terri back toward the others.

As soon as he scrambled to his feet, Golding grabbed the reins of Bob's mount and jerked upward so that the horse reared, dumping Bob on the ground in a heap, where Golding vented his anger by punching the helpless man

repeatedly in the face. Golding then turned his attention to
Terri, slapping her so hard in the face that the blow
knocked her to the ground. Giving orders for Maggie to
watch them, he retrieved Raif's rifle, and he and Crenshold
had mounted to go after their escaped captive. They were
not in a great hurry, confident that with his hands tied
behind him, Raif wouldn't be able to stay in the saddle for
long.

Left alone with the two captives, Maggie demanded
Terri sit up. She grabbed the woman's tethered hands and
dragged her toward her half-conscious father. Then, in a
show of anger, rammed her rifle butt into Terri's back,
knocking her again to the ground and leaving her gasping
for breath and writhing in pain.

"Well, you city folk has now been properly introduced
t' Wyomin'." She bent down low, holding her face only a
few inches from Terri's. "Your deputy ain't got a chance,
city girl! My man will bring him back here and then we'll
kill all three of you." The threat was made in a shower of
saliva and a flood of bad breath. Still in pain, Terri felt the
fear of this woman rise in her gut. She had never felt such
hatred from anyone.

Maggie then walked off a little distance and holding her
rifle in the crook of her arm sat down on a log to keep
watch.

Terri rolled over so she could see her father. "Dad, are
you okay?"

He nodded slightly. His face was bleeding in three
places and the flesh around his eyes was swelling badly.
Blood oozed from his nose. Terri's fear gave way to an anger
she had never felt before. They would take the chance Raif
had given them, and Maggie and her friends would pay for
what they were doing. She would make sure of it.

"Dad, we have to—"

Bob shook his head slightly. "No." He grunted in pain.
"Wait . . . wait for Raif. He . . . he'll come . . . back. . . ."

Terri could see her father was having trouble breathing. "Shhh . . . all right, all right." She lay still, letting time pass but growing more fearful as it did. How could Raif possibly escape under these conditions? With only Maggie to deal with, their chance was now!

She changed her position slightly so she could see Maggie. The woman sat staring into the trees through which Raif and her conspirators had bolted. Terri sensed no worry. A bad omen. She worked at her thongs, hoping a lust-filled Crenshold hadn't tied them well. After a few moments they seemed to loosen, but she still couldn't wriggle free. With further effort she felt her wrists chaff, sting, and begin to bleed. Though it was painful, she worked at the thongs, struggling even harder as large flakes of snow began falling and the wind picked up. How long had it been? How much more time did they have before Golding and Crenshold would return? She didn't have long, and she knew it. She ignored the increasing pain and worked harder at the thongs. Five minutes later, with her own blood acting as a lubricant, she worked her right hand free. Her feelings soared, deadening the pain as she unraveled the thongs from her left hand.

"Dad," she whispered, "I'm free." She tried to calm her emotions, keep her voice down.

"Terri, don't move! There is no way. . . ."

"Call to her. Get her over here! I can. . . ."

"Terri, you can't . . . Raif. . . ."

"It's been too long! If he were coming, he'd be here by now. We have to do this before her friends return or they'll kill us!"

Bob fought the desire to drift, to let the blackness he was fighting overcome him. He feared more for her than for himself. These animals would kill, but first Crenshold would rape his daughter. It made Bob shudder. If they didn't take the chance . . . if Raif were dead. . . .

He shook the blackness back. She was right they had to try. Had to!

"All . . . all right. But we do it my way." He whispered to her what she was to do. She nodded. Her breathing was quick now, her muscles tensed by fear and adrenalin.

"Dad?" she said lightly. "Dad!" She said it louder this time. Bob didn't move. Terri forced herself to her knees, her hands behind her as if still tied, facing Maggie across the still form of her father. She nudged him with a knee . . . rolled him slightly. She let the anger and fear show, as a skittish Maggie stood, the rifle pointed at them. "You've killed him! You've killed my father!"

Maggie's eyes went to Bob's still form, then to Terri's face. She strutted forward, disdain for Terri's concern showing in her smile and demeanor. With her eyes on Terri, Maggie used the rifle barrel to poke Bob. No movement. She poked again, harder. Nothing. She let her eyes drop to his hands. The thongs were still in place. The gun came up and away from Bob, and Terri saw her chance. She lunged upward, her lower legs acting as catapults, and grabbed the barrel shoving Maggie backward. The gun discharged as they struggled over it, and Maggie screamed a curse even as she used her stout body to shove back and regain her balance, forcing Terri to step over her father. The step was a large one and Maggie used it and her considerable strength to throw Terri off balance while releasing the gun with one hand and swinging a doubled up fist in an arc that met with the side of Terri's face, knocking her to the ground.

The blow left Terri's head ringing and things went black for a moment.

Maggie had turned her back to Bob, who squirmed toward her then used what strength he could muster to lift his legs and jam his boots into the back of Maggie's knees, folding her up like a wet rag and propelling her face forward into the deepening snow.

Before the bulky woman could lift herself, Terri jumped

astride Maggie's back. She grabbed the burly woman around the neck and pulled back as hard as she could. Maggie tried another curse but the choke-hold cut it off. Gasping for air she let go of the gun to claw at Terri's hands while bucking with her hips. She threw Terri off balance and was able to break free of her. Her eyes filled with hatred, Maggie lunged for Terri, knocking the lighter woman backward and falling heavily on top of her on the ground. Terri found herself fighting for her life and used every muscle in her body to roll. By a miracle she ended up on top and used the advantage to grab Maggie by the scruffled hair bangs sticking out under the front of the cap. She pulled upward, hard, then used her doubled up fist as a hammer against the woman's nose.

Maggie loosed another string of expletives as she held her arms between them to block Terri's punches and at the same time thrust her hips upwards, catapulting Terri off of her. They both scrambled to their feet and circled each other warily. Maggie wiped at her bleeding nose with her sleeve and said, "Tough for a city girl, ain't ya?"

Then her eye fell on the rifle lying in the trampled snow only a few feet behind Terri. She lunged for it, but Terri threw herself at the bulky woman's legs. Her superior weight carried Maggie over Terri's back, and she landed on her belly with the stock of the rifle directly under her face. Too quick for the larger woman, Terri was immediately astride Maggie's hefty backside. Filled with a rage she had never experienced, she ripped off Maggie's stocking cap, grabbed her by the hair, and yanked her head up before slamming her face down against the wooden gun stock. She did it again and again, until someone grabbed her from behind and pulled her to her feet. She tried to break free, to get at the woman again, to finish her off.

"Whoa! Terri, it's okay!" Terri turned on the unseen enemy, swinging as she did. Her fist caught Raif on the right side of his face, knocking his head to the left.

"Man!" he said, letting go and grabbing his jaw. In her blind rage, Terri was about to pummel him again when he grabbed her arm and stopped the blow in midair. He twirled her around and flipped her effortlessly to the ground.

She looked up in surprise. "Raif!"

"Yeah!" Raif said, holding his sore jaw. She looked quickly around at her father, then at Maggie who had rolled over on her back, and lay moaning on the ground.

Raif smiled. "Good thing I came back. You might have killed her."

Terri lay back in the snow, the pain and exhaustion flooding over her. "I wanted to," she said.

Raif stepped to Bob. "You okay?"

Bob was quiet but there was a slight nod from his head, and movement in the slits of his swollen eyes.

Raif opened his buck knife and cut the thongs that held Bob's hands, then helped him sit up. He glanced at Terri. "You gonna live?"

She lifted her head slightly, the cold snow melting the instant it hit her hot face. "Your concern overwhelms me." She let her head drop back, then lifted it again, a sudden thought occurring to her. "How long were you watching all this?" she asked.

Raif kept an eye on Maggie but cracked a slight smile. "Long enough to know I don't want to tangle with either of you."

She flopped her head back. "Great!"

Bob spoke. "The other two? What did you do with them?"

"Crenshold was unconscious the last I saw him. Golding has a broken leg and won't be going anywhere. They're both tied up about a mile west of here."

Raif leaned down and quickly searched Maggie's pockets, then unbuttoned the woman's coat and did an even more thorough search. He found a small .22 pistol suspended on a thong around her neck and under her jacket. He cut the thong and removed the gun. He checked it carefully, made certain the safety was on, and put it in his pocket. Then he checked the rest of her.

Terri forced a smile. "Thorough, aren't you?"

He kept searching. "I saw a cop take it easy with a woman once. She ended up sticking a knife in his back." He stood. "This is not a woman I would even want to have long finger nails. She'll rip out your eyes with them if you give her the chance."

"Yeah, I know. Strip her naked for all I care."

"A little cold for that." He rolled Maggie over and looked at her bleeding face. "She'll need stitches."

Terri didn't lift her head this time. "I'd be honored to help."

Raif laughed lightly. "I bet."

"How did you get away?" Terri asked.

"Later," Raif said, looking up at the sky as he handed her Golding's .45 from behind his belt. "Right now we've got to get some help up here. Keep an eye on her while I find the radio. There's already a shell in the chamber, but the safety is on. Don't kill her. You wouldn't like yourself in the morning," he grinned.

Terri gave Raif a wan smile, then looked up at the sky. The snow was coming harder. She let herself dream of a hot tub and a blazing fire. She had never been so grateful for a radio in her life. Now if they could only get a chopper, they'd be out of here before dark.

3

Raif pulled his collar up and glanced at the thick gray sky. The wind was growing stronger by the minute, and he suspected they would have a full-blown blizzard on their hands within the hour. He had to get them moving and off the ridge.

Terri saw the look of concern on Raif's face as he stuck the radio back in his saddlebags.

"When are they coming?" she asked.

"I don't know," he paused. "Like I told you, the Forest Service chopper is in Cheyenne for the winter, and the ranger at Buffalo says they can't get it here anytime soon. As I feared, the others are all grounded for one reason or another. On top of that this storm is worse west and south of here and has the valley socked in. Even if they were available, it would be hard to get them to us."

"How bad will it get?"

"Hard to say. It often snows several feet at a time up here." He took the .45 from Terri, checked the safety, then stuck it back in his belt under his coat. "We need shelter."

"What about Maggie's two friends?"

"They'll keep for an hour or so."

He stooped and did a quick examination of Bob's wounds. From the reaction to pressure on Bob's midsection, Raif concluded that his friend probably had a couple of broken ribs. Raif also noticed some blood in one of Bob's ears, a sure sign of a concussion. He'd have to be watched. Using a first-aid kit from one of the packs, Raif quickly doctored the cuts on Bob's face with disinfectant and called it good. He also checked Terri's face. She had some welts from being slapped by Golding and from the fight with Maggie and her wrists were chaffed from being tied up, but she seemed otherwise okay. He got a couple of blankets out of the gear on the pack animals and handed them to Terri. "Keep your dad comfortable while I see to Maggie."

The wounds Maggie had received when Terri slammed her face into the barrel of the rifle were in need of stitches, but for the moment his quick-fix bandages would have to do. He used snow to wash away the blood the best he could, then disinfected the worst of her cuts and bandaged them. She was conscious and cursing until he threatened to stuff her mouth full of cotton.

When he was finished dressing her wounds, she was still defiant. "According to the ranger you were an accessory to the robbery over in Cody. You wanna talk about it? Tell me who did what?"

Her only response was a belligerent stare. "How did you get here?" Raif asked.

"On them horses, how else?"

"It's a long haul, a lot of tough terrain. Just wondering about the way you came in. With Golding going to jail somebody is going to have to retrieve his rig, that's all."

"Don't matter. We didn't need it anymore anyway." She gave him a superior smile.

"Why kill the clerk, Maggie?"

Maggie looked away. Raif put a hand to her chin and pulled her face back, staring into her eyes. "It'll go easier on you if you cooperate."

She jerked her head back and up, pulling it out of his grip. The stare was full of hate. She said nothing. Raif went on.

"There were five of you when you left Cody. The clerk

you killed is in the ravine, or what's left of him after a grizzly licked him clean. But that still leaves us short one man."

The look of satisfaction on her face was enough. The fifth man was still at large. Raif stood, walked to Golding's pack animals and searched until he found the pistol and holster Benny had intended to steal from him. He strapped it on, then checked the cylinder. He always left the one under the hammer empty for safety reasons. Not now. Removing a bullet from his belt, Raif slipped it in, then holstered the pistol and attached the thong that kept it in place. Next he removed his .338 from his saddle scabbard, went to his packhorse and switched it for a lever action .30–.30. After filling the chamber with shells he placed the lighter weapon in his scabbard.

He considered it an easier, faster weapon, and figured he'd need every edge if the unknown fifth man showed up and started shooting at them.

He shook the snow off his Stetson for the fifth time. The white stuff was coming quick and heavy, the wind driving it around the clearing in flurries, decreasing visibility to less than a few yards in the dark gray of late afternoon.

Terri sat wrapped in a blanket under the protective umbrella of a large pine tree, holding Bob's head on her lap. His eyes were nearly closed from the beating he'd taken.

"We have to get out of here," Raif said. He looked at Bob. "Can you sit a horse?" He found himself raising his voice to be heard above the wind in the trees.

Bob raised his head and weakly nodded. He was nauseated but didn't say anything.

"We can't move him, Raif. Help will have to come here," Terri protested.

Bob tried to sit up. "No, Raif is right," he said. "We don't know when or if they'll be able to reach us." He coughed, pain etching his face. With Raif's help he sat up.

Terri pleaded. "Surely a chopper can get to us in the

next day or two. We don't know how badly you're hurt! I
don't think we should try this."

Bob laid his hand on his daughter's arm, but his eyes
were on Raif's. "There's more to it than that, Terri," he said.
"Raif?"

Raif looked away a moment, then, deciding they were
in this together, laid it out for them. "Two things. Up here
we'll take the full brunt of this storm. It will freeze us out
before help can get here. We have to get lower, get into a
protected area. Every winter we lose people to storms like
these. People who don't have enough sense to get out of the
wind and dig in."

He drew a breath and told them why Golding and his
two friends were on the run. "Five people left Cody, only
one of them a hostage. He's down in the ravine. That leaves
one unaccounted for."

"He could have left them, gone his own way, or maybe
they killed him, like they did the clerk," Terri said.

"Not this one." He hesitated for a moment longer.
"According to a rap sheet the Sheriff's Department got on
this bunch just before we left to come up here, his name is
William Two Shoes. The sheet said he and Golding have
been bosom buddies since they first knocked over a liquor
store in Laramie at the age of fourteen. Two Shoes is probably still alive. Where, I don't know, but I don't like the
idea of him catching us out in the open like this."

"How did they get here from Cody?" Bob asked.

"Most likely they went to Pahaska Teepee, east of
Yellowstone Park, and entered there."

"Then you think they planned the robbery, using this as
a burial ground and an escape route?" Terri said.

"Maybe it was planned, maybe it wasn't. Seems like a
lot of trouble to go to for a tank of gas and a little loose
change. The money had already been counted and placed
in the safe. They figure the clerk was locking up when
Golding and his bunch showed up. Maybe the clerk told

them he couldn't open the safe. Anyway, something went wrong, and they ended up killing him, then hauled the body up here for burial. No better place to hide a body that I know of. Unless you don't bury him deep enough."

"How did they know it was these people who killed the clerk?" Bob asked.

"A young couple happened to pass the place as Golding's rig was pulling out. Didn't think much about it until they heard news that the clerk was missing."

Bob attempted to get up. "Let's get going."

Raif and Terri stood and helped him. They got him to his horse then into the saddle, though it was all he could do to keep from crying out due to the pain in his ribs. Once up, he leaned heavily on the saddle horn but stayed put. For a city boy, Bob was tough, and smart enough to know that Raif's estimation of their predicament was right.

Terri mounted, and Raif handed her the rope of the two packhorses while telling her how to lead them. "Can you handle it?" he asked.

She nodded, pulled on a pair of lightly lined leather gloves, raised her coat collar, and wrapped the lead rope around her left hand. "Lead the way," she forced a nervous smile.

Raif turned to Maggie and pulled her to her feet. She stomped, shedding a layer of snow off her clothes while trying to pull away. He jerked her toward her horse, but she continued to resist. He turned and faced her.

"Let's get something straight, lady," he said. "Any trouble from you, and I'll string you up a tree like a butchered carcass. In this storm you'll freeze and keep 'til I can come back and get you in the spring. You may not realize it, but you need us now. Got it?" He yanked her arm again, but this time there was no resistance. When she was settled in the saddle, Raif removed her Morgan's bridle and quickly replaced it with one of his spare halters. He secured the halter's rope to the saddle of one of Golding's packhorses.

"Behave yourself, and I won't tie you to your saddle," he told Maggie. "You decide. We can do it either way."

What he got from Maggie was a dirty look and a flood of expletives.

"Have it your way," he said, then used a length of halter rope to lash her legs to the stirrup skirts and a leather thong to tie her hands to the saddle horn.

Mounting the gray, Raif reined him in a direction away from the canyon where Golding and Crenshold were tied. He didn't intend to leave them permanently to the elements, but right now they had to look to their own survival. It might take him a little while to get to them, and that might cause them to lose a few fingers and toes to frostbite, but it would be pain of their own making.

Raif found the trail he was looking for and dropped down the side of the ridge into a grove of aspen trees. A half hour later he was leading them upstream in the bed of a shallow creek. From where they entered the water, the stream looked as though it flowed directly out of the side of a granite mountain, but an outcropping of rocks hid the fact that the creek made a sharp bend, flowing out of a narrow opening between some tall cliffs. The passageway between the granite walls was only a few yards wide at its narrowest point, but a hundred feet farther on, the walls opened again into a box canyon filled with a thick stand of pine. The little basin was no more than a hundred yards deep and half that distance wide, but with steep granite walls on three sides, it offered them some protection from the storm and predators—both animal and human.

Dismounting, Raif tied Golding's packhorses then cut the thong holding Maggie's hands to the saddle horn and untied the ropes around her legs. As soon as she was free, she used one of her feet to push Raif away, but he expected it, grabbed her boot, and shoved, toppling her from saddle. She landed heavily on her backside, then, with her struggling all the way, Raif pulled her up, hauled her to the shelter of a tree, and lashed her to its trunk.

By the time Raif had finished with Maggie, Terri had dismounted and helped Bob do the same. Raif quickly unloaded his pack animals and removed their saddles, then got out a pop-up tent and erected it in the shelter of a stand of tall pines. Terri threw their sleeping bags in the tent, then helped her dad inside and got him settled. The wind was whistling hard through the trees high up, but was having less effect on the ground. It had continued to snow, but the accumulation where they were was less than it had been up higher, perhaps only three inches on the floor of the box canyon.

"Get your father into his sleeping bag. Keep him warm. The gas lamp will give you heat as well as light. You know where everything is." He pulled her rifle from Golding's packsaddle and handed it to her. "It's still loaded. Keep it handy."

Terri looked at Maggie. Snow was leaving a layer of white on her Levi's and light coat. Even though somewhat sheltered, a full night in the open, and she'd be buried, a frozen block of humanity.

"She'll freeze, Raif," Terri said.

"There's a tarp and blankets in Golding's gear. Cover her up, but don't untie her for any reason." When he was mounted he looked down at her. "The snow and wind will have covered our tracks by now. You should be all right if you stay here."

Terri got the impression he said it as much for his own peace of mind as hers. "We'll be fine." She forced a smile. "Can I start a fire?"

He nodded. "Keep it small. Use some jerky to make broth or there is some soup in the food box. Get it down your dad and have some yourself.

"Golding and Crenshold are about a mile away, just northeast of where Box Creek and Clear Creek come

together. It will take me some time. I left the radio in the
grub box. It won't pick up anything down here, but if the
storm breaks before I get back, ride out of the canyon and
climb to the top of the ravine. Call Moose Creek Ranger
Station. Tell them we've moved and where we are. I've
marked it on the map that's with the radio." He reined the
gray in the direction they had come, then stopped. "If I
don't get back it will be because the storm forces me to dig
in. Stay put until you can get through with the radio or I
return. Understood?"

The thought of his leaving made her mouth dry. As
much as she had come to love these mountains, she had
never seen them like this, and they frightened her. She
pushed her fear aside. Now was not the time to turn to jelly.
She'd have to do that later. "Be careful, Raif," she said, trying to keep her voice from wavering. What Raif didn't need
was a woman paralyzed.

He smiled. "Be back as soon as I can." He heeled the
gray's flanks and quickly disappeared into the trees. Terri
suppressed the temptation to panic, walked to Golding's
packhorse, and began removing the ropes. As she did, she
looked up through the trees at the gray and darkening sky.
It would be pitch black in less than an hour. How could
Raif possibly find his way around in these mountains at
night?

She shook out the tarp firmly as if to punish it for her
problem. She had come on this hunt for her father. His last
hunt, he had said, their last chance before her marriage to
be together, just the two of them, to talk, finish ironing
things out. And, for the most part, they had, but in the
process, the mountains, the cold crisp air, and changing
colors of the fall leaves had gotten to her, making New York
and everything she had there less appealing than they had
once been. Was that really the way she wanted to spend the
rest of her life? So busy she could hardly breathe, in a rat
race where the rats were winning? At first she had enjoyed

the excitement, the challenge, but now . . . she just wasn't sure anymore, and it bothered her that she wasn't sure. How could someone's way of life lose its luster so quickly if it were really worth doing?

Terri threw the tarp next to Maggie with a good deal of frustration. Taking a deep breath, she checked the time. Raif had been gone only ten minutes. She listened to the wind, and tried to ignore the constantly changing shadows, to keep them from reminding her that out there somewhere was a friend of Golding and Crenshold. Like them, he likely wouldn't hesitate to kill.

She felt suddenly cold inside, her heart doubling its beat and forcing her hand toward the .45 in her pocket. There was little comfort in cold steel, she thought, but with Raif gone, it was all she had.

Terri could only pray it would be enough.

* * *

Raif dismounted and led the gray into a stand of shrub brush and aspen. With few remaining leaves they didn't offer much cover, but the darkness would do the rest. The thick, heavy snow was growing ever deeper and the icy wind bit at his cheeks. Pulling his rifle from its scabbard, he flipped off the safety. Golding and Crenshold would be madder than a pair of wounded grizzlies by now, unless they had found some way to escape, which he doubted. The more likely problem would be that Billy Two Shoes might turn up and surprise him. He injected a shell into the chamber of his rifle then moved forward.

Working his way through the darkness to Box Creek he pulled a flashlight from his pocket and found a place where the water ran only a few inches deep, then crossed over. As soon as he got to the other side, he shut off the light. Its shining could be an invitation to a bullet, and that made him more jittery than the darkness.

Climbing the hill, Raif worked for a position above where he had left Golding and Crenshold. The forest was thick here, and the sound of the wind in the trees strong enough that two people standing next to one another would be hard-pressed to carry on a conversation. When he reached the position he wanted, he took a breather. It had been a long day, and he was bushed.

He felt the sound more than heard it. Something out of sync with the regular movement of wind in the trees. He wasn't sure what it was, but it was there, an unmistakable difference. He slid under the branches of a pine tree, then listened again. Something was moving through the forest above and to the left of him. Carefully pushing the branches aside, he squinted at the darkness. The white of the snow aided his sight very little, and the wind moved everything, making shadows jump and change. Picking out an image was nearly impossible.

His eyes centered on a spot fifty feet away where there was an unnatural steadiness in the darkness. An animal, large, powerful, wary, was there. Suddenly it leaped away, springing over deadfall and fleeing. Raif saw only a brief darkening against the snow, but knew it had been an elk who'd sensed human presence and fled from it.

Raif let himself breath easier while wondering if he or someone else had scared the bull. He listened, probing the darkness around him for some other foreign presence. Nothing.

Rolling out from under the pine, he got to his feet, then worked himself through the trees and downhill. A hundred yards later he neared where his gray had knocked the Morgan to the ground. He moved to his left and came up directly behind the tree to which he had tied Crenshold, careful not to make a sound. He removed the flashlight from his pocket and flipped it on. Crenshold was no longer tied to the tree. Instead the body lay spread-eagled under four inches of snow. Raif quickly flipped off the flashlight and ducked into scrub brush. Someone or something had gotten here first.

* * *

Raif waited several minutes before he approached the body again, trying to decide if whoever had gotten to Crenshold was still close by. There were no distinct tracks, only indentations covered with at least half an hour of snowfall. He heard no extraordinary sounds.

Before moving to where Crenshold lay, Raif wrapped his handkerchief around the lens of his flashlight. Then, flipping it on, he held it close to Crenshold's face and brushed off the snow. The eyes stared at the sky, wide and fixed. From the look of him, death had come as a surprise.

Raif brushed off more snow, working his way down the body. Pulling the coat and shirt open, he shined the light on a gaping wound where Crenshold's chest had been. Large caliber. Probably a hunting rifle like his own.

He flipped off the light and moved back into the shadows then through the brush to where Golding had been tied. The hillock in the snow told Raif what he wanted to know. He stooped down and brushed the wet stuff from Golding's body, then felt for a pulse. Nothing. He decided against using his flashlight this time, but removed his glove and felt the body until he touched the sticky substance that could only be blood. Same place as Crenshold's. Same kind of gaping wound. Probably inflicted by the same weapon.

He felt the body more carefully. Still warm. In this weather, Golding couldn't have been dead more than an hour. He felt his way to the leg that had been broken when Golding's horse fell on him. The bone was protruding out of the flesh. Someone had applied a good deal of force to make it this much worse. Thinking of the pain that must have caused, Raif cringed.

He pressed the buttons on his watch and read the dial.

He had left Crenshold and Golding here only a couple of hours ago.

Turning the body over, Raif found that Golding's hands were still tied, but the rag had been removed from his mouth. He had been questioned but, unlike, Crenshold, he had not been cut free.

Raif stood, miffed and very unsettled. He had never seen anything like this before. He tramped downhill to Crenshold and did a more careful inspection. Crenshold's I.D. was already in his pocket after their earlier encounter, but he did another search anyway. He found a book of matches, a half a pack of cigarettes, a buck knife very much like his own, along with a two-by-three-inch spiral note-book. Raif placed everything in his left coat pocket, and buttoned it shut. He shook the snow off his hat as he pondered what must come next.

He couldn't chance leaving them here, even though he doubted any grizzly would be wandering about in a storm like this one. Their bodies were evidence, and forensics might reveal more, give them a spent bullet or two that could be used at a trial. At close range, however, Raif figured the bullet from a .30-'06 or better would have exited and be difficult to find. Even so his humanity told him he had no alternative. He had to take the bodies back to camp, then on to Jackson with everyone else.

He picked up his rifle and turned back for the gray. He'd need the horse to pack them back to camp. They'd freeze up tonight, and that would keep the remains intact. Hopefully, by tomorrow, the weather would give them a break, and he could have someone from forensics flown in to take a close look at the scene. Deep down he knew it wouldn't happen, and even if it did, it wouldn't give them much unless the killer was dumb enough to drop his wallet.

As he reached the gray and mounted, he thought about Billy Two Shoes. Right now the renegade was his only suspect, but Billy and Golding had been good friends, even in crime. It would take a lot of money to turn Billy against Benny Golding. A lot more than you could steal out of some convenience store.

Raif shivered from inside out. Something big and terrible was happening.

He urged the gray across the creek. He must pick up the bodies and get back to camp.

* * *

Terri shoved her black thoughts aside as she fed more wood to the fire she had started. Gathering the wood and working on the flame, feeding her father and getting him to sleep, and giving each of the horses some oats from the camp pack, all this had kept her occupied, preventing the fear from paralyzing her completely.

After warming her hands for a few moments, she turned to look at Maggie. As she did, the woman's head came up. The eyes were in shadow, but Terri could sense they were filled with hate. The thought gave her goosebumps on her neck and arms. Maggie's hate made her think of one of her clients, an indicted murderer named Howard Manhope.

She had defended Manhope because no one else would, but because of the evil of his dark soul, she hated being in his presence. In their private conversations, Terri had never asked Manhope about his guilt. At first, she took up his defense because the law said he was entitled to a defense, even though she knew in her heart that he had almost certainly done the horrible thing of which he was accused. After she got into the case, she had proceded without regard to his guilt or innocence. It became a matter of playing the game, and she had played it very well. When she had her victory, though, it was a bitter thing. The satisfaction of winning the case and the prestige her victory earned her among her male colleagues in her firm were not enough to outweigh the remorse she felt for enabling Manhope to walk. And when he killed again, . . . well, it was almost more than she had been able to bear. She hadn't slept well for weeks after that. First it was the guilt, then it was the fear his new attorney might be as good as she was and get him off again. Luckily Manhope had been convicted of the second murder and was on death row awaiting execution.

Manhope and Maggie. Peas in a pod. They both made her blood curdle.

But she wouldn't let Maggie die, either. She stood and walked to where the woman sat in sullen silence. As Terri pulled the blanket closer around her and adjusted the tarp over her enemy, Maggie cursed her for her kindness. Terri refused to be intimidated by the abuse and instead tucked the tarp more securely between Maggie's shoulders and the tree trunk. Seeing that there was a good inch of snow on Maggie's cap, Terri removed it and shook it off. As she put it back in place the cursing stopped and Maggie looked away. Terri wondered when Maggie had last been the recipient of any sort of kindness.

Approaching the packs she removed her own hat and slapped it against her leg to knock the snow off. If the weather kept up like this, her Stetson would be nothing but a fancy set of wet earmuffs before morning.

While locating the gas lantern, Terri thought about Raif Qanun. He was a mystery. He was a man who talked little of anything, least of all himself. In fact, he had said more today than he had spoken the rest of the trip combined. She knew he hadn't gone to college, but she had never seen a man with more natural smarts and ability. She couldn't picture him in an office or with a day planner in hand. Nor could she see him in a double breasted suit and wool top coat. He'd be a fish out of water in New York, of that she had no doubt; but then Ted Hancock wouldn't exactly fit in out here, either. They were two very different men with two very different ideas about how life ought to be lived. Not that it made either of them wrong. Each of them used their environment to the best advantage, and each of them fit perfectly in their world.

Terri found the lantern and a box of matches, adjusted the fuel valve, and lit the mantle, then turned the knob to adjust the light. She would have preferred to have it burn brighter, but she feared lighting up the forest and hills around them.

She took the lantern inside the tent and checked on her father. It made her feel like crying to see his battered, swollen face, but she was grateful that he seemed to be sleeping soundly. After satisfying herself that he was all right, she zipped up the flap, and returned to the fire where she set the lamp on one of the nearby pack boxes.

The fire was going well enough for warmth and to provide a degree of comfort, but it cast strange, flickering shadows in the trees, giving her a bit of the jitters. She would like to have thrown more wood on the blaze but resisted the desire; Raif had said to keep the fire small. She glanced at the horses tethered together under the protection of several large pine. Their eyes reflected the fire, and they seemed comfortable enough, though one had his head up and ears pricked as if listening. She could hear nothing, but it still made her nervous, and she turned frequently to look over her shoulder at the trees behind her.

To keep busy she decided to make herself some soup and went to get the single plate gas cooker and a packet of instant soup from the packs. Placing them on the box, she took a kettle and went for water. She imagined that at this elevation it would be pretty clean, but she'd boil it just in case.

The farther she got from the circle of light, the more nervous Terri was. Reaching the creek, she quickly stooped and let the kettle fill, then hustled back to the grub box where she used a match to start the hot plate. Though it took longer than she would have thought, the water eventually came to a boil, and she added the instant soup.

Inhaling its welcome fragrance, she began to salivate and realized that it had been many hours since she had had anything to eat.

It was then Terri heard a sound that made her stiffen with fear. Someone was coming up the creek. She stood and started backpedaling, her mind in a panic. Maybe it was Raif. No! Too soon! Where was the rifle! Where had she set it when getting the tarp? She turned to search and stumbled over a packsaddle, sprawling face first in the snow.

She caught the glint of her rifle barrel where it stood near the tent and struggled over the pack boxes to get at it. Ripping back on the bolt, she fumbled to get it closed then turned to face the intruder that had emerged from the shadows.

But he was too quick. Suddenly he was upon her, a dark silhouette backlighted by the fire. Before she could raise and fire her weapon, he had seized the barrel and ripped it from her hands. Terri fell back with the unexpected strength of the pull and banged her head on the corner of a pack box. Trying to focus on the man in front of her, she attempted to get to her feet, but her knees buckled. Even though her mind willed it so, she couldn't get her hands to move, to catch her, and when she hit the ground, snow filled her eye sockets and burned against the heat of her face. She wanted to get up and fight the intruder, but her body wouldn't work. She thought it a great irony that she would only now remember the pistol in her pocket and the chance it would have given her to save herself and her father.

Then darkness flooded her mind.

4

Raif led the gray alongside the creek and into the box canyon. The two dead men lashed over the horse's saddle represented a considerable weight, and it had been slow going with him on foot leading the big horse in the deepening snow. Once through the narrow opening, he guided his mount through the trees in the direction of the camp.

Hearing a loud curse, Raif dropped the reins and pulled his revolver. Taking care to keep in the trees, he approached the camp. A fire burned a few feet to the side of where Maggie was tied, and a large man dressed in a buffalo hide coat was dancing away from Terri, his arms extended in an attempt to ward her off.

"Stop it, girl!" the man said. "Put that there fire down! I ain't gonna hurt you! I just. . . ."

Terri kept coming at him, the flame burning bright on the end of a piece of flaming pine branch she was using as a poker. The man stumbled over a fallen log, fell on his backside, then scrambled as fast as he could to get away from Terri, who was moving in for the kill.

"Look, I told you! I camp here all the time! I didn't know you was here! I didn't mean to. . . ." He stumbled again, then regained his footing as he worked in a circle around the fire. ". . . I mean I didn't try to hurt you. You fell backward and bumped yer noggin."

"Listen, you slimy piece of human flesh!"

Bob was watching everything from the door of the tent, a mystified look on his face. Raif decided he'd better step forward. Terri's victim saw him first and looked relieved.

"Raif Qanun, will you tell this gal I ain't got a harmful bone in my body! You tell her now, before she burns me with that stick. Again!" He rubbed the back of his hand.

Terri turned slightly, looking over her shoulder at Raif, still wary.

Raif grinned and shook his head. "You are the fightingest woman I have ever met." He turned to her victim. "Welcome, Prichard," Raif said.

She turned to face him, brandishing the fire brand at him.

"You let me go on again? I'll burn you to ashes, Raif Qanun!" She jabbed with the stick and Raif jumped back. Terri gave a frustrated gesture, then threw the makeshift weapon in the general direction of the fire, her eyes still flashing at both Raif and Prichard. She started to bite her lip and suspecting that tears might be coming, Raif stepped forward to provide some comfort. When he got close enough, she delivered a right hook to his midsection. His muscles were relaxed just enough that the blow sunk in and took his breath away. Then Terri turned on Prichard, who started backing away again.

"Now, wait, lady! I ain't done nothing! Just leave me be!" He was holding his hands in front of him in a defensive posture.

"Listen, you big hairball! You came barging into this camp like some thief! I ought to rip your eyes out for scaring me like that!"

Prichard moved to stand next to Raif, who was still catching his breath.

"Terri, take it easy. Sam didn't mean nothing!" Raif pushed the words out.

Terri, her face still red with anger, turned back to Raif as if to deliver another punch.

"He's right, little lady," Prichard said. "I told you, I camp here all the time. When you started scrambling for that gun I figured the best thing to do was get it outa your hands before you killed me on the spot!"

"You knocked me cold," Terri said, her anger subsiding.

"You fell backwards and bumped your head. I didn't mean to hurt you none, no, ma'am!"

"And who the devil are you, anyway?"

Sam glanced at Raif.

Raif wasn't quite over the effect of the blow to his solar plexus. "Sam Prichard, meet Terri Stevens," he said in a weak voice.

Sam only nodded.

"That's her father," Raif pointed at the tent with one hand while rubbing his stomach with the other. "They're clients of mine."

Eyeing the man looking out of the tent door, Prichard said, "It don't look like you been taking real good care of 'em, Raif."

Raif turned to Bob. "How are you doing?"

"I can't see what the devil is going on out there, but there's too much noise to get any sleep." He tried to get to his feet. Raif stepped to the tent to give him a hand, then helped him to a log near the fire. He was weak, aching from crown to toe, and when taking his seat he grimaced and held his abdomen.

Terri sat down next to him and took his hand.

"Did you bring anybody with you?" Bob asked.

Raif jerked his head in the direction he had come. "Two bodies. They've both been shot."

"You had to kill them?" Terri said, unbelieving.

"They were dead when I found 'em."

"I suppose you're gonna tell me what the devil you're all talkin' about," Sam said.

Raif recited the events of the last five hours. By the

time he was finished the fire was dying down, and Raif threw on the last of the branches Terri had gathered.

"The woman over there. She part of this?" Sam asked.

Raif had forgotten about Maggie. "Yeah. Golding's girl-friend." He looked in that direction. In the light of the fire, he could see the anger still hadn't subsided. He walked over to where she was to see how she was situated.

"What do you mean Benny was killed? If'n he was, you did it, Deputy. No one else—"

Raif cut Maggie off. "You run with a tough crowd, Maggie. Either Billy killed them or someone else. They were both shot through the heart at close range."

She swore, then turned away, but Raif had seen the glint of fear in her eyes.

"I seen your elk in the ravine," Sam said. "Wondered what big city fool had left good meat sittin' out."

"Haven't had time to even think about hanging it, Sam. Maybe you and I could go do it in the morning."

"Already hung. Cold as it is, the meat will keep until you can go for it."

Raif shook a head in thanks and turned to Terri. "You okay?"

"Your friend nearly scared the life right out of me, but, yes, I'm okay," she said.

"I apologize, little girl," Sam said. "I shouldn'a come up on you like that, but you can't always be sure you're walkin' into friend or foe anymore. Come into a camp one time, just about like this, and some drunken fool nearly killed me. Thought I was a griz."

Terri smiled while staring incredulously at his outfit. "Hard to imagine," she said.

Sam acted a bit embarrassed. "I suppose in the dark, I do look a bit fearsome."

Raif laughed lightly. "Truth is, you don't look a whole lot better in the light."

Raif stood. "I gotta get the gray unloaded and bedded

down." He walked to Maggie, threw off the tarp and blankets and undid her bindings. She got up slowly, rubbing her wrists where the thongs had been. "Come on, Maggie, I want you to see something." He pulled on her arm. She was reluctant at first, then went.

They walked to his packbags where Raif pulled out a blue plastic tarp. "We'll be back in a minute." He looked at Terri, who was watching him, a bit mystified. "Sam cooks a mean elk meat stew."

"Sounds good, but I'm fresh outa veggies," Sam said.

"Plenty in my boxes, Sam."

"What about the other guy?" Bob said. He couldn't remember the name. "The Indian you said was a friend of Golding?"

Sam looked curious. "Billy Two Shoes?" Prichard's expression changed to a thoughtful scowl. "Now there's a snake. You think he killed his friends?"

Raif shook his head. "No, but I wouldn't get too far away from your rifle. He's walking around these hills somewhere. Be back in a few minutes." He and Maggie disappeared into the shadows.

Sam stood and stirred the coals around. "Prime for cookin'," he announced. He showed Terri a smile meant to cure injured relations while giving her a good look at tobacco-stained teeth. "I've got a fair roast in my packsaddle. If you wash us up some taters 'n carrots, I'll get pots and pans, and we'll cook up a meal like you city folks are like to never forget."

Terri forced a smile as she glanced at Sam's greasy robes and dirty hands. As he turned and disappeared into the trees, she wondered just what kind of pain was involved when one died of food poisoning.

* * *

Raif used Benny's hair to lift his head and let Maggie get a good look. "Got any idea who did this?"

She turned away, a mixture of disbelief, anger, and fear on her face. Raif let go of her arm and untied the bodies, then let each one down onto the tarp he had unfolded next to the gray. He folded the remaining part of the tarp over the bodies. "You've got enemies, Maggie. Best tell me about them now, or we might all end up the same way."

Maggie's lips were pulled tightly across her teeth, her arms folded adamantly across her chest. It was obvious she wasn't talking.

"Suit yourself," Raif said. Taking the reins of the gray and Maggie's arm, he led them both back toward camp. Letting the reins dangle, he took Maggie to the fire and sat her down.

"They're out there, so you've got no place to go, Maggie. If you try runnin', I'll bring you back and tie you up tight as a roped calf." Maggie gave him a belligerent look, but Raif knew she got the message and would stay next to the fire.

By the time he was finished unsaddling and feeding the gray, he could smell the stew and realized how really famished he was. It had been nearly ten hours since they last ate anything other than jerky and Werther's caramels. Flakes the size of beer coasters were still coming down and he was grateful for the thick stand of trees that gave them partial cover. There was a good twelve inches of snow underfoot here, and if the storm kept it up they'd have another foot by morning. That meant several feet outside the box canyon and more on the peaks. It would be a difficult and lengthy process getting back to civilization. He picked up his rifle and saddlebags and moved back into the clearing.

"Smells great, Sam. You put in that special seasoning of yours?"

"T'aint worth eatin' without it," Sam said.

Terri and Bob sat on a log with plates in hand. Sam took Terri's first and filled it brimming full, then Bob's. Raif smiled as Terri sniffed it, shrugged her shoulders, and shoveled a chunk of elk meat onto her spoon and stuck it in her mouth. She was pleased with the result and the spoon quickly returned to feed her hunger. Bob was slower, and Raif could tell he was in a good deal of pain, but there was nothing left to do for him but be patient. Raif reached into the dish bag, removed a plate and spoon and let Sam dish it up before handing it to Maggie, who took it without a smile and started eating. There was hot chocolate in a pot settled into coals on the outside edge of the fire, and Sam's coffee in another pot next to it. While Sam filled his plate, Raif retrieved cups and poured and handed each a full one of their kind of brew. Filling his own with hot chocolate, Raif took a plate of food from Sam and both of them settled back to enjoy the hot meal without conversation.

Stepping forward Terri refilled hers. Her appetite had been healthy the entire trip, and Raif wondered how she could eat so much and stay so trim.

"Billy Two Shoes," Sam said, shaking his head and wiping his mouth and beard on the sleeve of the bearskin coat. "Last I heard of him he was serving time in the State Pen." He chewed on a piece of meat.

"He's been loose for about six months." Raif told Sam about the killing of the store clerk.

Sam responded with a disgusted shake of his head. "Sounds like something Golding would do. He's about as mean and nasty a man as lives. Can't say I'm sorry to see him go."

"Benny didn't kill no clerk, Billy did," Maggie said defensively. She didn't add anything, and Raif let it drop. This was a woman who spoke her mind when she was ready. To push her would only cause her to get her back up and keep her mouth shut.

Sam shrugged. "Billy is an ornery one all right. Letting

him outa jail is worse than letting a grizzly loose among them tourist types in Jackson."

Raif looked over at where Sam had dumped his gear. A number of hides, including that of a grizzly bear sat in a stack. Sam hunted for the Forest Service. When a bear wandered out of the park or went after tourists or made himself a nuisance, Sam was the one they called to kill it. He kept the hide, they kept or sold the meat, and tourists kept alive.

"I see you acquired another grizzly skin," Raif said.

"This one killed one of them backpackers. 'Twern't the bear's fault, though. Eastern fool was trying to get pictures. The bear didn't take to it. I keep tellin' the rangers they don't have no right killin' a bear for what comes natural, and eatin' intruders is what they's best at." He shrugged. "Animals got some rights, but only what them idiots down in Moose says they do."

Terri smiled. "Then why'd you shoot him? You didn't—"

"'Scuse me for sayin' so, Ms. Stevens, but there are only a few of us who can drop a grizzly with a single shot. Them rangers make 'em suffer. Wound 'em six or seven times, drive 'em mad! Ain't no way to die, and sometimes they take a fool ranger with 'em." He used his last piece of bread to wipe his plate clean, then removed a dirty cloth from his pocket and shined it up before depositing it in his dish bag. Raif saw Terri cringe and couldn't help but smile. "If it's gotta be done, at least I do it right," Sam finished.

"What do you do with the hide?" Terri asked.

"Fix it up proper. Make leather goods outa it. Moccasins, vests, that sorta thing."

"And sell it," Terri said.

"Not on yer life, girl! Too good a skin to sell. Make my own clothes. Use it for rugs and blankets. My Sunday go to meetin' clothes include a right fine bearskin coat. Not like this here buffalo. This ones for huntin'. Right serviceable, though."

Bob looked tired. He set his half-full plate aside and started to get up. Terri rose and helped him toward the tent. He said a weak good-night as she lifted the flap and let him in. Then she joined him. They were both exhausted, and Raif didn't expect either would come out before morning.

"Right pretty, that one," Sam said eyeing Raif, "and a fighter." He glanced at Maggie, who mumbled something. "What's her problem?"

Raif smiled. "Maggie learned first-hand, same as you and me."

Sam leaned forward and spoke in a quiet voice. "I seen tracks around that clearing where Golding and his bunch jumped you. Five horses with riders. They went west. I followed 'em until they crossed the meadows. The wind was kickin' up pretty bad so I broke off and made for this place." He sat back. "I reckon they're the ones that did the killin'."

Raif noticed Maggie stiffen then lean into the conversation.

"See anybody up close?" Raif asked it in a voice she could hear.

Sam shook his head. "Naw, too dark by then." He paused. "Near made myself known to them, to be friendly. Sounds like they were ornery enough to hang me next to that elk a yours."

Time passed without conversation. "Last time I saw you was in Jackson, about a week ago. You said you were finished up here for the year. What changed your mind?" Raif asked.

"That bear needed killing. I figured I'd get it done and get out in a couple days. Led me a merry chase before I cornered him."

"What's your feeling about this storm?"

"Here for at least tonight, maybe tomorrow. Three, maybe four feet. That was why I was headin' out. This country ain't no place to get caught in when Mother Nature kicks up a fuss the likes of this." He paused again, "I suspect this will be one of the hardest winters in knowable history."

Maggie was finished. Raif stood, took her plate and placed it by the fire. "Do you have a bedroll?"

She nodded.

He escorted her to Golding's packs, and she retrieved it, then he took her to her tarp and shook the snow out while she undid her sleeping bag. When she was comfortably inside, he stooped down.

"One of us will be up during the night, keeping an eye on things. It won't do any good to try and get out of here."

She stared at him coldly.

He started to rise, then decided to pursue her earlier remark. "You said Billy killed the clerk? Why did he do it?"

She hesitated, then seemed to shrug it off. "We needed gas. The guy had just closed the place and refused to give us what we wanted. He and Billy had gone the rounds before. This time Billy had been drinking and was loading a handgun. He just shot the clerk dead. Right there. No reason. Just killed him. While Benny took the keys and got gas, Billy and Crenshold stuffed the body in the trailer with the horses. Benny figured the best place to bury him was in these mountains, as far away from Cody as we could get."

"You were headed up here anyway. Why?"

"Money, what else. A lot of money, near as I could tell."

"Where was the money coming from, Maggie?"

She hesitated, "They never told me nothin' about it."

"Where is Billy?"

"Don't know. Benny sent him out this morning and planned to meet him on that ridge where we found you. I don't know what he was up to."

"Do you think Two Shoes killed them? With all this money you're talking about. . . ."

She shook her head in the negative. "They was friends. Blood brothers." She turned away from him. "I ain't got nothin' else to say to you, Deputy. Go away."

Raif stood, looking down at her, knowing she was through talking for now. In time she might give him more. He decided to give her a little motivation. "I'll try to get you a fair shake on this deal, Maggie, but only if you cooperate."

Maggie gave him a cold, 'don't need your help' kind of look, then turned her back to him. He tossed the tarp over her and walked away. Maggie was a hard woman, but a survivor. She had probably been forced to take care of herself almost from birth. She was a woman who'd do things her own way, but she'd also save her own skin. In time, that meant telling everything she knew. There was no need to hurry her.

He returned to the fire and sat down on half a buffalo robe Sam had moved near it. They both had their backs leaning against a log.

"Be cautious with that one, Raif. She'd kill you for half-chewed jerky."

Raif nodded. Each of them went to their own thoughts, watching the mesmerizing flames of the fire dance in front of them.

Raif remembered the first time he had met Sam Prichard. Sam had come to the ranch to look at some of the horses Raif's dad had for sale. By the time they were finished, Sam had bargained for one of his father's Arabian/Quarter Horse mixes, and Raif and his brother had an arrangement to take a two-week trip into the backcountry. This backcountry. It was on that trip, as a sixteen-year-old, that Raif had really fallen in love with the wilderness, and it was then that Sam had first shown him this box canyon. It had been a warm fall night then, and they had sat up by the fire much as they were doing now, talking—Sam telling his stories, and Raif and Hussa lapping them up like they were ice cream. The two of them had hunted with Sam a number of times after that, until Hussa left for Iran. Raif and Sam had kept on. Next to his father, Raif respected Sam Prichard most of all men.

"How's your pa?" Sam asked. "Still workin' miracles with other people's horses?"

Raif's father was well known for his ability to train, but even more for his ability to bring around even the most evil-spirited horses. "Yeah. Not as much as he used to, but he still likes a challenge." He paused. "You still riding the bay he sold you?" Raif asked.

"Third horse I bought from your pa, and this'n is the best yet. Never saw an animal can climb like this one, and its durable. Never quits."

There was a long pause. "Have you heard anything about Hussa?" Sam asked.

Raif shook his head. "As far as we know, he never came back from the war between Iran and Iraq."

"Hussa's blood ran hot, it did. Never seen anyone so bent on dying for a man who was the devil himself. No sir, never made no sense at all."

Sam was right. Husayn Qanun believed clear to his bone marrow that the Islamic Holy war would cleanse the world and that Khomeini was the prophet Mohammed reincarnate. Hussa wanted to be one of the *Jihad's* most heroic leaders. Raif had always looked up to Hussa—until then.

"I hear you're following in your pa's footsteps," Sam said, breaking the silence.

Raif looked up, then figured out what he meant. "I'm breeding some horses, if that's what you mean."

"Never heard much about this Shagya Arabian. And crossing them with Quarter Horses . . . what's the purpose?" Sam asked.

"The Shagya comes out of the Stallion Siglavi, born in Syria. Siglavi was imported to Babolna, Hungary. He bred many great stallions and most are at stud in Europe. I happened to get my hands on one and have him flown here. It's a practical horse and crossed with our Quarter Horse mares, we could have an animal more durable and stronger than even those my father has been breeding." He smiled. "As an added bonus, they'll have speed."

"Expensive, a stallion like that."

"I traded for him. Two Arabians I raised from birth, both with papered lines and excellent prospects for breeding. And they were trained saddle horses that could run and go the distance."

"The chestnut and that blacky?" Sam whistled. "Those were beautiful animals, Raif Qanun, and well-mannered. I hope you didn't get taken."

"I didn't. I have the Shagya in my barn. Nearly white, perfectly formed head, powerful withers, strong bones. He's a beauty, Sam. Ya gotta see him."

Sam sat back, smiling at his young friend's enthusiasm. Raif knew horseflesh better than Sam, and if Raif thought he had something that good, Sam would see it.

The snow now gathered on Sam's beaver fur cap resembled a stack of ice cream. Raif wondered what his own Stetson looked like even though they were both sitting in a fairly sheltered spot. He removed it and took a look. An inch. He shook it off.

"Tell me 'bout them bodies, Raif. How were Golding and Crenshold killed?"

"Up close, with a large caliber hunting rifle. At least a .30-'06, probably a .338. No tracks, no real physical evidence." Raif reached to drop a couple of sticks on the the fire. "Whoever did it knows they didn't tie themselves up, and out of self-preservation they just might decide to look for who did."

Sam only nodded his agreement.

"It's going to be a long day tomorrow. You had better get some shut-eye," Raif said. "I'll take the first watch."

Without argument, Sam got up and stretched, then left Raif looking at a dying fire, as he made his bed out of buffalo robes and blankets and burrowed into the pile. He'd sleep comfortably.

Raif stood, taking the buffalo robe they had been sitting on with him. He grabbed his sleeping bag and his rifle, then trudged through the deepening snow into the darkness to a point where he could see the entrance to the canyon. Finding a tree he could lean against, he rolled out Sam's buffalo robe, laid the bag on it, and climbed inside up to his waist. With his back against the tree, his hands were free to handle his rifle. The sleeping bag would keep him warm enough that he wouldn't freeze, but he would be cold enough that he wouldn't fall asleep, either.

The spot he chose was almost completely free of snow even though the wind in the trees up either side of the canyon still howled and the storm wasn't going away any-time soon.

The loneliness of it all felt comfortable to Raif, it always had. He let his mind sort through the events of the day, searching for something he might have missed that would provide a clue as to why the two men lying frozen fifty feet away had been killed. He wondered about the men Sam had tracked, who they were, what they were up to, and if one of them was Billy. If not, who were they, and how were they involved?

He let the details drift through his mind, and by the time he went to wake Sam to spell him, he had decided one thing for sure. He needed to see if he could find those men, and Billy Two Shoes. If they had some answers, he needed them. Needed them badly.

5

Raif woke up smothered in buffalo robe. Though it was a bit smelly, he relished the warmth provided by the heavy cover and let himself enjoy it for a few minutes before slithering to the top and poking his head out into a cold world. Though he lay in the cover of a large pine, a good foot of white fluff lay on top of the robe and the camp had a coat two feet deep. Sam was sitting on the same log, in the same spot he had occupied the previous night, a steaming cup of coffee in his hand. The fire was burning again and the flames looked inviting.

Shoving the robe aside but taking care to keep the snow from falling on the blanket, Raif grabbed his boots from near his feet. They were warm and easily slipped on. He glanced at the sky. The snow had temporarily stopped, but from the looks of the dark heavy clouds, they'd likely get a whole lot more before the day was over. He stood and buckled his holster on, then put on his lamb's wool-lined leather coat and his Stetson. Shaking the robe out, he laid it over the bed again then went to the fire. The dishes were sitting near their bag, still unwashed from the night before. He had been negligent, and now the leftover food was frozen to the aluminum surface. He ignored the dirty dishes, reached for the bag, and removed the last clean cup. The pots from the evening before were sitting next to the fire, steam rising from each. He picked up the closest, sniffed it, then poured himself hot chocolate. He hadn't thought much of the stuff until this trip. Terri, a Mormon, had brewed it each morning and convinced him to give it a try. He had come to like its warming and filling effect.

He looked around the camp while sipping his potion. Maggie was still in the sack, a lump under a layer of snow. As he looked toward the tent, he saw Terri coming out of the woods. She was combing her hair, and she looked washed and clean. Raif had to admit, she was a natural beauty and awfully easy to look at.

"Good morning," she smiled, putting her Stetson in place. Raif returned the greeting, while Sam only grunted, still staring at the fire. He wasn't a morning person.

Raif handed her his half-full cup. She saw the others were still dirty and took his with a "thanks." After taking a sip, she held the cup with both hands, letting it warm them.

Raif filled each of the dirty plates with snow, then placed them near the fire. Ater the snow melted, he dribbled some soap from the mess kit into each and used a rag to clean them. When he was finished washing the dishes, he added more of the hot stuff to Terri's cooling brew and poured one for himself.

"How's your father?" he asked.

"Sore, real sore. And he seems a little disoriented." She said it with a wrinkle of worry in her brow. "Any chance we can get a chopper up here today?"

Raif glanced at the skies. "Maybe. I'll get the radio, go to higher ground, and call the ranger station, see what can be done."

Terri smiled her approval.

"Sam, will you bring Maggie over by the fire?" Raif asked.

Sam nodded, set his cup down, and started for the spot without a word.

"He doesn't say much in the morning," Terri said quietly.

Raif smiled, "Unless it's something important, he won't

talk until about noon." He rummaged through his gear, searching the pack for the radio. Finding it, he put it under one arm, then pulled a pair of waterproofed fur-lined gloves from the same box and pulled them on. He took two more pairs from the same place, then walked to Terri and handed them to her. "Wear these today and give a pair to your father." He started away, then turned back. "Get him up if you can. Once he gets moving, some of the stiffness will go away. Sam isn't a breakfast person. If you don't get to it, I'll fix some when I get back."

She nodded but stayed seated, reluctant to leave the warm fire. By the time Raif had fed the animals and finished saddling the gray, she had gone for her father and returned to the fire. Bob's face was pulpy looking and badly swollen, but it looked as though he was standing a little straighter.

Raif mounted and headed out of the canyon. The creek had frozen along its edges, and the gray's hooves broke through it with a loud clap in the confines of the small valley. He checked the trail along Joy Creek for sign of animals. The snow was a couple feet deep and showed no mark of recent passage.

He reined the gray up a trail that traversed the far side of the ravine and was sheltered somewhat by trees. It was easier going here, and the big horse moved quickly, his nostrils blowing steam with each stride. Once at the top, Raif guided the gray along the rim until he reached a spot that allowed him a distant view of the direction of civilization. Nothing moved in the white landscape, which looked serene, smooth in its untracked coat. Looking again at the dark clouds overhead, Raif could see they would get dumped on again and wondered how many more feet they'd have settle on them before finally getting out of the formidable country that stretched before him.

Removing the radio from his saddlebags, he turned the

dials and pressed the button to speak. No response. He gave the numbers and greeting again.

"Raif, is that you?" It was the dispatcher in Moose.

"Yeah, Frank. How are things this morning?"

"Couldn't be better. This storm will close up the Park for sure."

Raif smiled. Frank Zimmer was with the Park Service, and they were, as a group, as much in love with the wilderness as Raif was. But most left in the winter. Some had no choice, some couldn't handle five months of relative isolation. Frank considered himself lucky to be a year-rounder because he loved the Park, most of all when it was empty of people.

"Got any good news for me?" Raif asked.

"How's the patient?" Frank asked, his tone more serious.

"Sore but serviceable. He's a bit disoriented."

"Sure sign of a concussion." A pause. "Can you bring him out?"

"The question tells me you still don't have a chopper."

"Nothing. It will be at least another day, maybe two. If you keep moving, you can be out by then." He said it in as convincing a tone as he could.

"Can you get the sheriff, give me a line through?" Raif asked.

"Hold on."

It took only a minute.

"Raif, where the devil are you?" The sheriff was always right to the point.

"Joy Creek."

"You still looking after Golding and Crenshold?" the sheriff asked.

"Yessir, but it's easier now. They're dead." He told the sheriff what he'd found and then what Maggie had told him. "Sam Prichard's with me. He wandered into our camp last night."

"If Sam's coming out, winter must be setting in permanent," the sheriff said.

"Get some people to cover the trail heads out of here, will you? Have them question everyone who comes out. Sam saw the tracks of five men in the area last night just before I found Golding and Crenshold murdered. They may have had something to do with it."

"Will do. We're still trying to get a chopper. Keep me posted as you start out so we can send someone in for your injured man if we're successful."

"I'm going to send Sam back along the trail with Bob, Terri, and Maggie. If you can't reach us, look for them there. I want to see if I can find any sign of Billy Two Shoes and the men Sam saw." He paused. "The clerk's remains need to be taken care of as well. For now I'll leave them where they are. Maybe we'll get lucky and forensics will be able to get in here in the next couple of days."

"Be careful, Raif." They signed off.

By the time Raif arrived back at camp, it was snowing again.

* * *

Finishing the last tie down on the pack animals, Raif confronted Maggie, her hands tied in front of her by Sam. "I'll make a deal with you," he said. "You give me your word you won't do anything stupid, and I'll cut the thongs."

She looked at him with doubtful eyes, then nodded. "Deal."

Raif removed his sheathed hunting knife and cut the thong. Maggie rubbed her hands and wrists as Raif motioned toward her mount. She walked past Golding and Crenshold on the way, their bodies hanging stiffly over Golding's pack animals. She hesitated, then mounted up, keeping her head up, an angry set to her jaw. Raif would hate to be the man or men who had killed Benny Golding. If she could, Maggie would tear him or them to pieces.

Bob needed help getting into the saddle, and Raif went to his aid. Sam and Terri had wrapped Bob's ribs, and though he seemed somewhat better, he was quiet. Pain would do that to a man, but Raif wondered if it was more than that. He knew that a long ride through rough terrain was something his friend didn't need right now, but there didn't seem to be any other option. Raif would have Sam keep a close eye on him.

Walking to Terri's mount, he gave her a hand up. She gave him a pleasant smile, but there was a look of apprehension in her eyes. They weren't out of the woods yet, and they both knew it. He mounted up and the group moved out of Box Canyon. At the fork in the trail Raif went his separate way.

The snow was falling only intermittently, and by the time the gray had carried Raif to higher ground, it had stopped. He watched Sam and the others turn the corner out of Soda Creek, then reined the gray in the direction where he'd found Golding and Crenshold.

The snow was sparse where the wind blew along the trail that lay on the west side of the canyon. In twenty minutes he was at the spot where the trail forked and Golding's horse had dumped its owner. He dismounted and let the gray's reins drop. The air was still. He was alone. He walked the snow-covered trail but the wind and snow had covered everything. Reaching the spot where Golding was killed, he shoved the snow aside until earth was visible. There were plenty of hoof prints all moving up the side of the canyon. He moved more snow to get a better look and discovered that one set had a unique marking; an "H" had been etched in the shoe of the right front hoof. He knew that mark. The animal carrying it belonged to a man named Hawkes.

He whistled and the gray trotted up the trail.

Mounting, he removed his .30–.30 from the scabbard and used the lever action to chamber a shell before releasing the safety. Placing the stock on his leg, he put his heels to the gray's flanks, and they started up the trail again.

Peter Hawkes had been a guide, of sorts. His license had been revoked, and he had served time for trying to extort money from clients. Since his release from the State Pen more than two years before, he had seemed to be making money without any visible employment. But, so far, no one had been able to prove he was doing anything illegal.

Hawkes was mean, but especially toward animals and anyone who disagreed with him. Raif had once given him a whipping for beating a Quarter Horse with a club, after the animal had thrown Hawkes during a horse cutting competition in Lander. In addition, it had been Raif who had arrested him on the extortion charges. Hawkes would not greet Raif with open arms if he had anything to do with Golding and Crenshold, especially if he had killed them.

The gray covered the last fifty feet of trail, and they came onto the ridge above the north fork of the Buffalo River. Reining the gray near the edge of a sheer embankment, Raif peered down into the gorge. He sensed movement in the trees, but it was too far away to see clearly. Pulling his binoculars from the saddlebags, he focused and took a better look. A bull and half a dozen cow elk. The bull was a tough old six-point with two of them broken off. Possibly the same one they had seen yesterday.

He let the lenses float over the land, his eyes looking for sign of a camp. There it was—smoke. Further north above the Buffalo. He stashed the binoculars and urged the gray to a gallop along the ridge, pulling his hat down over his eyes against the wind. Up here it was picking up.

Skirting a stand of trees, the gray took him around Joy Peak where they scared up a horse that bolted along the ridge. Shoving his rifle into its scabbard, Raif drove his heels into the gray and took pursuit. The animal veered right and left like the devil was on his heels, but the gray soon came alongside him, to a where Raif was able to reach over and pick up the Morgan's right rein.

"Whoa." He pulled gently back on the strap, slowing the gray to a canter, then a fast walk. Letting the Morgan feel his own mount's steady presence, Raif continued to speak in low tones. The frightened horse gradually settled down, and Raif finally brought both animals to a halt. Carefully he dismounted, removed his glove, and ran his hand along the Morgan's head, down his neck and leg, speaking all the while in a soothing tone. It was Golding's horse. After spending a night on the mountain, the animal had every right to be a little nervous. He walked around the Morgan, checking each leg. He seemed sound, just frightened. When Raif had him settled down, he tied him to a tree branch and removed the beat-up saddle, then the bridle, replacing it with a spare halter he carried. He removed the bags from Golding's saddle, ditched it underneath a tree, and threw the saddle blanket on top. Old and worn, the saddle wasn't worth packing out.

He and the gray led the Morgan back the way they had come. The animal was sturdy and large for one of its kind. Raif estimated fifteen hands. He was a bay with one white stocking and a well-formed head. Although not a particularly beautiful example of the breed, Golding hadn't picked it up at a barn sale either. Raif guessed the cost was at least a couple of thousand dollars.

When they reached the trail and started down, there were actually spots of blue sky overhead and the sun even broke through momentarily, making the white surface of the land glisten like a sea of diamonds. Another half hour ride through majestic scenery and cold air and he was nearing the camp where he had seen smoke.

He found a thicket and tied the horses. Pulling the .30–.30 out of its scabbard, he skirted the trail, working his way carefully through the thick trees. He could smell the smoke, but heard no voices and saw no movement. The camp was in a deep ravine where the wind was nearly non-existent and the forest created a natural quiet that eased Raif's tension some. Just the same, he kept low as he topped a small outcrop that overlooked the camp. Nothing, the fire only smoldering embers. He had his binoculars and put them to his eyes taking a detailed look at what lay below.

Though the snow had been stamped down it had a covering of new flakes. From this distance it looked like they had broken camp early in the morning, before the last snowfall. He did a second scan but saw nothing in the way of humanity except garbage around the fire ring. They had left without cleaning up after themselves—either lazy or in a hurry. Walking back to the gray, he mounted and led the Morgan through the trees to the trail, then down to the camp. He dismounted before actually entering the area, afraid the animals might disturb something. What that might be, he didn't know, but it was a precaution he knew he must take.

In the trampled area, there had been two large tents placed in the shelter of the trees. From the foot-marks, most of them wore cold weather packs with broad toes and rubber treads, hard to fit in a stirrup but not unusual gear for even veteran hunters in this kind of weather. The impressions in the snow where the tents had been indicated five sleepers.

He walked to where the horses had been tethered. Six spots. He could see that the end one had been a packhorse, the prints of the packs themselves still in the snow. He found that curious. Five hunters with only one pack were either moving fast, or living off the land and unafraid of the elements, unless they had a base camp nearby. The hooves had worked through the snow leaving marks in the dirt, and he found the telltale "H" imprinted in the space next to the pack.

Removing his sheathed knife, Raif cut a small branch

from a nearby pine then walked to the fire ring. Half a dozen beer cans lay next to the ring, another dozen lay in it, charred, the paint on the aluminum missing, each crushed. Some were crushed in the middle, some from end to end. Difference in habit. The unburned ones outside the ring might contain fingerprints.

He walked to the gray and removed an empty food bag from his saddlebags. Returning to the fire ring, he deposited those cans that hadn't reached the fire inside the bag, then used the branch to stir further into the dying coals. Bones from the rib cage of an elk, a couple of more cans that looked as though they'd been there for months, and two coiled pieces of copper wire. One was partially encased in half-melted plastic, the other bare. He deposited them with the cans, snapped off a larger branch, dug out some of the ashes, and lay them on the snow where they sizzled a few minutes before cooling enough to handle. Stirring in the remains he came up with three spent cartridges. Two were .306 caliber, and one belonged to a .338. He removed them, careful to grab them at each end between finger and thumb, and deposited each in his bag. After digging more out and stirring around in the coals for another five minutes and finding nothing, Raif washed his hands with snow and wiped them on his pants for want of something better. Walking back to the gray, he dug around in his saddlebag until he found his camera, then took pictures of everything, including a close-up of the horseshoe print with the letter "H" etched in it.

He surveyed the entire area, looking for anything else of interest. His eyes stopped on indentations in the snow. They led out of the far side of the camp into a thick stand of trees. Getting a closer look, he found three separate trails, probably made by those answering the call of mother nature. Making a path of his own he followed, but came up short ten feet into the trees. A patch of scrambled snow in the middle trail revealed that someone had fallen, and red splotches were visible underneath the latest layer of white fluff. Brushing the snow aside, he took another picture before moving on.

The signs of blood were heavy and the trail muddled. Whoever had made it was badly wounded. The other two trails split away here, forking left and right as if to encircle the bleeding man. Obviously someone had tried to escape, had been shot, tried to keep going, but was chased. Raif felt the hair on the back of his neck stiffen. The stillness around him had suddenly become ominous, foreboding. He drew his handgun even though his head told him whoever had done the shooting was long gone. The cold bone handle helped slow his heart beat.

From the amount of blood on the trail, Raif figured the runner had taken a second bullet here, large caliber. He followed the trail into heavier timber.

The path led around half a dozen trees, the trail of blood becoming more prevalent. The hunted had stopped several times as if looking for those who looked for him, possibly returning fire. The amount of blood told him one thing for sure; the wounded person was suffering, probably dying.

Raif moved with caution as he came to an outcrop of rocks, circled them, and found what he was looking for. Billy Two Shoes sat against the rock, dead as the fallen tree next to him.

As he took a closer look, Raif figured Billy had been a prisoner, had seen what his captors had done to Golding and Crenshold and knew it was only a matter of time before they killed him, too. He had waited until the middle of the night, then tried to escape. His captors hadn't cooperated. Then again, maybe they just didn't like the way he combed his hair.

Raif swallowed hard several times to keep his breakfast down as he pulled back the clothing and took pictures until his camera told him he had used up the last of the film.

As he started back to his horse, he tried to make sense of it. Maggie had said Billy had gone to meet someone—that it involved a lot of money. It was apparent they, whoever they were, and at least one could be Peter Hawkes, had decided not to pay. The only thing Raif could figure was drugs. These mountains had been used as a staging place before, probably a lot more than anyone knew.

Raif shoved the camera back in his packsaddle. Chasing the killers was enticing. He would like nothing better than to corner Hawkes and send him and his murdering friends to prison—for life. But he was alone, and if it were Hawkes, he had at least three others still with him. From the look of the trail, they were probably two hours ahead of him. Catching up in this country wouldn't be easy, while ambushing a single law officer would. In anyone's book the odds were against him.

Raif had another, more immediate, worry. Getting his clients and Maggie safely out of the hills had to take priority. Best thing to do was get to the radio. Hawkes and his friends had to be heading out. If they weren't, they were fools. It would take them a full day in good weather, two with conditions as they were. The sheriff could find their rig and be waiting.

Raif tramped back to the body and buried Billy by covering him with rocks. Not much defense against predators but hauling him out held even less promise. Simple truth was that Raif needed to move fast, and taking Billy's body would hinder that. The kid would just have to keep until someone could come back for whatever was left of him.

He returned to the gray, deposited Billy's personal belongings in the evidence bag that hung from his saddle horn, then mounted and reined the gray back the way they had come, spurring him into a lope as soon as they cleared the ridge. The Morgan seemed happy to keep up and gave Raif a slack rope. He figured by three o'clock Sam would be at the conjunction of the Buffalo and Soda Forks and would stop to rest. If Raif kept moving he could intercept them there.

Pulling his hat down against the wind, Raif noted the sky was blue above him but in the distance to the west he could see the dark gray of the storm's second wind. The trip home would be hampered by more snow, possibly even worse than they had received in the last twenty-four hours. He nudged the gray for a little more speed and was moving at a fair pace along a bald ridge when he heard the chopper.

He figured Sam must have gotten through to the sheriff and planned a rendezvous, now they were looking for him. He reined in the gray and looked for the green and white of the Forest Service McDonnell Douglas 500E, the only craft with even the remotest chance of getting up here this quickly. The chopper was just under the thickening clouds and coming head on from the north. Odd direction.

Raif squinted to see the markings. It wasn't green with a white background, but red. He didn't recognize it, and his stomach churned a bit. It flew low overhead, blowing the snow around him into a cloud and making the Morgan rear, then back away. Raif let go of the rope rather than be ripped from the saddle, then turned the gray to go after the fleeing horse while cursing the pilot. As Raif sped after the Morgan he realized the chopper was circling, coming in again. Mad enough to chew nails, he pulled his mount up short and tried to wave the idiot off.

It was within a thousand yards before he realized there was a man hanging out each side, and both were heavily armed. He felt a sudden surge of panic and drove his heels into the gray's flanks in attempt to get under cover. Responding to Raif's urgency, the gray was at full speed in six strides, his strong legs plowing through the snow.

Raif kept low in the saddle but managed to look behind him. The chopper was coming in at tree top level and the distance between them had all but disappeared. He knew he wouldn't have a chance if he held his present course.

Pulling back on the reins, he turned the gray hard right and drove him into the trees. Bullets struck all around him, creating a shower of of woodchips that pummeled his heavy leather coat but bounced off its thick skin. The gray screamed as a large piece stuck in his rump, another in his neck. It was all Raif could do to keep the animal from total panic and get him deeper into forest.

Once under the shelter of the trees, Raif changed the gray's direction and worked him quickly down the side of the ravine. Coming to a halt under a thick stand of pine, he pulled the chips from the gray's neck and rump and used an ungloved hand to soothe and get him under control. The tension seemed to ease a little even as the chopper was returning, coming from directly ahead. Removing his .30–.30 from its sheath, Raif quickly dismounted and took cover behind the stout trunk of a big pine.

Raif figured he had an advantage. They wouldn't know his exact position until they were right on top of him. He could get half a dozen shots off before they spotted him. Then, if they were still wanting a fight, he would have to move fast for the heavier timber further down the ravine.

The chopper exploded into view. Raif fired, working the lever action in three quick, successive movements. A man at the door seemed to hesitate even though he had a perfect shot and Raif fired. The chopper swung away as the man fell back inside the craft. Raif figured he had placed at least two bullets in him for his hesitation.

He launched himself back into the saddle, slammed the rifle into the scabbard, and redirected the gray downhill toward thick timber, a steep incline that could be deadly to negotiate and for which he'd need both hands and a lot of luck.

Suddenly the side of the moutain fell away at a sharp angle, and they were in the open. Raif threw himself back in the saddle, gripping the gray's shoulders with his knees. The horse somehow kept his balance, and they were halfway down the slope when the chopper was suddenly overhead again. Raif felt a bullet rip into his leg, then the big horse began to stumble and pitch forward. Raif felt the sudden pain of losing a friend even as he realized he had to get free or he'd be crushed. He propelled himself away from the saddle and was thrown forward. Hitting the ground with his shoulder, he made a painful effort to roll himself into a ball as the ground pummeled him again and again. The incline was steep and he picked up speed, rolling for long yards before slamming into a tree, glancing right, and sliding another ten feet to where he came to a sudden and heart-pounding stop.

Raif felt sick to his stomach and fought the desire to black out. Forcing himself to get up, pain shot through the bullet wound in his leg and nearly put him down again. He heard the chopper coming and hobbled toward deeper cover as fast as the pain would let him. Glancing back at the lifeless body of the gray, which had slid to a stop against a thicket of scrub brush, he felt anger mingled with anguish well up inside as he grabbed hold of a tree and dragged himself into thicker timber.

Stopping to catch his breath and gritting his teeth against the pain, Raif realized how Billy must have felt those last minutes of his life. Unlike Billy though, Raif could still fight.

Leaning against the tree to take the weight off his leg, Raif reached for his revolver. It was gone. He looked at the scabbard attached to the lifeless body of the gray. His Winchester was still intact. The chopper was coming cautiously, but it was coming. It was now or never.

He took the few steps as hurriedly as he could, grabbed the rifle by the stock, and jerked it free of the scabbard. Just as the chopper appeared overhead, Raif launched himself behind the cover of some rocks and a downed tree. A spattering of bullets slammed into the spot where he had been, and he cuddled up to his cover and held his head in his hands as lethal projectiles tore at the dead wood like a high-powered chain saw. Flattening his body against the backside of the log even more tightly, he jammed fresh shells into the Winchester's loading gate while picturing in his mind the positions of the shooters. As the barrage let up, he lifted and fired three times in quick succession. The first bullet caught one of the men leaning out of the chopper in the chest and dropped him from his lofty perch still holding his weapon in his hand. Raif's second bullet hit the plexiglass window, drove through, and lodged somewhere inside the helicopter.

The pilot immediately pulled the lever back and the bird jerked left. Raif emptied the rest of his rifle at the craft as it veered quickly up and away. He was gratified to see a puff of black smoke erupt from the rotor housing as the helicopter disappeared over the trees. He listened as the sound of the rotors moved farther and farther away, until the sound disappeared altogether. They were beaten but still flying. At this point Raif didn't care just as long as they were gone.

He collapsed onto the log that had shielded him. Without the strength to hold it any longer, he his rifle next to him, and stared blankly at the body spread-eagled in the snow on the side of the hill. The man was wearing a heavy white winter parka, the hood neatly in place around his face. Funny, it hadn't been that way before he fell from the chopper.

Raif shook his head. Another body. Not exactly the kind of hunt he had in mind when he left Jackson a week ago.

After resting for a long moment, his mind emptied from exhaustion and pain, the cold chill of a brisk wind brought him to his senses. He had to get moving. Using his rifle as a crutch he stood and hobbled the twenty yards to where the gray lay, then lowered himself into the snow next to his lifeless friend.

He ran his hand over the soft damp hair along the neck, the body still hot to the touch. He had lost horses before, but not like this one and not in this way. He had raised the gray from a colt, trained him for cutting, calf roping, and hunting. They had come into this wilderness together for seven years, and the gray had never failed him.

He felt the warm blood on his leg, changed his position by placing his back against the saddle and took a close look at the damage. From the feel of it, the wound would pain him a good deal but he wouldn't die from it. Pulling his buck knife from his pocket, he cut open his blood-soaked Levi's and insulated underwear to find that the bullet had entered and exited the outside of his calf without hitting anything vital. No bone was broken and apparently no arteries violated. The entrance hole of the wound was about half an inch round, the exit about twice that. The torn muscles were what was causing him the pain. Under the circumstances Raif considered himself lucky.

Removing his saddlebags, he opened one side and pulled out a small first-aid kit in a Ziploc bag. Gritting his teeth, he used the Mercurochrome in it to sanitize the wound before bandaging it. He felt a great tiredness, but he was also angry at his unknown assailants. Who were these people who valued the lives of others so little? Drug runners? Maybe. Men like them had used this wilderness as a delivery point before. Receiving their product here, they would then take it to Salt Lake and Las Vegas. If they were drug runners, it had the signs of being a major operation. Two-bit operatives didn't have million-dollar choppers and well-trained assassins.

He put the kit back in his saddlebags. Maybe they were, maybe it was something else. What, he didn't know, but one thing he did know was that, before they died, Golding or Crenshold had told someone that a county deputy sheriff was in the mountains and messing around in their business.

After the storm had died down, Raif hadn't been the only one who called for a chopper.

Peter Hawkes? He wondered. Hawkes was a small-time criminal, smart but without that kind of financial backing. Golding, Crenshold, and Billy Two Shoes, though mean and willing to kill, weren't as smart as Hawkes and had even less access to the money needed.

That meant outsiders—professionals with money and little patience for some small-time, half-a-kilo drug smuggling operation. Someone who might need a middleman like Hawkes but who would push all the buttons themselves, and who would not hesitate to get rid of loose ends. If he was right, Hawkes was nothing more than a brutal pawn doing the bidding of an even more brutal boss. The thought of such men made Raif's skin crawl.

Raif looked for his Stetson and spotted it caught in some nearby shrubbery. Using the saddle to push himself to his feet, he steadied his frame, and then limped over to retrieve his hat. It felt like someone was applying a hot branding iron against his flesh, but at least he could walk. He worked out the dents in his hat and replaced it atop his scruffed up, wet hair.

Returning to the gray, he loosened the cinch and dragged the saddle free. Then the blanket. Last was the bridle. He undid the saddlebags, opened the left one, and removed his camera. It was apparently undamaged. He pushed the automatic rewind, removed the film, and placed a new roll inside, then limped to the dead assailant. He had never seen him before—dark skin, dark hair, dark eyes. He took several photographs of the dead man then stooped and went through his pockets. There was a wallet containing a California driver's license, a Visa and Mastercard in the name of John Turner, along with five, one-thousand dollar bills. There was also a receipt from the Moynihan Gallery in Jackson. The man had purchased an original Bev Doolittle painting for fifteen thousand bucks. Raif knew her work. The painter's wilderness scenes were currently a hot item, and they didn't come cheap. Whoever this dead man was, he had money, he'd been in Jackson, and he had a taste for original western art. Now he would enjoy none of it.

While laying the items out on the man's chest and taking a picture, he wondered if five thousand dollars was the price paid to assassins for a man's life nowadays. He didn't think much of being worth so little.

After snapping the shot, Raif picked up the items and placed them in his saddlebags while etching the man's face in his memory, another suspect in a growing circle of them. Raif didn't like the idea of leaving the body, but he had no choice. He would have to string him up a tree. Removing the lariat from his saddle, he found an acceptable branch up a tall and sturdy white birch. It was hard work, but ten minutes later Raif had the man hanging by his heels ten feet off the ground. It was a gruesome sight, but Raif was fresh out of compassion for cold-blooded killers.

He must get moving. Staring up the side of the ravine for the first time, Raif saw how lucky he had been to survive. He and the gray had plummeted over a virtual cliff and onto snow-covered shale. That fall alone should have killed him.

And the climb to the top surely might.

Throwing the saddlebags over his shoulder and picking up his rifle, Raif took a deep breath and started up the steep slope. At the half-way point he stopped to rest and noticed the glint of metal on a spot of shale where the snow had been cleared away by the sliding gray. He was thrilled to see it was his revolver. Raif struggled the few steps across the loose rock and picked up the weapon. It was scarred but operable. Placing it in his still attached holster, he felt less naked. He was running low on ammo for the .30–.30, and if the people who wanted him dead returned, he'd need something to welcome them, even though they'd have to get a lot closer for the handgun to do much good.

After climbing up the slippery slope for half an hour, Raif finally reached the top. He was breathing heavily, and his leg was throbbing. It was too much to hope that the Morgan might still be somewhere near, so he was surprised to see the bay standing less than a hundred yards away. When he approached, the horse looked at him with sleepy eyes, then went back to gnawing at a few blades of grass he had cleared of snow with his hooves. He looked as tired as Raif felt.

Reaching for the halter rope, Raif saw why the Morgan hadn't gone far—the knot in the end of the rope had caught up in the branches of a downed tree. The Morgan had dragged it nearly fifty feet before deciding it wasn't worth it. Untangling the rope, Raif fashioned it into a makeshift bridle, then positioned the horse next to the fallen pine. Standing on top of the downed tree, Raif took hold of the Morgan's mane and painfully threw his leg over the horse's bare back. Once aboard the slippery, broad back of the horse, he decided to take the time to go back for his saddle and bridle. Then he'd hurry to catch up to Sam and the others. He only hoped he'd get it done before the coming storm dealt him another blow and accomplished what the assassins couldn't.

6

The snow was dry this time, but it was coming at Raif nearly head-on. A wind that he estimated at thirty to forty miles per hour picked it up and flung it at him, making it nearly impossible to see. Worse still was how it obscured the terrain, making him wonder if he were even headed in the right direction. Finally he knew he had to stop. Moving the Morgan into the shelter of a thick stand of pine, he slid from the saddle and leaned against the animal's side for support while he worked up enough energy to move into deeper cover.

Raif was hurting. The wounded leg was stiff and sore, but that wasn't his major problem. It was the storm that was taking it out of him. The freezing wind stung his face with brutal force and sucked the heat from his body, draining his strength. The snow was two to three feet deep in most places open to the weather, and it was drifting. His toes felt like cubes of ice, his face was numb, and his fingers, even inside the fur-lined gloves, were like sticks. The Morgan's skin was beginning to ice over in places, and he knew that if he lost the animal, it would be all over for him.

In addition, he was unable to see anything by which he could get his bearings, and felt like he had been wandering. Even though the trail looked familiar, he wasn't sure, and he knew that to continue would be foolhardy. He might survive the continued cold, though he doubted it, but it would do no good if he were going the wrong way.

He found a small clearing encircled by large pines that served as something of a windbreak. Dismounting, he loosened the cinch and removed the saddle. Then, using his gloved hands, he dug through the snow to uncover some long grass beneath for the Morgan. Raif couldn't remember ever being so cold, and his frozen fingers hurt like the dickens when they scraped against solid earth.

After he had fed the horse a fair sum of grass, he broke some dry twigs off the lower branches of the trees and lit a fire. Adding larger branches, he built up a big enough flame to warm both him and the horse. Gradually, the frost in his mustache melted and the chill left his face. Taking his cup and a small bag of elk jerky from his saddlebags, he made a broth using snow for water. While he waited for it to heat, Raif removed his gloves and let the fire get at his fingers. As they thawed they began to throb, a painful but good sign that he wouldn't lose any of them. While drinking his broth, he ate more of the jerky, intermittently turning his body so the heat could thaw all parts. He noticed the Morgan was smart enough to do the same. Raif only wished he had some oats and a bed of straw to reward the sturdy animal for his work and suffering. He smiled at the thought of Golding looking down, or up, as the case might be, and cussing his horse for saving a lawman.

Raif peeled a small fallen log out of the snow and placed it close to the fire. Like a fool he hadn't brought his bedroll along and he'd have to stay close to a well-fed fire through the night. If he didn't, by morning he might be greeting Golding first-hand.

He packed his cup with snow several times until it was two-thirds full of water again and added instant soup base from a small container in his saddlebags. Normally he didn't like the stuff, preferring the real thing to a crushed powder with half the nutrients and a lousy taste, but tonight it went down like honey.

He thought about Sam, Terri, and Bob, wondering if the assailants considered them as much an enemy as they did him. He didn't think so. There was really very little to which they could testify, little that they knew.

Maggie was a different story. She was a liability, someone able to tell what she had heard and seen. If they knew she was running around loose they might come after her, putting the others in danger by simple association. The question was, how much did the killers behind all this really know? They would have pumped Two Shoes and discovered Maggie was along. Self-preservation is a strong motivator.

Sam was good with a gun, good at keeping out of sight and turning bad odds into even odds—even better than Raif was. Hopefully, Bob was feeling well enough now to handle a rifle, and he was a good shot. Terri had proven she could use a gun and was a fighter. Back her into a corner, and someone would regret it.

He smiled. He had seen feisty women before but, in his experience, they were usually crude or had a strong distaste for men, much like Maggie. Terri was neither, but the way she had handled Golding's girlfriend, the punch she had laid on his own jaw, told him she'd do her share if anyone tried to stop them.

He hobbled a short distance away from his circle to a still standing but very dead tree and tore a dozen good-sized branches from it. Returning to the fire, he tossed four on. The snow had soaked his Levi's clear through but the heat was making them steam, drying them out. The white stuff was still coming down in sheets, the wind still pitched, but he was grateful for the storm—it would keep his enemies' chopper grounded and give him enough time to find his people and prepare if their new enemies refused to let them alone.

He wondered where Sam had decided to wait out the storm. There were several good places along the trail, but there was one better than all others. Sam called it Bear Hole because he had once followed a grizzly there.

It was a good-sized recess underneath a solid piece of granite, tucked away in a thick stand of trees. A person would have to walk right into it to know it was there. On a night like this, Raif knew he'd never find it. But then neither would the enemy, if they were even looking, which he doubted. Only a fool would be stumbling around in these hills now.

He picked up the saddle blanket and saddle and dragged them nearer the fire. He would use them for a make-do bed. Grunting with the pain, he spent the next twenty minutes stripping the dead tree of the rest of its reachable wood and stacking it nearby. When he figured he had enough to get him through until morning, he made a bed of pine boughs next to the fire, and laying down, put the wet saddle blanket on top of him. Thoroughly miserable, wet and in pain, he lowered his hat over his eyes and tried to get some sleep.

He had only one dream all night.

When it woke him up, he was in a cold sweat.

7

Raif hated his dreams even though most were like everyone else's, harmless, confused, idiotic settings in which fantasy and the ridiculous played the primary roles.

But there had been others. This was one of those. His dead brother was taunting him with Raif feeling angry and mean, wanting to beat in Hussa Qanun's thick skull.

The dream woke him, and he was grateful. The fire was nearly out and the cold had almost overcome him. After getting up and forcing the blood through his veins again, he saddled the Morgan and was moving in the first gray light of dawn. The wind had settled down considerably, but the snow was still coming, laying down a coat of fine powder that would have been the envy of most ski resorts. The trail was buried under three feet but the top half was fluff, making the Morgan's job easier.

He had been able to get his bearings and was closer to his destination than he had hoped. Another half a mile and he reached the trail Sam would have taken to Bear Hole. He slid from the saddle, his leg still paining him, pushed aside the snow and looked for some sign of their horses. It was there.

Mounting again he spurred the Morgan up the trail. As he came onto an open section of a ridge, he felt the cold wind at the back of his neck, and rolled his lamb's wool collar up against it. When he reached the point he knew

was above and west of Bear Hole, he reined the Morgan
into the trees. He found himself fighting the Morgan, having to rein and urge him through snow-covered deadfall
and across the slope, something the gray did instinctively
because of his training. But the Morgan was willing, just
cautious. With a little work, he'd be a fine mountain horse.

Raif saw the outcrop of granite a hundred feet away, but
saw no smoke and smelled no camp. It worried him some,
but it was early. They were probably still in bed or Sam had
refused a fire this morning for fear others might be close by.

He slipped from the saddle and tied the Morgan to a
tree limb. Removing his Winchester from its scabbard, he
quietly injected a shell in the chamber, then began working
his way into the bottom of the ravine. He moved cautiously
but a bit clumsy, his leg being stiff and sore.

The sound of the gun sent him diving to the ground.
The bullet hit a small tree before it hit Raif, lodging in
wood instead of flesh. He slithered through the snow to a
group of small boulders that formed a circle and planted
himself flat on his belly in the middle of them. He cursed
under his breath. This crap was getting old!

Hearing movement above and to his right Raif took off
his Stetson and warily raised his head above the top of the
snow-covered boulder, trying to get a bead on the shooter.

He located a man-made path in the snow that led into
a stand of trees with a large boulder at their center. Lifting
his rifle he prepared to fire. The muscle in his index finger
pulled down on the trigger as a piece of fur hat lifted above
the distant boulder. The bullet struck the object and thrust
it ten feet away from the boulder. Raif heard a curse.

Raif couldn't help the grin. "Sam, is that you?" he
yelled.

No answer, then Sam's head bobbed up above the rock.
"Raif?"

Raif didn't stand. "You took a shot at me, right?"

Silence. "Uh, yeah, s'pose I did."

"Nobody else out there. That was you?"

"What do you want, a signed confession?"

Putting the safety in place, Raif stood. "Sam, how many times have you been told you need to get some glasses!" He started out from behind the boulders and toward his friend.

"Don't need no glasses," Sam mumbled, picking up his fur cap and checking for holes. His finger exited near the top. He wiggled it. "See what you done?"

"Be grateful it wasn't two inches lower," Raif said.

Sam mumbled something as he put his hat back on, then jerked a gloved hand in the direction Raif had come. "You ain't riding the right horse. When I seen that Morgan, I thought you was them boys that killed Golding."

Raif laughed lightly, deciding to rub it in a bit even though Sam was a better shot half-blind than most men were who had 20/20 vision. "Blind as a bat! You probably woulda killed me, hung me, and had me half-skinned before you noticed who I was!"

Sam spat a wad of brown juice at the ground. "You gonna sit and jaw all day or come into camp?" He yelled it across the distance between them even as he placed the barrel of his .338 leisurely on his shoulder and started walking. Raif came out of the rocks, pushed through the snow, and joined him.

"I don't smell anything cookin', so I take it you had a cold camp last night."

Sam noticed his limp, glanced down at the blood-stained bandage and Levi's, but kept walking.

"When you didn't show up, I figured someone had rung your number and was lookin' to do the same to us." He paused. "Unless you shot yourself and somebody stole the gray, I'd say it was a right smart move." Another pause. "How bad?"

"Clean through, but I need some of that concoction of yours for infection."

Sam got a wicked grin on his face. "Glad to oblige."

Raif knew Sam's stuff burned, but it healed better than anything he had ever used, heard of, or seen. It was a painkiller, too. Something he would need if he was going to ride out of these mountains today in any kind of comfort.

Leading Raif through the trees, Sam skirted an outcrop of rock and ducked into the sheltered overhang of the Bear Hole. Terri, Bob, and Maggie were positioned behind a flat-topped boulder under the granite overhang he and Sam had always used as a table. Even Maggie seemed relieved to see him, and all three stood, Terri putting her rifle down.

"What did you do, cowboy, get lost?" she asked, smiling.

The relief in her voice pleased Raif and he returned the smile. "You could say that."

Terri noticed the wound and shot him a concerned, questioning look. Seeing them still healthy he had forgotten the pain, and what she was concerned about didn't register until he looked at the spot where her eyes rested.

"Nothing serious," he said. He turned to Sam. First things first. "Where's the radio?"

"In the saddlebags, but ain't no use tryin' to use it."

Raif had already started toward Sam's gear in its usual resting spot under the overhang. He stopped, turned around, waiting for an explanation.

"Don't work," Sam said.

Raif continued his journey, found the radio and pulled it free. The plastic and metal cover were broken and one section was missing. He could see the circuit board inside. It had a neat little crack running from side to side. He held it up, looking at Sam.

"Fell. Horse stepped on it," Sam said, matter-of-factly.

Raif glanced at Bob, Terri, and Maggie. Bob shrugged lightly and Terri nodded. Maggie had a slight smirk on her face.

"It wasn't anyone's fault, Raif," Terri said. "It bounced out of the saddlebag. Sam's packhorse stepped on it before I could let him know."

Somebody had to have left the saddlebag unstrapped, but he decided to let it be and simply dropped the thing back in the bag. "Get comfortable folks. I'd better fill you in on what this means." He spent the next fifteen minutes explaining what had happened, who he suspected was involved, and that they probably hadn't seen the last of them.

"Hawkes is mean," Maggie said. She paused, thinking, then decided to continue. "He's the one that put this deal together. Least that's what I heard.

"Benny has a brother name of Jasper." She shifted her weight to her left foot nervously. "Jasper was in this with Benny, but he started to get cold feet and Hawkes told Benny to kill him before he ruined everything. Benny didn't want to do it, but when he talked to Jasper, Jasper told him he was going to the cops because what Hawkes and his friends were doin' was bad, real bad, and it weren't right." She paused, turning slightly pale at the memory. "They argued and Benny shot him." She hesitated, looking down at her feet. "Benny gets crazy sometimes. Doesn't know what's he's doin'. But this time he knew, and it pained him some, but he did it anyway. Said it was necessary if we was ever goin' t' have a decent life." She sniffed, her eyes focused on the ground. Raif figured she had probably witnessed the whole thing.

"But Benny never told you who Hawkes's friends were?" Raif asked. "What it was that Jasper knew?"

She looked at the ground again. "I heard him say they was foreigners and they paid well enough we could retire anywhere we wanted." She seemed weak, scared, a disappointed girl whose dreams of getting out of a life full of misery had all been riding with Benny Golding. Raif thought that was like getting aboard a boat shot full of holes and still believing it would get you up river.

"What did Benny do with Jasper's body?" Raif asked.

"Buried it in the barn at his old lady's house. Told her

Jasper went away to see his divorced wife and kids in Colorado for a few weeks."

"Was it Hawkes who Benny sent Billy to meet yesterday?" Raif asked.

"I don't know for sure." She was trying hard to think. "There were others involved. Benny said they was all Hawkes's people and that they'd be here to take delivery."

"Any of 'em know you were involved?" Sam asked.

She nodded.

"They'll be coming after you then," Sam said.

"I didn't do nothin'," Maggie said.

"Tell us what you were delivering, Maggie," Raif said.

"Crates we had brung on a couple packhorses." Her hands were clasped, and she started wringing them. Possibly it was the cold.

Raif took a deep breath. "What was in those crates?"

She hesitated.

Raif figured he knew why. Even Maggie was smart enough to realize that she had been an accessory to some kind of serious crime, even if she hadn't known exactly what it was. Added to being an accessory in Benny's brother's death, not to mention the clerk's, it meant a long prison term. She was understandably scared.

"Maggie, what was on that packhorse?" Raif asked again.

Maggie didn't look up as she said, "I heard Hawkes tell Billy that stealing from the federal government could get them all hung, and that Billy, Benny, and Burt Crenshold should make sure that no one got drunk and started bragging about what they done."

"Do you know what he was talking about?"

Maggie fidgeted. "Two weeks ago they went to Cheyenne. Benny said it was business, and he told me I wasn't going along. When they came back, they were scared, but talking big—like they'd just pulled off the robbery of the year. Crenshold was struttin' around like he was

Jesse James or something. Billy just sat there, quiet and somber like, drinking vodka straight until he passed out. Benny and me . . . we . . . we went to bed."

"But he never told you what they stole?" Raif asked.

Maggie shook her head.

"Was it drugs?" Raif asked.

"Don't know. Maybe. 'Cept Billy liked drugs. If'n they'd a been stealin' drugs, Billy woulda been usin' 'em to get wasted, instead of Vodka."

"How did this Hawkes know to send that chopper after you, Raif?" Terri asked.

"I figure Golding told 'em I was involved before they killed him," Raif said.

Maggie got irate. "Not Benny! Never. Now Crenshold, he might . . . he would. He was a stinkin' coward! Benny wasn't afraid of Hawkes."

"Then Crenshold, woman!" Sam said impatiently. "Don't matter who, but even I can see they knew. And they know about you, too. All of us are loose ends, seems to me. And they'll be waiting for us somewhere along the trail out of here, and if Raif's shootin' it full of holes and this weather don't keep that chopper grounded, then we'll see that thing again, too!"

It was quiet. Raif was wishing he had the radio and figured everyone else was thinking about the same thing. No use crying over what couldn't be fixed.

"Will the sheriff come after us?" Terri asked.

"If he can get a chopper and get it in the air," Raif said.

"And if he doesn't hear from us, will he send in a search team?" Bob asked.

"Radios don't work well up here in the best of conditions. Too many rock mountains. Bad weather makes it worse. He'll believe that's the problem first. Probably start to worry about us in another few hours, but he won't send anyone in until this storm calms down. If we get moving, we can be out of here tonight."

"Unless someone tries to stop us," Sam said.

Raif looked up at the sky. The storm was socked in and the snow would only get deeper, making their chances even smaller. They needed to get out while they could.

"All right, let's break out a couple cans of peaches and some jerky, then we pack up and get movin'," Raif said.

Terri seemed glad to have something to do. She stood and told Maggie to help her ferret out the fruit.

Sam got up. "Time to fix that leg," he said.

Raif took the opportunity to talk to Bob. "Are you feeling all right?"

Bob looked down but nodded. "Y . . . yes."

"You're stuttering Bob. Sure sign of a concussion. I could stay here with you and send the others for help. The storm won't go on forever and they'd get a chopper into us. Riding out could make you worse."

Bob shook his head adamantly. "I . . . I'm okay. Help won't get here any quicker if we stay behind."

Sam returned. Raif decided to let it go for now. He removed his sheathed hunting knife and cut away the gauze bandage. The wound was red around the edges, and Sam wrinkled his thick brows as he looked it over. Without saying anything, he took the lid off a jar full of greenish-black goo, stuck his fingers in up to their first joints, and lifted a glob of the smelly stuff out of the jar.

"This wound looks like it was made with an automatic weapon. An M-16 unless I miss my guess."

Raif nodded. He was one of the few people in Jackson who knew Sam had been in the military. Vietnam. A volunteer with an ability to use a rifle as few men could. The Army made him a sharpshooter. They'd drop him into the backcountry, where he'd find a nice perch over a trail known to be used by the enemy, and pop as many of their leaders as he could before disappearing into the jungle. They had caught him once, but he'd escaped and worked his way back to his own lines, half-dead from the beating he'd been given and the exposure he'd suffered without food and decent water. They sent him home. The second day he'd been back in Jackson, he'd bought two horses, gear, rifles, other odds and ends and disappeared into the backcountry. He seldom came out until after Thanksgiving, then retreated to a small place down on the Hoback River. Some called him a hermit. Others, who knew his story, called him a war casualty.

Raif had often wondered how a man with about as many manners as a baboon and with only a sixth-grade education had ever survived basic training, let alone become one of the war's most decorated soldiers. But from what he had learned the few times Sam had opened up about his war experiences, his talent with a rifle made up for a lot of weaknesses.

Raif grabbed his leg above the wound as Sam none too gently spread the goo on the wound. It felt like someone was holding a hot frying pan to his skin. He gritted his teeth, sucking air through them. Sam only smiled.

"Cuss you, Sam! You enjoy this!" Raif protested.

Sam chuckled. "Only when it's someone else who's gettin' the treatment."

Bob had a look of disgust on his face. "Whew! . . . What the devil is that stuff?" He wrinkled his nose at the strong smell.

"A little o' this, o' little a that," Sam said. "Mostly roots, a little ground antler paste, a few odds and ends." He chuckled. "The good Lord's ointment for rectification of about any sore spot you might have."

"The smell alone could kill the patient," Terri said, returning with cans and opener in hand. "If anyone is out there, all they'll have to do to find us is take a hearty sniff."

"Seldom lost one that way," Sam said, putting on a serious face. He brought his fingers to his nose, then jerked his head back. "Never noticed! Sorta smells like my Aunt Jane."

Knowing what was coming, Raif couldn't help smiling.

"Jane died of flesh rot. Ya know, skin starts peeling first, then big hunks of flesh jist start fallin'." He shook his head. "Never was no funeral fer Jane. Couldn't find enough of her to plant. Animals just kinda followed her around, knowing anytime they'd be served up breakfast." He paused as if thinking. "Was somethin' to see, dogs and cats following her along like she was the Pied Piper." He laughed, then lifted the jar. "This here goo is made from the last part that dropped."

Raif was glad to see everyone smile, even Maggie, once the others did. Smiling was something none of them had done much of the last day and a half.

Sam finished doctoring Raif by packing the wound again with clean gauze. He returned the jar to his gear, removed a rag, and ripped a long strip from it, which he used to tightly wrap the wound.

"How's the burnin'?" He asked Raif.

"Still hot enough to fry eggs!" Raif said. "But even at that it's cooled off some."

Sam just nodded then used the remainder of the rag to wipe his hands as clean as he could before washing them with snow, then wiped them again before replacing his fur-lined bearskin mittens. "Raif, I think we had better stay clear of the main trails," he said.

"You know this country better than I do, Sam. If you know another way, I'm all for it."

Sam rubbed his shaggy beard. "We'll have to stay on it for a bit, then we can follow Soda Fork Canyon and go over east of Terrace Mountain, before dropping down into the South Fork of the Buffalo."

Raif thought about it for a moment. "It'll work, but that's tough country on a sunny day in summer." He explained to the others what lay ahead as Terri handed them each a couple of pieces of jerked elk meat then placed three opened cans of peaches in the center of the group.

Maggie handed each a spoon. While Raif talked, they took turns retrieving slices of peaches. No one seemed to care about sharing. When the peaches were gone, each ate what meat they could, then stuck the rest in their pockets to gnaw on as needed through the rest of the day.

"I say we do it," Bob said with forced bravado. Everyone nodded agreement.

After feeding the horses, they saddled them and packed up. Terri helped Raif tie the last of the ropes over one of his packs.

"The gray was a beautiful animal, Raif. I'm sorry," Terri said.

He nodded. Feeling the time was right, he approached her about her father's slight stutter.

"I know. He started talking like that yesterday afternoon, but I haven't seen any more bleeding in his ears, so its hard to know just how bad it might be." She was looking at Bob as he stood, watching the others, seemingly confused about what to do.

"I tried to get him to stay here with me," Raif said, "while you and Sam and the others go for help. He said no."

Terri nodded. "It's almost like it's slowing him down half a gear." She had a worried look on her face. "Let's just get moving, okay?"

Raif nodded. He felt helpless, like it was his fault. He handed her the halter rope. "I'll get the Morgan I'm riding. Sam and I talked and decided one of us will ride wide of the rest. Scout things out a little, make sure we're not being followed. That'll be me. You stay close to Sam and keep an eye on your father. Any further deterioration and we stop. Sam or I can stay with him until the rest of us can get help."

She nodded. "Be careful," then smiling, she added, "You're beat-up enough for one day."

He returned the smile, then turned away and headed out of the Bear Hole, the burn in his flushed face stronger than anything Sam's goo could cause.

He mounted, his wound feeling more numb than comfortable, and reined the Morgan in the direction Sam was taking the others.

Physically he felt better. Food in his belly, less pain than he'd dealt with in the last sixteen hours, and an optimistic feel for their chances now that they were together again. A good day of travel and they'd be back at his rig, loading up, ready for a hot bath and a warm bed.

He took off his hat and shook it even as he saw the train of horses, Sam in the lead, passing along the trail on the far side of the ravine. Stopping the Morgan, he watched them for a moment, then headed directly down his side of the same canyon. If they were going to get out today it was time to get moving.

CHAPTER

8

They stopped for something to eat at about midday. The snow had continued coming and was a good six inches deeper on the meadows than it had been that morning. Though the snow was light and dry, it was getting deep enough that pushing through had been difficult for the horses. They stopped and rested them a dozen times to avoid exhaustion. Their riders weren't much better off, fighting the cold, wet, chill of the storm that dragged heat and energy from them.

Now that they were over the top of the natural saddle east of Terrace Mountain and headed into lower elevations, the snow depth should diminish and their work get easier. At least, that was what everyone hoped.

Their cold camp was three quarters of the way between Soda Fork to the North and the South Fork of the Buffalo River. When they hit the Buffalo, they would turn west and follow it through Bear Cub Pass. After that there was only one correct trail to take. Hopefully, going this way, hard as it was, had kept their whereabouts secret, but there were still plenty of places for an ambush and they'd have to be on their toes.

They used two single-burner hot plates to heat soup for those who wanted it, but didn't start a fire. Though all of them were cold and wet and would have relished the warmth, the risk was too great that the smoke or the smell of burning wood would give away their location.

Bob's condition hadn't seemed to worsen. In fact he seemed to speak with less of a stutter than he had that morning, which made Raif feel a little better. While the others filled their bellies and rested up for the last push to home, Raif and Sam fed the horses some oats and let them drink a little from a small stream. After an hour they were remounted, tired but enthusiastic, able to see the proverbial light at the end of the tunnel.

Sam left camp first this time to ride point, and Raif led the others. They had a hard stretch of the pass to go through and Sam knew a spot from which he could get a good look at things before they did.

Taking the lead rope of Sam's string of packs, Raif headed out, the others falling in place behind him. He felt strong enough, but the wound was giving him some pain and discomfort. He'd be glad to see the end of the trail and knew the others felt the same, especially Bob.

The forest was quiet, the snow muffling much of the sound of their horses. When snow came to the high coun- try, everything seemed to rest, the cold and snow insisting everyone and everything be still. Raif felt like an intruder.

After an hour of enduring blowing snow and near zero weather, they entered a small meadow and Raif saw where Sam had left the main trail to get above them. They dis- mounted and gathered in a small shivering circle.

"This will be the tricky part of our journey. The river falls away rapidly just below us, creating a deep canyon that ends in a waterfall of more than fifty feet. The trail along- side is narrow and steep. With wet weather it will also be slick. Over the next ridge this trail joins with the main one that meanders along the Buffalo. It's a perfect spot for an ambush. That's why we came this way. If they're waiting for us they'll be watching that direction and we have a chance of getting around 'em." He paused to see if there were any questions. "Stay put, get a couple of the gas burners out and warm your hands, and get something hot in your belly. I'll look things over, then be back."

While they removed the burners, Raif retrieved his binoculars and went along the trail to a spot where he could see the canyon below. Using the glasses he checked what trail he could, but saw nothing. Changing positions he searched for signs of Sam where the ridge above jutted out, giving his friend an even better look at the trail ahead. He was there, half hidden by trees and stooped in front of his horse, his own binoculars at his eyes. It was a long five minutes before he turned and looked in Raif's direction, giving him a thumbs up sign that they should go ahead.

As Raif watched, Sam retrieved his rifle and returned to the same position. It made sense. From where he was, Sam would have a good shot at anyone waiting to surprise them. It would give them a chance if someone showed up in the middle of their getting to the bottom of the canyon.

Returning to the group, Raif found them bunched against the storm in a small stand of trees.

"Sam's staying up there. He's ready with his rifle. Most of the snow has blown off the trail but it's sure to be icy from the mist created by the falls. We lead the animals down one at a time. That means making several trips." He turned to Bob. "You take only one."

Bob started to protest, but Raif cut him off.

"That's the way it is, Bob. No arguments." He turned to Maggie and Terri, "Be sure of your footing, but let the animals find their own. They're good at it." He smiled. "When we get to the bottom there is a place, a camp, we shelter them there while we come back for the others. Bob can keep an eye on them," he paused again. "The worst spot is down about forty feet. You'll see the falls on the right. At that point the trail turns hard left but slopes to the outside. Loss of footing there will send you into the drink below the falls. If the fall doesn't kill you, the current and cold water will. It drags you swiftly to the right and away from the bank. You'll be able to see that you can't get out on that side and if we don't get to you in time, the current will carry you into rapids that even good swimmers would have a tough time beating. The real problem will be the cold. Stay in that water too long, and it will suck the heat out of your body like a sponge." He paused to see if there were any comments. There were stunned looks mingled with fear on their faces, but no one had anything to say.

"Stay out of the drink. If a horse starts to go, let him." He forced a smile as he picked up the reins of Golding's Morgan. "I take mine down first. No one else for now. If I don't come back, you'll know this wasn't such a great idea."

No one laughed.

Raif led his mount to the trail and started down. He slipped a couple of times, but nothing serious. When he reached the spot that concerned him most, the trail looked even narrower than he remembered it. He figured that it was still wide enough, took a deep breath, and started over it. The Morgan, reluctant, held back. He used a soft, gentle tone and firm hand on the rein to coax him forward and made it without a problem. Working his way to the bottom over half a dozen slick but passable spots, he tied the Morgan, removed his rifle from its scabbard, and did a quick reconnaissance of the area. Satisfied to find no sign of human presence, he put the rifle back in its place then climbed back up to where he had left the others. The trip down and back had taken nearly half an hour, and they were all glad to see him.

"All right, I'll take one of Sam's packs, you bring your mounts. Bob, you go first, then Terri and Maggie. I'll bring up the rear." They made it to the bottom in a little under fifteen minutes. Raif took a second to look up at the ridge high above him. Sam was still there. He was grateful that his old friend had shown up in the box canyon two nights earlier.

The three of them went back and brought three more horses down the trail. Maggie was leading one of Golding's packs through the narrow spot when it decided to turn back. She jerked on the reins and swore at him, but he still refused. She jerked again, but he pulled back again, a little frightened this time. It was obvious he was headed over the edge in no more than two additional steps when Maggie, with another string of curse words, and another jerk, got him moving in the right direction again. Not the way Raif would have done it, but on the narrow trail he had no way to go to her rescue. He breathed again when the stubborn animal was nearing the bottom.

It was a hard walk; he could see Maggie and Terri were tired and his leg was paining him badly. They rested before returning for the last four animals, two of Raif's and one each belonging to Sam and Golding. He considered making a separate trip for the fourth animal, but they had already taken up more time than they could afford. He decided he'd take two and let Maggie and Terri worry about one each.

He eyed Golding's last packhorse. It was a moody, cantankerous cross between a Morgan and a Standardbred. A poor one at that, and the animal least willing to be loaded this morning. Having watched Maggie deal with her last assignment, he decided she had better take Sam's bay pack, the easiest of the four to get along with. Terri would take one of his. He'd bring up the rear again, with a firm hand on Golding's pack, and by tying the halter rope of his last animal, a Morgan he called Jake, to the crossbreed's pack gear. Jake was steady and normally easy to guide. Most important, he wouldn't get nervous without awful good cause, essential if the crossbreed decided he wanted to turn back.

"Terri, you go first, then Maggie. I don't want anyone behind me if one of these two decides to get nervous."

Terri looked up from the log she was using to take a breather. "Two at once?"

Maggie joined in. "Crazy's what you are. Bingo don't like strangers, and even at his best, he's worse to get along with than I am!"

Raif smiled. "I appreciate the magnitude of the warning, Maggie, but it will be getting near dark in another two hours and we've still got a ways to go to get out of these mountains. I'm afraid another trip is a luxury we can't afford. Now, let's get moving." He undid the halter ropes and hooked Jake to Bingo's gear. Bingo stepped away, but Raif calmed him with a firm hand on the halter and a word in his ear. "Listen you cantankerous piece of glue base, you give me any trouble, and I'll throw you over the side. You can swim your way home." He pulled firmly on the halter and Bingo moved with him.

Overhearing Raif's version of gentle persuasion, Terri smiled as she untied her animal and headed for the trail. When they arrived at the worst corner, Terri went around smoothly, but Maggie's charge slipped on the slick surface. The bay screamed, fear in his eye, but caught himself and made the turn. The motion upset Bingo who jerked back on his halter rope. Raif sensed it coming and held firm, so did Jake. Bingo knew he had no choice but to go forward. They made the corner, but Bingo, happy to be past what he saw as a threat, lunged forward. The rope between the two animals went taught, jerking Jake off balance at the worst spot in the trail. He struggled to keep his footing, but the surface gave way, leaving him sliding toward the edge and scrambling for his very life. Bingo was pulled back, Raif with him, and they were all three headed over the edge. Knowing that it would mean he'd lose Jake, but that if he didn't cut the horses loose, he and Bingo were bound to follow, Raif ripped his knife free from its scabbard and sliced through the rope that bound the two animals together.

Screaming in fear, Jake floundered in vain to keep his

footing then fell over the edge. Bingo caught himself with his rear legs, but in a desperate effort to get away lunged forward.

Unable to get out of the horse's way, Raif was knocked aside by the animal's haunches and fought to keep his balance. Grabbing for anything and everything that might keep him from going over the edge as he slid down the icy slope, he found nothing and was suddenly airborne. Then he plummeted into the icy water.

The shock of hitting the water drove the air out of his lungs in one big rush. He kicked and drove himself upward, his head finally breaking the surface of the water just as he thought he couldn't hold his breath another instant. Something hard and heavy hit him and he grabbed for it. It was the top of Jake's packsaddle and Raif realized the animal was still under it and would drown unless set free. He still had his knife in his hand and took a deep breath before putting himself under. Finding the cinch he drove the knife between it and Jake and cut it through. The packsaddle broke free and floated away, allowing Jake a chance to get his head above water. Raif filled his hand with Jake's mane and held on as they both desperately struggled against the current that was dragging them away from shore. Gasping to catch his breath in the icy water, and just as he was about to give in to the cold current and quit struggling, Raif felt something hit him. It was a rope! He reached out and grabbed for it then hung on to both the lifeline and his animal, as if he had a hope of bringing Jake to shore; but the current ripped them apart and the horse was swept away.

Raif felt the anguish of making a bad decision to try to bring both animals down at once and the subsequent loss of his second horse in a week. Seconds later he was pulled, half-frozen out of the water. He wanted to help them as they strained to get him to his feet, but his muscles wouldn't work. He felt cold clear to his bones and was shivering so hard it made him sick. Dragging him free of the river, they laid him temporarily in the relatively warm snow. Seconds later they picked him up and placed him on one of Sam's skins. He knew they were speaking to him, but he was too cold to respond. They pulled at his clothes, removing all but his boxers, then threw the bear hide over him, fur against his flesh. He was shivering uncontrollably even as he felt two bodies slide in next to him. They sandwiched him between them, rubbing his hands and arms while letting their own warmth penetrate his skin and work its way into his frozen muscles and bones.

When his shivering died down some, one of the bodies slid from between the skins but the other hung on, willing her warmth into his. She was handed a towel and rubbed his face and head with it, drying the water off. Pressing her body against him, she held him as close as possible until the shivering completely disappeared.

Raif opened his eyes in the dim light and found himself looking directly into those of Terri. She smiled, relieved, but then her face changed to something he had only hoped he would ever see. She placed a hand behind his head and kissed him gently. He responded, letting himself feel the softness of her lips, the warmth of her body. She pulled away slightly, looking into his eyes as she moved a strand of damp hair away from his forehead with a soft finger. "You have a sorry way of picking up girls," she said with a smile. Then she lifted the skins and was suddenly gone.

Raif had never felt so warm and figured he was probably delusional and would come out of it once he woke up.

Seconds later the light filled his eyes as the skin was pulled back to reveal Sam kneeling above him. The mountain man smiled. "Some folks have all the luck." He looked down at the water-soaked bandage. Retrieving the goo and gauze Sam quickly had Raif's wound redone. "Found these in your packs." He handed Raif some clothes. "Get movin'. We're almost out of daylight, and we need to find shelter before it's too dark to dig in." He dropped the robe back over Raif.

Raif used it for cover and quickly removed the boxers and dressed. The clothing felt warm and made the goose-bumps go away. When he had pulled on fresh socks, he sat up and stuck his head out of the skins. His boots were sit-ting close, but were soaking wet, along with his lined coat and Levi's.

Good thing he had extra boots and a coat in his pack.

But that part of his gear had been aboard Jake. He looked around, knowing that he wouldn't find the animal, or the equipment he had cut free to save the animal's life.

Stooping by Raif, Sam handed him a pair of calf-length boots made out of bear skin, the fur still attached. Raif slid them on, knowing they would be comfortable and water-proof because Sam had made them by hand and knew what was needed in country like this. He also handed Raif a waist-length buffalo skin coat. It was warm but heavy, with buttons made of antler and leather cord. The hat was a Stetson. Or it used to be. Well-worn, the brim flopped down so low it was hard to see. He thought he must be quite a sight, but at least it would keep the snow off and his ears warm.

"I know you ain't used to such comfort, but don't get spoiled. I want 'em back when we get outa here." Sam smiled, then his face went serious. "Your pack went through the rapids. Not much chance of survival, but we'll take a look when you're ready." He stood and walked back toward the others. Raif got up, gathered the robes, and started after him. The others were huddled around the cook stove, fix-ing something hot to drink. All gave his new outfit a good look. Bob looked away, hiding a smirk on his battered face. Terri laughed lightly and Maggie out loud. He knew his face was a deep red color, but there wasn't much to be said. It was his own fault. Terri handed him a cup filled with steam-ing broth.

"Thanks. For this and . . . uh . . . warming me up." He glanced at Maggie. "Both of you." It was the first time he had seen Maggie turn a color other than angry.

"You're welcome," Terri said.

"The pleasure was all mine," Maggie added, sugar in her voice. Sam nearly choked on a throat full of hot coffee and spewed it into the snow.

"That stuff will kill you," Terri said with a smile. Sam only mumbled.

Raif, still a shade of red, took the offered cup, thanked them generally and turned back to retrieve his wet clothes.

They were stiff and ice cold to the touch. As he picked them up, then turned to go back to camp, Terri was standing there looking at him.

"You pick strange times and places for a swim," she said.

He smiled. "What happened after I left you stranded up there?"

"Bingo nearly forced all of us over the edge. We let the horses go and scrambled to the inside of the trail. They got away, but somehow we didn't get trampled."

"Who threw me the rope?"

"Dad. He said you taught him how to use one after last year's hunt."

"Glad I took the time. It's nice to hear he can do that. A bad concussion usually leads to a lack of coordination and straight thinking."

They started back toward camp. "I thought you were going to stay out of trouble." She put an arm through his and leaned into him.

He looked down at her. "Yeah, me too." He didn't know what else to say, her warmth and closeness continued to scatter his brains around the inside of his skull.

"We need to round up the other three packs before we can move outa here," Sam said. He was standing a few feet away cinching the saddle on his mount. "You comin' or are ya gonna dilly-dally 'round here all day?" There was a slight grin on his face.

Raif handed Terri his cup and clothes, then checked his own saddle. He watched Terri walk toward the others. Couldn't help himself. Terri Stevens made his heart race and his temperature go up like no woman he had ever met. He mounted the Morgan then spoke to Bob. "Thanks for hauling me out of the drink. One of you watch for signs of strangers. If any show, fire three shots in succession." Bob nodded as Raif reined the Morgan around and loped after Sam. What was happening with Terri would have to wait. Night was coming. They had to be out of the mountains before it arrived.

CHAPTER

9

They found Jake first. Wet and roughed-up. His head
hanging down between his forelegs, he was the picture of
tired bewilderment. As Raif dismounted and rubbed his
hand along the neck, back, and legs looking for injuries, he
glanced upstream at the rapids through which Jake had
come. Raif marveled that the horse had lived at all. As he
handed Sam Jake's halter rope, he noticed bits and pieces of
his gear washed up along the bank. Picking up what he
could, he placed them near a fallen tree. He'd return for
them on their way out.

He saw his Stetson next. It was beached on the bank
fifty feet away. Reining the Morgan to the spot, he retrieved
it. Not that the Stetson itself was worth much now, but the
band was. A half-inch wide strand of pure silver his father
had pounded out, etched, and decorated. Too wet to wear,
the hat rode astride the horn of his saddle.

They found the enemy next.

Following the trail left by the three horses, Sam had
reined in his bay and put up a hand that told Raif to be still.
Sam had an uncanny ability to hear things in the wild, or
the absence of them. Sam said it was something he had
picked up in Vietnam and that it had meant the difference
between death and survival too many times to count.

Sam quickly reined his horse into the trees and dismounted, rifle in hand. Raif did the same but brought his

binoculars along. He followed a cautious Sam up the side of the hill. Fifty yards from the top they went to their bellies and crawled until they could look down into a small canyon. A dozen horses, only two of them packs, were teth-ered with their saddles still cinched. Men milled around the fire eating, talking, and drinking coffee. Through binocu-lars Raif spotted Hawkes immediately.

"How the devil . . . ?" He put the binoculars back to his eyes, double checking. It was Hawkes all right, but how had he gotten in front of them if he had been the one who killed Billy?

He handed the binoculars to Sam, who took a look. "Seems we were wrong about Mr. Hawkes's whereabouts," Raif said.

"Seems. Hawkes must have loaned out an animal still carryin' that "H" in its shoe."

"Don't suppose he caught up, got around us," Raif said, already knowing the answer.

"This bunch come in ahead of us, not out of the same country we been pushing through," Sam said, handing the binoculars back. "Look at them animals. Fresh. Men, too. They called in that chopper. When that failed, Hawkes decided to come himself, cut us off." He spat in the snow. "Unless, o' course, they's just out huntin' in this blizzard, sharin' a good time with friends," he said sarcastically.

"How do you suppose he got around the sheriff at the trailhead?" Raif asked.

"Easy enough. Came up the trail northwest of Angel Mountain. Half a day ride on a real bad day like this one. I'd say he's been sitting here for a couple hours. Know any of the rest of them polecats?"

"Two. Walters and Gitry. Dumb but deadly. They beat up a Mexican in an alley one night a few weeks ago. Nearly killed him. They were bailed out but waiting trial." Raif stopped there. The Mexican was an informer for Raif. A growing community of seasonal workers from south of the

border was living in Jackson and among them was a growing number of drug runners. Moses Rodriguez didn't like it
and came to Raif. When Raif told him they'd need proof,
Moses said he'd get it. The next thing Raif knew, Moses was
in the hospital emergency room with a broken arm and a
face that would never be the same. He itched to get at
Walters and Gitry.

"Any way around them?" Raif asked.

"You know this country. There is, but it would be worse
than what we already been through, and them people of
yours are plumb tuckered out. I say we get on through here,
and quick."

Raif knew Sam was right. This was where the two trails
joined. A perfect spot for an ambush.

"They must have somebody watching out for us so they
can jump us. We'd best locate him," Raif said.

They slithered away from the hill and worked their way
along the backside of the ridge. They found the lookout
easy enough from the smell of burning tobacco. One man.
They got around him and continued a search before returning to their mounts.

"One guard watchin'. Hawkes is either a fool or doesn't
have much respect for your ability," Sam said.

"He'll learn. What do we do about the runaway horses?"
Raif asked.

Sam rubbed his chin. "Can't be far away, and on this
side of the ridge is my guess. We give ourselves an hour to
find them. After that we hope they survive long enough we
can get back and bring 'em out later."

Raif knew what it meant if they left the animals behind.
They had left the gear and skins somewhere as well, and
getting back to both would be near impossible unless they
had sudden spring in winter. But right now they had no
other choice.

When they returned to a warm but small fire, they had
the lost horses in tow. The animals had been pawing at the

snow, digging up grass in the shelter of some trees half a mile further down the valley. Over a cup of hot stew the women had put together, Raif told the others what they had found and what he thought they ought to do, then turned to Maggie.

"You sure about Hawkes?"

Maggie nodded. "I figure he as good as killed Benny, Deputy, and he's here to do the same to us. If it was me I'd take a rifle and shoot him clean, then I'd know he wasn't at my back somewhere, ready to pop me off."

"No killing, Maggie. I've got something else in mind." He told them his plan, and they all agreed.

But agreement does not necessarily ensure success.

10

Raif had asked Sam to provide a diversion. Something that didn't involve gunplay. Sam seemed pleased with the request and responded simply by telling Raif all he needed was someone to coldcock the guard at the top of the hill, then get the animals through when the world seemed to be coming to an end. Raif wasn't sure what his friend meant, and Sam wasn't offering to tell, but Raif agreed. Sam knew what he was doing.

Raif lay flat on his belly in the darkness less than ten feet from the guard while Maggie, Bob, and Terri waited a hundred yards down the trail, near the bottom of the canyon. They wouldn't come out of hiding until Raif had the guard removed and sent them a signal. Then they would move up the north side of the ridge and ready themselves to bring the animals down the south side and through Hawkes's camp when Sam provided his diversion.

Taking a deep breath and holding it, Raif slithered toward the small dot of fire burning on the end of the guard's cigarette. When he was close enough he simply stood up. The guard, shocked by the sudden appearance of something resembling a large fur-covered animal, let his mouth drop open, his cigarette falling into the snow. In the same moment, Raif stepped forward and pummeled him with the butt of his .30–.30, dropping him like a fly hit with a swatter. Gitry.

Score one for Moses Rodriguez.

Raif quickly tied and gagged him and threw his weapon in the trees, then removed a flashlight and gave the signal. A light flashed back at him, and Raif knew Bob and the others had started moving.

Scrambling along the backside of the ridge until he found Sam's tracks, Raif followed, careful to keep plenty of trees and distance between him and Hawkes's camp. Once at the bottom of the valley, he sneaked closer, then slipped into some scrub brush to wait for Sam's promised diversion.

Five minutes seemed like a full day. Raif got antsy, but stayed put. Sam's specific instructions were that Raif was to wait at a spot where he could see the enemies' tethered horses. When chaos broke out, it was his job to cut the tethers and send them packing, then get to Terri and the others on the far side of the camp. There Maggie would wait for him and Sam, their mounts in tow. After that it would be a run for the base camp several miles down the canyon.

Raif looked at his watch. It showed 5:45 P.M., and it was dark, cold, and the storm was still putting down another layer of snow. Sam was five minutes overdue, and Raif was getting impatient.

A minute later he heard something behind him. It was Sam, running through the woods, yelling obscenities over his shoulder. Raif watched, mesmerized. What was he doing!

Then he saw it. A grizzly, its large body romping on all fours after Sam. He was roaring, grunting, and mad as the hosts of Hades!

Raif swore and smiled at the same time, suddenly realizing what Sam intended. The camp was coming alive as the racket Sam and the grizzly were creating worsened, and Raif leaped for the tethered horses.

As Sam charged into Hawkes's camp, with the bear only twenty feet behind him, Raif cut the ropes, and the horses bolted, the smell of grizzly strong in their nostrils. He ran with them, using them to keep his presence obscured. He heard more than saw Terri and the others leading the string of horses down the path of the canyon wall. It sounded like they were at full throttle, but with men yelling and scrambling around Hawkes's camp, it was hard to tell.

Sam came blazing through the camp, leaped the fire, and ran into darkness again. As the fire loomed up in front of him, the bear came to a sliding halt. The men who hadn't bolted for the horses suddenly found themselves confronted by a grizzly the size of a small car. Two ran, tripped, picked themselves up, and ran again. Four others, paralyzed by the sudden appearance of the animal watched as the grizzly lifted onto its hind legs and roared, his long claws bared and ready to rip at anything that moved. Walters, standing next to Hawkes, grabbed a rifle that lay against a tree, dropped it, tried to pick it up, dropped it again, then decided half a second too late he'd better run. The bear swatted at him with his paw, and Walters screamed as the claws laid him bare to the bone across the shoulders. He stumbled away as the grizzly turned its attention to others too close for the grizzly's comfort.

Score two for Moses Rodriguez.

Raif was enthralled by it all and nearly forgot to run himself. When it dawned on him that he could be a target in an instant, he ran for the trail at the other end of the camp, a grin on his face. Sam had delivered one whale of a diversion—that was for sure! Now it was time to use it up and go home.

He reached the trail and was relieved to find it somewhat clear of snow, probably from Hawkes's group coming in. It would make their dash to civilization easier.

Terri came through the darkness and raced passed him with most of the horses in tow. Seeing the path partially cleared she drove her spurs deep and had her animals into a full gallop and past him in seconds. Bob followed, then

Maggie flew out of the darkness, practically dragging Sam and Raif's mounts behind her. She yanked on the reins of her horse and swore such a streak at the others that they all came to a screeching halt at the same time. Not pretty, but serviceable.

As panic continued in the camp, Raif untied the Morgan from the last pack. Sam did the same with his bay. They mounted the excited horses with some difficulty, the dreaded smell of grizzly strong in the animals' nostrils. The Morgan danced in a complete circle before Raif got him under control and got aboard. He turned to yell at Maggie to get going only to see her dismounting. Sam grabbed for the reins of her horse, but it broke away down the trail after the others before he could get a good grip.

Raif yelled at her. "Maggie! What the devil . . . !" Then he saw his .338 rifle in her hands. He gaped at his scabbard in disbelief! Empty!

As Raif jumped from his horse, reins still in hand, the gun thundered. He looked up to see Hawkes thrown back, landing in the snow half a dozen feet behind him. He didn't move. Maggie looked satisfied even as Raif jerked the rifle from her hands. He tossed it to Sam, who had a shocked look on his face.

"Tarnation, woman! You've done it now!" Sam said.

"Go!" Raif yelled at Sam as he mounted the Morgan.

Sam put spurs to his gelding, driving the animal down the trail.

Raif offered Maggie an arm, which she grabbed, ready to swing up when a gunshot thundered. Maggie went lax in his grip. He lifted, but she was dead weight. Too much of it even for his hardened muscles. The rifleman put his gun to his shoulder for a second shot and Raif had no choice but to let the Morgan go. They raced down the trail, Raif half-dragging Maggie. Hearing more gunfire but knowing he wasn't hit, he glanced over his shoulder to see the grizzly demanding more immediate attention. The shots were to bring the animal down. Knowing the bear didn't have a chance Raif thanked him for at least giving them one.

A minute later, in frustrated anger, Raif stopped the Morgan and let Maggie slip to the ground. He dismounted and knelt beside her, opening her coat to a blood soaked shirt. From the location of the wound he could see there was nothing he could do. She opened her eyes and focused them on Raif. He could see the life leaving her even as she smiled lightly.

"He killed Benny. I . . . ain't nothin' . . . without Benny." She wrenched with pain, then her eyes fixed and the air went from her lungs.

Maggie was dead.

11

They reached base camp about seven. They hadn't stopped moving since Maggie's death, except to give the horses a brief rest. Both riders and animals were exhausted.

Along with Forest Service officials and a few men from Teton County Search and Rescue, the sheriff and two other deputies were there to greet them. While the three bodies were being removed from the packs and placed on tarps to wait for the coroner to pick them up, Raif helped Bob and Terri into the back of a vehicle belonging to a Search and Rescue volunteer and sent them to the hospital. Terri had coaxed Raif to come along and get his leg checked. As usual Sam's concoction had worked, and though the wound was paining him some, there had been little bleeding, and Raif determined it could wait. He promised he'd be along soon, then watched them go with considerable relief. Bob needed a doctor.

While the two deputies and several from Search and Rescue took care of loading his and Sam's horses in the six-place horse trailer attached to Raif's rig, Raif and Sam sipped hot soup next to a fire the sheriff had built.

"Gitry and Walters are part of Hawkes's group," Raif said after giving a general overview of the last two days.

"The men suspected of beating up Moses?"

Raif nodded. "Maggie killed Hawkes, then was killed by one of his men." He couldn't help the smile. "Walters will be sporting a nasty wound. A griz swatted him, and I gave Gitry a good sized headache, probably a broken nose."

"Sounds like they should be easy enough to get along with, once we catch them," the sheriff said.

Raif told them about the chopper and the body of the gunman. "Strung him up a tree. If the weather clears we can retrieve him. He carried these." He took the wallet, money, and receipt belonging to the would-be assassin from the evidence bag he had tucked among the blankets on the packhorse. "The driver's license says his name is John Turner. I doubt it, but fingerprints should tell us for sure," he said.

"As soon as the storm clears, the Forest Service chopper will fly in from Cheyenne. We can go after the gunman's body then if you're up to it."

Raif gave an approving nod. "The enemy chopper was red. No numbers or identifiable markings, but we need to check with the airport to see if the thing flew high enough to get into radar. If not, it could still be in the Valley. Seen anything like that around?"

The sheriff shook his head. "Choppers have been a rarity the last few days. I searched every hangar, called every private concern and individual known to have one. Came up empty."

Raif nodded as he removed the items from his other pockets and lay them on the campground table. He identified what belonged to whom and carefully marked each item. He handed the sheriff the bag with the cans and other items from the camp where he had found Billy Two Shoes.

"Let's get you to town and a doctor." The sheriff stood as another department vehicle pulled in. At the wheel was Jess Farrell, detective lieutenant, and Raif's boss in investigations. His passenger was Shad Petersen, investigator, and Raif's sometime partner. The sheriff instructed Shad to take Raif into Jackson. He would stay behind and fill Jess in while they waited for the rest of Hawkes's group. The sheriff also instructed two deputies to see that the animals and gear followed in Raif's rig.

He turned to Sam. "Where to, and what about your horses?" he asked.

"The animals can go to Raif's. Just take me to town. I figure I'll sleep at my sister's place tonight."

"Will you be around when we go back in with the chopper?" Raif asked Sam.

Sam nodded but didn't reply. He hadn't said much since Maggie's death and their escape and seemed more tired than Raif had ever seen him, but then Raif figured he looked just as rough. Running for your life and watching people die took their toll.

There were still Golding's horses to take care of. As Raif stood he spoke to Jess, "I'd appreciate it if something could be done for those animals of Golding's. The bay Morgan I was riding is a right good animal, and worth some money. All of them ought to be returned to his people in Cody. Unless he stole 'em."

"A distinct possibility," the sheriff said. "We'll take them to my place until we find out. If they're his, we'll notify someone in his family and make arrangements to have them picked up."

Raif nodded his thanks and accompanied Shad and Sam, glad to have the pressure off.

As he passed by Maggie's body, he hurt inside. Here was a woman whose whole existence had hinged on Benny Golding. Her still form was mute testimony of how little future there was in relying on someone without a lick of sense and a mean streak the size of Soda Mountain.

As they pulled away from the camp, he looked in the rearview mirror on his side of the vehicle, glad to be finished with the whole ugly business, at least for now. He rested his head back against the seat, lowered Sam's floppy brimmed hat over his face, and closed his eyes.

It was the first time in his life Raif had ever been glad to leave the mountains.

12

Shad had delivered Raif to the emergency room of the Teton County Hospital then left to take Sam to his sister's. Raif sat in the emergency room, watching a doctor bandage his leg, when Terri stepped in, a tired but satisfied smile on her face.

"Hi," he said. "From the look on your face, I'd say the news is good."

"Dad does have a slight concussion but with some rest he'll be fine. They want him to stay the night for observation. His ribs are cracked and bruised, but nothing broken."

"They'll have to tie him down."

She laughed. "Actually, he's fast asleep and did little arguing. I think he's exhausted."

She moved to Raif's side, watching the doctor bandage his wound. "How are you doing?"

"I'll live."

"Unless blood poisoning, gangrene, or losing half his blood supply kills him," said the doctor.

"Terri Stevens, I'd like you to meet Adam Nethercott, local doctor and *former* friend of the family."

"And the doctor who has bandaged your wounds, fixed your broken bones, and sewed you back together more times than he can begin to remember," Nethercott said. He nodded at Terri, then looked back at Raif. "It's dangerous to be around this man, Ms. Stevens. He's a walking series of accidents that would kill most people. It might be catching."

She laughed lightly. "So I've noticed."

The doctor removed his rubber gloves. "Keep that wound clean, Raif. There is a little inflammation, probably brought on by Sam's goo." His eyebrows lifted showing his disapproval of Sam's homemade healer. Even though he had seen it work, Adam Nethercott was a traditionalist when it came to medicine. Antibiotics worked, super goo didn't. He handed Raif a prescription. "Take three a day for infection until the bottle's gone. The wound will pain you some, but the worst is over." He turned to Terri. "I'm glad your father is doing well. Get this one something to eat. His body thinks someone sewed his lips shut." He started for the door. "And Raif, please, don't come back." He closed the door behind him.

Raif smiled at Terri. "Are you hungry?"

"Famished."

He looked at his clothes or what was left of them. One pant leg was cut off almost at the groin. The other was still intact but stained with blood, mingled with water, food grease, and dirt. Sam's buffalo-skin coat and fur-lined boots lay on a nearby chair, the floppy brimmed hat resting on top of the disgusting pile.

"Not exactly formal attire," he said. "I'll need to pick up a few things." He let himself off the table, shoving the prescription into his pants pocket. Then he put on his shirt and Sam's boots.

"I'd like to go home, get a shower, and clean up," Terri said. "How about we pick up your things and go there? We can both wash the trail off, then get something to eat."

He nodded. Her place was in town, his was thirty minutes away if you counted both directions, more in a storm like this. And there was nothing in the fridge to feed his hunger anyway—unless you counted TV dinners and microwave burritos. And, the thought of spending more time with Terri Stevens was more than pleasant and worth waiting a few hours to get much needed sleep.

She started for the door. "I'll say good-night to Dad and meet you at the entrance to the emergency room. Five minutes?"

He nodded again. After dressing, he picked up the buffalo coat and floppy hat and left the room, heading for the pay phone.

The first call was to a friend who had a sort of taxi service. He made arrangements to be picked up in five minutes.

Then he called his parents but kept explanations simple. He was back from the hunt, and one of his clients was hurt, but okay. He was going to get something to eat then go home for sleep. He'd see them for breakfast in the morning. He figured that would be soon enough to fill them in on the rest.

He turned around to find Terri standing across the hall, eyes fixed on him. "You're a mess."

"Umm. I'll bet you say that to all the men you pick up."

"Are you up to this?" The question was full of concern.

"Like the doc said, my stomach needs to know my mouth still works." He held the door for her. "Shall we?"

They stepped outside to catch their taxi, and five minutes later were at a western clothing store on the south end of the center square in Jackson. He asked the driver to wait while he and Terri went in to get what he needed. The other customers gaped at him in disbelief, but he ignored them and walked directly to the men's section.

"You're quite a hit. You must entertain here often," Terri said.

He gave her a wry grin. They were joined by Allison Winters, a clerk Raif had dated a couple of times until she married some tourist from California, who had come to Jackson for a ski weekend. He had heard that the surf bum beat her, so she left him and was back at her old job—still looking for Mr. Right. The only thing Raif knew was that it wasn't him and it wouldn't be, even though they had gone out a time or two. Allison was one of the few ladies he had ever been able to relax with a little, but she was always talking about getting out of the Valley to some place she called "civilization." He would never leave Jackson and didn't want a woman harping at him about it twenty-four hours a day. It came to mind that the same thing might apply to Terri Stevens, but it didn't take much to ignore the reminder.

"My, you're looking fine this afternoon," Allison laughed. Then she saw the bandage. "Let me guess, one of your clients didn't like the service."

He ignored the dig and introduced Terri.

Allison gave her a smile. "Be careful, Terri. He's a heart-breaker, this one."

Raif busied himself looking for a new shirt. He found one, grabbed it and moved to find a warm but lightweight coat. Allison followed, but replaced the pinkish shirt he'd selected with a blue one. "Matches your eyes." She smiled.

Terri watched as Allison helped him pick out a coat, then the right size in Levi's, then socks. They headed for the boots. "Elk skin, calf hide, horse? Or something exotic, like armadillo?" Allison asked.

Raif stared down at Sam's homemade boots. They wouldn't do for an evening out unless he wanted to garner attention like honey garners bees. "Work boots, but polished enough for a night out. After that, it won't matter, so I want 'em durable." Allison went to the back while pointing at the dressing room. "Make sure the rest of that stuff fits. I'll get the boots." She disappeared as he headed for the underwear section. Terri followed.

"You two were a number once, weren't you?" Terri said, grinning.

Raif looked up then returned to his search. "She likes surfers or men with money. I don't fit in either category."

"She'd make an exception for you. It's in her eyes. Head-over-heels."

Raif quickly picked out a pair of boxers and an undershirt, then retreated to the small dressing room, unsure of what to say. Terri stood next to the closed door. "Do you have this effect on all the girls, or is this one the exception?" she teased.

Raif didn't answer, concentrating on undressing and redressing as quickly as he could. The blasted shirt was too small. He removed it and threw it over the top of the dressing booth. "Make yourself useful, Terri. Find that in a 17" x 34–35, will you?"

She laughed lightly but went to change the shirt. Raif eased on the boot-cut Levi's. Good fit. He left them on. Terri returned with a shirt and handed it over. It was a different color.

"You look better in browns," Terri said.

He put it on, just glad that it fit, then put Sam's floppy brimmed hat on absentmindedly. Next came the snaps on the long-sleeved shirt and tucking it in before feeding his belt through the keepers.

"Here, try these." It was Allison's voice. A nice but durable, size eleven boot appeared over the top of the door. He tried it on.

"Perfect," he said. She handed over the other one, and he slipped it on as well, then stood and stamped his feet to settle them in the new leather. Lastly he changed things from his old pants pockets to the new, opened the dressing room door, picked up Sam's gear and his own clothes, and stepped out.

Allison and Terri studied him, a look of curious disapproval on their faces. Terri turned to Allison. "It's the hat."

Allison smiled and nodded. "Definitely."

Raif looked out of the top of his eyes at the floppy brim. He'd gotten used to it. He removed it as the two women led him to the hats. He picked out a gray model, similar to the one he had nearly lost to the river. He placed the new hat on his head and pulled it down. It needed a little shaping and his father's silver band, but for now it would have to do. He noticed Terri's frown.

"What?" he asked.

She smiled. "The truth? You look better without it."

He glanced at himself in the mirror. He'd be naked without a hat.

"No offense, Terri," Allison said. "But folks around here wouldn't know Raif without a Stetson. They think he was born with it on."

"Yeah, I've noticed. I didn't know he had hair for the first three days of the trip."

They laughed and Raif pushed the Stetson firmly in place and walked to the cash register. "You ladies have no respect for a well-established American tradition. Baseball players wear caps, lawyers carry briefcases, and horsemen are naked as a jaybird without a Stetson." He smiled.

"In that case," Allison said with a seductive grin. "I suggest you forget the hat."

Terri's snicker accompanied Raif's obvious embarrassment. He clumsily removed his still damp wallet and fished out his Visa. Two hundred fifty dollars later, he was thanking Allison, then he and Terri headed for the door, his hands still full of Sam's clothing. He told his taxi-driving friend to pop the trunk and he put the clothes inside, then gave him Terri's address.

Terri and her father were staying just south of Snow King Mountain Ski Resort in a spacious, one-level condo of about four thousand square feet. With four bedrooms, three baths, a large kitchen, a recreation room, and a formal living room complete with grand piano and vaulted ceilings, Raif figured it was costing a bundle.

Terri directed him to a room down a long hall. It looked unused. He had deposited Sam's homemade gear in the mudroom at the back of the house, and was glad he had.

The white carpet, bedspread, and light-colored easy chairs, looked better unsmudged. Terri acquainted him with a few of the necessities before going to her own rooms at the other end of the house.

Before Raif showered, he slipped into the kitchen and scoured through the cupboards looking for some Saran Wrap. Taking the roll back to the room, he stripped and wrapped the bandaged area on his leg with the plastic wrap. Then he got into the shower, letting the hot water soak clear to his bones and relieve the tired ache there. It was a long while before he forced himself to turn off the water and get out. He toweled himself down and slipped on the one-size-fits-all terri-cloth robe he found hanging next to the shower door.

The medicine cabinet contained everything he needed for shaving. When finished, he removed a new toothbrush from a cellophane wrapper and pushed a dab of Crest onto it and cleaned his pearly whites. Curious, he surveyed the rest of the cupboards to see what else lots of money could buy. There was everything from extra toilet paper to various forms of headache reliever and bottles of three, name-brand mouthwashes. In one drawer he found half a dozen men's swimming suits. In another the same number for women, in various sizes, probably, he thought, for use in the hot tub, for which rules were posted on the back of the door. There was also a list of telephone numbers to call if anything was needed or if there were problems of any kind. It was twenty-four hour service. The lifestyle of the rich and famous. He wondered how Terri would react to his own bathroom, where it was hard to find toothpaste, there was only one brand of deodorant, and no mouthwash, and the only thing that was one-size-fits-all was his razor.

The eight-foot-long vanity was fitted with two oversized sinks with gold fixtures and a well-stocked bar underneath one end. He slid it open to find a dozen different kinds of hard liquor and a small ice box that did nothing but make ice cubes. All of it looked unused. He closed it. Raif had quit using hard liquor when he realized that drinking was becoming a habit. When you met with friends, you ordered drinks. When you felt low, you poured yourself a stiff one. When you ate out, drinks were in order, even if they made the food tasteless and the conversation stilted. He hadn't ever really liked liquor. The stuff burned his throat, was too sweet or too bitter, and it impaired his judgment and his memory. He hated being controlled by anything or anyone, and for him, addictions robbed him of control. Alcohol had been the cause of his becoming an orphan. His mother was half-Cherokee, half-Irish, and both halves loved liquor.

He heard the knock on the door just as he finished pulling on his last boot. Opening it he found Terri standing there working at putting on an earring. She smiled. "You men take so long."

She was beautiful. The white slacks and loose fitting red turtleneck sweater were perfect for her dark complexion and hair. He saw that she still wasn't using much makeup and it pleased him. No sense ruining a good thing. He reached for his coat and hat as she turned and walked back down the hall toward the main living area.

"Did you find everything you needed?" she asked.

"Yes," he said as she faced him. "You're a pretty lady, Terri Stevens."

She smiled. "Thanks, and devoid of bearskin and facial hair you're not bad, either." She smiled as she pointed toward a door near the front entrance. "I have a coat in there. Black leather lined with thinsulate or something. Would you get it, while I grab my purse?"

Raif walked to the closet and opened it. There were several coats, two of which he recognized as Bob's. He found the waist-length black leather jacket and removed it, knowing with the first touch it was the finest money could buy. She returned, and he held it for her to slip on.

"I guess you know, a perfectly good cow died for this," he said.

Buttoning it, she turned and faced him. "Touché."

"Now I suppose you'll want to go to some steakhouse and finish him off," Raif went on.

"You can't prosecute a person twice for the same crime, Raif. If he's dead, he's dead. I might just as well get the full benefit if I'm going to have to pay the full penalty." Her smile was growing on him.

"That's my motto: If you kill it, use it." He placed his hat on his head and opened the front door. "Where to?"

She smiled. "Well, first we go to the garage, unless you plan on walking."

Sheepishly he closed the door. "Forgot. No wheels."

She took his hand and led him through the kitchen to the garage where a new Ford Expedition sat in one of three bays. She removed the keys from her purse and handed them over. "I like the Gun Barrel Steakhouse. Okay with you?"

"Expensive, but for the lady from New York, only the best." He opened the door and let her in, then stepped around to the driver's side. Two shiny Arctic Cat snow machines stood perched on a trailer in the second bay, a later version of his own machine, except these were the souped-up models, had no dents, and probably ran without being worked on every mile or two. Against the wall stood several pairs of skis in a rack, with boots, gloves and poles all neatly lined up beside them. He slid underneath the wheel and pointed to the skis.

"Yours?"

She nodded. "Mine and Dad's."

"They look new."

"Last year's models. We haven't had much chance to use them."

Raif thought of his own skis. Six, seven years old, sides nicked, one busted binding. He hadn't had much chance over the last few years, either. Besides, the sport was too expensive anymore, unless you worked the hill as an instructor or had a spot on the ski patrol. At least for the average man working in the Hole. In fact, the last year he had been able to afford new skis was the last year he had patrolled Rendezvous Mountain at Teton Village.

He started the engine, and Terri pushed the remote door opener. He backed the vehicle into the plowed driveway, then the street, as the door descended back into place. The ice-covered road would have been slick except that it was well sanded, and they arrived at the Gun Barrel in ten minutes. Without even going in, they could see it was standing room only and there was a long line. They tried the Cadillac Grill next. Same story. Deciding the wait back at the Gun Barrel would be worth it, they returned.

Raif approached the hostess and signed in. Not so long after all. Half an hour, maybe less, she told him with a nice smile. He returned and took a seat next to Terri. "Would you like a Coke or something?"

She shook her head. "My bones still seem to have a chill. How about some kind of herb tea? Black with honey, please."

He ordered the tea and brought it to her, then sat back to enjoy his own Coke on the rocks.

The silence between them was comfortable. She leaned against his shoulder, her legs crossed, the cup held in the fingers of one hand and cradled in the palm of the other. Her closeness made him feel good. As he placed his hat on the chair beside them, he noticed one of the other deputies coming through the door with his wife and another couple.

Raif stood, Coke in hand, and made the introductions as Terri stood to meet them.

"You had quite a week. More excitement than the rest of us experience in a lifetime." As the deputy spoke, his wife was giving Terri the once over. She shot Raif a sly glance of approval. Thank the powers that be she didn't say what Raif knew was on her mind! Every wife in the department was constantly trying to line him up, get him married. Luckily for Raif, the other two couples had reservations and were immediately dragged away to their table by the hostess. As they walked away, Raif began breathing again.

As they sat Terri put her arm through his and let her fingers rest on his palm. "News travels fast in Jackson," she said.

"Yeah, my money says it will be in the paper by morning."

"Umm. I wonder how it will read when two of the main characters haven't even been interviewed yet," she smiled.

"Sparse, with a light touch of fiction and a whole lot of speculation."

She laughed. "It sounds like *The New York Times*."

He grinned. "I guess some things remain the same, regardless of the size of the city." He paused, then said, "That's a pretty fancy place you're staying in."

"Dad's company owns it, and several others at various locations around the country. Good customers use them mostly, but the last few years Dad has taken the time as well."

"Your dad is a self-made man. I admire him for that. But from what he told me, he lost a lot getting there."

"If you mean his family, you're right." She sipped her tea. "My mother left him because their worlds never seemed to intersect, especially after he started his own business. She took me and my brother with her. Donald was upset because Dad couldn't afford Ivy League schools and fast sports cars at a time in Donald's life when those meant everything. Because of it he's always blamed Dad for his dead-end job and dull life and probably always will."

"But partly justified," Raif said.

"Yes. Kids deserve live-in parents, but having decided to make my living in that dog-eat-dog world of business and finance, I'm beginning to understand why Dad wasn't there. It's a horrible commentary on our society, but if you're going to survive in my world, really make it, there is a cost, and that cost is often your family." She paused, smiling.

"Is that why you've never married?"

She looked a little surprised.

"Sorry. Sometimes I spout off without thinking," he said.

She touched his arm. "No, no, it's not that. In fact your honesty is one of the things that sets you apart from most men I know. It's just tough to be confronted with the truth, that's all." She paused to sip her tea. "Yes, my career has come first, for a long time. Getting ahead, proving myself in a man's world, was everything. That all changed a couple of years ago."

The hostess approached them to tell them she had a table ready. She led them to one next to a rock-faced fireplace, where Raif seated Terri, then took his own chair. Both were famished and concentrated for a minute on the menu. The waitress soon returned, and Terri ordered a 16-oz. T-bone. Raif asked for the prime rib.

"What changed?" Raif asked. "Why did your career seem less important?"

"Me, that's all. The world stayed the same, the career, the people around me. All of it stayed the same. I just began looking at them differently." She sipped her water. "I wasn't yet thirty, had an apartment downtown, was a junior partner in one of the country's biggest law firms, and was socializing in New York's most wealthy and influential circles. I had it all."

She paused as if trying to decide how to express herself. "In that world, you are caught up in a continual round of excitements. As long as the excitement keeps coming, you have something to hang onto, a reason to keep going, fulfillment. But when you really look at it, you see that much of it is empty and meaningless. I think that's why there is so much infidelity and intrigue in that world. It creates that excitement, keeps things alive, gives people something to do. If there is nothing to do, there is nothing, no purpose to life, and you suddenly realize how empty you are. Nobody wants to feel that way, so people in those circles eat, drink, and are merry to avoid looking into that emptiness."

She shook her head. "I woke up one day and saw what a crock it all was. I tried to ignore what I saw, to go on as if it were the most wonderful life a woman could have, but I couldn't." She smiled at a memory. "I started seeing a shrink like everyone else. His advice was that I was still too inhibited. I had to let myself go even further, enjoy the life I had, live it up! Have an affair or something! Travel, see the world!" She laughed. "More excitement—that was his answer—the culture's answer, for every depression, every moment of emptiness. Fill it up with excitement!" She shook her head sadly again. "It's a manual full of lies."

"What made you change your mind?"

"Believe it or not, there are a few people in that arena, at least on the fringes, who have their heads on straight. One of them asked me out."

The waitress brought their salads. Terri picked up her fork. "I'm ruining dinner for both of us." She forced a smile. "Better eat."

Raif figured she was talking about Ted Hancock. Bob had told Raif about Ted. He sounded like a good man. A Mormon, he had reintroduced Terri to her religion. Bob said it had saved his daughter, given her something to live for when she needed it most. Ted Hancock was an important part of Terri's life.

Raif's appetite seemed to have waned a little, but he picked up his fork and started eating. Halfway through the prime rib he found his appetite again and concentrated on renewing his depleted fat supply. While eating, they made small talk about his parents and family, her mother and brother. She had a lot of questions about the Valley, especially the business community. She said her father was thinking of moving a recently purchased subsidiary to Jackson.

For dessert Terri ordered apple pie à la mode while, full to the gills, Raif tinkered with his Coke. He was once more amazed at how she could put away so much and show so little. Her figure was perfectly proportioned and trim. But then he had never seen a woman with so much energy. In the mountains, she had never really been able to sit still. If she wasn't helping with the cooking, she was gathering wood, or taking care of the horses, or bathing in a cold stream. He could easily see what she might be like in a law office. He imagined her male colleagues, with their macho egos, thinking they could outrun and outwork any woman, having to concede there was at least one exception.

"You're amazing," he said. It was only an admiring thought, but it came out sounding differently than he had intended.

Terri was just taking the last spoonful of her ice cream and pie. With a puzzled look on her face, she asked, "What do you mean?"

Raif tried to cover himself by treating it lightly. "I mean, if I ate like that I'd look like a bloated steer." He leaned forward. "You seem to use it up faster than you take it in."

She smiled. "Thanks for the compliment. . . . I think."

He felt a little flustered. "I guess what I really mean is that I've never met anyone quite like you, Terri. You're amazing in a lot of ways, that was just one that occurred to me at the moment."

Wiping her mouth with her napkin, she said, "You're a bit amazing yourself, and, to return your compliment, I've never met a man quite like you. Most are tripping over their egos most of the time. You aren't, although on the mountain you were still a little . . . protective—like you didn't think I could handle it."

"You couldn't. Not at first."

"Ahh, a sign that he does have an ego." She smiled.

"No argument, but the fact that I didn't trust you completely at first is not a sign of it." He paused. "What makes you a good lawyer?"

The question caught her off guard and deflated a response near the end of her tongue. "Hard work, great schooling, working with attorneys who know what they are doing."

"Same thing makes a person good in the mountains. But it takes time. You weren't ready to be trusted with the big cases, so to speak, the first day, or even the second. And only because you were willing to learn, and to work hard were you ever trusted at all. Too many come up here with the belief they can handle anything. They get all upset when I won't trust them with my animals or to just wander off on their own. They think that their position or their money buys them ability, trust. It doesn't. Ability is learned, trust comes after that. You're a quick learner, and I came to trust you as quickly as any man I've ever taken into those mountains, but you still had to earn it."

"And my gender and muscle tone were never an issue?"

"Brains and initiative can offset physical deficiencies, in some instances completely negate them. The physically challenged show us that everyday, but there are limitations to what all of us can do." He paused. "A person has to do the best he or she can, then accept their limitations and let others pick up the slack. If they don't, they slow everybody down and get caught up in an ego trip that drains the energy needed for important things. That's what my father calls a fool's errand."

"No one is an island unto himself?"

"Something like that. When you're in a pinch, the greatest asset a person can have is the ability to involve others, give up his or her ego for the good of the whole."

"Like your reliance on Sam," Terri said.

"I hadn't thought of it in personal terms, but yeah, I suppose that's an example. Without Sam, we might not have made it, but you and your father were a part of that success as well." He paused. "I know men, Easterners who head corporations, who, in that situation, would have gotten us all killed."

"How?"

"By insisting we defer to their leadership skills, even though they were operating in a foreign arena. Frankly, Sam and I were the best qualified to lead in that environment. You and your father, and even Maggie, recognized that and gave us your undivided support. Some would have tried to take over, tell us what to do. They think because they have expertise in one area, they should be followed in all others. Success can breed egos the size of that grizzly Sam conjured up and be just as deadly."

"And if Dad and I had egos like that, and we had tried to take over, what would you have done?"

"Chopped you down to size and saved your neck anyway." He smiled. "But the point is, you didn't, and your willingness to concede that someone else was better suited to getting the job done added as much to our success as we did."

He fingered the rim of his half empty glass. "Now, I've got a question for you."

She smiled. "Shoot."

"Why did you defend Howard Manhope? He was as guilty as anyone I ever saw come before the courts. You must have known."

She shook the ice in the bottom of her glass. "Because no one else would and every man has a right to a proper defense." She looked at Raif. She might have taken offense, but looking into his eyes, she felt this wasn't some kind of attack on her as a woman, or even as a lawyer. It wasn't an attack at all. He was obviously genuinely interested, she just wasn't sure why.

"Why the interest?" she asked.

"I'm a cop. I'd like to know what went wrong with a case that seemed signed, sealed, and delivered. Call it your contribution to my education."

"Two of the witnesses hadn't actually seen what they told the court. I showed that. Even if a man is guilty, you have to convict him on real evidence, not supposition. The detectives on the case let people get away with lies, may have even encouraged it. I caught them at it, and the jury had no choice."

"Umm. The press painted you as a witch out to destroy the system." He smiled. "Never did trust the press much. How did you handle it when he killed again?"

"With two weeks of deep depression, then I came to grips with it, and moved on."

"On to what?"

"Other cases." She paused. "Actually, I considered leaving law altogether. I still might. The system has too many holes in it anymore. If you're not fighting lies and corruption, you're fighting the law itself, which is so full of loopholes it acts like a sieve. In the past, laws were made to protect the innocent. They've changed, now they protect the guilty, especially if the guilty have a lot of money or power. The little guy hasn't got a chance against the corporation with deep pockets. Worse, the people haven't got a chance against criminal millionaires who tie the courts, juries, and the law in knots with so much bull you'd think you were standing in a barnyard." She paused, calming herself. "After a while you start feeling dirty."

"So what is the answer?"

"In criminal law? Seal off the loopholes with good legislation and get judges who don't try to legislate with a gavel. In areas where attorneys file frivolous or unworthy suits just to get a settlement, make 'em go to court, and if they lose, they and their clients pay all costs. You'll cut cases by two thirds and give judges a chance to do their homework on cases that really matter."

"And put a lot of attorneys in the poorhouse."

"Better them than the rest of the population. The cost to the citizens of this country to cover such cases is billions in higher insurance payments alone. And the sad thing is the people who really deserve the money don't get it. Attorneys take half of everything, minimum. If a case has merit, they should get paid for their defense. Paid well enough to provide a living, not a penthouse in downtown New York."

"I sense a rebel in the ranks."

"Makes me sick, that's all." She gave a sheepish smile, realizing she had been on her soap box.

"Ever thought of running for public office?"

She gave a wry grin. "Moving from one corrupt business to another wasn't what I had in mind."

Raif was laughing when the waitress approached the table and asked if they wanted anything else. Terri shook her head.

"Are you sure you wouldn't like coffee?" Raif asked.

She smiled. "Knowing you know that I don't drink coffee, I'll take that as a bad stab at humor."

"Oops. Sorry." He smiled, then handed the waitress his Visa card. She took it and went to figure up costs.

"Dad has invited me to work for his company. I'm considering it," she said.

"Which division?" Raif asked.

"A new one," was all she said.

"Thus, all the questions about the Valley and its business community."

She nodded.

The check was returned, and Raif filled out the tip and signed the receipt. The waitress gave him a copy and thanked them both.

Shouting from the parking lot greeted them as they

exited the restaurant. Two men stood face to face, yelling at each other. Next to them were two vehicles, one a pickup and one a Cadillac Eldorado, which seemed attached to one another. As the name calling heated up, Raif excused himself, went to the two men, showed his badge and asked what the problem was. Each tried to out-yell the other and gave Raif nothing but a headache.

"Sir," he said to the driver of the Cadillac. "Please go to your car. I'll get a city policeman here, and he can take down your view of things."

Grudgingly the man turned to leave when the owner of the Ford pickup shouted an obscenity at him. The Cadillac owner, a young and husky man of about two hundred pounds, came at the pickup owner like he'd been shot out of a cannon. Raif just happened to be in the way.

The Cadillac owner tried to shove Raif aside, while the pickup owner tried to come over his back. A doubled-up fist came at Raif's face from the Cadillac owner, but Raif ducked, came around the back of the man, grabbed an arm and jammed it up between his shoulder blades. He drove the man forward, forcing him into the owner of the pickup, knocking him to the ground. Raif kept his captive moving, slamming him against the side of the pickup. He had no cuffs or weapon on him, so he grabbed the first thing he saw—a piece of bailing twine in the back of the pickup. He had roped for enough years that tying up a calf's legs was second nature to him, and in less than five seconds he had the first man's hands bound. He shoved him to the ground on his belly and told him to stay put unless he wanted to spend the rest of his vacation in the county jail.

He turned just in time to see the second man getting up and coming at him, a scowl on a face and a tirade of profanity pouring from his mouth. Raif ducked to one side as the idiot swung at him. A slight shove knocked him off balance and a tap with a booted foot did the rest. Mr. America ended up lying next to his opponent. Raif grabbed another piece of twine and tied his hands behind him while reading him his rights. He then stood and turned to Terri. "Call a cop will you?"

She smiled and nodded her head then worked her way through the crowd that had gathered in front of the restaurant entrance. Raif went back to the two and read the other one his rights.

Terri returned just as a city police car pulled into the parking lot. Explaining the situation to the officer, Raif turned it over to him, promising to file a report in the morning. He then escorted Terri to her Expedition and unlocked the door.

"One thing about time spent with you, Raif Qanun, things are never boring." She smiled as she got in the vehicle and he closed the door behind her. His leg wound throbbed, and his muscles ached, and, frankly, he was tired of being a lawman on his vacation.

They drove back to the condo the way they had come, neither saying much, both tired and comfortable enough with each other to settle into a relaxed silence. Normally Raif would have been a nervous wreck to sit in silence in the presence of a pretty woman. It was different with Terri.

As they approached the condo, they saw a white Taurus bearing a Hertz bumper sticker parked in the driveway. Raif pushed the remote and the door to the garage lifted. As he pulled the Expedition into its bay, he asked, "Are you expecting company?"

She shook her head as she let herself out of the car. Before she and Raif reached the door leading from the garage into the house, a well-dressed stranger opened the door.

In obvious shock, Terri inquired, "Ted, what are you doing here?"

The man in the Wall Street business suit only smiled, then took Terri in his arms and kissed her. Raif felt sick to his stomach.

* * *

Turning the Expedition off the main highway and into his lane, Raif drove the half-mile to his self-built log home. All the while he stewed, thinking about Terri. He had known it was a long shot from the beginning. Terri Stevens was a prominent lawyer, a big city girl, beautiful, and about as westernized as a New York Deli. He had never liked the East, the big cities in particular. He hated operas, longhair music, and novels by Danielle Steele, or whatever her name was. Terri probably went nuts over all three.

Religion was another problem. She was a Mormon, he was Islamic. They both believed in prophets but beyond that the two religions were as different as they could be. He had grown up with Mormons as good friends, had even listened to their missionaries. It was a good religion, and the Mormons he knew in Jackson were good, honest people, some of the best. But his family was Islamic and would stay that way, and the two religions simply couldn't be reconciled. He knew the odds against making interfaith marriages work. They weren't favorable, and Mormons were especially set against such things. They believed marriages lasted beyond the grave but only if you married inside their temples. To do that you had to be of the faith. A covenant they called it. Not that he minded it, in fact the idea held considerable pull. Too many in the world had lost sight of such binding commitments, but if he had to join the Mormon faith, leave his own . . . well, it was a lot to ask. And if that was what Terri believed and wanted, it left him out and he wasn't about to pursue a relationship that made things difficult for everybody. No sense in it.

Those were his thoughts as he drove home alone from Terri's condo, the memory burning in his brain of Ted taking Terri so confidently in his arms and kissing her.

Still, he had let himself believe there was something happening between him and Terry—something he had never felt in just the same way before. He thought about the softness of her lips against his, when she kissed him under the buffalo skin.

Then he shook it off. He had no claim on Terri Stevens, and it was apparent Ted Hancock did.

Pulling the Expedition to a stop in front of the house, he noted his rig parked next to the large barn several hundred feet away. He clicked off the lights, but let the motor continue to run for a few moments, glad to see home again.

He had built the house himself, from foundation to roof. It had been necessary in order to afford it. At twenty-eight hundred square feet on the main floor and with a full unfinished basement, it was something he could grow into over time. But for now, it had only one finished bath and no garage. The furnace wasn't in yet, either, and neither were most of the interior walls. He hadn't had the time nor the money. He heated it with a wood-burning stove and considered himself lucky to have such a large room in which to sit and watch his thirteen-inch television. At present, there were few kitchen cupboards, and no tile, carpet, or hardwood on the plywood floors, except in the kitchen where he had laid some Spanish tile he had been lucky enough to find at a foreclosure sale. Everything else would come in the future, but right now they were only a dream.

In comparison to what Terri Stevens was used to . . . well, there just plain wasn't any comparison.

He turned off the key and let himself out of the vehicle. Hitting the remote, he locked it, then opened the door and let himself into his house thinking he'd find the place cold, but it wasn't. His parents seemed to know what he needed most and when. He walked to the woodburning stove and opened the door, adding a couple of split logs from the stack near the wall.

The real fireplace wasn't finished. Raif had only half the river rock laid, so the woodburning insert a friend had built for him filled the square hole and heated the house. He finished shoving in enough wood to keep things warm until early morning, then closed the door and dampered the stove.

He walked to the north end of the house and entered his bedroom through the only door in the entire interior. The spacious bedroom had double-insulated windows that looked out over the river and up at the Tetons, although tonight there were too many clouds and too much darkness to see anything at all. In the daytime, the windows in his bedroom provided a view he never tired of.

His house and barn sat in one corner of his father's one-hundred-acre ranch on the west side of West Gros Ventre Butte. The ranch was bordered on one side by the Snake River, which was lined with trees. The place was secluded, beautiful, and a dream partially come true.

Going to the master bath, the only bath, Raif brushed his teeth and removed his clothes, tossing them over a chair he had built from pine logs and lined with comfortable cushions. It was the only chair in the house and was a project he had completed on cold nights while working near the hot stove.

Turning out the lights, he climbed under the covers of the bed that he and his father had built and stared up at the vaulted ceiling. He was exhausted, but his mind wouldn't shut down. It was the first time for several days that he had really had a chance to think about what had happened to him and what he would have to do next, but his mind avoided the subject, focusing instead on Terri.

Bob had told Raif about Ted Hancock, not by name, but by way of information given about his family. This was the man who was enamored with Terri—a Wall Street front-runner who Bob considered something of a boor, but who had been kind to his daughter and would never mistreat her, even if he probably couldn't really love anything without Ben Franklin's picture on it. Too cold, Bob had said. Too involved with business, with making money, to really love a woman like Terri.

And yet Ted, whatever his name was, had flown thousands of miles to see Terri. Not exactly the sign of man who didn't care.

He turned on his side, closed his eyes, tried to black out his mind. An empty void, no thoughts, no feelings, that's what he needed. Then he could sleep.

He tossed onto his other side. No chance for a void, so he'd try and change the subject. He thought of Crenshold first. Crenshold was local. He lived with his mom. They'd have to get a warrant, search the place, see if they could find anything out about what the small-time crook had gotten into.

Then he remembered the notebook.

Raif threw off the covers and walked barefoot into the living room. His personal gear was piled in one corner near the door, his still-wet clothes lying in a heap next to his saddlebags, where the deputies had deposited them. He went through the pockets until he found Crenshold's notebook.

The wood in the stove flared up as he opened the door and gave enough light so that he could see the writing on the pages.

There were several addresses and phone numbers, all of them local except one. That one was in Cody, probably Golding's. Empty pages, more empty pages, then a small hand-drawn map. He turned it this way and that, trying to figure out what it was. Then he saw it. Soda Mountain, the Yellowstone River, an X near the junction between it and Castle Creek. It lay a few miles to the north of where they had been when Terri killed the elk. Had that been the spot where Billy went to meet others for his delivery?

He had hunted that country and tried picturing it in his mind. A meadow, open at one end with sheer cliffs at the other. Raif and his brother Hussa had both killed elk there on the same day. A beautiful, secluded little valley, with water and shelter. Something to check out when they went back.

More empty pages, more. Burt Crenshold wasn't a great note-taker. On the inside of the back cover was an address and phone number. This one was in Cheyenne. Raif retrieved his phone where it sat on the floor and returned to the fire.

Using his business calling card number, he dialed Cheyenne. The phone rang several times before being picked up.

"Fort Cheyenne. Night Watch Officer speaking."

"What is your name, soldier?"

"Corporal William Stanley, sir. May I help you?"

"This is Raif Qanun, Sheriff's Deputy in Teton County, Wyoming."

"Yessir?"

"Corporal Stanley, have you had anything unusual happen on the base as of late? Anything stolen?"

"No, sir, not that I know of." There was a silence. "Sir, does this have anything to do with Corporal Roberts's death?"

"It may. Can you fill me in?"

"I would refer you to Colonel Adam Blakely, Night Watch Commander, sir. You can reach him in the morning, here, sir." The voice had stiffened into formality. It was obvious he was following strict instructions.

"I'll do that, but can you answer just two questions for me? It's very important to an investigation we have going on here."

"If I can, sir."

"When was Roberts killed?"

"A week ago, while on this same watch."

"Cause of death?"

"I'm not at liberty to say, sir. Perhaps Colonel—"

"Yes, I'll give the colonel a call tomorrow. Anything come up missing the night of Roberts's death?"

"Sir . . . really, I'm not at liberty. . . ."

"Thanks, Corporal. Tell the colonel I called and that I'll get in touch with him." Raif hung up. "Looks like Roberts got in deep water," he said to himself. He thought of the crates Maggie mentioned. Ammunition? Guns? Something worse?

He thumbed through the notebook again. Nothing else of substance, except the map.

He put the phone down and went back to his bedroom.

It was another hour of thinking things through before his exhausted mind shut down and he went to sleep. He had the questions but the answers would have to wait until tomorrow.

13

Raif was in the office by seven o'clock. He logged on to his computer and did the paperwork on the argument in the parking lot first, getting it out of the way. Then he started writing up the events of the last few days. Shad walked in at nine, said his hello, and started his own bit of work. Jess came in five minutes later.

"Sheriff wants all of us in his office at nine-thirty," Jess said. As chief of investigations, Jess assigned cases, and Raif worked directly under him. When he gave an order, Raif listened. But if Raif disagreed, they could talk it out. Jess was good that way most of the time.

Raif nodded as he hit the print key on his computer. The printer gave him hard copy as he picked up the phone and called the Cheyenne military base and asked for Colonel Adam Blakely. If Golding had taken something from the base and sold it, it was time to find out what it was. He was soon on the line with Colonel Blakely, Night Watch Commander and director of stores. Raif introduced himself and went over the questions he had asked the corporal last night. When he encountered even greater reluctance, it made Raif angry, so he launched into new ones.

"How did Roberts die?" he asked.

"You have to understand, Deputy, that this whole thing is under investigation. At this point I can't make any comment. I'm sorry. . . ." The colonel seemed nervous, tense.

Raif tried to keep his cool, knowing that losing it would only make things worse. But it was obvious the colonel was hiding information, and Raif didn't like it.

"I understand your position, Colonel, but we have an ongoing investigation here as well, and we were told by an informant that two of our suspects may have stolen something from your base. Now if that something were weapons, or explosives, or something like that, and a danger to public safety. . . ."

"Suspects? What suspects?"

"Two men—Benjamin Golding of Cody and Burt Crenshold from here in Jackson, along with a man by the name of Billy Two Shoes."

There was a short silence. "We'll be in touch. Until then there is to be no mention of any possible involvement by personnel on this base. Is that understood, Deputy?"

Caught off guard, Raif didn't respond before Blakely disconnected.

He hung up the phone with some hesitation, his mind on what had just happened. He had always hated liars, but he especially disliked the kind who try to shove people around while they do it.

He leaned back in his chair. Something had definitely gone wrong at Fort Cheyenne, and Colonel Adam Blakely was trying to hush it up. The question was, why?

"Time to go," Jess said, as he clicked "save" on his Word Perfect file menu. Raif glanced at the stack of papers on his boss's desk and knew what they were. Last night's arrests, calls, etc. They all had to be carefully checked and entered in the computer before handing them over to the prosecutor. Even if it was minor, if the deputies on patrol made a mistake in their paperwork, attorneys would jump on it like trout to a fly hatch.

They crossed the parking lot to the main offices. Growth and overcrowding had forced the detective section into temporary quarters, but it was just as well. Being away from everyone kept them focused on their work.

"Just to bring you up to speed," Jess said, "we booked Gitry and Walters and four others." He smiled lightly. "After we treated both of the former at the hospital. You broke Gitry's face, and Walters, well, he had fifty-eight stitches in his back. Looked liked someone ran over him with a very sharp hay rake." Jess couldn't help the laugh, then cleared his throat before going on. "Gitry said they left Hawkes's body. Said they couldn't find all the horses you spread around the countryside and some had to ride out double. No one wanted Hawkes as a riding companion, so they buried him in a shallow grave. They also said they had to kill that grizzly. The animal wold have killed all of them, and they had no choice."

"The one sad note in the whole affair," Raif said.

"Yeah, well, all of 'em, but Gitry and Walters, made bail."

"Made bail? This is murder, Jess. How—?"

"The others said it was Gitry who shot Maggie. He claims it was in self-defense. They were just up there hunting, minding their own business, when you guys came plowing through. We haven't connected anything to Hawkes yet, Raif, so we can't hold them without some evidence that they were involved in a crime. Even Gitry and Walters will be out before long if we don't come up with something more than what we've got." They stopped at the door to the main building. "It gets worse, but I'll let the sheriff fill you in." He didn't smile, and Raif didn't like the feeling he was getting.

Heading past the main counter, they walked back to the sheriff's personal office. Several patrol deputies hanging around gave them a nod and an inquisitive look as they passed. The deputy who had been at the restaurant had a smirk on his face and said something under his breath to the one next to him, who looked over and grinned. Raif felt his dinner date with Terri Stevens had become the talk of the office.

The sheriff nodded a good morning and told them to take a seat. Then he shut the door.

"Has anyone besides Hawkes's group come out of the wilderness?" Raif asked.

"Not yet. I don't expect them to. Hawkes had a high-tech radio in that camp. Gitry or one of the others probably warned whoever is out there." The sheriff sat down behind his desk. "We have people covering the trailheads they might use, and the Forest Service is looking for their rigs. They had to unload their animals somewhere." He shook his head. "The weather doesn't help. We can hardly get off the main road, let alone into the backcountry."

"They'll probably wait it out. Dig in and let the snow cover their tracks until they get word it's safe enough," Jess said. No one disputed what he was saying. A storm like this brought things to a standstill in the Valley. In the high country it was worse. If they didn't get out when Raif brought his own people down, they'd have to dig in. Mother Nature wouldn't leave them any other choice. Raif had the thought of them all freezing solid until summer and it wasn't all that unpleasant. He shoved it aside knowing this bunch had other means of escape.

"They'll come out by chopper when the skies clear," Raif said.

"Shad, is Search and Rescue on alert?" the sheriff asked.

Shad nodded. "When the weather breaks, we'll get some planes in the air, see if we can find any sign of 'em. Airport control has been notified to let us know of any planes flying anywhere near the area, especially any that don't identify themselves." He paused. "But everyone in here knows that a chopper in those mountains would be hard to detect if it kept low and in the canyons. We didn't detect it once, we might not again."

"Nothing from other airports? No choppers needing a

sudden landing spot?" Raif knew the answer before asking, but he gave it a stab anyway.

Shad shook his head. "Nothing. My guess is you wounded that bird, and he went down out there somewhere. We'll find it sometime in the spring if we're lucky." He didn't sound anymore convinced than Raif felt.

Raif said, "This isn't some Po-dunk operation, we all know it. They've got a safe house somewhere, and that bird is parked, waiting for parts." Nobody disagreed. He had another question. "Something this big usually brings a state forensics team in. When can they get here?" They didn't have their own forensics people, no small town did. All of them relied on the state office in Cheyenne, and they were usually swamped and at least two weeks behind on most cases. Raif felt like this one should be an exception, jump to the front of the line. He was hoping the state felt the same.

Shad broke in, "The Forest Service chopper left Cheyenne this morning. A team was on board. Weather isn't as bad over there. But they only got as far as Pinedale before they were grounded. We're hopeful they can get in here this afternoon, allow us to retrieve some bodies." He looked at Raif with a smirk on his face. "Heaven only knows you left enough of 'em laying around."

The sheriff smiled but moved to his next question. "Any chance they might find something if we fly them back to that campground you found?" He asked the question with a hopeful tone, even though all of them knew a storm like this would cover physical evidence until spring thaw. Then it would be mostly useless. Raif verified that knowledge with a tentative shrug of his shoulders.

"Chances are maybe one in fifty. Two days ago there was two feet on the ground. I expect there's four by now. Take a lot of diggin' just to get to solid ground. Time would be better spent looking for the killers." He leaned forward, his elbows on his knees. "Gitry and Walters know what's goin' on. I wanna talk to 'em, get some answers."

Shad glanced at Jess who was shaking his head in the negative. "Larry Noble was waiting for us when we hauled the entire bunch in. It was under his direction that the four went free and Gitry and Walters went mute," Shad said.

"Noble?" Raif said. "Since when can Walters and Gitry afford Noble?"

"Beats me," Shad said. "And Noble doesn't give breaks to the poor."

"Whoever is paying Noble is making promises. Big ones," Jess said. "Walters is a stubborn mule and wouldn't talk if you hung him from his thumbs, but Gitry has the heart of a chicken, and just the thought of doing time would normally give him uncontrollable shakes. But, this time, the air of confidence he's wearing on that ugly mug of his makes you want to throw up breakfast."

"Gitry needs to understand he's expendable, the walking dead," Raif said. "If he doesn't think so, he needs to be reminded about Golding and Crenshold. Whoever is behind this will shut him up, permanently, if they have even the slightest idea he's a threat."

"We reminded him. He didn't even break a sweat," Shad said. "Same with Walters. My bet is if we could check their bank accounts we'd find out why."

The sheriff spoke. "Noble wants them out of jail. He says we have no right to hold them. It was self-defense." He leaned back. "At this point I think the judge will agree."

"Then I suppose Noble is pushing to get this before a judge soon."

"The judge left town before the storm hit. Some sort of meeting in Cheyenne. Could be a few days. Probably Monday."

"I want to talk to Gitry more 'n ever," Raif said.

The sheriff leaned back. "You can't go near 'em, Raif."

Raif stiffened. "What?"

"Noble is after your hide. He's trying to make you responsible for the death of Hawkes and claims that if anybody should be in jail, it's you, not his clients. He says you had no right tearing up their camp and claims you allowed Maggie to shoot Hawkes, and that makes you at least an accessory to murder. So far he's got about half a dozen witnesses who claim they'll swear to that story."

"Maggie told us Hawkes was involved with the bunch trying to kill us. We had no choice. If we'd waited, they had enough firepower to bury all of us." Raif paused. "As for Maggie killing him, it was done before I had a chance to stop it."

"Bob and Terri Stevens back you up, Raif," Shad said. "They heard Maggie tell you Hawkes was connected to Golding, and they say it was a group decision to take the offensive."

The sheriff glanced at Shad. "You're getting signed affidavits?"

Shad nodded. "I have Terri Stevens coming in this morning, and I can get one from her father at the hospital anytime before noon," he said. "Can't find Sam. He left his sister's place early this morning."

"By now he's probably out at my place picking up his animals," Raif said.

Jess made a note.

"What about your own report, Raif?" the sheriff asked.

"I filled it out this morning." He leaned forward and handed the sheriff the brown envelope in his hand. "There are photographs in there. I had them developed at that fifteen-minute film shop on my way in."

The sheriff opened the envelope and removed the 8" x 10" photos, spreading them out on his desk. Raif leaned forward and picked up one, handing it to the sheriff. It was the shot of the horseshoe print with the stylized "H" on it.

"Hawkes had a thing about identifying his equipment. That print was found in the campground where Billy Two

Shoes was killed. It should help make a connection to Hawkes," Raif said.

"Maybe," the sheriff said, "but Noble can use it against you as well."

Raif was confused and it showed on his face.

The sheriff went to a map on the wall. He pointed to a spot. "Hawkes was killed here. The horseshoe print was here, right?" Raif nodded and the sheriff pointed to another spot. "Noble is going to ask how he could have gotten from one place to the other without wings."

"He didn't. Only his horse was in the campground, and whoever was riding it musta borrowed it from Hawkes. Everybody knows he has his animals reshod when he sells 'em."

"That's not the point, Raif. He'll use it to throw doubt on your decision to believe Maggie. He'll ask why you didn't talk to Hawkes and his people, why you just believed Maggie when you knew Hawkes couldn't get from here to here that quick." He poked at the two places on the map to emphasize his point. "Second, Noble is already claiming that the horses were stolen from Hawkes a week ago. This photo will do more damage than good."

Raif saw it. Noble was trying to make him look like an amateur. And maybe he had trusted Maggie too quickly. He had done it more on instinct, believing in his gut that she wasn't lying to him. He had been careful to keep gunplay out of it, and Sam had strongly agreed, but had he let his dislike for Hawkes affect his judgment? He hadn't thought so until now, but maybe.

"You've arrested Hawkes twice. Beat the crap out of him for mishandling a horse once. Noble will make you look like a vengeful cop, too quick to jump to conclusions. At the very least, Raif, he'll discredit you as a lawman," the sheriff said. "It could get nasty unless we come up with some solid connections, and I don't want you hassling Gitry and Walters, adding fuel to the fire." He leaned forward.

"Get more. I want Hawkes, Gitry, and Walters directly tied to that bunch still in the wilderness, and to those who used that chopper. I want evidence that justifies your conclusions, Raif. It's the only way we'll get Noble off our backs."

Jess looked at Raif. "I heard you on the phone to Cheyenne. Some colonel. What was that about?"

Raif told them about the death of Corporal Roberts. "I was talking to his commanding officer, a Colonel Blakely. He's unwilling to fill me in, even warned me to keep the base out of it, but I figure Roberts was an accessory. If we search deeply enough, I think we'll find a connection to Golding and Crenshold."

"He *warned* you?" the sheriff asked. "And didn't give you a thing?"

"Nothing. I think somebody important oughta lean on him." Raif turned to Jess. "The Army's Criminal Investigation Division would be involved in this wouldn't they?"

"CID? Yeah, they would. They investigate anything that happens on military bases," Jess said.

"You told Shad and me you roomed with a CID investigator during your last training session at Quantico. Any chance he might be able to find out what happened in Cheyenne?" All deputies, in fact most law enforcement investigators, got training at the FBI Academy at Quantico. Raif had been twice, so had Shad. Jess had been double that and had connections all over the country. It was a sort of unofficial web everyone used when investigating something or someone just outside their official domain.

Jess nodded. "Jed Stringham. It's worth a call." He made a note.

The sheriff picked up the pictures of the man Raif had shot out of the helicopter. "Send this one to the FBI ID center. See what we can get." He opened a plastic bag carrying the things Raif had gathered from the wilderness.

They were careful to keep their hands off the items so as not to smudge any possible fingerprints. The last item discussed was the receipt from the Moynihan Gallery. The sheriff assigned Raif to check that one out. "We should get some prints from some of this stuff. Near as I can tell, Raif, you did as good a job as you could under the circumstances. Anything else here we ought to pay special attention to?"

Raif handed him the notebook and explained the map. "If there is time and the weather permits, we'll check it out when we go back in for the bodies."

He picked up the pictures. "I'll need these."

The sheriff stood, and Raif and the others got to their feet, knowing the meeting was over. He spoke to Jess again. "Get a patrolman out to Hawkes's place. Until we get a warrant, I want it watched. Anyone comes or goes, we're to know. And Jess, I want this tied in so many knots it will take Noble a lifetime to unravel them, and I want it before noon tomorrow."

As they left the room, Raif spoke to Shad. "Crenshold lives around here. Get a search warrant. Jess, maybe you could call Cody. I'm sure they've searched the place where Billy Two Shoes and Golding were living, but we ought to see what they came up with."

"Looks to me like we're after weapons," Shad said.

Raif nodded, "Or explosives." He had an unsettled feeling churning up his stomach like a post hole digger. He had seen what the enemy was willing to do to its own people when there was even the slightest chance they might become liabilities. This wasn't some small-time weapons dealer selling automatics on the street. This was major weapons theft, and these people killed at the drop of a hat. That worried him a good deal more than Larry Noble or the loss of his job. If the enemy thought they were getting too close, more people could get hurt. People like Shad and Jess.

He cautioned them to watch themselves and headed for his pickup. It was still snowing heavily, and he had to brush several inches off his windshield.

The Moynihan Gallery was located on the town square in Jackson. Raif found parking across the street and dodged a Toyota Forerunner with a ski rack full of skis as he crossed. The boardwalks were covered and fairly clear of snow. He walked to the entrance and went inside.

Raif enjoyed art, especially anything that portrayed wildlife in the backcountry or the old West. An imposing sculpture stood just inside the front door, a bronze of an Indian on horseback, chasing half a dozen buffalo. He studied it carefully for a minute, admiring the detail. He glanced at the tag, caught his breath, and moved on. Art work that cost as much as a couple year's feed for his horses would not be greeting people in the entry of his home.

"May I help you?"

The man was new. "Is Tilly around?" Tilly Whitehead was a young Indian woman of the Shoshone tribe, well educated, and a good artist in her own right. She worked at the Moynihan to feed her addiction to oil paints and Jackson Hole.

"No, I'm sorry sir. It's her day off. Possibly, I can help you."

"I'm Deputy Qanun with the Sheriff's Office." Raif took out his wallet and showed his badge, then the receipt, still encased in its plastic container. "You sold an original Bev Doolittle painting to a man on the second day of the month. Dark hair, dark complexion, paid in cash."

The man viewed the receipt through its plastic shell. He was thin, with the stoic face of a butler, his head balding from the front backward. It appeared to Raif that he let the right side grow very long then combed it over the top to hide some of the shiny scalp that glistened in the overhead lights. Vanity did strange things to people.

"I'm sorry, I didn't make the sale. As you can see. . . ." he pointed to initials at the bottom of the receipt, " . . . the salesperson was the manager."

"Is he around?"

"She. Just a moment." He went through a door into the back. The Moynihan had recently changed managers, and Raif didn't know this new woman. He had heard she was stiff, formal, and a bit unfriendly unless you smelled of money. But Raif had found it didn't do much good to listen to rumors.

A woman appeared and walked toward Raif. She looked to be about forty and was dressed to impress. Her red suit covered a white silk blouse set off by extravagant Indian jewelry. Her potent perfume reached him before she did.

"Officer," she said, "what is it you wish to know?" She forced a smile.

Raif showed her the photo of the dead assassin. "Do you know him?"

She got a little pale. Raif glanced at the picture. The guy wasn't exactly presentable for a photo session. He put the picture back in the envelope. "Sorry."

She forced the corners of her mouth upward a little. "He . . . he is the man who purchased the picture you're asking about. What happened?"

"He fell out of a plane."

She gave him a disbelieving look.

"Can you tell me anything about him?"

"He wore an expensive business suit then, and a knee-length wool coat of the same quality. He said he was staying out at the Village for a few days. One of the condos." Raif perked up.

"Did he take the Bev Doolittle with him?"

"No, he wanted it shipped. A place in San Francisco. I have the address if you want it."

"Please."

She walked to a counter and reached underneath, bringing up a binder. Thumbing through it she turned the binder so he could read it and showed him the address.

"Do you have a copy machine?"

She nodded. "Yes, just a moment." She removed the

sheet and stepped through the door into what Raif thought must be the office, then returned a moment later, copy in hand.

"How long ago did you send the painting?" Raif asked.

"The date we decided on is written on the receipt." She showed him. "Seven days ago."

"Was he alone when he made his purchase?"

"No, there was a woman with him." She seemed to think of something. "Wait." She pulled a day planner from under the counter and thumbed through the pages. "This is the number of the condominium he was using. I delivered receipts of the mailing and insurance information to him just the other day." She seemed to get pale again. "He can't be dead," she said softly.

Raif borrowed her pen and wrote down the number and name of the condo on the sheet she had copied. "Thanks. Anything else?"

"Both seemed well-educated, wealthy. She wore expensive clothes and jewelry. Dark hair, black actually, and very large eyes, dark brown. A beautiful woman, but . . . cold."

"When they left did you see them get into a vehicle?"

"Yes. It was parked across the street there. A Lincoln, I think, with a Hertz sticker on the bumper."

Raif folded the paper and placed it in his pocket. "Thanks. You have a good eye for detail."

She smiled, genuinely this time. "I always take a close look at my customers, their identity papers, and their license plates. In this instance, however, it was more a matter of habit than anything. They paid in cash."

"Thanks for your help." He started for the door.

"I am sorry he won't be able to enjoy the painting." She paused. "How on earth did he fall out of a plane?"

Raif deadpanned it. "Head first."

He tipped his hat and left the gallery. As he drove back to the office, he mulled over what he had discovered.

Money. Lots of money. A woman involved, but was she only an innocent bystander or part of whatever was going on?

Returning to the county buildings, he parked his vehicle in the slots left open for official use only, turned off the key, then headed for the office. He'd need another search warrant.

14

It was nearly noon when they arrived outside the condominium at Teton Village Racquet Club. Raif and Shad approached the main desk at the club's reception center and flashed their badges to the clerk on duty. They showed him the search warrant, and the clerk went to get the manager, a slim-faced man with a body to match and the air of a stuffed-shirt snob.

"We don't make it a practice of interfering in the affairs of our guests," he said.

Raif smiled. "We don't make a habit of delivering search warrants. And this is a search warrant. So I suggest you get your pass key and lead the way."

The manager retrieved a set of keys from a cash drawer, banging it shut to show his displeasure. "This way." He said it with bored disdain.

They left the building and walked the short distance to a condo. In the grayness of the day, Raif noticed lights on in a couple of windows he suspected were a bath and bedroom on the second floor.

They stepped to the door, and the manager knocked before Raif could stop him. He grabbed the stuffed shirt by the arm and yanked him to the side. The manager tried to jerk his arm away but Raif held it.

"Are you really this stupid or just having an off day? Warrants are issued for bad people, bad people carry guns,

guns shoot through doors. Any questions?" Raif asked. The manager's face changed to an off-white, and Raif let go of his arm. He and Shad positioned themselves, one on each side of the door, their guns out of their holsters, safeties in the off-position. The manager turned another shade of white and also flattened his back against the outside wall. As he knocked on the door, Shad couldn't help smiling at the change in the manager's demeanor.

There was no answer, but Raif thought he could hear muffled noises. He rapped his hand against the metal door one more time.

"We're with the sheriff's department. We have a search warrant. Open the door." Nothing. Raif turned to the manager. "Keys." Shaking fingers placed them in the palm of Raif's hand. "Which one?" Raif asked.

The manager nervously shuffled through them, selected the right one, and held it up.

Keeping himself to the side of the door, Raif shoved the key into its slot and turned it. Shad pushed on the door with one hand, and it swung inward. He positioned himself and went in first, his gun extended in front of him. Raif followed, using the same technique, at the same time hearing quick steps behind him. The manager had fled to his office for a less exciting exercise in paper shuffling.

Shad worked left, Raif right. They finished on the first floor and went to the second. Two bedrooms, two baths. Expensive clothes in each closet. Both rooms appeared to be occupied by men, although a single, designer dress hung in one of the closets.

Determining the place was uninhabited at the present, Raif stowed his gun and began a more thorough search of the second floor while Shad returned to the first and shut the front door. He began his own drawer-by-drawer search on that level.

Raif found luggage, men's clothing, underwear, and jewelry in each room, all top-of-the-line. He removed a couple of pieces of luggage from the closet of room number one and opened each case. In the second he found an American passport for John Turner, the man who fell from the chopper. At least they had the right place. He finished searching that room more thoroughly but found nothing else of significance.

In room two, he pulled the suitcases from the closet and put them on the bed. The first two were empty, the third contained a passport for a younger man, brown hair, blue eyes. Name of Bunnell.

He left the luggage lying on the bed and looked under the bed. Nothing there.

In bathroom number one there were the usual toiletries, costly electric razor, colognes, shampoos. In bathroom number two he found similar items, but the items lay on the counter as if recently used. Even the mirror dripped of condensation, and the shower walls and curtains were still wet.

Mr. Bunnell hadn't been gone long.

He searched the medicine cabinet and found a prescription for Pepcid, issued in San Francisco to a Lucinda Bell. Glancing around the room, he saw nothing more than the dress hanging in the closet. Had whoever owned it left for parts unknown or just moved to another condo or hotel?

Raif left everything untouched. Forensics wouldn't like him messing up their work before they could get to it.

He walked into the small hall at the top of the stairs, checked a small utility closet, then heard a creak in the ceiling above him. He froze, his eyes moving to the ceiling. Overhead in the closet there was a panel that appeared to access the attic.

"Shad, come up here, will you?" Raif pulled his revolver.

Shad let the cushion in the couch fall back in place and came up the stairs. Without speaking, Raif pointed to the ceiling in the closet, and Shad drew his own weapon. Raif was beginning to sweat. If there was someone up there, and he knew how to use a weapon, trying to get him out could be bad for their health.

He looked down at Shad to make sure he was ready and then using the end of a broom handle, gently pushed up on the panel. The squeak of a rafter was followed by a spray of bullets ripping through the ceiling. Raif dove to the floor and rolled away from the closet. Shad fired three shots randomly then threw himself inside the bedroom to avoid being hit with a second barrage of bullets. Raif rolled for the other bedroom, firing his .45 randomly at the blank ceiling above. It exploded with more gunfire as the unseen gunman tried to locate them. Raif kept rolling even as he emptied his own weapon into the ceiling. The shooting ceased. Raif replaced his clip as he heard a dull thud directly above him, then the plaster board in the ceiling bulged and fell apart. Raif rolled away as a body crashed through it and landed on the floor next to him, face down. Raif scrambled to his feet and placed the muzzle of his gun firmly against the back of the man's head as Shad came to the door, his weapon in front of him. Raif turned the gunman over. There wasn't any pulse. Just what Raif needed—another body!

"You'd better call the office and get some people out here, then we need to seal this place off," Raif said. The adrenaline rush had left him shaking.

Holstering his pistol, Shad started for the door. "And, Shad, get the city on the line and tell them we need someone to investigate this mess." Raif knew that when an officer was involved in a shooting, a team from another agency was called in to investigate. That way, claims of a cover-up could be averted.

Raif went to bedroom two and retrieved the passport he had seen earlier. Comparing it to the face of the dead man, he got an exact match. Mr. Bunnell was accounted for. Raif stared at the passport. It showed that the date of issuance was nearly five years earlier. And yet the face was the same, exactly.

Rolling the body slightly, Raif removed the man's wallet from the right-hand back pocket of the stonewashed Levi's. Twelve hundred thirty-six dollars, mostly in large bills. Credit cards issued by Chase Manhattan Bank in New York and half a dozen other banks, and one from Chevron Oil. The California driver's license picture matched the one in the passport. The credit cards all carried expiration dates in 2001. He placed the wallet on the bed. Later he would run a check on what was there, but his gut feeling was that Mr. Bunnell was not Mr. Bunnell at all. The name would lead nowhere—the billing address, a post office box no one could trace. His mouth went dry.

They were working against professionals.

* * *

Raif glanced at his watch as he sat forward on the couch and looked over the items they had found in the condo attic. The weapon the gunman had used in his attempt to throttle Raif and Shad, half a dozen other guns, including a sharpshooter's rifle, two M-16A's, and three high-powered handguns. All the weapons, even the pistols, had laser-guided scopes with nighttime capability. In addition there was a large stash of ammunition, explosives and detonators, and a sackful of money in combinations of tens, twenties, and hundreds that added up to twenty-six thousand dollars and change. The money had been found inside a laundry bag buried in the insulation. There was also a deposit slip in the bag that indicated better than five hundred thousand dollars had been placed in the bank account of Peter Hawkes just two days before. It was the piece of evidence that pleased Raif most. It made the connection between Hawkes and the men who killed Golding, Crenshold, and Billy Two Shoes, and who had attempted to kill him. It also connected Walters and Gitry to the whole mess. Now they could be held for killing Maggie and for trying to kill the rest of them. A silver lining in a dark cloud.

Raif and Shad had finished filling out their report and answering the questions the city police had to ask about the shooting. The independent investigation of the shooting was conducted according to department procedures and would likely clear them of any wrongdoing. They were ambushed, plain and simple; but the policy was a good one, and they followed it.

By the time they were finished at the condo, it was nearly three o'clock in the afternoon, and Raif was both tired and hungry, but they needed to wait for the forensics team. The team had arrived at the Forest Service chopper pad an hour ago and had been at the hospital since then, looking over the bodies before being notified of what had happened here. They were being driven out in Suburbans owned by the department.

The sheriff sat in a chair across the coffee table from Raif. "According to the desk clerk and maid service, the woman's name was Lucinda Bell, the same as that on the prescription bottle. She took a long-term lease on the condo six months ago and paid cash. The maid says she didn't sleep here much and figured she had a boyfriend stashed somewhere in the Valley. Then, about four weeks ago, John Turner, the man you blew out of the chopper, arrived. He represented himself as the woman's boyfriend and said he was joining her for a vacation."

"Sounds like an afternoon soap."

"It gets better. The clerk said the woman left with another man the second day after Turner's arrival and hasn't been seen since. A day after that, a new gentleman moved in."

"Bunnell. The guy in the attic," Raif said.

"Yeah. The manager says they were gone for days at a time, and the maid saw them wearing camouflage gear on several occasions. She thought they were doing some hunting."

"It didn't concern the manager that the woman who leased the place was no longer its occupant?" Raif asked.

"Everything was paid up-front, including a five thousand dollar deposit. The clerk says they had no need for concern."

"Were they Americans?" Raif asked.

"One man had a slight accent—the one shot from the chopper."

"The manager said the woman left with a third man," Raif said. "Any description?"

"Older, maybe middle forties, gray to silver hair, cut short, with a matching silver beard and moustache. Height was about five-feet-ten inches. He was either well-tanned or of dark complexion, and the maid said he had dark brown eyes that made her nervous."

"Sheriff?" The voice came from the entrance to the house. "Forensics is here." Both Raif and the sheriff were on their feet as the deputy finished his sentence. They met Warren Kristoff and his people in the hall. Kristoff was the top man at the State Forensics Lab in Cheyenne and one of the best in the nation at his job. They greeted each other with handshakes.

"You look a little pale, Warren," the sheriff said.

"I had nine lives when I left Cheyenne. I have maybe three left." Kristoff went on to describe their harrowing journey by chopper through Hoback Canyon, south of Jackson. "Only the pilot's quick reflexes and steady hand kept us from crashing into mountains we couldn't see and the valley floor we could." He ended by swearing he'd never ride in another chopper as long as he lived. He made assignments to his team, and they started doing their thing.

"Now, let's take a look at that body," Kristoff said, rubbing his hands together in a macabre imitation of Doctor Jekyll looking forward to becoming Mr. Hyde.

Together they went upstairs. Kristoff looked at the hole in the ceiling and the dead assailant, then glanced at Raif. "Shooting blind and yet you hit him three times. You have radar or something?"

"Just luck."

Kristoff laughed lightly as he removed a small tape recorder from his pocket and stooped down beside the dead man. He began dictating a detailed report of the position, state, and look of the body even as his photographer took pictures from a dozen different angles. Raif and the sheriff waited as Kristofff checked the wounds, the eyes, and generally poked and pushed in a dozen other places before slipping on a pair of rubber surgical gloves and opening the man's mouth to search with a finger. "Dental work: four fillings, all recent, probably done at the same time by the same person." He checked the wounds more carefully, went through the same reporting procedure, then began a check of the limbs. When he got to the fingers, he stopped talking and pulled the hand closer to get a better look.

"Well, well, what have we here?" He grabbed a finger and shoved it toward them. Raif and the sheriff stooped to see what it was Kristoff was seeing. "Notice the little scars around his fingertips?"

Raif squinted. They were hard to see, but evident if you cared to look close.

Kristoff went on. "This man has had his prints surgically changed. They will match all of your passport pictures I would guess, but somewhere there is a very dead man who is missing the ends of his fingers and thumbs." He dropped the hand, and it flopped onto the floor with a thud as Kristoff straightened up. "It's my guess that the dental work was done to match the man's whose fingers were removed. These are professionals, Sheriff. Origin, still unknown, but they have gone to great pains to keep their identities hidden. It will be only by a miracle or a mistake on their part that we find out who this man really is." He smiled.

"However, I'm good at what I do and after we're finished here, and with the others, maybe I can give you more." He waved his hand toward the door. "Now, if you gentlemen will clear the area of nonessential personnel, we'll continue our work."

Raif and the sheriff went downstairs, and the sheriff gave orders for everyone but the guards at the door to leave the condo. They were headed for the front door when Shad walked in.

"Neighbors didn't see much more than the maid and desk clerk. When they were around they say that the occupants of this place seemed to sleep during the day, then at night there was more activity. Coming and going, even had a truck deliver some stuff on one occasion. Other than that, they didn't see much."

"Did you show them pictures of Golding, Hawkes, and the others?" Raif asked.

Shad nodded. "They hadn't seen any of 'em."

Kristoff was coming downstairs as they got to the door. "By the way, the guy called Golding was shot with a .338 at close range, but it was a light load, probably .170 grains. One of the slugs was lodged in the guy's spine. Get us a weapon you think might have been used, and we'll be able to make a match. In addition, Golding's face was all messed up. Apparently somebody used him for a punching bag before he died. And that broken leg. . . ." He shook his head. "They finished breaking it by degrees, and if he didn't talk, he was just plain mean and stubborn or he didn't have the right answers." He paused to catch his breath. "Crenshold was killed with the same gun, but no bruises. I'd say he gave them what they wanted, hoping they'd let him live."

"Maggie said Golding wouldn't tell, even if they beat the crap out of him," Raif informed them. "She was right. He knew he was dead and was just stubborn enough to keep his mouth shut. His way of getting revenge on the people he knew were going to kill him. Too bad Crenshold's weakness under pressure made it all for nothing."

They thanked Kristoff and left the condo.

"That explains how they knew to come after you," Shad said.

Raif nodded. "Crenshold's hands were free when I found him. I figure it was like Kristoff said. They played him for a fool, made him think they were setting him free. In his gratitude he told them about us, then they shot him. They may have tried finding us, but the storm set in and wiped out our tracks." It wasn't the first time since the ordeal had begun that Raif had been thankful for the storm, but he hadn't realized until now how lucky they had been.

"That was when Sam saw them," Shad said. "And when they didn't find you, they called in a chopper as soon as the weather broke.

"Which brings a question to mind," Shad said. "Why use men and horses to take delivery on whatever Golding had? Why not just fly the chopper in, make the deal, and fly out with whatever they had purchased?"

"Golding might not have trusted Hawkes and his people, so he set up a system he felt he could manipulate. We won't know for sure until we get our hands on someone directly involved. Someone who can talk."

"I can't figure out why Hawkes would use Golding's crew in the first place," Shad said.

Jess spoke. "I talked to the Cody Police earlier. Crenshold was stationed at Fort Cheyenne when he was in the military."

"Let me guess," Raif said. "He was a security guard at the armory."

"Not quite. He was a materiels handler. Ran a forklift. Real familiar with the layout and with some of the personnel there." Jess removed his notebook and referred to it. "He was given a dishonorable discharge three years ago, a full eight months before his time was up. Petty theft from a dozen foot lockers over a six-month period. He spent some time in the brig, then got the boot. Before he got into trouble, guess who his bunkmate was?"

"Roberts?" Raif answered.

Jess nodded. "Hawkes has known Crenshold since they were kids in preschool. Probably knew the man couldn't handle grand theft from a military base on his own, so he brought Golding in. Billy Two Shoes was included because of his knowledge of the backcountry and because he and Golding are tight. It's my guess Hawkes played all three of 'em for suckers and intended to get rid of them all along."

"That explains using the wilderness for delivery. Not many places in this world where you can commit murder and have a chance of getting away with it," Jess said.

"When I put out the bulletin on this case this morning, one of the deputies on security duty at the airport called and told me something interesting. Four or five weeks ago a bunch of militia types flew in from up country in Lovell. Hawkes met them at the airport," the sheriff said. "They had gear enough for a long stay."

"Any idea who they were?"

"He didn't know any of 'em." Jess leaned against the side of his truck. "Looks to me like Hawkes set up an arms dealing ring. Used Roberts and Golding's group to get inside Fort Cheyenne, got all they wanted out of them, then killed the corporal."

"Question is, what kind of weapons were stolen, and who was he selling them to?" Raif said.

The sheriff had a distant look on his face as if thinking. He had an idea. "Jess, call Lovell. See if they have a militant bunch up there, and if they do, have him check on 'em. See if any have been out of town for the last few weeks."

Jess nodded. "You're thinking Hawkes was selling weapons to fanatics within the militia movement?"

The sheriff nodded.

Jess shook his head. "It doesn't fit. Turner and Bunnell

were professionals, not half-witted militiamen with some macho agenda. Someone else is involved, and they have a very large bankroll."

"It's a start," the sheriff said. "I'll go back to the office and run Bunnell and Turner through the FBI identification system, and through Interpol, see what we come up with."

"Somebody is using Hawkes to get weapons," Jess said. "Now there's a scary thought."

"Have we heard from Army investigations about what was stolen from Cheyenne, what kind of weapons we're dealing with?" the sheriff asked Jess.

"My friend in CID is looking into it. If it's an arms deal, this case belongs to them, or the FBI."

Raif found it interesting that he had mixed emotions about turning the case over to federal agencies. On the one hand, he had a bone to pick with the professionals behind Hawkes. He didn't like getting shot at and wanted to see them caught and prosecuted. On the other hand, he was beginning to feel like they were in over their heads. The feds had expertise in this field that they didn't. He didn't want to muff it, but he didn't want to give it up, either, not yet.

The sheriff seemed to read his mind. "It's still our case, and I think we're on the right track, but I want to know for sure by tomorrow at noon. I'll notify the FBI then." He removed a legal document from his pocket and handed it to Raif. "You'll need this to search Crenshold's place even though he's dead. His mother is the owner of the house. It's rumored she's in a rest home, but you'd better do it right."

Raif looked it over as the sheriff wished them luck and got in his vehicle. Raif turned to Jess. "Now that we can prove Hawkes was involved, we should be able to get one for his house, too."

"I'll let you know when I have it. We can meet there."

"Anything else from Cody?" Raif asked as Jess opened the door of his car.

"They searched Golding's place along with the dump Billy Two Shoes used as a house. No weapons, nothing else that would help our cause, at least not yet," Jess answered. "Get to Crenshold's place. Let me know by radio what you come up with." He got in his car and pulled away.

Raif and Shad walked back toward the Club parking lot where Raif had left his rig. He had an unsettled feeling in his gut. He knew being a lawman was dangerous, but this was the first time since pinning on a badge that he had felt death crawl under his skin, and it gave him the shakes.

It was going to be a long day.

15

Crenshold's place was a pigsty on the west side of Jackson near a strand of the Gros Ventre River. They watched the shabby house for fifteen minutes but saw no signs of life and decided it was deserted. Getting out of Raif's rig, they walked across the street, through a broken-down gate, and onto the partially snow-covered and sagging wood porch. Shad took up a position to the left side of the door, Raif to the right.

"I want you to know this is getting old," Shad said.

"Tell me about it," Raif replied.

Raif knocked. "Deputy Sheriff. We have a search warrant. Open up!"

No response.

"Maybe you should say please," Shad said.

"I'm tired of being Mr. Nice Guy." He tried the knob. It was open. Not a good policy in Jackson these days. Unless you had nothing to steal.

The door creaked. No other sound. The windows were covered with moth-eaten blankets, leaving the room only dimly lit. Raif reached around the door and found a light switch. Flipping it on he ducked in first this time. They checked each of the three rooms and small bathroom. No one home. Still skittish from events at the condo, both kept their revolvers in hand while looking up at the ceiling.

"I don't suppose there is an attic," Shad said.

"Low roof, not enough room," Raif answered. "But there might be a crawl space. Your turn to get shot at if there is." They couldn't find one.

The living area was filthy. All the dishes were either on the small kitchen cabinet against the far wall or piled in the sink, and the smell of old and rotting food permeated the place, even in the cold.

They searched through the junk and clothes but found nothing. There were two bedrooms off the main living area, a grime-encrusted bath between them. Shad took the room on the left, Raif the one on the right.

Raif found himself in a small bedroom with a large, beat-up bed and a closet full of dirty clothes and a heap of shoes tossed on the floor. It was the mother's. The dirty sheets were gathered in the center of the bed and didn't look like they'd been changed in the last year. He looked through the filth but found nothing and joined Shad. "Anything?"

Shad was bent over a pile of clothes in the closet. "Fungus, and a smell that makes me want to throw up lunch."

Looking under the bed, Raif found a beat-up suitcase and pulled it free. Heavy. The latches were old and stuck. He hit the front of the case with his hand and they both flew open. He had one almost like it.

Shad stepped closer and took a look. Literature. He went back to his own search while Raif went through the suitcase. Propaganda from one . . . two . . . three . . . maybe a dozen militia organizations. The first was the one called MOM in Montana. Old stuff. The second was from one in the Midwest, and the third was from Hawkes's own Freedom Foundation. It was a manual on how to sell weapons on the black market. There were half a dozen names jotted down on the back along with phone numbers. Next to them was the name of a particular weapon, then a number. Most of them were for M-16As, and Colt .45

handguns. There was one for a thirty-caliber machine gun, and another for five pounds of plastic explosives. Raif wondered how long Hawkes had been using Crenshold and Roberts to steal from the base and sell weapons. "Seems like these boys had their own little home sales program," he said. "Did you find any weapons?"

Shad shook his head. "It will take an army a good day to work through this mess, do a good search."

"Call for help," Raif said. "Let's have this place taken apart. While you're using the radio, check to see if Jess has a warrant for Hawkes's place yet." Shad headed out to the pickup.

By the time Raif had finished a cursory search of the rest of the house, Shad had returned, a sheriff's deputy two steps behind him. Raif instructed the officer what they wanted done and why, then he and Shad headed back to the pickup and were soon on the road toward Hawkes's place. Jess had the warrant and would meet them there. He had also received a report from the deputy watching Hawkes's place. A woman had gone into the house. He identified her as Allison Winters, a clerk at the store where Raif had purchased clothes only the night before. Raif found it ironic that Allison had gone from a beach bum who had beaten on her regularly, to a dead ex-con, who had beat on everyone else. Nice woman, but when it came to men, she seemed to be a target for losers.

They left the city going west toward Teton Pass. At Teton Village Road they turned right and went half a mile before turning back toward the Snake River.

"I heard you were out with a pretty lady last night," Shad said, a half smirk on his face. "Wouldn't be the lady you tried to get killed in the wilderness, would it?"

"It sounds like my private life was the topic around the coffee pot this morning."

"You're as a good a topic as any," Shad said, smiling. "Any truth to the rumors?"

"We had dinner, that's about it."

Shad glanced at his friend a bit amazed at the tone of voice. "That's it? I met Terri Stevens this morning—took her written statement about what happened in the mountains. Seems to me she'd be worth going after with more than dinner."

"She has a boyfriend. Big stock broker from New York. He showed up on her doorstep last night."

"Must have been the guy with her this morning. I thought it was her brother or somebody. Acted like he had starch in his shorts."

Raif laughed. "From everything I hear, he's a great guy." He paused. "I'm not even in the running. He's from New York—she loves New York. He's Mormon—so is she."

Shad was Mormon. He understood the difficulties. "So are you—just not baptized yet," Shad said.

Raif smiled. Shad had been trying to get him wet for years. "I'm sure she'd be willing to overlook that minor detail," he said wryly. "I'm Islamic, Shad. As hard as you have tried to get me to change it hasn't happened, and won't. Not even for Terri Stevens."

Shad started to say something, then thought better of it, opting for a simple shrug. By then, they were at the intersection leading to Teton Village, and Shad turned right.

The house was little more than a fancy log cabin sitting on what Raif thought was probably a half acre. Houses like this went for anywhere from half to three quarters of a million dollars in the Jackson Hole market, but nowadays the Hole was a rich man's summer residence. You didn't get much for three hundred grand anymore.

"Jess told me Hawkes bought this place more than a year ago. Paid cash," Shad said.

"It would take more than selling stolen .45s to common crooks to buy this place."

It was late afternoon, and the heavy cloud cover brought an early gray-black sky. Lights were on in the front room, and Raif could see Allison sitting on a couch watching television.

This time Shad and Raif would handle the front door while Jess covered any back exit. As they walked up the sidewalk, Raif watched Allison through the window. He let Shad ring the doorbell and watched her get up to answer it. He left his pistol holstered.

The door opened, and Allison stood there, a defiant look on her face. "What's the matter, didn't the clothes fit?"

Raif showed his badge as Shad looked at him curiously. Allison backed away from the door, and Raif walked past her and entered the small foyer. A stairway ascended to the second floor from here. Next to it there was a hall, and the kitchen was at the far end. "Is anyone here with you, Allison?"

She shook her head. "No. You're fully aware that Hawk isn't coming home. Why didn't you tell me last night you had killed him?"

Hawkes had always liked the short version of his name and insisted that his friends call him that. His enemies usually called him everything else, but never Hawk. "I didn't know last night you were dumb enough to take up housekeeping with him," Raif answered.

Her back stiffened. "Do you have a warrant?" The chill in her voice told him he'd hit a raw nerve.

Raif showed it to her. "For the record, I didn't kill him," he said, evenly.

She glanced at the warrant then crossed her arms in front of her, a belligerent pose, though she was sweating a little and seemed nervous.

Shad walked down the hallway and opened the back door, letting Jess in.

"Anyone else taking up space here?"

She shrugged again and moved to the couch, riveting her eyes on the television in an attempt to ignore him. But she also went to biting her nails. Something was wrong. He motioned to the others, and they started a complete search of the house and grounds. "Watch your step," Raif said.

Shad gave him a wry smile, his .45 already out of its holster and the safety off.

Raif went to the television and shut it off. Allison looked annoyed.

"I have some questions."

She looked away, her jaw set.

"Hawkes has been out of jail less than two years. How can he afford a place like this?"

She shrugged. "We've only been together for two months. He doesn't . . . didn't . . . share his business dealings with me," she said coldly.

"You've hit an all-time low with Hawkes, Allison. You should have stayed with the beach bum."

She gave him a cold stare. "At least Hawk never beat me like the beach bum did. It seemed like a fair trade at the time." She said it bitterly.

"Sorry," Raif said. "I was out of line."

She looked at him, making sure the apology was genuine.

"You have no idea what Hawkes did?" Raif questioned.

"I never asked." The nervousness reappeared.

"Do you know any of his friends?"

"A few. They come here for meetings sometimes, and we went to dinner with one or two."

Raif opened the packet of pictures and fanned the photos out on the coffee table. "Pick out the familiar faces."

She rolled her eyes, but glanced at the photos. "Him." She pointed to the man Raif had shot out of the chopper. He seemed to get around. "What did he do?" she asked.

"He was the one who put a bullet through my leg, requiring the new wardrobe you sold me last night. He was in a chopper at the time. The picture was taken just after he fell."

"And Hawk was involved?" She wrinkled her brow.

"Yeah. Any others you know?" He pointed at the other pictures.

"This one."

It was the man killed at the condo, Bunnell was his supposed name.

"Was he accompanied by a woman?"

She nodded a yes and looked away.

"Allison, if you know anything . . ."

She looked back at him, uneasy. "The woman was beautiful but cold. Dead eyes, ya know, empty. She gave me goosebumps." She rubbed her arms. "Hawkes was even afraid of her." She paused as if deliberating. "Part of the downstairs apartment here was turned into an office by a friend of hers."

"But he's not in these pictures?"

She shook her head. "He's from San Francisco, very rich, and the person Hawk dealt with the most, other than the woman." She hesitated. "He . . . he's been staying in the basement, using it for business. Hawk said it was all about making him a lot of money. Millions he said."

"Did you ever hear his name?"

"Hawk called him Dan. I never heard a last name. He was about five feet, ten-inches tall, gray hair, dark skin, dark eyes." She shrugged. "He was okay, nice, ya know?"

Raif nodded. "Have you seen him in the last few days?"

"I don't stay here all the time and haven't been here in more than a week. Hawkes said he had things to do and wanted me to stay away. When I heard about what happened, I decided to make a trip to pick up some things." She shrugged. "I decided to hang around awhile. I like the place."

Raif understood. Rent was exorbitant in Jackson, and he knew Allison was staying with her parents. Her dad was a drunk and seldom worked. Her mother did janitorial stuff at the hospital and was rumored to be living with somebody else half the time. Going home wouldn't be much fun.

"Do you think he was an American?"

"Yes, I think so. He owned his own company. 'A rich benefactor,' Hawk called him."

"Did Hawkes deal in drugs?"

"Not since I met him."

"You seem awfully sure."

"I would know, that's all. I. . . ." She looked away, rubbing her hands against each other nervously.

Raif knew she was telling the truth. As a former user, she would know if Hawk was dealing. Addicts, even rehabilitated ones, could smell the stuff in a brisk mountain wind blowing away from them.

"You know Burt Crenshold don't you?" he asked.

"He's dead, too. I heard it on the radio."

"Somebody had him killed." He waggled the picture of the man who had fallen from the chopper. "This guy lived in a condo at the Village, and your gray-haired businessman was seen there. So was the woman. They're dangerous, Allison, and they don't like loose ends. The fact that you know something makes you a liability and them nervous. I want you to take a vacation. Go down to your aunt's place in Alpine, but don't tell a soul you're going."

She was biting her nails again, a distant, frightened look on her face.

"Do you hear me, Allison?"

She snapped out of it and nodded.

"Stay put for now, all right?"

"Am I in trouble? I mean . . ."

"Not unless you're hiding something."

She thought a moment. "No, I'm not. Not about Hawk, anyway."

Raif went into the entry as Shad came downstairs from the upper level. He shook his head in the negative. "Nothing up there," Shad said.

"Stay with Allison, will you, Shad?"

Shad nodded as he holstered his gun.

Going through the kitchen to the back door, Raif found Jess in the yard near a shed at the back of the property. Jess came toward him.

"Anything back there?" Raif asked.

"Fishing gear and a new boat. Brand new. Nothing we're looking for."

"The man was getting rich, on the verge of living the American dream. Amazingly lucky."

"Yeah, lucky."

"Did you see an entrance to the basement?" Raif asked. Jess nodded. "It's locked."

"Time to unlock it." They walked to the end of the red-wood deck and took some steps down to the basement door. They drew their guns and Raif placed himself against the stairwell wall and jammed his foot against the steel door, splintering the door frame.

Opposite the spacious living room kitchen area stood an expensive, professional style pool table. Passing through they checked each room. The large bedroom was empty—the closets open, even the bed stripped of its coverings. Whoever used it left in a hurry but made sure there would be little trace of them.

The other door off the main area was locked. It was Jess's turn to give them entrance, and he did so with a slam of his size-twelve boot.

Inside they found a ham radio setup. Along the wall to the right stood a gun rack filled with weapons of various kinds—most of them illegal. The most impressive, in size at least, was a fifty-caliber, automatic machine gun. Next in line was a Russian-made Dragunov sniper's rifle, one of the finest of its kind in the world. It was equipped with a massive scope with both day and night sights and the stamp of the U.S. Army on the end of its stock.

"Seems the Army buys only the best," Raif noted.

"Your tax dollars at work. Makes you wonder who they had in mind when they bought that thing, doesn't it?"

The drawers underneath the rack held ammo of all kinds, and reloading equipment sat atop a work bench on the adjoining north wall.

"Hawkes was a collector. Trouble is, he collected everything illegal," Jess said. "At black market prices, you've got twenty thousand bucks worth of weapons here. We better have the serial numbers copied. From the look of the markings, they're missing out of Fort Cheyenne's arsenal."

While Jess made a list, Raif searched the drawers. He found paper for writing and booklets containing instructions for a dozen programs used in the late model computer sitting atop the desk.

"Pentium III with gobs of memory, fax, high-speed modem, the Internet, the works," Raif said. He hit the switch and the thing hummed to life. While it was booting up, he looked through several other drawers. A password box lit up on the screen with a double beep from the speakers. He tried several that dealt with Hawkes's name but had no luck and shut the thing off.

"After forensics is finished here, I'll take this to Allen Dansie. Have him take a look at it, see if he can get around the password. Maybe Hawkes and his gray-haired friend got careless."

Jess agreed with a half absent-minded nod, his concentration on the weapons and their serial numbers.

Dansie was a computer whiz, who ran his own computer consulting business in the Valley. He set up machines and taught everyone from top management to secretaries and receptionists how to use them. He knew the Internet backward and forward and helped build everything from home pages to spread sheets. But Dansie's greatest talent was in saving businesses a lot of grief by "undoing" messes they had made in their computers, or destroying viruses sent long-distance via the Internet.

Raif found more of the militia propaganda in the form of letters. They addressed Hawkes as the president of the

Wyoming Chapter of Freedom Foundation. As far as Raif knew, the Wyoming Chapter was the only chapter. He decided to leave all of it alone. Fingerprints. And Kristoff wouldn't like him messing around. While Jess finished, Raif filled him in on what Allison had said.

"And the guy was from San Francisco? That's where the painting was sent, wasn't it? We'd better have the police there check out that address."

Jess folded his sheet of paper and put his pen away. "Let's close this place off. You've got Kristoff's people enough work already, and they won't get here until morning, but we're likely to mess things up if we don't get out of here."

"For professionals, these boys are messy," Raif observed.

"Messy?"

"Using guys like Crenshold, even Hawkes. Then they leave guns like this lying around. Messy."

Jess smiled. "Maybe, but remember, if you hadn't stumbled onto them up there, we wouldn't be here. Near as I can tell, they hadn't made any mistakes until they ran into you."

"I'll apologize when I catch up to 'em," Raif said dryly.

After leaving the basement, Jess went to his vehicle and retrieved a roll of yellow tape and cordoned off the area, while Raif returned to the main floor of the house where he told Allison to pack her things. It was a crime scene now, and that gave him even more reason to send her off to someplace where she wouldn't be quite so vulnerable. She was reluctant, less than happy at the idea of leaving Jackson, but Raif had done all he could.

When Allison was gone, they finished locking things up and left in their own vehicles. Jess went ahead as Raif and Shad stopped to tell the deputy on duty to call for another officer to help patrol and keep everyone off the property. Twenty minutes later they were sitting in the parking lot of the county buildings. Normally it took less than ten minutes, but with the snow still falling, things had slowed to a snail's pace. Raif wondered aloud how many inches they had gotten since it first started snowing two days before.

"Two and a half feet down here. Four to six up where you were a couple days ago," Shad answered.

"If the people who killed Billy and the others aren't out by now, they won't get out. Not with their horses."

"They'd better know how to live off the land. If they don't, they'll be dead before we find 'em."

"Plenty of elk and deer trapped in the canyons. Easy pickings if they have proper gear to get after them. Makes you wonder what kind of plans they made. They must have bought equipment of some kind. It might do us some good to check out supply stores tomorrow."

Shad nodded. "I'll get on it in the morning."

"What does the weather service say?" Raif asked.

"Clearing off late tonight. Blue skies tomorrow by sunup. Then another storm. Not as bad as this one, but up in that country they'll get another foot or more." He shrugged. "Maybe we can get some planes up before it hits, find their trail. I'll let you know."

"Then you're not going back to Alta tonight?" he asked Shad. Alta was in Wyoming, but on the west side of the Tetons, and at the very base of Teton Canyon. To get there Shad had to go over Teton Pass to Idaho, then through Victor and into Driggs. Then he turned east and worked his way along Teton Creek to Alta, crossing into Wyoming again, just before arriving home. Shad's family was from Alta, and he could afford to live there. He couldn't in Jackson.

"Jess offered me a bed. I'll stay there tonight, so I can join the search if there is one." He frowned. "Besides, the pass into Teton Valley is closed. Best to stay put. See you tomorrow."

Suddenly the radio came to life and both men listened. Raif was wanted in the office. The FBI had shown up.

* * *

Shad stood to one side, sipping a soda. He looked nearly as tired as Raif felt. The sheriff had joined them and sat at one end of the table. Raif sat across from Milo Sharps, Senior Investigator for the FBI out of San Francisco and the man now in charge of the investigation.

Sharps didn't seem like the abrasive type. In fact Raif figured in the right time and place he might even be likeable. It was his partner who made Raif grit his teeth. Over the last hour of discussions, it had become obvious the guy had an ego the size of the three Tetons.

As near as Raif could see the two men were exact opposites. Shawn Moen was tall, blond, and meticulous in how he dressed. His hair was something out of the movies, impervious to forces of nature such as wind and water. Raif wanted to reach out and touch it, just to see what the devil held it together, but he resisted the urge for fear he might get his fingers stuck in something that would require surgery to extricate them. So far, Moen's suit coat had seldom been unbuttoned, and his tie was knotted tightly enough to shut off oxygen to the brain. Maybe that was why he kept shoving his undersized Italian loafers into his oversized mouth.

Milo Sharps wore a suit, but it looked like it was last year's model from JC Penney. He was short, but solidly built. His eyes were set in a square head that had a flat nose at its center. Short, dark hair sat nearly on top of his eyebrows and made him look like a bulldog with an attitude. The eye sockets were deep and sat above his flat cheek bones. But it was those gray-green eyes that told you the squat but square body could probably rip you into small pieces and have you for breakfast.

"Do you understand Arabic?" Moen asked.

Raif nodded. "Some," he said noncommitally.

"Have you ever heard the name *Ibn al Nizari?*" Moen said.

"*Ibn al Nizari*—translation—Son of the Nizari," Raif said evenly.

Sharps looked up from the folder he was reading. "'Sons of the Present' is more accurate. Plural. More than one." He went back to his folder.

Moen doused his cigarette in the tray and Raif was grateful. Ordinarily Raif didn't mind other people's smoke but Moen floated it out there like bug bomb, hanging the stuff overhead until it squeezed your lungs and made them burn.

"It's a new terrorist group out of Iran," Sharps finally continued.

They were finally getting somewhere. "And you think we're dealing with them. I suppose you have proof," Raif said.

"We aren't here to prove anything. Especially to some back-country cowboy. . . ." Moen stopped in midsentence as Sharps's eyes bore a hole in the man's skull, as though looking for his pea-sized brain.

"Moen, get us all some coffee." Sharps ordered, saying it with such a cold edge that it gave even Raif goosebumps.

"They don't have . . . I mean the coffee machine doesn't work. . . ."

"Then go to McDonald's."

Moen's face went hard, but he started for the door. He reminded Raif of a wildcat that has been defanged and declawed. He wanted to tear Sharps into small pieces but didn't have the tools. Sharps was still sizing up Raif from across the desk when they heard the outside door slam.

"He seems to have a problem with cowboys," Raif observed.

"Not just cowboys, with anyone from a town of less

than a million people." He shrugged. "His mother locked him in the closet until he was twenty. What can you expect?" he asked dryly.

"How'd you get stuck with him?" Raif asked.

"Long story."

"It's still early." Raif leaned back on two legs of his chair.

"I'll give you the short version. I screwed up a while back. Moen is the company watchdog, and he likes to lick the hand that feeds him."

"A truer rat was never born," Raif said.

"Every company has one."

"Not mine," Raif said.

"No, I don't suppose so. Any openings?"

"Nearly."

Sharps smiled for the second time—a humorless grin. "Yeah, I hear you about bought it yesterday, and the day before, and the day before that. Maybe I should hang around. An opening is bound to come up."

"Don't bet on it."

"Yeah." He reached down and pulled another file from his briefcase. "Your very talented medical examiner has identified the man you shot out of the chopper as being of Arabic descent. We've done one better." He removed a paper and handed it to Raif. "His name is Shamil. Yusuf Shamil. He was supposed to have died in the war with Iraq in the late 80s early 90s." He paused. "He's Iranian."

"A member of the *Nizari?*" Raif asked, briefly scanning the report.

"He fits the profile."

"Profile?"

"Members of the *Nizari* are all individuals who have been declared dead, then given new lives. They are Iranian, and their fanaticism is well documented. They are the worst of the worst."

"If this guy was supposed to have lived in Iran and been killed in a war with Iraq, how could you get a file on him?"

"Trade secret." He paused. "Those guys in the back-country. Have any idea where they are?"

"None." Raif glanced at the sheriff who nodded agreement. "My guess is they'll come out in the next few days, or they won't come out at all, unless they get their chopper fixed."

"You think you wounded their bird that bad?"

"He was blowin' smoke. I wouldn't be surprised if he didn't get out, either, but I'm not bettin' on it." Raif stood. "Keep their chopper grounded long enough, and they'll either freeze or starve to death. Easy pickin's in the spring." Raif put on his hat. "I'm glad you're here, Sharps. Glad to hand you this one, with all its problems." He looked at the sheriff. "My vacation isn't over for another forty-eight hours. I'll see you then."

Sharps broke in. "Sorry, Qanun, but you're the only one who knows where the bodies are. When the weather clears, I'll need you to go back for them."

"Then you'll pay me time-and-a-half."

"Whatever it takes, but you go."

Raif nodded and closed the door on his way out.

"You need anything else from us?" The sheriff asked Sharps.

Sharps shook his head in the negative. "Thanks for your cooperation, and, Sheriff, if Moen gets testy, a good right to the chops usually straightens him out," he smiled, this time a little more genuinely.

The sheriff grinned back at him as he closed the door, leaving his office to Sharps.

Left alone in the room, Sharps gazed for a moment at the door then let his eyes fall on the sheriff's case folder in front of him. Qanun had discovered more in the week he'd been hunting than a dozen FBI agents had discovered in six months.

The door opened, and Moen walked in with a McDonald's sack. Sharps slipped the file back into his case. Moen's eyes would never see it.

Moen set the sack on the table, removed two cups of coffee, and some cream and sugar. He pulled off the plastic top of his own and poured in a container of cream, then added a small envelope of sugar. Sharps flipped off his own lid and put the black stuff to his lips.

"Where is everyone?" Moen asked.

"In bed." Sharps stood, downing the last of the tepid coffee. "And that's where I'm going." He started for the door, pulling on his newly purchased calf-length parka as he did. "Coldest place on earth," he mumbled as he closed the door behind him.

Moen waited for the distant door to bang shut before removing his cell phone and dialing a number. The man who picked up the phone sounded like he was half asleep. Moen glanced at his watch and smiled. It was past midnight in Washington. "Sorry to wake you, but you said you wanted updates."

"Yes, but at this time . . ." the voice took a deep breath. "Fine, what's going on?"

Moen told the man in Washington what he had learned.

"Good. If they find anything—"

"I'll let you know," Moen said. The man at the other end disconnected.

Moen downed the rest of his coffee and tossed the cup at the waste can. It hit against the wall and landed on the floor, but he ignored it.

Moen hated hick towns like this, and he despised the half-baked law enforcement organizations that pretended to protect them. They knew little to nothing about real investigative procedures and always, always, screwed up any big case that landed in their laps. It had happened a dozen times when he was the head agent for North and South

Dakota, and it had nearly ruined his career. If he hadn't had contacts in Washington, known the right people . . .

He shuddered just thinking about it.

Now he was back on track again, and he wasn't about to let any hick deputy or an old horse like Sharps ruin it.

Because of things beyond his control, mostly screw-ups by locals, Moen had been slighted when promotions had come, and his career seemed dead in the water. It didn't seem to matter what he did, things just weren't coming together. He considered himself of above average intelligence, scoring high on all tests, and had more knowledge of Middle Eastern culture, policies, and religion than any man in the Bureau. His skills on the firing range were excellent, and he knew procedure backward and forward, and yet in spite of all that, they had sent him to the Dakotas! Sure, he was a bit caustic, but so were a lot of other agents, including Sharps. It was a man's way of staking out ground, making himself a place among both good and bad. He had used too much force once or twice, but it was part of the job. There were no real reasons for passing over him, just ambiguous statements about his personality and his "overzealous approach."

Then Simms had contacted him. He needed someone to babysit Sharps in San Francisco. Moen figured it might be a way out of the dead end where he was stuck—a way of getting his career back on track. Simms had promised him a position on the Middle East desk in Washington if he'd take the job. Moen wanted that post.

But he was a bit nervous. He was being asked to spy on one of his own, and if Sharps found out, Moen knew his face would be nothing but pulp when he woke up. If he woke up.

He picked up the picture on the desk. Sheriff's family— nice enough. He sat down. He couldn't get used to Sharps. The man was a study in opposites. He looked like a bum off the street, but behind that unwashed veneer was a shrewd, calculating mind that seemed to read the thoughts of others. Cold-hearted as a rock in winter when it came to crooks, Sharps had the strength to break them in half if they pushed him. Most seemed to recognize that from the moment they looked into his gray eyes, others had it to think about while having their faces repaired at the nearest hospital emergency room.

Moen pushed it aside. Sharps was a good agent, but a flawed one. He deserved a watchdog.

He stood and pulled on his thick scarf and designer top-coat. Made of pure wool, they had served him well in the Dakotas and would serve him well here. He never could stand the idea of a parka.

Picking up his hat, he placed it on his head, turned off the light, then left the office. Moen figured it wouldn't be more than a couple more weeks before he'd be reassigned to Washington. As he stepped into the frigid night, it was a thought that kept him warmer than either hat or coat. In Jackson, plain wool never was enough.

16

Raif was awakened by a knock at the door. It was still dark outside, and he glanced at his alarm clock. Five o'clock. Fifteen more minutes and it would have sounded reveille anyway.

Pulling on his Levi's, he tramped through the cold rooms to the entrance of his cabin. Before opening the door he glanced out the window and saw a Ford Expedition parked in front. His heartbeat picked up as he opened the door to find Terri standing at the top of the stairs, wearing a fashionable wool, full-length coat. Its oversized collar was pulled up around her ears, and she was dancing lightly to ward off the cold. Her breath was heavy with frost.

With a stupid grin and a somewhat baffled look in his eyes, he asked her in.

"You're up early." It sounded trite, but it was all his brain would give him.

"A friend of mine had to catch an early flight." She rubbed her gloved hands together and smiled. "I hope you don't mind. I mean . . ."

"No, I was just getting up, anyway. Chores to do." He walked barefooted across the cold plywood floor to the stove. Opening the door, he stirred at the coals, then threw in small pieces of pine to catch flame. Larger and larger pieces were added until he could stuff in several log quarters. When he was sure they were blazing, he closed the stove and lifted up the handles to tighten the seal before dampering it for greater heat. Terri still stood near the entrance, watching him and looking around the empty room.

"Not exactly the penthouse at Caesar's Palace is it?" Raif said with a sleepy smile.

Her face was in the shadows, and he couldn't see an expression. He pointed at his bedroom. "I'll grab a shirt. You can sit on the hearth, closer to the stove." He disappeared through the door and shut it behind him as she sat down by the stove and extended her hands to warm them.

Quickly pulling on a heavy turtleneck sweater and socks, Raif went in the bathroom and ran a brush through his hair and one over his teeth. He could see the clock on his end table reflected in the mirror. 5:10 A.M.

He joined Terri, lined work boots in hand. "I see you found your car okay," he said, setting the boots to warm by the stove.

She nodded. "Shad gave me the keys when I gave him my written affidavit. How did you get two cars into town?" she asked.

"Dad and Mom were going in. They brought my pickup along."

She rolled her coat collar down. "That thing really puts off the heat," she said.

"Umm. Usually it keeps the place warm through the night, but after chores last night, I was too tired to stoke it properly when I got in."

"How did things go yesterday?" she asked.

"Well enough that I won't need an attorney. At least not at this point." He filled her in.

"Allison?" She shook her head. "She can do better."

"She draws the wrong kind of men. Sorta like a magnet."

"You dated her." She smiled lightly.

"See what I mean," he grinned back.

"From what you've found, all this sounds like some sort of gun-running business."

"Could be."

"No idea what kind of weapons Billy delivered in the wilderness?"

He told her about the weapons they had found at Hawkes's place. "They'd be hard to stop with that kind of stuff," Raif said.

"Another Waco," Terri said.

Raif nodded as he pulled his boots away from the fireplace a little and told her about the emergence of the FBI. "It's their baby now, and if they're not careful this could make Waco look like a job well done."

"Meaning?"

"When the Army decides to shine some light on what they've lost, I think the FBI might find out that Hawkes was selling things even more deadly than we've discovered to this point. Trouble is the colonel in charge of the investigation at the Fort isn't the sharing kind."

Raif stood and dampered the fire some so that it would give off less heat, then he told Terri about Corporal Roberts. "I figure Hawkes and his friends enlisted Roberts to help them get those weapons, then they killed him."

"Roberts wouldn't have had the keys to the armory, even if he were at the guard station, Raif."

He looked at her a bit surprised.

"I had a case a couple of years ago. Theft of military goods from storage at a base in New York. They tried to blame the guard. In the end he turned out to be part of the plot but not the man with the keys. Roberts might have been used in a minor role, but they would need someone further up the chain of command to get at weapons like those. Someone with full access."

"Maybe a colonel?"

"Possibly."

Raif was watching her. He couldn't help himself. And

that made him nervous. She already had attachments, and they had differences. He stood and walked to the window as if checking the skies or the weather. "It's getting late, and I've got chores and horses to give a workout."

She stood and put her coat on. "I don't suppose you need help?"

Raif turned, looking her over, then smiled slightly. "Yeah, I could use a little. But that coat and those pants won't work. You'll freeze your backside in the first place, and, forgive me for saying so, but you're not exactly dressed for mucking out stalls."

She smiled. "I just happened to bring along warm clothes and proper boots for, 'mucking out.' They're in the car."

Raif smiled. "Didn't get enough in the mountains, huh?"

She was already headed for the door, but turned to face him. "I know a good thing when I see it." She left.

He faced the window, his face flushed. Maybe Ted Hancock wasn't master of all he surveyed, after all. This time he did check the skies. The coming sun, still far below the horizon, was turning the heavens above the mountains a dark blue, but stars still glistened there. The sun would be out today, and it would be frosty cold in the Valley, even worse in the backcountry. His arms developed goose bumps as he thought about taking a bitter cold trip into the mountains to bring out the bodies.

He turned, went to the bedroom, and retrieved his own cold weather gear. Terri was coming through the front door as he returned, and he pointed her toward the bedroom. "Excuse the mess. I'll be in the barn when you're ready."

"Thanks." It was cooler in the bedroom, but she had gotten too hot so it was somewhat refreshing. She stripped to her underclothes then pulled on thermal underwear and 30-oz. wool hunting trousers. Instead of being baggy and making her look like she had a horse's rump and an elephant's legs, these fit like any other pants. She was told that her maroon Windstopper sweater was good for both outdoors and in. She liked the feel of it the moment she put it on and wished she'd had it while in the mountains.

After pulling on a pair of wool socks, she pushed her feet into the same Canada Hunting Boots she had used on the hunt. The parka was new, the other coat being at the cleaners. This one was a Sierra Down Parka with hood. The gloves were the pair Raif had given her in the mountains. She had never had warmer ones, and this morning she'd need the best.

She put her other clothing in the car on the way to the barn. The frosty air nipped at her nose, ears, and cheeks, and she removed a tight knit wool cap from the parka's pocket and pulled it down over her ears. The yard light near the house showed the barn to be massive and strongly built. Her father had told her that Raif had built it himself. She lifted the latch and pulled the door open enough to get through, then closed it behind her. The smell of hay and manure mingled in her nostrils. A row of lights in the rafters gave off only a little light, but filled with pungent odors, the place was tight and a lot warmer than outdoors.

Raif was saddling the most beautiful horse she had ever seen. The deputy glanced at her with a smile. He noted that most women looked like they had posts for legs when dressed in winter gear and that their figures seemed to melt together into one block of straight lines. Not so with Terri. There were definite breaks in Terri's frame, and he had to return to the job of saddling to keep from staring.

"He's beautiful, Raif. The gray was wonderful, but this one is magnificent."

He smiled as he slipped the bridle over the Shagya's perfectly formed head. After fastening it in place, he handed her the reins.

"Uh-uh," she protested, "This is too much horse for me."

"I just need you to hold him until I get your mount saddled."

She breathed a sigh of relief. "What do you call him?"

"He already had a name when I traded for him. The English word is Powder."

"A wonderful name," she said, rubbing the Shagya's nose.

Raif tightened down the cinch and slipped the bridle on Storm, then led the Quarter Horse to the side of the Shagya. "You see the difference in size?"

Terri was a little confused. They seemed very close to the same height.

"In the withers, and quarters. By breeding the Shagya with a Quarter Horse like this one, I hope to have a mountain horse that has the quickness and strength of the Quarter Horse and the endurance and beauty of the Arabian." He handed her Storm's reins and took those of Powder.

Terri placed a boot in the stirrup and hoisted herself into the saddle. Once settled in she patted Storm on the neck with a contented smile. It was good to be aboard again.

"I thought we were going to clean stalls," Terri said with a smile.

"I appreciate your enthusiasm for the fun stuff," he grinned, "but the horses need exercise. They come first."

The Shagya stood perfectly still as Raif swung easily into the saddle. Terri knew enough now to realize that a lot of horses didn't stand still, especially spirited mounts such as Raif loved. Most moved away or danced forward while the rider was trying to get aboard. Even though high-spirited, Raif's horses were well-trained and understood what was expected of them.

Raif nudged Powder in the flanks and walked him to the door. Reaching down and lifting the latch, he shoved it open and both horses danced through. He then pushed it closed and the latch fell neatly in place again. Raif prided himself on the tight construction of his buildings.

The sky was still dark enough that they could see stars from horizon to horizon. It never ceased to amaze Terri how different the nights were here than in New York, where either smog or the glow of city lights prevented such a daz-zling display of the heavens. Added to the stillness of the frosty morning, the starlight and coming dawn were exhil-arating and made her feel wonderful. She was beginning to understand why her father was thinking of moving part of his company here, why he said he wouldn't retire anywhere else.

Raif settled his mount, making it stand still, and Terri's horse did the same. "Listen. Can you hear it?" he asked her.

Terri smiled. She had been around him enough now to realize how he used words. "The quiet? Yes. It's wonderful."

He smiled even as he nudged Powder into a lope. Terri booted the Quarter Horse and quickly moved to his side.

The ride was brisk but comfortable, and as they went they talked of her father, her job, the ranch, and Raif's plans for it. In the growing light, they moved along a fence line until they reached a gate. Raif leaned down, lifted the latch, and they entered a lane leading into some trees along the river. The snow was deep in the open fields, but in the cover of the trees, it was only a foot and a half at best. Raif reined Powder back to a walk and Storm fell into the same gait, both horses blowing and tossing their heads.

Terri rested her gloved hands on the saddle horn and let the reins hang slack. She knew the horses were glad to be moving by the strength of their motion and lift of their legs. Her mind turned to the last couple of days, and to the deci-sions she had made. Her life had changed dramatically.

She took a deep breath and spoke. "I didn't come out here just to help you muck out, Raif." She gave him a smile.

He didn't answer.

"Ted came uninvited. I'm sorry the evening ended that way."

Raif smiled, looking at her. "Yeah, I admit, it was kind of a bummer." He looked away.

"I want you to know what happened last night. Not because I owe you any explanation but because I want you to know. I told Ted he shouldn't have come. I told him I was grateful for all he had done for me because I really am grateful, Raif. But lately I've felt more and more that there just isn't anything, . . . well, romantic between us. It doesn't feel right, anyway. I told him we needed some time off from each other. He agreed."

She finished, and Raif smiled but said nothing. They rode on in an awkward silence, listening to the rhythmic dull thud of the horses' hooves, the squeak of leather, and the horses' breathing as the two animals moved in cadence. They came to an open field and turned left. Terri felt she should say something more but that anything more would have to be about Raif, and she was half fearful she might get it wrong.

They approached a large log house, barn, and an enclosed exercise arena, and she gave herself to riding. The rest would have to wait.

Raif urged Powder to a lope, and she followed behind.

The immense chimney of the house billowed a stream of thick white smoke into the chilly morning air, and even though she couldn't see anyone, she sensed they were there, already busily working at chores, getting an early start on a busy day.

Entering the yard, Raif guided Powder to one of the large doors of the arena. He dismounted and opened it as Terri jumped down. They led their animals inside to find several horses with riders trotting in a circle at the far end. A silver-haired man, wearing Levi's, a woolen shirt, a downfilled shell, and a flat-brimmed, black Stetson stood in the center of the near end, working a beautiful chestnut stallion on a rope. The man was slightly built and had dark skin and eyes, set above high cheekbones. Nostrils flaring and his ears pointed forward, the Shagya whinnied and danced nervously until Raif placed a hand on his neck and spoke soothing words. Then the horse settled some as Raif stroked his neck until he stood still, alert but content to watch the chestnut.

Terri's own mount, still breathing heavily from the ride, shook his neck and bridle, but stood calm, seemingly indifferent to all the activity.

"My father. The horse he's working is an Anglo-Arabian. Notice the height. Larger than most Arabians, he's a cross between a Thoroughbred stallion and an Arabian mare. The neck is longer, the head that of a Thoroughbred. They're a strong breed. Not as fast as the Thoroughbred, but they make good saddle horses and above average jumpers. Jumping requires strict discipline and concentration, and my father's the very best at teaching such things to horses."

Raif's father led the horse to a young man standing nearby, giving him instructions and handing him the halter rope. The chestnut was led to a door on the opposite side of the arena and out.

"He'll take him to the barn, rub him down, and make him comfortable. Dad will work him at least two additional times today for an hour each."

"How long will he have him here for training?"

"Anywhere from three to six months. His method is slower than some others, but the results are proven."

Raif's father walked to them as Terri removed her knit hat and shook out her hair.

"Good morning, son," he said. He and Raif hugged.

Terri hadn't noticed how short Raif's father was until then. He stood a good head under Raif.

"From the sound of things on the news and in the paper, you're keeping busy."

Raif only smiled, then turned to Terri. "Dad this is Terri

Stevens, one of the clients I had with me on this trip. Terri, my father, Raoul Qanun."

Raoul smiled at Terri. She extended a hand, and he shook it. "Everyone around here calls me Ray. Raif's mother will have breakfast ready in half an hour, and she'll expect both of you to join us."

Terri smiled. She was hungry. "Thank you. I'd like that."

"I suppose you wish to work with Powder for a few minutes," Raoul said to Raif.

Terri watched with interest as Raif quickly removed the saddle and bridle and put a halter on the Shagya and attached a long halter rope. He led Powder a short distance into the ring and began working him in a circular fashion, similar to the way his father had worked the chestnut. Even Terri noted the difference between the two men's techniques. Raoul had been relaxed, patient. Raif's was more hurried, stiff, and Powder seemed to sense it.

"Raif will be good at this someday, when he learns that he must force his will upon the horse less."

"What do you mean?" Terri asked.

"The horse has a mind of its own. What it will become is already stamped on its whole being genetically. One cannot change that anymore than he can change the direction of north to south. The trainer simply lets the horse find that in himself by going through deliberate, thorough, and patient actions that ignite those inherent qualities within."

Terri watched for another half hour, until Raif finished the exercises and brought Powder toward them. Tying the Shagya to a ring bolted on the wall, he resaddled him but left the cinch fairly loose. His father pointed out a couple of things while Raif tied Terri's horse and loosened his cinch as well.

"Patience, Raif, patience. Remember, this one has more in him than meets the eye, you cannot force him another way."

They walked toward a nearby door and left the building then crossed the snow-covered open yard, before climbing the front steps to the large covered porch of the log ranch house. Raif and his father discussed several business matters, including the progress of Raif's cutter team. This was all new to Terri, but she listened with interest, wanting to learn. She noticed that Ray never talked down to his son, that he treated him as an equal, even though training him like he would one of his equine interns—with love, patience, and care.

After walking the length of the house under the covered porch, they entered a heated anteroom. There they discarded their top layer of clothing, then washed their hands in three of six sinks lining one wall. Entering a large kitchen, they found Raif's mother standing at an iron stove, spatula in hand. Approximately the same height as Ray Qanun, with a build very much like Terri's own, Raif's mother's hair was dark but with a showing of gray. She wore it straight and long, but had pulled it back and over her ears into a ponytail that fell to the center of her back. She brightened at the sight of Raif, who walked over and planted a kiss on her cheek.

"You have a lot to tell us," she said, her eyes shining.

Terri could see immediately that though Raif was not of her womb, she certainly loved him as if he were.

Raif put one arm around his mother and made the introductions.

She handed Raif the spatula, reminding him he had been taught how to use it, and walked to Terri and gave her a hug. "I was sorry to hear about your father. Is he okay?"

"He's doing very well, thank you. In fact, I'll check him out of the hospital this afternoon, and he'll board a plane for home tomorrow night." Terri glanced at Raif who turned to look at her as she spoke. "He'll be fine," she said, her eyes back on those of Sarai Qanun.

"Good. Could I get you to help me? I'm almost finished,

but I need someone to make several gallons of orange juice."

Terri nodded. "I'd feel bad if you hadn't asked."

After flipping a few pancakes, Raif turned the spatula back over to his mother, and he and his father disappeared through a doorway into another part of the house.

Sarai removed a half dozen large cans of concentrated orange juice from a pail of warm water in one of three large sinks, then pointed at a lower cabinet to the left of them.

"There are pitchers down there," she said.

Terri retrieved the pitchers as Sarai worked expertly with three different parts of the stove. It was a novelty— massive, with four separate burners at one end, a solid metal gas grill at the other, now well-covered with pan- cakes, eggs and sausage. Each burner held a large coffee pot, the smell of which mingled with everything else. Together, all of it made Terri salivate.

Terri quickly opened the juice cans and prepared three different, two-gallon pitchers of the orange concentrate. Ten minutes later she was helping Sarai carry the full plat- ters, brimming pots of coffee, several pitchers of milk, and the orange juice into a dining area. A lengthy table and nearly two dozen chairs filled the spacious room. Then Sarai slipped through the back porch to an iron triangle and sounded the call for breakfast.

"Do you do this every morning?" Terri asked when Sarai returned.

"Three times a day for some of the men." Sarai smiled. "I love it, but I usually have help. A maid of sorts. Spanish. Her husband is in the hospital; she needed to take him home this morning." She paused. "Raif may have told you about him."

Remembering the story of how Moses Rodriguez had been beaten, Terri winced. By then the first of the hired men came into the washroom. After stopping at the sinks, they passed through the kitchen in their stocking feet, each of them nodding politely and some of them offering a cheery hello. All of them seemed happy to be up before dawn. An amazing feat in itself, as far as Terri was concerned. She counted sixteen.

Sarai continued talking as they pulled platters of food out of warming ovens and handed them to two of the young men to take to the table.

Getting back to the reason why she had no help this morning, Raif's mother said, "Her husband informed Raif that drug dealers were working out of the Spanish community here. Raif had to have more than Moses could give him at the time, so Moses began watching things more carefully. Others didn't like it so they sent two men to give Moses a beating."

"Walters and Gitry," Terri said. "Raif did mention something about them beating up on someone. They're in jail now, charged with murder and attempted murder after trying to ambush us." She gave Sarai an abbreviated version of their escape. Terri felt comfortable with Sarai; she had an instant friend.

The last of the hands had joined them and all were seated at the table. As Terri and Sarai entered the room, Raif and his father came from the opposite end. Ray pointed to a chair and invited Terri to sit there. The hired hands were all silent, watching her. She flushed pink and quickly sat in the chair pulled out by Raif.

"This is Terri Stevens, attorney-at-law from New York City. We spent an exciting week together, with her father, in the backcountry. She killed an elk with one shot from nearly two hundred yards and beat up one very mean lady with her bare hands. So watch your manners," Raif informed the men.

The group laughed lightly, and Terri wondered just how much redder her face could get without catching fire.

Ray seated Sarai then took his own place at the head of the table. As he did so platters were passed and emptied,

pots of coffee soon drained to the last drop, and orange
juice and milk flowed over tooth and tongue like a flood.
Except for coffee, Terri took something of everything that
came her way and ate heartily. She noticed a young man
across the table from her, who also passed the coffee by and
wondered if they had something in common. The chatter
and bantering were constant but refreshing, and Terri found
herself laughing along with the others as tales were shared
about experiences in days gone by. When all had finished
eating, Ray stood and gave orders for the day and made
assignments for those who would spend the night with foal-
ing mares and calving cows. Two of the young men were
even assigned kitchen duty and had to take good-natured
ribbing from the others. It was obvious all of them took
turns.

"And now an announcement." He looked at the young
man across the table from Terri. "As all of you know, and
some of you won't let him forget, Matt is going to serve a
mission for his church. He got a letter about it yesterday."
The table fell silent, all eyes on Matt. "Well, boy, tell us," a
crusty man at the other end of the table said.

"Australia. Brisbane." Matt said, a bit flushed.

Congratulations came fast and hard, and Terri noticed
that Raif and his parents seemed pleased with all of it.

"Let's see, that was a penal colony wasn't it?" Raif asked
good-naturedly. "A community of rough and tumble knot-
heads from England, the way I hear it."

Matt grinned. "I'll feel right at home," he said.

"Congratulations, Matt," Terri said. "I have a friend
whose brother is there. His name is Elder Kjar. I hope you
meet him. He'd make a great companion."

They talked about what it was like and everyone listened, then, while good-naturedly ribbing Matt, everyone
excused themselves, carting their dishes to the washing
room, scraping them off and placing them in a monstrous
commercial dishwasher. The two assigned to clean up busied

themselves with it while others left and went back to jobs in the yard. Only the four of them remained at the table. Raif glanced at his watch, but made no effort to leave.

"All right, Raif, your turn," his mother said.

Raif rattled off a condensed version of all the events that had taken place over the last six days, including an explanation of Terri's fight with Maggie, but leaving out the gun battle at the Raquet Club condo. His father laughed, enjoying the picture conjured up by Raif's colorful retelling of the fight between Terri and Maggie, then Sam and Terri. Sarai especially enjoyed that one.

It was apparent to Terri that these people really loved each other. Though they were very businesslike in their conversation and made few public displays of affection, they clearly took pleasure in one another. She thought their reserved mannerisms were probably a result of their Islamic culture. But in their eyes, in their smiles at one another, when they thought no one was looking, Terri saw genuine feeling. She was impressed.

They made small but important talk, asking about her family, her work, and the trip into the mountains—not the part when they were running for their lives, but about the beauty of the place, how she felt about killing the elk. Terri was frank to share her feelings after the kill, but said she had learned that elk stew was better than beef and admitted that had changed her mind about the hunt as much as anything.

Raif looked at his watch again. It was nearly eight. He excused himself and left the room. He was gone for only a few minutes, and when he returned he said, "Search and Rescue has some planes up, but the Forest Service chopper is being used to pull some skiers off the backside of one of the ski runs at Teton Village. Several teenagers spent a cold night up there, and the living have priority over the dead."

Ray Qanun shook his head. "Happens every year. These out-of-towners have no respect for the weather around here and get themselves in the darndest predicaments." He suddenly realized he was talking to an out-of-towner. "Whoops. Sorry, Terri."

Terri laughed lightly. "No need. I understand perfectly what and who you meant. Raif, however, is at fault in my case." She smiled.

"Hate to eat and run, but I've got a few things to do before they call me for the flight," Raif said.

Fifteen minutes later, he and Terri were riding back toward Raif's place where she helped him curry the horses and feed them both oats and hay before they left the barn. "Dad said he'd bring some hands over when he comes to work out the cutter team. He'll see that the stalls are cleaned out and fresh straw put in. I have to go to town. Would you like to tag along?"

"Tag along?" She smiled. "That sounds like something you'd ask a little sister."

"Umm. Hardly appropriate then." He smiled. "I'd like you to come."

"Now that's an invitation that's hard to turn down, but on official business . . . ?"

"Until we go back in for the bodies, my time is my own."

"Why do I sense it will still be business?"

"Umm, perceptive. I got to thinking about Hawkes's computer. I'd like a friend to break into it before the FBI hauls it away and sticks it in some lab for a month before they get to it."

"You'll step on somebody's toes," she said.

"Sharps will thank me later."

"And the other one? Moen?"

"Better move his big feet."

They walked to his pickup. He let her in the passenger side, then went to his own, slid in and started the vehicle before scraping the windshield while it warmed up.

Ten minutes later they were at Hawkes's place. Kristoff

and his forensics crew had already arrived, and the computer had been dusted and otherwise checked for prints. Raif was glad to see the FBI were late-sleepers or still sipping coffee. Kristoff delivered the computer to Raif on the sly but with a promise that if it were missed it would be Raif's hide hanging on the wall at FBI headquarters, not his. Raif knew it was true when Kristoff made him sign a receipt.

It didn't take a space scientist to know the computer was important, and Raif couldn't pull himself free of this mess until he had it checked out. Suspecting that it really would be sent to some lab in Washington that was swamped with too much work and had too little manpower, he had thought of a way to help the case along. He had a pro only a few miles away. He salved his conscience by telling himself that in the end, Sharps would be grateful for his quick thinking and his ingenuity.

Or he wouldn't.

Ten minutes later, he and Terri were in Jackson, pulling up to an older house on King street.

"Who lives here?" Terri asked.

"Allen Dansie, computer expert and avid movie buff. Come on, I'll introduce you." He went around and let her out, then removed the computer and took it with them.

He rapped on the door several times before it was answered by a squat little man with enough freckles to cover an entire state. His stomach hung over his pants and from under a T-shirt that was too small. The many food stains on it made Terri think that if it were washed and wrung out, the drippings would make a filling soup.

"Allen Dansie, meet Terri Stevens, a friend of mine." Allen looked at Terri over bifocals as he let them in, then worked to get the stubborn door closed behind them.

The house was cluttered with everything from Pepsi and Coke containers to greasy Subway sandwich bags with leftover oil oozing through them. The walls were plastered with large movie posters. The clutter and mess was too much to take in all at once.

"Miss Stevens." He shook her hand. After he released it, Terri resisted the impulse to wipe it off. She had never considered herself finicky, but she wondered if in Allen Dansie's case, she ought to make an exception for the sake of her health. At the same time, she admired Raif's genuine acceptance of Dansie. She had decided that if Raif Qanun was anything, it was genuine. Possibly that was what she found herself drawn to more than anything else. She found herself a little embarrassed for being so fastidious.

Dansie took the computer from Raif and led them to his work area where he set it on a table and began plugging in wires and cords. Terri counted four other computers, all with separate 17" monitors, connected by a maze of wires and cables. A high-speed laser printer sat off to one side and all kinds of other electronic machines she had never seen before were stuffed in any available space.

Raif explained what he wanted. Allen nodded agreeably at every request, asserting "we can do that," with each one.

When Raif finished, Allen cracked his knuckles as he spoke. "Well, here goes nothing." He hit the "on" button, and the machine whirred then beeped as numbers sprang onto the upper left-hand corner of the screen. The computer zipped through a dozen or so operations, then a box, asking for a password appeared.

Allen frowned. "I don't suppose you know what it is?" he asked Raif.

"That's why I'm paying you the big bucks."

"Who did this belong to? I need all the details you can give me."

Raif told all he knew.

"Channel three says he's dead. Can you send me a copy of his rap sheet? Parents names, is he married, if so, to whom, etc. etc."

Raif picked up a phone, dialed the sheriff's office, and ordered the file brought over, then hung up. It would be delivered in the next twenty minutes.

"Come back in an hour." Allen said, waving good-bye, his eyes glued to the monitor, and his fingers fairly flying over the keys.

When they were outside Terri spoke. "Unique." She smiled.

Raif laughed lightly as he let her in the pickup. "One of a kind. As you noticed, personal hygiene is not his first priority. Movies and computers, computers and movies. The man is addicted to the screen. He has a woman come in once a week to clean house, but it doesn't seem to do much good."

"That was only a week of food containers!"

Raif smiled. He closed the door, walked to the other side, and climbed behind the wheel. "When it comes to computers, Allen Dansie has no peer, not around here at least. So we put up with him. Actually he has a heart of gold, AND, he manages to bathe and change clothes every Saturday night."

They turned left on Pearl. "I'll take you back to your rig. I've got a few chores I can do, then I'll come back and see what the whiz kid has been able to do. By then the chopper should be ready."

Terri removed her gloves and unbuttoned her coat. The pickup had a very good heater. "I see what you mean about your family. They are not typical Islamic."

Raif shrugged. "Father prays five times a day as he should, has made his pilgrimage, fasts during the thirty days of Ramadan, although I have seen him shorten the day for various reasons of health, and he gives more to the poor than most people know, some of it through the local Mormon bishop." He smiled as her head turned. "They're friends. Bishop Barry and Dad take care of several families. Matt will also be supported on his mission by my father."

"You pray five times a day, but not at meals," Terri observed.

"Meal-time prayer is a Judeo-Christian practice, but some Muslims pray then as well. Usually they'll repeat *Sura I*. A *Sura* is sort of like a chapter out of the Koran. He recited:

Praise belong to God, the Lord of all Being,
The All-merciful, the All-compassionate,
The Master of the Day of Doom.
Thee only we serve; to Thee alone we pray for succor.
Guide us in the straight path,
The path of those whom Thou has blessed,
Not of those against whom Thou art wrathful,
Nor of those who are astray.

"This one is often repeated in the five prayers of the day. It was the one I grew up with, as you might have been with the Lord's prayer or a child's prayer."

"Now I lay me down to sleep, I ask thee Lord my soul to keep . . . or something like that," Terri said. "My parents weren't into religion when I was growing up, nor anytime thereafter."

Raif glanced at her. "I sense some regret."

"Some. Parents owe it to their kids to teach them things no one else will. Now-a-days God certainly falls into that category. Don't misread me, Raif, I love my parents, but their world revolved around getting things. The more the better. All their energy, all their love was focused on that one goal back then." She paused, as if remembering, and from the look on her face the memories bothered her. "But things can't love you back. I won't let that happen to my kids."

"No offense, Terri, but as much as you have, won't it be hard to worship anything but things?"

She smiled. "You mean the condo, my father's toys?" She shrugged. "In the first place, only the skis are mine, but that's not the point. I have my share in New York." She paused. "A great man once taught that the danger comes when you let your possessions possess you. A thing is something to be used not just for your benefit but for the benefit of others. If it doesn't do that, I don't need it."

"Pretty lofty view from the top."

"Maybe, or maybe it's just ashes in my mouth." She smiled.

He returned it. "Ashes in your mouth?"

"Yeah, it's been a bitter experience learning what can happen when your parents put everything in the world before you. Do you know where they were for Christmas when I was five? Hawaii. The maid woke us up and tried to play Santa Claus. The next year it was the Caymans, the year after that . . . you get my drift. Until Mom and Dad split up, I didn't know Christmas was for families." She took a deep breath. "I suppose ashes in your mouth can make you pretty opinionated, sure of what you will or won't do." She paused, turning a bit to face him. "You have a few ashes of your own."

He looked at her surprised. "Me?"

"Yes, Raif, you. Your feelings about your brother. Ashes in your mouth."

They drove a ways in silence as Raif thought it over. She was right. Although he would never admit it to anyone, not even to Terri Stevens, he was bitter towards Islam because of what it had done to Hussa and what Hussa had done because of Islam. He wasn't sure he would ever get over it, good examples such as his parents to the contrary.

Driving down the last portion of the lane, Terri glimpsed a team of horses pulling a chariot toward the barn. Ray Qanun stood in it and had the reins.

"My cutter team, and the main reason Dad comes over. He loves to work them."

As they drove to the barn, Sarai came out driving a tractor, loader attached and filled to the brim with sodden straw. She waved, then drove some distance away from the barn and dumped the load. Raif let himself out, and Terri slid across the seat and joined him. Inside the barn the sharp smell of manure bit at their nostrils much more heavily than this morning.

"Ouch!" she said, wrinkling her nose.

"The mucking out you missed. A washing of the concrete waste ditches with hot water and disinfectant then fresh straw makes a difference."

Sarai came through the door on foot and called to Terri. "I could use your help again."

Raif stayed to help his father with the team, and Terri went inside the barn. One of the hands was using a steam compressor to do the washing. Sarai handed Terri a pitchfork and the two of them began a liberal spreading of straw in the two stalls belonging to the team. By the time they were finished and had placed fresh hay and water in the proper places, Terri was sweating. It felt wonderful and she resolved not to lose the muscle tone she had gotten over the past ten days.

She sat next to Sarai on a hay bale while the two men worked the team. Terri glanced at her watch. Nearly noon. She was surprised by how late it was. Days seemed to fly by in the out-of-doors.

"You have two daughters," she said to Sarai.

"They don't live close enough to see all the time. Dua lives over in Laramie and Aziz on a place outside of Pocatello, Idaho. Her husband trains Quarter Horses for racing. They have a cutter team as well, and we see them more often than Dua and her brood. I wish they lived closer, but I think a child's marriage is as much an adjustment for parents as it is for children. Something suddenly comes up missing in your life."

Terri thought of a question she had wanted to ask since first meeting Raif's parents. She glanced at Sarai, then decided to go ahead. "You raised your children to be

Muslim, and yet there is so little about you that attests to your belief. The traditional clothing for women, what most Muslims think about the role of a woman and how she ought to act, . . ."

Sarai laughed lightly. "I find it very difficult to help a cow with her calf wearing the Muslim woman's traditional clothing, although I know it is done." She set her pitchfork aside. "We are Islamic, but our families have lived in America for three generations. Our grandparents moved away from Iran because traditions are forced upon people, and because the rulers of the day did not take kindly to criticism. The first thing those ancestors discarded was the clothing, may Allah be praised."

They watched as Raif took the reins and directed the team to the field used to exercise them. "The things you see in the media about how women are to dress, and how they are treated are old traditions, based on the dress of Arabia a long time ago. For many in Islam, these customs have been hard to give up; they consider anyone who breaks with tradition as breaking with Islam. Others do not. We worship after the teachings of the Koran, we celebrate the holy days, and we fast during the month of Ramadan, but we don't feel the traditional dress for men or women is essential to that. Then again, if Ray and I wanted to wear it, we could, that is the wonder of the freedoms we have in this country. It gives us choices others don't have about how we worship the same God.

"As far as the treatment of women is concerned, in the early history of Islam, women were given more freedom than they had ever had before in Arabia. Those freedoms were curtailed later, under the rule of the *Abbasid Caliphs*, and others curtailed them even more in later years, but only in certain cultures."

"Such as Iran, and under the *Taliban* of Afghanistan?"

"Yes. And in our view they are wrong. Islam's view of salvation is equal for men and women before God. Women should not be treated as inferiors. For the male *Taliban* to insist that women not be heard when they walk is nothing more than abuse, and Allah does not approve." Her face reflected sadness. "The suicide rate among women in that part of the world has soared in the last few years. A horrible testimony of what is happening."

"There was an article in *The New York Times* a few months ago that said a woman's testimony in a court of law is not as highly regarded as a man's in some Islamic countries. As an attorney, I find that not only repulsive but dangerous. If a jury or judge disregards a woman's testimony because she is a woman, how can justice be done?"

"It can't, but what you are talking about is not Islamic, but cultural interpretation. It is like the Christian differences regarding sacraments. In some cultures the service is very elaborate, while in others it is nonexistent. Different spiritual leaders interpret your Christian scripture different ways. That is also true in Islam. Do you know that most people see Islam as a patriarchal religion, but in some instances it is matriarchal, such as in the Sahara and parts of Africa? A woman has few rights in some countries where culture and tradition have invaded religion and changed it. It is sad, but under some governments and religious fanatics, it is the way of things."

Sarai removed her hat to cool down a little. "If you were to read the Koran, you would find that it is not out of harmony with American religious ideals of marriage, family, and even the roles of men and women. There is to be unity before God. As one *Sura* in the Koran says, 'the world needs believing men and believing women, obedient men and obedient women, truthful men and truthful women, enduring men and enduring women, humble men and humble women, men and women who give in charity, men and women who remember God oft, for them God has prepared forgiveness and a mighty wage.'"

Raif and his father came through the door of the barn,

each leading a horse and talking about the mountains where Raif and Terri had been hunting.

Ray looked at his wife. "Raif got a call over his radio. He has to be at the airport by half past one. The chopper will be ready by then."

While the two men removed the harnesses and rubbed down the animals, Terri and Sarai meandered to the door of the barn, taking in the beautiful view. Clouds were scattered and moving across the sky at an unhurried pace. The whole panorama was covered in a glistening white sheet of purity.

"What has happened over the last few days seems so out of place here," Sarai said.

Terri understood and nodded. Killing was commonplace in New York. Here it marred the serenity—the untouched beauty—making it somehow even more horrendous.

Raif spoke from behind them as he and his father shut the large doors. "You have to pick your father up at one?"

Terri nodded.

"Gotta go myself. Just enough time to stop by Allen's place and still get to the airport by one-thirty. I'll walk you to your car," Raif said.

Sarai hugged Terri this time, and Ray held her hand warmly, then Raif escorted her to the Expedition. She slid behind the wheel; Raif stood next to her with the open car door against his back.

"I would like to see you before you go back to New York. When—?"

"I'm not going back for at least a week," she said. "I've agreed to run Dad's new division here. I'm staying to get a handle on things and to meet with an attorney about local zoning laws and a realtor about a building."

He looked into her eyes, shocked, trying to figure out what to say, and how to say it. He was glad, and yet knew that it had nothing to do with him and that created some confusion, which slowed down his mental processes and bound his tongue. He stood there, a stupid look on his face.

She turned and faced the steering wheel and had the key in the slot and the vehicle started before he came to his senses. Then he did the only thing he could think of. He put a hand behind her head, pulled her to him and kissed her. Then he turned and walked to his pickup.

Terri watched him go, her arms unable to move, her brain empty of everything but the buzzing in her head. He was to his own vehicle and starting out of the yard before she gathered enough strength to close the door to the Expedition. It took another few seconds to remember what came next and how to do it. Finally she got the vehicle headed in the direction of the lane. She waved to the Qanuns as she passed their pickup and couldn't help but wonder if they could see the flush in her face.

CHAPTER
17

Raif bounded up the sidewalk and knocked on Dansie's door. He didn't have much time, and he wondered what the computer whiz might have been able to learn.

No one answered. He knocked again. Still nothing. With all that had been happening the last few days his stomach automatically tied itself in knots. He tried the knob and opened the door. "Allen?"

"Yeah, back here."

Raif breathed easier as he walked to the work room. "Don't you answer your door?"

Allen kept his eyes focused on the screen. "No. Just a nuisance and usually means more work. That gives me less time to play."

"What did you find?" Raif asked.

"The initial password is his mother's maiden name, Lilly." He pointed at the screen. "I've been looking through the directories. There's been a lot of stuff deleted in the last few days."

"You're just full of good news."

"Actually, it isn't that bad, but let's look first at the ones not deleted. They are mostly letters. In case you're unaware, which I doubt, Hawkes was a member of the militia movement. In fact a leader of his own group." He pointed to the screen. "This letter was sent out to membership." He clicked on another file. "This one is a copy of a speech given in Chicago back about a year ago. Hawkes would have made a good American Hitler. A speech like this one could incite the wrong people, the wrong way. Everything else undeleted is like this. Pretty general, but caustic, all of it dealing with his involvement with the militia movement."

He hit more keys. "Now, let's get down to business. Whoever used this computer is not very knowledgeable of what he's doing, but then most people who use computers aren't. He didn't know there is a recycle bin in this outfit. Anyway, a deleted file goes to that bin and can be recovered from there. We get an enhanced picture of Mr. Hawkes and his militia involvement with these."

Dansie punched some keys, entered a different directory in Word Perfect, and brought up the first file on the full screen. It was a list of names and addresses under the title "Members of the Jackson Hole Freedom Foundation."

"There are sixty-two people on this list, a lot of them from around here, some who would surprise you." He smiled as he went down the list with the cursor. "Like this one."

The selection was Jeff Grant, but it didn't surprise Raif as much as Allen thought it might. Grant was an officer on the city police force, who had been brought up on charges of using deadly force unnecessarily a year or so before. He had been fired, but returned to the force when his attorney brought suit against the city for firing him without due process. A review board agreed, and he'd escaped prosecution when his attorney started applying more pressure. Raif remembered now who Grant's attorney had been. Larry Noble, the same guy who had come to the aid of Walters, Gitry, and the rest of Hawkes's people the night they were arrested. Raif doubted it was a coincidence.

Grant had a fetish for weapons, had even brought a sawed-off, double-barreled shotgun to work with him as part of his arsenal. He had been reminded that it was not a legal weapon by the chief and told to leave it home. From what Raif had heard, Grant hadn't. Instead he carried it in the trunk of his patrol car.

Grant was also antigovernment and big on anti-taxation. He also frequently got on his soapbox to preach against what the militia movement called "The New World Order." He treated Jackson's Spanish population with disdain and had rousted a black couple in a hotel bar, who had downed one too many drinks but who weren't being that big of a problem. He definitely fit the militia mold.

Raif let his eyes wander over the rest of the list. He recognized half a dozen other names, one a prominent local businessman. Several others were part-time residents, who made lots of money in the big city and had summer homes in the Hole. They probably had what Raif called the Jesse James syndrome. Frustrated, wanna-be-tough-guys, who were desperate for a little excitement. Normally Raif didn't give much thought to militia organizations except as they affected his job, but he didn't think much of men who got their kicks at some out-of-the-way militia training camp, firing real bullets into targets shaped like other humans.

In recent years, too many had overstepped common sense as well as the law on such issues as taxation and states' rights. The more radical of these people had gone from trying to effect change through legislative means to resorting to violent action that hurt the very people they professed to protect. They were becoming the new American terrorists; demonstrating the same extremism and screwed-up thought processes and rationalizations as their counterparts in the Middle East. Clearly Hawkes's group was one of these, and Raif had no tolerance for them.

Allen clicked on another file. "These letters are to other militias. They ask for information and are downright scathing in their denunciation of everyone from the feds to you guys in the county. The guy was a true believer, Raif."

"Information on what?"

"Different things. One asks for names of what Hawkes called 'team players, willing to give their all for the Constitution.' Having read them, I got the idea he was try-ing to pull together a bunch of people for some kind of schooling. I shudder to think what he had planned after that."

"Anything else that caught your attention?"

Dansie pointed to a half dozen file titles. "These. Letters to a company in San Francisco. AMI Chemicals, Daniel Beni, President." He clicked and a letter appeared. "This is one of the last ones. Hawkes talks like he was providing some kind of service. Read it for yourself. You know things that are going on in this guy's life that I don't, so it will probably make more sense to you." He picked up a quarter of a beef sandwich and shoved it in his mouth.

Raif started reading the letter from the screen.

"AMI Chemical Corporation—San Francisco.

Attention, Mr. Daniel Beni."

Bingo. Allison's Dan with gray hair.

He read on: "In reply to your question of me in your letter of the 15th, about the promised supplies for your company's stopover here, I wish to let you know that pur-chase is proceeding as planned and we should be able to make delivery on the 5th of November as you asked. Your representative has already arrived and arranged to take delivery, with my assistance. However, there seems to be some confusion regarding payment. Our terms were that the payment would be placed in my account on October 16th. She indicates that you now wish to delay payment until after delivery. That is unacceptable, and I hope you will clarify the issue with her soon so that there will be no delays.

"Training for company employees has been completed, and I have asked several to stay with your man at the train-ing facility, as the delivery date is only two weeks away. They will aid him in retrieving the items and in disposing of the problems we discussed. I understand your concern in that area, as it has been my own all along. We look forward to your arrival and final planning meeting. Sincerely, Hawk. President, Jackson Hole Freedom Foundation."

That explained the cash deposit slip they found at the condo, and it added credence to the idea that Hawkes had no intention of letting Golding and his party live. The date given for delivery was the day Terri had killed her elk. It was also the day they had all nearly been killed by Golding and Crenshold.

The idea of a training camp was a new one, but it fit. Question was, what were they being trained for? And who exactly was Daniel Beni? The letter raised as many questions as it answered. He rubbed his forehead. He was getting a headache.

"One other thing you might want to know. An encryption program was used to send these. Hawkes didn't want anyone reading his e-mail."

"And the others are like this?" Raif asked.

"Similar stuff. They all deal with some sort of supplies to be delivered to AMI."

"But what it is isn't ever mentioned directly?"

"Not in these letters, and unusual I would think, so I'm assuming the real product was something they didn't want published. When I first saw that Hawkes was contacting a Chemical company, I had visions of another Oklahoma City, but in this instance, Hawkes is providing the product, not the chemical company."

"Weapons. Hawkes was stealing them for sale to the highest bidder."

"Then AMI is a buyer, an arms' dealer. Horrid thought."

"Any record of responses to any of these letters?"

"These were written in Word Perfect, then transferred to e-mail, so I was able to pull them out of the recycle bin. The deleted e-mail files were also deleted from the sent files

so they aren't retrievable. All except one, but that is a different animal altogether."

"You're just full of surprises aren't you? Different in
what way?"

Dansie moved the cursor and clicked into another program. "This was received two days ago, at 6:14 in the
evening."

Raif recalled that that was the day Hawkes was killed
and figured Daniel Beni was the most likely candidate to be
receiving messages. Raif wondered if he was still in the
Valley.

Allen continued. "It's in a foreign language; therefore,
whoever wanted to read the file had to use a language conversion module. What that does is convert the computer
over to a specific language—keyboard, typeface, everything. Once that is done, he can read it.

"The bad news is, I don't have the slightest idea what
language it is because I don't have the language conversion
module. Let me show you."

He pulled up the directory and pointed to the file title.
Marks similar to chicken scratches existed where a word
ordinarily would. "These must be converted to readable
script by use of the module. So if this were Spanish and a
module of that language were applied, it would come up on
the screen as Spanish and people who speak Spanish could
read it."

"And the proper conversion module is not on the hard
drive?" Raif asked.

"Nope. My guess is whoever received that file brought
his own module with him."

"Let's say we find out what language was used and get
you the module, could you get into the file then?"

"In, yes, read it . . . maybe. Depends on if it is password
protected in that language. It's hard enough to try to figure
out passwords in English, I wouldn't know where to begin
in Spanish, or any other language, but it's rumored the

government has programs that decipher codes and passwords in a number of languages. I might be able to get my
hands on one of those." He smiled. "If they actually exist."

Raif knew better than to ask how, but he also knew
Allen Dansie had connections. He had worked as a pro-
gramer for the NSA for two years until he got tired of the
day-to-day hassle and having to wear a tie and fight traffic.
"Do language modules exist for all languages?"

"All the major ones. Some of the lesser used languages
aren't profitable enough for the software companies to
make the programs. Once we know which language we're
up against, we'll just have to check to see if a module exists.
My guess is it does, because something was used here, and I
don't think it was decoded one letter at a time. You don't
have any idea what the language might be?"

Raif didn't know, but he did know they were dealing
with professionals, probably people who wanted weapons
and couldn't buy them on the open market, professionals
who were also involved in training violent men harbored in
the militia movement, and the FBI was leaning toward
Iranian-backed terrorism

"Order Arabic, Russian, and Farsi," Raif said.

"Never heard of the last one."

"Few have, that's why it might be used. It's the language
of Persia and Iran and the one they've used in the past for
things like this. How long to get modules here?" Raif asked.

"Overnight mail in most cases, but I'll see what I can
do. I might talk them into an internet transfer."

"Get everything you need, Allen, as quick as you can."
Raif looked at his watch. "Gotta catch a chopper. I'd better
get going. Put everything you can on a backup disk for me,
will you? I'll have a courier pick it up."

Allen grabbed a small disk and shoved it into his "A"
drive as Raif turned and headed out of the house. Once
inside his pickup and the motor was running, Raif removed
his mike from the dash hook and called in as he put the

pickup in gear and headed for the airport. "Get me the sheriff, will you, Nancy?"

Raif filled the sheriff in on his thinking.

"A training facility. It fits," the sheriff said.

"Any word on the guy who died at the condo?" Raif asked.

"The identity belongs to an American college student, who decided to travel alone in Europe. His parents haven't heard from him for better than a year."

"What country was he last seen alive in?"

"France. Paris to be exact."

"I'd bet my ranch that the dead man's real origin is the same as the guy who did a nose dive out of the chopper."

"Safe bet. Both are Iranian. Sharps is trying to come up with his name," the sheriff said.

"I had Allen order language modules in Arabic, Russian, and Farsi. Give him a call will you, and have him get them in Kurdish and Turkish as well," Raif said.

"Farsi?"

"The language of Persia, now Iran."

There was a pause. "I don't like the way this is coming together," the sheriff said.

"National law enforcement has been warned for the last two years the terrorists intended to regroup after losing in that attack on the World Trade Center—repay us for imprisoning some of their people. Looks like somebody was right." Raif paused long enough to turn a corner. "If that is who we're up against, and they're training radical militia elements here for some kind of terrorist activity to close out this century, it will be hard to stop.

"Tell Sharps that Allen has connected Hawkes to a business in San Francisco. AMI Chemicals."

Raif could hear the message being passed on. Apparently Sharps was in the office. He wouldn't like being left out of the loop.

When the sheriff's mike clicked on again, it was Sharps

who spoke. "I hear you, and I want that computer," he said gruffly.

"Allen needs more time."

There was a pause. "I'll have men, specialists, here from Washington by sunup tomorrow. He's got until then."

"That'll be long enough."

There was a pause. "Don't circumvent me again, Qanun, or I'll have your head."

Raif bit his tongue. It would take more than Sharps to take his head, and both of them knew it. "What about the prints at the condo or at Hawkes's place?" Raif asked.

"Kristoff got several different but very clear sets at the condo. We had Hawkes's on file and got a match to both of the dead men with false prints. Most of the others matched those of Allison Winters. The rest will take more time. Sent the ones on the beer cans you found in the fire at the campground, and copies of the photos as well."

"Has anyone heard from CID about the theft at Fort Cheyenne?" Raif asked.

"Nothing yet." They all knew that the longer it took the greater the chance they had stumbled into a bigger mess than they imagined. An empty spot in the pit of Raif's stomach was growing to black hole proportions.

"Terri Stevens defended a guy like Roberts in New York under similar conditions. She says Roberts couldn't have accessed those weapons on his own. Someone higher up has to be involved." Raif told Sharps about Colonel Blakely's stonewalling.

"Did you say Blakely?"

"Yeah, his response to my questions over the phone gives me reason to believe he might be protecting more than the good name of Fort Cheyenne and the American Army. Maybe he just wasn't minding the store and got his pocket picked and he's not anxious to admit it. Then again, he could be the Army's newest millionaire." Raif turned into airport road. "In one of Hawkes's letters to AMI, he mentions that a representative of that company had arrived earlier. It was a woman. Hawkes helped her make necessary arrangements for delivery of the weapons, housing, etc."

"Lucinda Bell, the woman whose dress you found at the condo."

"Probably. According to the clerk at the Village, she was only at the condo for awhile, but my guess is she's probably still in the Valley. Shad was going to check real estate sales, rentals, and stores that might have sold winter and camping equipment that fits what is going on here. You might want to have Moen get it done, now that you're in charge," Raif suggested.

"A bull in a china closet," Sharps said, "but I'll enjoy his misery."

"At least it will keep him out of the way. There is something else you and the sheriff ought to know, Sharps."

"My brain is already on overload, Qanun, but go ahead."

"Hawkes has organized a group called the Jackson Hole Freedom Foundation. Golding and Crenshold both belonged; so did Gitry and Walters. Some of the others who came after us on the trail are members as well." He paused. "There's one more name on this list you oughta check out: Jeff Grant."

Sharps had clicked on his mike to respond, and Raif heard the sheriff swear in the background as he explained who Grant was.

"If Grant is involved, it would explain Noble's quick response to the arrest of Gitry, Walters, and the others," Sharps said.

"Noble was Grant's attorney when the Jackson police wanted to boot him," Raif added.

"We'll check into it."

"Don't let Noble pick anybody's brain for information. Tell everyone to keep their lips buttoned from here on out. The enemy has enough advantage as it is," Raif said.

Sharps and the sheriff signed off as Raif pulled into a parking spot at the airport. The entire lot was banked high with snow. He glanced at his watch. He was five minutes late. Slipping out of the vehicle, he went to the rear of the Topper covered bed and removed a pair of Alumalite snow-shoes and a prepackaged survival kit. Such things, along with a couple dozen other items that could be used to get themselves and others out of deep snow and layers of ice, were standard fare in both his and his father's outfits during the winter.

His .30–.30 lever action rifle was locked in a metal case attached to the bed of the pickup. Raif unlocked the case and removed the weapon along with two boxes of shells. He wasn't concerned about grizzlies, they would be burrowed in for the winter now. It was predators of the two-legged variety that worried Raif.

By the time he reached the chopper, the blades were already churning. He opened one of the side doors and climbed into the seat next to Sam. Shad sat in the front by the pilot. Raif shut the door, and the Forest Service chop-per immediately lifted off into the crisp but clear air. As they gained altitude, Raif looked to the south and west near Teton Pass, then let his eye wander along the range clear to the three peaks. The sky was mostly clear, but as the chop-per lifted higher, he could see a bank of gray clouds lying on the distant horizon in Idaho. He figured they were safe from the fury of Mother Nature until after dark at worst. After that, he didn't know. This early in the season the clouds moved in without much more than a scattering of flakes, but sometimes, as in the past few days, they'd dump enough white stuff to bury a full-sized pickup.

The three major peaks of the Teton Range glistened in the afternoon sun. As many times as he had gazed at them, they never failed to create a sense of awe in Raif. Their rugged majesty and distinctive shapes were unparalleled in his experience. He had climbed them several times over his short life, and he knew they could be as deadly as they looked, but the view from the top was more than worth the struggle and the potential danger encountered in climbing them.

But then the whole Valley was that way. Rugged and beautiful, unforgiving and majestic, all at once. Modern conveniences and technology made things safer, more accessible for even the New York weekender, but if you underestimated the strength of her nature, the Hole could kill you.

They flew over trees blanketed with a layer of snow, creating a scene such as you'd see on an old-fashioned Christmas card. While driving to the airport, Raif's digital thermometer in his pickup had read ten above, making it unseasonably cold, even for the Hole. In the mountains, the temperature would be at least twenty degrees colder.

He took out his sunglasses as protection against the bright glare and settled back for the ride as Shad turned in his seat and pointed to the headset next to Raif's head. When they were in place, Shad spoke through the intercom mike attached to his headset.

"Search and Rescue had planes up at dawn. Nothing yet, not even a track, but the snow we've gotten since you came out of the mountains has covered everything." He paused. "A bit of good news. The Forest Rangers found a '96 Model Chevy truck with a four-place horse trailer that has carried animals in the last couple of weeks. They also found a lease agreement under the name of John Duren from Lovell." He smiled. "According to the sheriff over there, John had a guide license for this area. Had it revoked for killing animals out of season three years ago. Ever since then, he's been militant. The sheriff in Lovell says he's got a son who has come up missing, too. Mean as his father. Only twenty but with a real knack for the outdoors, and he loves guns. Rumor around Lovell is that he had a collection of automatics banned by law, but the authorities could never prove it. The younger Lovell and a bunch of his friends put themselves together a unique firing range on private property. Moving targets of men. Mostly cops."

They were flying fast and low, making good time. In another five minutes they'd be at the spot where the body of the clerk had been found. The storage well of the chopper contained stretcher beds that could be attached to the chopper's runners, along with emergency equipment. Raif glanced at Sam who seemed a little pale. Raif knew it wasn't a fear of flying in general; rather it was a fear of choppers because of the memories they brought back. Memories of rice paddies and kill or be killed. Nightmares were born into Sam's life in Vietnam, and Raif had watched him wake up shouting more than once when they were camped out hunting. On those nights Raif had heard enough to be thankful he had been spared the hell of Vietnam.

After twenty minutes the chopper veered hard left, sailed over a ridge, maneuvered for landing, and sank into the snow clear to it's belly before hitting solid granite. They were still attaching their snow shoes when the blade came to a standstill; the wind whistled through small cracks in the chopper's metal body. Sounded cold enough to freeze up hell, and as Raif stepped onto the snow he felt he was there. The wind was harsh, raw, and biting, filling the air with blowing, stinging snow. As Sam and Shad joined him, Raif pulled on his insulated mittens, then moved the fur-lined hood of his parka over his head and ears, tightening the cords around his face. From the look and feel of the temperature, it was at least ten below zero here, with wind chill making it much worse. The layer of snow thinned with the wind and created drifts and snow bridges that could swallow a man whole. The stuff was deceiving, looking solid enough for snow shoes, but Raif knew different. It was one reason Raif wanted Sam along. In the past Sam had trapped in winter, coming as far north and east as they were now. He knew the dangers and what to watch for.

He removed a rope from his survival bag. It was sixty feet long and would be attached to the waist of each man. Another rope would be attached to a snow sled they'd need to remove the remains of each of the men lying dead and frozen in three different locations.

Raif could see the chopper had landed on the ridge where Golding and Crenshold had taken them prisoner. In the blinding snow, he saw no sign of anyone's presence. He fed bullets into the holding chamber of his .30–.30 then slung it over his shoulder by use of a strap he quickly attached. Shad followed suit with his own rifle. Sam had already done the same with a hand-woven cloth scabbard with matching strap. Raif thought the scabbard would con-tain Sam's favorite weapon, a .30–.30 with lever action, but it bulged in the wrong places. He had seen those bulges only once. When Raif was still in high school, he and Sam had gone out to the county range for some target practice. Sam had used an M-16 automatic rifle, an earlier model of the Army's M-16A. Raif had fired a few rounds with it. They were legal then. Now the laws had changed, but Raif let it go. If any two-legged predators did show up, Sam's weapon would help even the odds.

When everyone was ready and attached to the rope, Sam led them along the ridge to where it sloped to the east. He couldn't take them directly to the bottom of the ravine as Raif and Terri had done the day she'd killed the elk. The loose shale underneath would slide easily and the heavy snow would likely do the same and bury them. They would have to follow the slope for half a mile to a trail that worked its way down, then come back to the west where the clerk's remains were. It took them nearly thirty minutes to get to the bottom, carefully brush away the snow, and package the frozen body in a black body bag, then another forty-five minutes to return to the chopper.

While Shad and Sam were packaging the grisly remains of the clerk, Raif trudged to the spot where Sam said he had hung the elk. It was gone, but a two-foot length of cut rope was still tied to the cross beam Sam had cut and put in the forks of two trees, evidence that someone had cut up the animal for their own use.

Raif was glad in a way. He didn't know when he would be able to return for the meat, and it was best someone was getting the use of it. The question was who? Friend? Or foe?

With the clerk's remains secured in the cargo hold, the chopper lifted off the ridge and banked west. A few minutes later they were over the camp where he had buried Billy Two Shoes. The pilot attempted a landing in the small clearing near the camp, but the deep snow prevented it. He opted for another ridge and Raif and others found themselves walking some distance to the trail Raif and the gray had taken into the camp itself. Although the spot was covered by snow, Raif pointed out the approximate points where the horses had been tethered, the tents placed, and the spot where he had found the beer cans and other items in the fire ring.

From there he led them to the spot where he had left Billy. Working in the wind and cold, they removed the snow, then the rocks over the shallow grave Raif had fashioned, and pulled the body free. After stuffing the corpse into the body bag, they struggled back to the chopper. There they laid the body on the first of two stretchers now attached to the runners by the pilot, then strapped it in. Raif climbed aboard and plopped into the seat. He was bushed and cold to the bone, but they still had enough sun to make the last stop and get back to the airport before dark. He caught his breath as the doors closed against the cold and the pilot started the engine.

They were soon hovering over the area where Raif figured he had fallen with the gray and hung the assassin's body for pickup. He had been hopeful that they would see the body from the air, but dense trees and the full-blown winter landscape changed things enough that he couldn't pinpoint the spot with any precision. He told Sam about the place. Sam said they were one ridge too far west and redirected the pilot to a spot where he figured they could get to the corpse.

The pilot set them down, and the three men snowshoed toward the site. The first sure sign something was wrong was a trail they crossed in the snow. It was evident that either two men or a very large animal had come through before the last foot or so of fluff had covered the trail again. It wasn't fresh, but fresh enough that all three men took their weapons in hand. Raif noticed Shad smiling at Sam's M-16.

"A man prepared," Shad said.

Sam spat tobacco in the snow. "Some things take more killin' than others."

Sam and Shad split away from Raif, going about fifty yards to east and west. They checked the area for other tracks, newer ones, as all three of them pushed on toward the spot Raif figured the body should be waiting, but found none.

The rope was there, its cut end dangling several inches above the now much deeper snow. The indentations indicated someone had dragged the body on some sort of makeshift sled into the depths of the ravine.

Raif debated. Following the tracks could lead them into a trap. Then again, it might mean finding the enemy and the stolen weapons they carried, weapons that Raif figured had the capacity to kill a lot of people.

He looked at the sky to the southwest. Gray to black clouds were sliding over the Tetons and into the Hole. It wouldn't be long before the sky above them would turn from intermittent blue to solid gray. Snow was imminent. Worse, sunlight was quickly disappearing.

"Where are they headed, Sam?"

Glancing at his watch, Sam spat in the snow. "Don't know, but they've left a pretty trail to follow, even from the air if we stay low."

They started back for the chopper, Raif picturing Crenshold's notebook map in his mind. By the time they arrived at the helicopter, he was sure the canyon from Crenshold's pocket notebook would be at the end of that trail.

"How'd they know where to find that body, Raif?" Shad asked as they pulled off their snowshoes.

Raif wasn't sure and said so, but he had a good idea. He had given a detailed report of the area the night of his return. Jeff Grant would have had access to those notes.

Raif told Shad about Grant. As a Mormon, Shad didn't swear much, but the disgust he had for a cop gone bad deserved a little extra punctuation that made even Sam smile.

The chopper lifted, and Shad directed the pilot to the spot where the body should have been. The trail below was visible from the air but only intermittently, and they had to stay at tree top height and fly at reduced speed to see it at all. Raif could see why the search planes hadn't picked it up.

It led over rough terrain but eventually ascended another ridge and dropped into a third, then a fourth valley, the one on Crenshold's map.

The pilot, Will Sayers, had flown for the Army for a few years and, rumor was, had been involved in the conflict with Iraq. Raif figured his experience would come in handy if they confronted any opposition from the trees, but he still felt the helicopter provided an awfully big target and that they were at an extreme disadvantage. He wondered if the ones who had attacked him a few days earlier in another chopper had felt the same way.

Suddenly they were over a ridge and into the valley. Sayers pushed on the throttle and the chopper swooped across it at tree top-level. Cliffs protruded from the valley floor at the other end and they were quickly closing on them.

"Nobody moving," Sayers said as he pulled the chopper into a hover just before dashing them all in small pieces against the solid granite wall. "But there is a man-made trail down there against the cliffs. Looks like fresh tracks. What do you want to do?" He looked at Shad, then at Raif.

"I want on top of those cliffs," Sam said. Sayers nodded, a grin on his face. "And I don't wanna break no leg gettin' out of this piece of junk, so get it low enough so's it's nothin' more than a big first step." Sam said. He looked at Raif. "I suppose I'm deputized?"

"Yeah, you're deputized. I'll go with you," Raif said. "Shad you stay with the chopper, make another pass and see if anyone decides to take us on. If not, land this thing somewhere and check out those trees." He pointed to a thick stand of trees in the canyon to the west of them. "Unless I miss my guess there are horses in there. We've got two transceivers. Keep one, and Sam and I will take the other. If you run into trouble or see anything of overpowering interest, let us know. We'll do the same."

Shad nodded his agreement.

Sayers had his machine hovering over the top of the cliffs in a matter of seconds, then he lowered it to within about five feet of the snow-covered rock. "As ordered," he shouted with another grin.

Raif felt vulnerable, his heart in his throat as Sam opened his door and, with snowshoes in hand, jumped. Raif followed, and the chopper quickly dipped its nose and then sped out of sight. Raif was still crawling out of the pit he made when landing as Sam finished putting on his Alumalites.

Pulling some binoculars from his backpack, Sam scanned the canyon walls, then the trees below them. "Nothing nor nobody," he said half to himself. "I smell a fire, though. Come on."

Sam headed down the ridge until he found a trail, half hidden by trees, at the base of the cliff. "These boys know what they're doin'." Sam said it softly. "Watch your step, Raif." Raif nodded.

The trail had been recently used, and the snow was packed. Raif looked both directions. Ten feet back in the direction they had come, it veered to the left and went toward the stand of trees Raif had pointed out to Shad. Sam stooped down and checked something in the snow.

"Blood," he said. Gathering some in his ungloved fingers, he rubbed it between finger and thumb then smelled it. "Human. Not critical unless whoever's bleedin' don't take care of it."

Raif gave him a curious look of disbelief.

"Smelled enough in 'Nam. A man's chemistry smells different than an animal," Sam said. He pointed toward the stand of trees. "Someone went that-a-way. Gotta be after a horse."

Removing his radio, Raif called Shad, warning him someone might be in the area and to use caution. Even as he spoke, he could hear the chopper's rotors winding down somewhere above and to the east of them.

Sam was already moving along the cliff face, and seeing Sam take his safety off the M-16, Raif did the same on his .30–.30.

A hundred feet later they came to a thick stand of deadfall that Raif figured they'd have to go around, but then noticed the tracks disappeared underneath and near the rock wall of the cliff. He watched as the slope of the hill dipped suddenly and an opening appeared in the deadfall. Sam vanished through the hole and Raif followed. They entered a spot cleared of debris that looked to be about twenty feet square. The deadfall had lodged against the cliff above them, giving the place a canopy and making it invisible from the air. Below it, there was a cave entrance in the cliff face.

"I take it you've been here," Raif said softly.

"Used it as a camp once or twice. Hussa and I found it during that hunt with you boys. Inhabited by grizzly once. Seems animals of a different kind are using it now. You got a flashlight?"

Raif pulled one from his survival pack and flipped on the switch. They moved to the cave entrance and he flashed it inside. It was of substantial size near the opening but narrowed some as it turned to the right about twenty feet in. They both listened and Sam pointed to the smoke that hung near the cave's ceiling and was escaping around the top edge of its entrance where it dissipated in the deadfall.

Sam started in and Raif followed, careful to keep the light away from his body. The opening took a turn to the right. Raif placed himself against the cave wall, then shone the light around the corner.

Camping equipment and cases of food goods were stacked against the walls of the cave, with pack equipment, saddles, sleeping bags, tarps and other gear strewn about the floor. The last embers of a fire were burning in the center of the large cavern. A body lay next to it, face to the ground. Raif scanned high and low, every nook and cranny with the light, but saw no other sign of human kind and stepped farther into the cavern. A Coleman lantern sat on a table near the fire pit. Next to it was a box of matches, half the contents strewn across the table. Raif handed Sam the flashlight and lit the lamp. The bright light immediately filled the interior of the cavern, giving some comfort to taut nerves.

"Looks like they left in a hurry," Sam said, stooping down by the body and feeling for a pulse. "Warm, but barely." He rolled the man over then said, "John Duren." Sam opened the man's coat and checked the wounds. There were two, one in the stomach, the other probably through a lung. Sam pointed to a gun lying near Duren's right hand. It was a Colt six-shooter much like the one Raif used when in the saddle. "Looks to me like he was a little slow on the draw." He stood. "We'd better get him aboard that chopper and back to Jackson or he'll die on us. Might anyway."

"How many do you think camped in here?" Raif asked.

"From the look of the used sleeping bags and dishes, I'd say five."

"One dead, one wounded and trying to get to the horses. That leaves three unaccounted for." Raif pushed on the send button of the radio, but got only static. The granite walls of the cave were too thick to allow for any reception. As Raif headed for the exit, Sam was tending to Duren's wounds. When outside, Raif called Shad and told him what they found. "Have you seen anyone?" he asked.

"No, but we found where they bedded down the horses. Five of 'em are still here. There's a trail going west and somebody took two animals and headed out. Trail looks real fresh and I'd say he or they haven't gotten more than a mile or two, considering the depth of the snow. The animals will be pushing the stuff all the way, and it'll wear 'em out real quick. You probably already know this, but one of 'em is bleeding." There was a pause.

"Sayers found a spot where another chopper landed sometime this morning. There is a packed trail that leads to it from the direction of the cave and a couple of indentations in the snow in the shape of boxes or crates of some kind. He figures three or four people left aboard it."

Raif pushed his own send button. "Have him get on his radio and notify Search and Rescue. Ask if their planes have seen any helicopters besides ours, and get hold of the tower at the airport, find out if anything has shown up on radar. If it has, we want location. And, Shad, we need a stretcher down here. We need to get Duren to a hospital."

They signed off, and Raif returned to the cave to help get Duren ready for transport. Ten minutes later Shad and

Sayers had him on a stretcher and were headed back to the chopper with a promise to try and return for them before dark. Raif only nodded, knowing it would be impossible. Just as well, there were at least two others who needed tracking.

Sam was rummaging through things and Raif joined him. "Find anything of interest?"

"Mostly camping stuff and food." He pointed toward the back of the cavern. "They dug a hole back there to bury waste. I dug around some and as near as I can tell there have been a lot of people in here over the last few months, but not all at the same time. Sorta like a guide's trail camp where he brings in four or five clients for a week or two. Lots of coming and going."

"A training camp." Raif told him about Hawkes's letter. "My bet is they've been arming and training militants in the militia movement in here. Or worse. Looks more and more like we have a foreign element involved, doesn't it?"

Sam was scratching at his beard as he nodded. "There's boxes back there, empty now, but they contained night vision goggles. Over on the table there are some maps. I figure they played war games at night." He walked to the table and Raif followed. They looked through the maps and Sam stopped at one that was hand-drawn. "This one here is a plan of attack. Shows three teams of three each, approaching the target from different directions." He pointed to a map. "There's a river to be crossed by one of two teams. Probably under cover of darkness. One team then does some climbin' to get into position while the second team stays on the water for some reason, and the third team is located here." He pointed. "My guess is the third is a reconnaissance unit, deployed to eliminate anyone who gets too close to the operation."

"Any idea what or where this target is?"

"No names, but it looks like a bridge or maybe a dam. My guess is they trained for it, but don't know exactly what the target is either. I saw it in special ops in 'Nam all the time. It was a security precaution. When we were on our way we were given names, final details, and explosives if they were needed. These folks mean business, Raif." He pointed again. "See how far their final positions are from the actual target?" Raif nodded. "And this dotted line hooking up the target to their position? My guess is that's a missile."

Raif's mouth felt dry, and he licked his lips. "Any more maps like this?"

"Partials, but nothing this complete. I'd say they're planning at least three major hits, but have trained for more than that." He lifted a sheet of paper. Raif could see a detailed drawing of a large airport. "My guess is one is an airliner." He paused. "This stuff was left behind by mistake, or because they were in a big hurry and didn't figure anyone would be coming along soon. Come with me." He led Raif toward the back of the cavern, flashlight in hand.

"Couple of fair-sized crates sat here," Sam said. He shone the light on the soft ground. "I figure they came in here in the past couple of hours and took 'em out. Could be the missiles they're gonna use." He walked a short distance to another part of the cavern and pointed. A man's finger could be seen sticking out of the earth. "That'd be the man you hung up the tree, but he'll keep for now unless some griz decides to take up residence here before our chopper gets back."

Raif told Sam that Sayers had found signs of another chopper and that Shad had found the horses and figured two or maybe three were missing. Sam's brow was furrowed with worry. "My gut feeling is they ain't friends. Not any more. Somebody's chasin' the wounded man. They must consider him a threat. We'd better find him before they do," Sam said, even as he started for the entrance. "And we'd better keep him alive if we want any chance of finding those missiles before these idiots decide to use 'em."

18

Raif led the buckskin he had selected into the trail before stopping to adjust the saddle. Sam had been checking out the trail.

"Two horses packing light riders, probably carrying only essential gear. The second left after the first. Like I said, one is chasing the other." He glanced up at Raif who had mounted. "I should be going with you. Both are dangerous, both will be watching their back trail if they seen us fly in here."

The sheriff had called Shad on the chopper radio, and Shad had relayed the message. They wanted forensics in the cave tonight and someone had to stay behind to light landing fires and get Kristoff's team to the cave. The sheriff made it clear that Raif was the deputy and should do the chasing. That left Sam.

"That storm ain't going to allow no chopper in here, Raif. I just as well—"

"Sheriff's orders. Besides, you can use the chopper to catch up with me in the morning. Without Shad coming back in, you'll have to show the pilot the way."

Sam was about to protest again then decided it was no use and kept his mouth shut. He handed Raif the halter rope of a second horse loaded with a sleeping bag and other gear. "You'll need this stuff, but more important, when the buckskin gets tired, switch to the bay. You'll make better time and keep these animals from cashin' in on ya."

"I'll see you in the morning," Raif said. He reined the mount in the direction the others had gone. His mind went quickly to business. If the second was after the first, the chaser would be forced to move cautiously for fear of an ambush, but he would be able to move with less difficulty because the first would be breaking a trail through the deep snow. That evened things out between them.

Raif figured that because neither of the men he was following knew his whereabouts at this point, he had a chance of catching up and nailing both of them. If they did discover he was on their back trail . . . well, chances were he'd get his fool head blown off.

No time to worry about it. The wounded man was becoming a key figure now, probably had needed information. He wanted the man alive.

After an hour of tracking it got dark enough that Raif was forced to dismount and walk the trail in front of the buckskin in order to see it at all. He had made good time and felt he had closed the gap significantly between himself and the others, but the darkness was quickly becoming a two-edged sword. On the one hand, if he kept moving, he could narrow the gap, possibly even surprise them. On the other, they could go into hiding, ambush him, and he'd be dead before he realized it.

He paused a moment, listening. The wind in the trees prevented him from hearing much, and that stretched his nerves even tighter; he decided to keep going. The man in the lead would want to put as much distance between him and his pursuer as he could. Raif figured he had to keep going or be left behind.

He tramped along the trail for another fifteen minutes when he came to a spot that had been cleared out some. Needing to get a better look, he removed a flashlight from his saddlebags and covered the lens with a hankie. Turning it on was taking a chance, and he held his breath as he pushed the button. He exhaled when there were no immediate repercussions, then he concentrated on the trail in the snow.

Someone had dismounted to rest, sitting on a boulder to the right of the trail. From the look of the red stains in the snow, it was the man being hunted. The second man had come this way as well, stopped, but then moved on. The hunted one had lost a lot of blood. Raif figured the hunter would move in for the kill. He switched off the light and led the buckskin back into the trail, shaking the snow off his hat as he did. It was picking up, falling in large flakes and lots of them. The snow-filled tracks before him indicated he was still an hour behind the hunter, further behind the hunted. He had to keep closing the gap, even if it meant walking through the night.

He found himself wishing Sam were along. An extra set of eyes and Sam's sixth sense for tracking would come in handy, but the sheriff had been adamant, and Raif hadn't argued. Now he was wishing he had.

Thirty minutes later, Raif led the horses out of the trees and onto a ridge above a deep canyon. Howling wind drove the snow at him in great sheets of white, and the trail disappeared. He decided to stay on the backside of the ridge, where the wind wasn't as bad. He knew this country, thought he knew the trail they'd take. It was an uncommon trail, one seldom used, steep, and unfriendly. He and his brother had followed an elk this way years before. It had led them to a deep ravine, then up an even steeper slope on the far side. That was in middle fall, in a rainstorm. Hussa's horse had slipped, broken a leg. They had learned a hard lesson. Now here he was, about to take the same path. He could only hope the trail would be kinder to him.

He missed it on his first pass, but found it on his second. As he and his animals dropped down the side of the ravine in the cover of thick trees, the trail got clearer and the wind lighter. He stopped at the bottom long enough to check the animals and give them some oats from a bag in his pack-saddle. In some ways the trail had actually been easier than he had remembered, but the steep part of the slope was still ahead. He wasn't looking forward to it.

The boots he wore were the best, and his feet had stayed warm. He pulled a thermal mask over his head and face to prevent frostbite, then put his parka hood back in place. He wondered if the men in front of him were pre-pared for this kind of weather. The second had probably taken the time to dress warmly, pick out what he needed to keep himself alive. The first had been forced to flee and might be in trouble, especially with the amount of blood he was losing. Soon or late, the weather and physical weakness would force him to dig in. Then it would be a matter of who could kill who, first.

The trail told Raif he was getting close to the hunter. As Raif had thought it through he figured this man would be Duren's son. He had experience in these mountains and knew how to survive, and he would want to avenge what he had probably thought was the death of his father. That would make him dangerous, unwilling to let anything get in his way.

He wondered about the first man. Who was he? What had he done? Was he just another man they were trying to get rid of? It was obvious he knew these mountains, knew how to travel through them, even in the worst possible weather. That would make him a local, possibly another man from Lovell who had worn out his welcome. Whoever he was, Raif knew he was just as dangerous as the man who chased him.

He was up against two experienced men in the use of weapons; men who would kill to survive. Raif knew he'd better be at his best.

He removed some jerky from his bag as he tried to put himself in the shoes of the hunted and read his thoughts.

He was on a trail that few knew about. It was the shortest route to the North Buffalo River, and, though extremely difficult, it was the most direct way out of the backcountry. It would climb to the very edge of the tree line, and wind and exposure would drop temperatures to thirty to forty below freezing at night. At that temperature, exposed flesh froze within minutes. Darkness and the snowstorm would make it impossible to get any bearings. He would dig in. No other choice. But when and where? And would the hunter follow suit, or would he continue the hunt? These were questions Raif could only guess at, but it had better be a pretty good guess, or his body wouldn't be found until summer.

He switched his saddle to the bay and the gear to the buckskin. Putting the halter on him he tied it to the saddle horn, then put the bridle on the bay. It was taking a chance, but he removed the flashlight and masked it with the hankie again. It was too dark to do otherwise. That done he set out on foot, leading the two horses. He had learned years ago that trying to ride up this slope would be foolhardy. He couldn't afford to lose a horse this time.

Cautiously he worked his way to the top and was grateful to arrive there winded and sweaty but in one piece. The wind worsened, pummeling him with snow he couldn't see in the pitch black darkness. Surely the other two must have stopped. No man in his right mind would fight this! He looked for their tracks and found them nearly filled with blowing snow. He moved into the protection of a stand of trees and shut off his flashlight while debating his next move.

The trail was hard to follow, and if they had dug in he could stumble into them and get himself killed or miss them altogether. Neither was an exciting prospect. The only other chance he had was to get around them, cut them off along the trail. Could he do it in this storm? He knew this country, was dressed warm enough to survive, though even then he was taking a big chance.

But if he didn't take it, if the hunter got to his prey before Raif did, they'd never know what was going on, where those targets were. He had to chance it.

There were two trails that ran parallel to this one; the first would take him back the way he had come, then east through the valley at the foot of the mountain, over several ridges and back to the west, exiting near the Buffalo River. It would be long, but out of the wind, easier on both him and his animals. The problem was, if the men he chased kept moving, he'd never arrive at the Buffalo in time.

The second one was high up and went around the eastern edge of Soda Mountain. It would be cold, miserable riding and hard on his animals. He would need to rotate them more often, make them take turns blazing trail; could lose them to the cold. But, it was shorter and still out of sight of those he pursued. He could travel without fear of discovery and most likely be ahead of them when morning came.

For a moment he questioned his sanity, then he picked up the reins of the bay and led him along the ridge searching for the trail he wanted. As he found it, mounted, and started down the side of the ravine, the snow seemed to increase in its intensity, trying to beat him back. He lowered his head into it and nudged the bay forward. One thing was certain: it was going to be a long and very cold night.

19

Raif threw aside the snow-covered, waterproof tarp with some difficulty and found himself surrounded by mounds of drifted snow. He was relieved to discover the wind had stopped blowing and that the sky was a brilliant blue color. The night before, he had traveled for another two hours before being forced to find cover in a storm unlike anything he had ever experienced. Stumbling into a stand of rocks and trees, he had made the horses as comfortable as he could before making his own bed and falling into it.

He glanced in the direction he had left his animals. Both were still erect, heads hanging low between front legs, their bodies draped with the tarps he had managed to tie around them to try and keep them from freezing up during the night. As cold as it had gotten, he hadn't expected to see them still alive. He was grateful to find them breathing.

In the face of the worsening storm, it had seemed a foolish decision to take this other trail. He had spent a futile two hours in which he made little headway and had finally been forced to blaze his own path to lower ground and the cover of thicker trees. His only consolation was that the others would also have been forced to find cover or die fools.

He looked at the mountain towering above him. Reflecting off the field of bright snow, sunlight turned the

273

expanse into a field of glittering diamonds, forcing Raif to squint to save his eyes from damage. The deep snow hung on the the cliffs and cornices above him like heavy blankets. This much snow accumulating so quickly increased the danger of an avalanche ten-fold.

The air was crisp enough that it turned his breath almost crystalline as he stood and worked out the kinks, then looked at his watch. Nearly eight. He had slept longer than he had intended. Working clumsily with the frozen ropes, it took him longer to do everything, and it was some time before he had the buckskin saddled and the rest of his gear lashed on the packhorse. He knew the weather had been too bad for the sheriff to fly in last night, but this morning would be a different story. He tried several times using the radio to make contact but soon realized that the mountain stood between him and civilization. He'd have to wait, hoping they were already on their way and that they would be able to find him and the men he chased.

Shoving the radio back in his saddlebags, Raif took a piece of frozen elk jerky from a pocket. He would eat this morning's breakfast while trying to locate his prey—assuming they had also survived the cold temperatures of the storm.

Moving out of the trees, Raif passed under a cliff of sheer granite and directed the buckskin toward the lower trail he figured his quarry would take. The intermittent rays of sun coming through the trees felt good against his face. He was exhilarated by the crisp, clean air, but he knew that he'd better get his flesh covered or risk frostbite. After pulling on his face mask, he fed a shell into the chamber of his .30–.30 then pulled his gloves back on. The buckskin proved itself to be tough, and continued to plow its way through the three feet of snow that blocked the trail.

He could see no sign of man or beast; no imprint in the snow, no fresh track. Had they gone a different way or had he gotten in front of them? He pulled the buckskin up short and turned him back the way they had come. When he reached the spot where he and his animals had entered the trail he dismounted and led his horses into the protective overhang of a thick bunch of ancient pine. After tying up the horses, Raif strapped on his Alumalites. He figured that if his quarry had gone another way he would never catch them, but if they were on this trail, just behind him, he was still in the game with a chance of getting to the hunted before the hunter did. He snowshoed back to the trail and began moving north. When he came to a spot where the trail descended, he followed it down into a small meadow. There, he found a fallen tree and dug himself a place in the snow behind it. Now it would be a waiting game.

He made sure he was well-concealed, checked the chamber in his rifle, made sure the safety was off, and took a look around him. He noticed the steep slope rising above him to the west and noted the heavy blanket of snow that had accumulated there. He hoped he wouldn't have to use his rifle. The report would likely set off an avalanche that would rumble into the meadow like a huge tidal wave. Not a comforting thought.

After all his exertions, lying motionless in the snow, he began to feel the cold settling in on him. He fantasized standing by a hot fire, holding something warm to drink. The minutes passed, and he began to think he was stupid lying in the snow, waiting for someone to come—someone who was probably miles away from this spot. Several times he thought of giving up, then he would imagine hearing something moving through the trees on the far side of the meadow. He would ready himself, only to be disappointed when nothing appeared. His hands and feet grew ever colder, and he frequently removed his thick gloves to blow on his hands to try and warm them.

Then he heard it. The distinct sound of a horse forcing itself through heavy snow.

He lowered himself behind the log and held his breath, afraid the fog created would surely give away his position.

He listened with all the power of that sense he could muster. Yes, someone was coming, coming through the trees, approaching the far side of the meadow. Was it the man he hunted, or was it the hunter? Had the second achieved his goal of killing the first, and was he now just working his way out of the mountains? Either way, Raif intended to stop him.

He noticed his breath making a small cloud and pushed his lips into the cold snow in front of his face. He must stay hidden a few more minutes; wait until whoever it was had cleared the trees and would stand defenseless in the middle of the meadow!

The quiet air around him seemed to go even more still. Had the rider stopped on the other side of the meadow? Had he been there at all? The temptation to look was nearly overpowering, but Raif kept his face buried in the cold snow and waited.

"Giddup," the voice said in a low, distant tone.

He was coming out of the trees.

Raif's heart thundered in his chest. He pulled his face out of the snow and checked the safety on his rifle. He'd count to twenty, then he'd stand and take whoever it was crossing the meadow!

"One . . . two . . ." The numbers echoed off the inside of his head. He could hear the horse pushing, grunting with the effort as he floundered in the deeper snow of the meadow, heard the rider urge him forward.

" . . . eighteen . . . nineteen. . . ." Raif scrambled to his feet, his rifle at his shoulder, the log covering the lower half of his body. A dark-colored Morgan stood near the center of the meadow, but the rider was gone! Raif looked left and right, then caught a glimpse of a dark form disappearing into the trees. He was about to fire when he remembered the mountain of snow above him and cursed. Quickly lowering himself behind the cover of the log, he thought hard about what to do next. Then it hit him.

"You in the trees," he yelled. His voice carried over the snow like some foreign object, its dull tone hardly able to carry the distance. He raised it five decibels. "You in the trees. I'm not your enemy! I'm a deputy with the Sheriff's Department sent to keep you from gettin' killed! Your enemy is behind you!" He paused, the next part would be guesswork. "His name is Duren, the son of the man you nearly killed back there at the cave. Give yourself up and let's get outta here."

No answer. No sound. Nothing.

Raif waited, his eyes just above the top of the tree, scanning the forest for a sign he might have been heard. It was a long minute before he saw some movement in the stand of trees. Then the man stood, his hands in the air. At that distance, Raif couldn't see him very well, but could tell he was poorly dressed for the cold and bad weather and wondered how he'd ever survived the night. As he drew closer, it was evident that his parka was nothing more than a pullover, heavy windbreaker with the hood pulled tight around the bearded face by its pull strings. He was wearing only a pair of regular leather work gloves, and his pants were light-weight, army fatigues. Raif could see he was shaking and figured the cold played as much of role in his decision to surrender as the fear of his enemy.

Raif stepped from behind the log and began snowshoeing his away across the meadow toward his captive. He was nearly to the Morgan when he noticed movement to his right and turned quickly enough to see the hunter raise his rifle and aim. The hunted man dove for the ground a second before the report of the rifle shot reverberated around the canyon walls and the bullet missed its target. Raif leveled his rifle at the hunter.

"Move and you're a dead man!" he yelled.

The hunter, his white winter parka hood laying on his back and shoulders, stood motionless. It was young Duren, and it was apparent from his posture that he was trying to make a decision.

"I've killed porcupine at this distance," Raif called out. "One shot right between the eyes. Compared to him, you make a big target."

Duren hesitated, then dove to his left, and Raif fired. The bullet hit with enough force to change Duren's trajectory, but Raif never found out if the shot killed him.

The report of the second shot on top of the first set the snow above them into motion. Turning, Raif attempted to run, but the snowshoes were cumbersome and his effort was futile. Cascading down the mountain like a monstrous wave, the snow was suddenly upon him.

Helpless to prevent it, Raif was picked up like a twig and swept along. He felt himself tossed, twisted, and pummeled by the sea of snow as it rolled along, carrying trees and even rocks along in its flow toward the bottom of the ravine. Finally, after what seemed minutes but was probably only seconds, the movement stopped and darkness engulfed him.

* * *

Raif had never liked tight places, so when he awoke to find himself completely covered in snow, he totally panicked. Had he been able, he would have screamed in terror, and it was all he could do to keep from throwing up and drowning in his own bile. But, he was still alive, and once he realized that, he gained a little control. He sensed he was lying on his back with his right arm pinned in front of his face. That had created a small pocket of air, making it possible for him to breathe. He could also see some light above him.

He tried to move but couldn't, then tried again. It was as though an obscene weight lay on his torso and legs and feet, pinning him down and making it difficult even to breathe. His left hand and arm were extended away from his body, and after struggling for a time, he found he was able to move that hand slightly. By wiggling it, he was eventually able to create a little space, which he worked to enlarge. It took all his strength, but he was finally able to break through a six-inch crust of snow and get his left arm free. Frantically, he clawed at the snow covering his face, clearing it away. When he was finally able to see and breathe freely, the relief was so great he thought he might weep.

With his two hands free, he worked to dig himself out. He had always assumed the snow in an avalanche would be light and fluffy, but he found it heavy and dense, and it took great effort to dig through the relatively shallow layer under which his body was trapped.

His head and chest finally free, Raif sat up and threw his head back, sucking in the deep, cold, clean air, then used his hands to dig out the snow that had forced its way into his parka hood and made the sides of his face and neck cold as cubed ice.

Still shaking from the ordeal, Raif looked around him. The avalanche had cleared a path a hundred yards wide through the trees and was piled up below him like a huge mound of plowed snow. Trees and other debris stuck out of it at absurd angles, bearing witness of the tremendous power behind one of Mother Nature's most deadly forces.

Twenty yards to his left and below him, Raif saw a horse's foreleg and hoof sticking out of the snow—the Morgan hadn't been as lucky. Though saddened by the loss, he was also glad he had left his own animals a half mile up the trail.

Raif spent the next ten minutes digging himself free and finally climbed out of what could have been his grave. As he lay on the snow catching his breath, he wondered what had happened to Duren and the man they'd both been hunting. Could either have survived as he had, or were both buried under ten feet of snow?

Getting to his feet, he realized he had lost his gun. Shading his eyes against the bright sun he scanned the surface of the field of snow and rubble, knowing there was no chance of recovering the weapon.

Turning, he climbed uphill toward the trail. The snow underfoot was loose and deep, and he remembered he'd had the Alumalites on. He looked down at his feet to see marks on his boots where they'd been ripped free. He was lucky he hadn't lost a foot or at least broken it good at the ankle.

Wading through the deep snow, it took him half an hour and two rest periods to get back to the where the trail had been cut in half by the avalanche. Turning south he reached the spot where he'd been lying behind the log. It looked untouched. If he'd stayed put . . .

But he hadn't.

He walked back to his horses and was elated to find them resting. As he stroked the buckskin's neck, there was a movement next to a tree a half dozen yards away. Startled, Raif jumped back. The man he'd been hunting stood leaning heavily against the trunk, an arm dangling loosely at his side, his head hanging down in exhaustion. Raif moved quickly to his side and eased him to the snow. As he pulled the man's hood off, then his mask, Raif stared in disbelief at the man's face. He blinked and cleared his eyes, not certain that he wasn't dreaming.

The eyes opened into thin slits and a weak smile creased the older, worn-out face. "Raif. Nice to see you again," the man murmured.

Raif felt a wave of revulsion. The years of frustration bordering on hatred welled up inside him like acid, but his mouth was so dry he couldn't speak, his brain so muddled he didn't know what to say. He swallowed hard, his fists clenched into tight knots as he stood staring at the man slumped in front of him.

"You!" he said angrily. "What the devil are you doing here!"

The mouth twitched into another tired smile, but there was no response as the eyes closed against the pain and he passed out.

Raif eased himself onto a snow-covered log and sat staring at the unconscious man's face. It was a face Raif had sworn countless times that he would beat into a bloody pulp if he ever saw it again. It was the face of the man who had given his parents such pain—the face they had all assumed dead! It was the face of his brother.

Husayn Qanun had come home to the mountains.

20

Raif sat in the waiting area of St. John's Hospital emergency room. They had flown Hussa directly here from the mountains, and he had gone immediately into surgery. That was less than an hour ago. Though Hussa had regained consciousness, he had not spoken. Neither had Raif, afraid he would lose his cool and strangle his prisoner before he found out what Hussa might know.

Sharps sat nearby, his new coat unzipped, a wool stocking cap in his hand. He had nothing to say, and both he and Raif sat deep in thought about the appearance of this new apparition in their case.

While they waited, roadblocks had been set up, searches conducted in out-of-the-way places, and every lawman in the area put on alert. All their efforts were aimed at finding the still missing weapons and those who held them. So far, no luck.

Raif forced himself to his feet as his parents appeared at the door of the emergency room. He hadn't told them anything, only that he was here, and that they should come quickly.

Ever since finding Hussa in the mountains, he had been trying to decide how to inform his parents their lost son was not dead. After years of grieving, his mother was only now getting over Hussa's supposed death, and to bring him back to life, then lose him again . . . this time to prison . . . well,

Raif didn't know if she could handle it. His father would be equally shocked. He'd been blaming himself and hating Khomeini for so many years, it was ingrained. Now Hussa was miraculously back, and Raif didn't have answers yet as to why or how. Would Hussa be able or willing to clear the air? Would he finally tell them what had been going on for the last dozen years?

The look of fear on his parents' faces changed to relief as Raif met them in the hallway. His mother latched on to him with a full embrace, then looked up into his face. "Are you okay?" she asked.

He nodded, but his face was a dead giveaway there was something more.

"Is it Shad?" his father asked. "Sam?"

Raif shook his head even as he pulled them toward a couch and two chairs.

His voice quavering, he said, "Sit down."

"Raif, you're scaring me," his mother said. "What is wrong?"

Raif somehow managed to croak out his unbelievable story. His mother turned pale, leaning back against the chair. His father searched Raif's eyes for some sign of an awful joke, even though he knew Raif wouldn't pull something that cruel. Then he, too, sagged back in his chair.

"What is he doing . . . here . . . in Jackson?" Ray asked.

Raif told him what he could. "Beyond that I don't know, Dad. All we know is that he was on the run, trying to escape. Apparently he knew too much and these people felt they had to catch him, to shut him up. Maybe when he gets out of surgery, wakes up—"

"Then he wasn't involved in what they were doing, in this killing and the attempt on your life?" Sarai said, hopefully.

"I didn't say that, Mom." Raif realized he sounded impatient, and he took a deep breath. The anger had to be kept under control. His parents, their feelings, must come first.

"Where is he?" Sarai asked in a weak voice.

"In surgery. A bullet through an arm, some broken bones, and he's lost a lot of blood."

"Then he'll be all right." His mother's expression didn't change. Raif had seen that same look on her face the times they had been told Hussa was probably just lost in the mass of humanity of Iran, then that he'd surely turn up in the army, then. . . .

It had gone on and on until no hope was left, and here it was again, the hope that led to dead-ends and depression when the dream didn't come true. Hussa might survive, but chances were he'd go to jail, or worse. His mother could hope it would all go away all she wanted, believe she'd get her family back again, all nestled safely around her, but it wouldn't happen. Ever.

Ray put his arm around Sarai and pulled her close as Raif worked on sorting out his feelings. Leaning back in his chair he ran a hand through his short hair. "I keep thinking it's a dream and I'll wake up."

It had been a dream. It had come to him in the same wilderness days ago. Hussa had been there, deathly pale, stuck on a precipice that hung over a deep cavern. Then he had fallen even as Raif had tried to reach for and save him. Though the end had been more deadly, the feelings horrible, the dream didn't hold a candle to reality.

The look on his mother's face suddenly changed, her jaw hardening and her eyes filling with determination. Standing up, she declared, "I have to see him."

"You can't, Sarai," Ray protested, standing in her way. She tried to shove him aside.

"I must! I must ask him why!" Abruptly, her hard determination melted away, and, convulsed by great sobs, she laid her face against her husband's coat and surrendered to her tears.

Ray wrapped his arms around her and held her tightly,

stroking her back in an effort to wipe away years of emotional upheaval.

"How could he do this!" she wailed. "How could he! Why? Why hasn't he contacted us? Does he hate us that much?" A hand beating against her husband's chest, she sobbed so that Raif could no longer stand it, and he stood up and moved away from his parents.

Nothing caused him greater anguish than seeing their pain. He had watched as they fought with Hussa, pled with him, tried to get him to see that he was wrong to want to go to Iran, to join that miserable war led by fanatics! But he wouldn't listen! Their mother had cried for days after Hussa ran away, and it had been even worse when they were told that he had probably been killed. Sarai Qanun was just getting off that emotional roller coaster, and now this! A feeling of rage flooded over Raif, so dangerously close to the surface he felt he might explode.

More deep breathing. He had to help her, help both of them.

He put a hand on her shoulder. "Mom, I'll talk to Doc Nethercott. If he thinks it would be a good thing, I'll get you into the operating room."

Sarai looked up at her son while wiping at her tears. "I must see him, Raifim. I must know . . . see for myself. . . ."

"I know. I'll do what I can." He forced a smile.

Turning, he walked to the nurses' station where he quickly told the head nurse what he wanted. She shook her head adamantly before he even finished. "It can't be done! Surgery—"

Raif interrupted her. "I want you to go in there and ask!" he said firmly. "Tell Doctor Nethercott we'll abide by his decision, but ask, or I'll do it myself!"

She stared angrily at Raif, then pushed through some swinging doors and disappeared.

Five minutes later she returned.

"He agrees," she said with a stiffness that bordered on

being rude, but Raif had no time for an injured ego and let it go. "Tell them to come this way. They will have to change clothes and wash up."

Raif motioned to his parents, who immediately followed the nurse to begin the process. Fifteen minutes later the nurse returned.

"How long?" Raif asked.

"I'm sorry, I really don't know." She said it coldly, still nursing her wounded pride. Sensing his displeasure, she quickly disappeared on another errand—a good move for both of them.

Raif returned to the waiting area where Sharps joined him.

"I just talked to our Salt Lake office," Sharps said. "They found Colonel Blakely at the Marriott Hotel making plans for an extended European family vacation. They've taken him into custody."

"What's he tellin' 'em?" Raif asked, almost without interest, his mind still embroiled in his own problems. He tried to shake it off.

"Not much, but they've completed an inventory at the fort—two Javelin anti-tank missiles and four Stinger air-to-ground missles turned up missing, along with a handful of assault weapons. That fifty-caliber machine gun we found in Hawkes's house was one of them. So was the Dragunov and half the other guns. As near as they can tell, Blakely has been giving Hawkes and his people access for about eight months. Small stuff at first, then they trapped him with the threat of blackmail and the promise of big bucks. That's when they went after the missiles."

He brushed some melted snowflakes off his new parka. "Blakely says he thought Roberts had removed the firing mechanisms. The guy must think we're stupid."

Raif noticed Sharps looked extra tired. "What else?"

"One small nuclear warhead used on the Stinger may be missing as well. Blakely won't say a word about that."

"What do you mean 'may' be missing? You'd think they'd be sure about a thing like that, wouldn't you?"

Sharps shrugged. "What can you expect from an organization that gets charged five hundred dollars for a toilet seat and doesn't notice it?" he glanced at his notes. "Some sort of paperwork screw up. A company assigned to its development for future use might actually have it. They're checking on it."

Raif sighed. "Let's hope it doesn't take them as long as it did to find out they were being overcharged for those toilet seats." Then he added, "It's apparent Hawkes was running Blakely. Question still remains, who was running Hawkes?"

Sharps flipped to a page in his small pocket notebook. "Putting what we have with what you've given us, it's Daniel Beni, the all-American boy living the all-American dream in the Bay Area. He started AMI just ten years ago and built it into a powerhouse—a multi-million-dollar-a-year enterprise. By the way, the Bev Doolittle purchased by the man who fell from the chopper was sent to a building owned by Beni—some kind of loan company. My people in San Francisco say the picture was delivered and was awaiting the dead man's arrival. Needless to say it's been impounded as evidence. We also searched the place. They have one secretary and don't do many loans, but nothing else was found, either."

"A front," Raif said. He looked up as a doctor came from the operating room hallway. Wrong one.

Sharps continued, "Yeah." He took a deep breath. "I've been working on this case for a year, Qanun, and didn't even know these guys existed. Disgusting ain't it?"

Raif didn't answer.

"I thought the enemy was a guy by the name of Andrews, a Middle East transplant who had all the markings of terrorist backing. Spent all my time chasing shadows."

"There might be more than one," Raif said.

"Yeah, maybe." Sharps pulled himself out of a slouch and shook off the desire to beat himself over missing Beni. "Deputy Petersen called Delta Airlines. They have record of Beni flying into Jackson a dozen times over the past few months. The last time was on a round-trip ticket about ten days ago. He hasn't used the return fare." He flipped to another page in his notebook. "Rented a Bronco from Hertz. It hasn't been returned, but they don't mind. He secured it with a Visa that has a thirty thousand dollar limit. Kristoff pulled some fingerprints off the paperwork, and they match those in the majority in Hawkes's basement. You've made my case. Beni's in this up to his neck."

"Does he have a family, a background?"

"A wife and daughter. The maid says they're on vacation in Paris, France. We have the gendarmes looking for them, but my guess is that Beni sent them into hiding."

"Are they part of the hoax or just innocents he picked up along the way?"

"We can't find any proof of the woman's existence more than ten years old. No families, that sort of thing. Same for Beni. The kid is only seven and probably an innocent."

"Do the *Nizari* use women?"

"Some of their best operatives."

Raif stood and stepped toward the door of the operating room, checking his watch. They should be out of surgery by now.

Sharps flipped to another page of his notebook. "There was a positive match on the fingerprints on the beer cans you found where Billy Two Shoes was killed."

"Duren?"

"Yeah. By the way, he died. The bullet screwed up too many internal organs."

"It's murder then," Raif said matter-of-factly.

"Maybe."

Raif turned to look at him. "Hussa shot the man, he died. Where's the maybe?"

"You know as well as I do, we haven't got a shred of evidence your brother pulled the trigger. Second, if he did, he can make a nice case for self-defense." He pulled an envelope from his pocket. "But even if he did kill him, this will keep him outa prison."

Raif took the envelope. It was standard white, the kind you could buy in K-Mart. The letter inside was a fax copy, but he could still see the seal of the President of the United States in the bottom right-hand corner. To the left of the seal was the signature of the President himself, and below that there were several lines for more signatures—two for witnesses, one for a notary, and one for Husayn Qanun.

"The original will arrive by special courier sometime tonight or tomorrow morning," Sharps said.

Raif read it carefully.

"You don't see many of these floating around," he said, when he'd finished.

"Presidential pardons don't get printed by the gross."

"When was this decided?"

"The moment we knew we had someone who had seen the inside of the *Nizari*, more to the point, the inside of this operation."

"Still pretty strong antidote. Clemency, an offer of a lighter sentence, there are a dozen other options."

Sharps reached for his briefcase and removed a folder. "Not in your brother's case." He removed a single sheet of paper and handed it to Raif, who took it and unfolded it only to find another fax copy of information. On this one there was a barely distinguishable picture of Hussa in the upper right hand corner. The rest was written in Hebrew. "What's this?"

"An Israeli warrant for your brother's arrest. Interpol sent it to us. Your brother is wanted on five counts of murder, the result of terrorist bombings they figure he planned and carried out. His fingerprints were found on the wheel of one escape vehicle, and he left a phony passport in a safe

house in Tel Aviv, Israel, on another occasion when terrorists set off bombs in Jerusalem. The Israelis want his hide
nearly as bad as the President wants his information. If the
President doesn't get what he wants, the Israelis probably
will. Do you understand why a presidential pardon is
necessary?"

He handed Raif the rest of the folder. As Raif took it he
felt faint. He had figured his brother was a soldier in Iran,
at least for awhile, and had probably killed people, but this
. . . a terrorist who killed the innocent with bombs and missiles! He had not expected this! He sat down, afraid he
might topple.

After regaining his composure, he opened the folder
and thumbed through the sheets. Pictures of his atrocities,
of what Hussa Qanun had done to innocent men and
women, with names jotted on the back of them. Raif felt
suddenly sick to his stomach and closed the folder.

"He doesn't deserve a pardon. He deserves to die," he
said softly.

"And if keeping him alive prevents others from ending
up like that? Does he deserve it then?" Sharps asked.

Raif couldn't answer. His mind was filled with blackness, and his heart ached.

"He may lie, lead you the wrong way," Raif said.

"Then God help us because at this point I haven't a
clue which way to turn," Sharps said. "And another thing,
if we turn him over to the Israelis, his real identity will be
known. Your parents will have to go through the misery of
having their lives dissected by the press. Worse, the *Nizari*
always, always, take their revenge on the family. They'll
come after you, Raif. They'll come after your parents." He
leaned forward. "You and I have one job, and one job only,
to convince Husayn to cooperate with us. If we fail, a lot of
people will get hurt."

Raif knew Sharps was piling it on, making sure he had
an ally. He didn't need to worry.

"You're a hard case, Sharps."

The FBI agent only shrugged. "You with me or not?"

"Yeah, but if he doesn't cooperate, what then?"

Sharps grinned. "You can take him out behind the barn and beat some sense into his thick skull. After that, we'll see." He cleared his throat. "Uh, about Moen . . ."

"Your partner? What about him?"

"He's in the dark on most of this, I'd just as soon keep him that way."

"You'll get no argument from me."

Sharps seemed relieved, and Raif wondered if there weren't more to the problem between Sharps and Moen than met the eye.

"Who knows who the prisoner is on the operating table?" Sharps asked.

"The doc, us, that's about it. We're keeping it tight. Security is heavy. He's registered under a different name. We've got two armed officers at every door into the building."

"Good, let's keep it that way," Sharps said.

Raif knew that if Hussa's friends-turned-enemies wanted him badly, they wouldn't likely concern themselves with guards at the doors, nor would they mind hurting a lot of innocent people, but there was no reason for them to come. Few knew what had happened out in the wilderness, least of all the enemy.

They went into the coffee shop and each picked what they wanted. Raif didn't have much appetite and selected milk and a bear claw. They were headed back to the waiting area when they saw Doc Nethercott come through a set of swinging doors and motion to them. He gave them a quick rundown on Hussa's condition.

"When will he be conscious, Doc, able to talk?" Raif asked.

Nethercott was shocked by the abruptness of the question. "Well, the anaesthetic will wear off in an hour or so, but he is weak from loss of blood . . . rest is needed, Raif. I don't think—"

"I want someone with him every minute," Sharps said. "We'll have guards at the door, and at the reception desk. Tell your staff no one is to know who he is! Do you understand?"

Nethercott was nodding, but he had a confused look on his face. "What is this all about, Agent Sharps?"

Sharps looked at Raif. "You tell him, I gotta make a call." He headed for the phone.

Raif told the doc what he could. "His enemies may think he's dead. If we keep it that way, they won't try again, but if they find out he's alive, no telling what they might do. That could put everyone around him in extreme danger."

"I understand." Nethercott had a deep wrinkle to his brow. "Your parents will be out in a minute."

"Has he said anything?"

"No, but you should know there are two sets of rope burns on his arms and ankles and that there are signs of both recent and past torture. The old ones date to many years ago, and it must have been quite horrible for him."

"And the more recent?" Raif asked.

"All I can say is that he is a lucky man to have escaped these men. They must be highly sadistic." As Doctor Nethercott walked away, Raif thought it was somehow appropriate that a sadist be punished by his own kind.

And he hated himself for it.

21

After another hour of waiting, Raif decided he'd call Terri and Bob Stevens. He needed to say goodbye to Bob and just plain needed to hear Terri's voice. Lifting the receiver he remembered he didn't have her number. He called an operator only to discover the number was unlisted. With disappointment gnawing at his gut he hung up and turned to face Terri standing a dozen feet away. To Raif her smile seemed to be mingled with a good deal of relief.

He nodded at the phone. "I just tried calling you."

"Umm. I'll bet you say that to all the girls." She came closer, then embraced him. Raif gathered her close. Some of the pain seemed to melt away with her touch, and he held on as long as he could without embarrassing her in front of hospital personnel who were watching them.

"I called your house," she said. "Then your parents. I was told they were here." She looked up at him, biting her lip. "I was afraid . . ." She smiled, "I'm glad to know it wasn't you they came to see. What's going on?"

They sat down, and still holding Terri's hands, Raif told her about his trip to the mountains and finding Hussa.

She sat back in the chair as she tried to assimilate it. "I guess there is a resurrection."

"Even for those from hell?"

She hesitated, trying to assess the bitterness she felt emanating from him. "Yes, even for them."

"This is no resurrection."

She decided to leave it alone. "How is he?" She asked.

"Still under sedation from the surgery, but his vital signs are good, no real damage. Sad, isn't it? The wicked never seem to get beat up like the righteous."

"Maybe the bruises are just in places you can't see."

Time to change subjects, Raif thought. "Where's your father?"

She looked at her hands. "Headed for the airport. He needed to get there early and file a flight plan for our trip home."

"You're going? I thought . . . what about the new business?"

"We just found out this afternoon that the bank in Minneapolis wants a face-to-face meeting before they loan us the start-up money. If I'd known you were going to try to get yourself killed again, I would have scheduled our meeting for a later date," she joked.

"Sorry. I take it you're not on commercial."

"The flights were sold out. Dad booked a Lear."

"How long before you come back?"

"A few days. Why? Did you have something in mind?"

A smile creased his lips. "The mucking out has to be done again, and you are the only one I know who will work for ham and eggs."

"You just haven't got the rest of my bill, that's all."

He looked at the clock on the wall. "What time does the flight leave?"

"In about an hour."

Raif stood. "Come on. You can still make it," he said, taking her hand and heading toward the door.

"That was a quick change in direction."

"I want that subsidiary in Jackson," he grinned. "It will be good for the economy." She slugged him lightly on the shoulder.

"Let me rephrase. I want the boss in Jackson, and I figure

getting that subsidiary here is the best chance of having that happen. Is that better?"

She returned the smile, her ears turning a light red. "Unpolished but serviceable."

They were about to leave the building when one of the deputies called to Raif. He hurried toward them.

"Doc Nethercott says the patient is awake," he said, his eyes apologizing for his intrusion.

Raif nodded. "Tell him I'm on my way, and find Agent Sharps, let him know." The deputy went back the way he had come and Raif escorted Terri through the door, across the covered drive, and into the lot where her car was parked. He opened her door but before she got into the vehicle, she turned to him and they held one another.

After a moment, she pulled away. "Promise me, no more close calls," Terri said, her eyes looking up into his. "No gunplay, no avalanches, no picking on choppers loaded to the gills with people who hurt people."

He laughed lightly. "I'll lock myself in the house."

Suddenly she moved her face close to his and their lips met in a gentle kiss that quickly became more urgent. Raif finally forced himself to pull away so that Terri wouldn't keep her father waiting. After closing the door, she rolled down the window. Her face was flushed as she handed Raif a cellular phone. "Let me know how he's doing. I'll be on the ground for another hour."

He took the phone. "Won't you need this?"

"I have another and Dad has two. Hit the button on the lower left and it will give you the numbers to call. My phone is listed as 'Ms. Legal.'"

"Charming." He reached through the window and touched her face lightly with his finger tips. "I hope you have a pilot who knows what he's doing."

"I do." She grinned as she backed out of her parking spot and drove away.

Raif watched the Expedition turn into the street. When

it had disappeared he went back inside. Time to talk to his
long-lost brother.

* * *

The sheriff was standing next to Hussa's bed when Raif
entered the room. Sharps was in the room also, standing at
the foot of the bed. Hussa's eyes were open, but only partially so. He looked weak and was pale from loss of blood.
If he was listening to the sheriff, it was without any interest,
and he wasn't answering any of the questions the sheriff was
asking.

The sheriff was obviously frustrated. He took a deep
breath as he glanced at his watch. "Read him his rights and
arrest him, Raif. I want guards on this place around the
clock, and he's to be booked as soon as the doc says he's
well enough to put his feet on the floor." He went to the
door.

"What's the charge?" Raif asked.

"Murder, attempted murder, conspiracy to overthrow
the government of the United States. Take your pick. I'm
headed up to the cave with Kristoff. I'll let you know what
other charges we can throw at him when I get back." He
looked at Hussa. "You've changed, kid. Nasty-tempered as
you were twelve years ago, it was nothin' compared to what
you've become." The door closed behind him.

Raif glanced at Sharps. It was apparent he hadn't shown
the sheriff the letter of pardon. Then he concentrated on
Hussa.

"I guess you still haven't read *How to Win Friends and
Influence People*," Raif said, his own face as devoid of emotion as Hussa's as he read his brother his rights and put him
under formal arrest.

In the few moments it took to do that, Raif came to the
realization he was looking into the face of a man who might
look like an older Hussa on the outside, but who on the

inside had become someone else; someone changed and very dangerous. What had happened to the boy who'd left home so many years earlier was anybody's guess, but he no longer lived in the shell Raif saw before him. Time to find out who the new resident devil was.

"You wanna tell us who you are?" Raif asked.

The cold eyes remained empty, but the lips formed a tired smile. "Mustafa," the man in the bed replied.

"Well, Mustafa, you're in a heap of trouble. What went on up in the hills?"

"We were hunting. Things went bad."

"So you tried to kill Duren. What did he do, burn your eggs, make weak coffee, what?"

Sharps was intrigued by the interaction. The two had been raised brothers and yet they were feeling their way like blind men. Mustafa seemed the most baffled, and Sharps could tell he wasn't convinced Raif deserved the respect an equal would get. He'd learn, just as Sharps had learned, just as half a dozen others had learned in the last few days. Bad as Husayn Qanun might have become, his brother was up to handling him. Of that, Sharps was confident, and he'd enjoy seeing it happen.

"I beat him at cards. He didn't like it. We got in a fight. . . ." He shrugged.

"Cut the crap, Mustafa!" Raif said. "Let me fill you in on what we know about you and your little entourage of Iranian radicals." He proceeded to tell him about the condo, Daniel Beni, and Hawkes, then the information they had found in the computer. Sharps could see Mustafa was impressed.

"You were sent here to train American misfits. Targets were designated, missiles stolen to use on 'em. Then some sort of disagreement raised it's ugly head, probably between you and Beni. He told Duren to kill you, but you resisted and escaped." He took a breath. "If I'm missing anything just speak up."

Mustafa smiled. "No, you're doing pretty well. Please, go on."

"Duren junior took offense to your shooting his pa, so he went after you, and if Mother Nature hadn't intervened, Duren would probably have put a bullet between your shoulder blades, and we wouldn't be having this conversation." Raif looked at Sharps. "Regrettable, isn't it? Now a trial and all that goes with it will cost the county thousands. Probably cause an international incident when we prove Iran sent a butcher here to slaughter Americans just like in Israel. You want a lawyer?"

Mustafa's face lost the slight sign of humor it had gained. "I'll give it some thought."

Raif noticed there was no accent. All the time he'd been away, all the time he'd been an Iranian, Hussa hadn't picked up an accent. He expected he'd at least have an accent. "The targets? What are they?"

No answer.

"How many men did you train?"

No answer.

"Beni picked up the missiles yesterday. Where are they?" It was a bit of guess, but not much.

No answer.

"They can't have left the Valley. They're trapped and we'll get them. It's just a matter of time."

"You'll regret cornering them," was the answer. "The man you call Beni is worse than anything you can imagine, even of me."

Raif lost patience but grabbed the side of the bed instead of Hussa's throat. "Oh, I don't know, I've managed to conjure up some pretty nasty things about you over the last twelve years. Your boss would have to be the devil himself to be worse than you, you traitorous piece of humanity!"

For the first time Sharps could see Mustafa was affected by Raif's talk. It rattled him.

"You . . . you don't understand . . ." He bit his tongue,

the old self taking over. "My attorney is in New York." He looked at Sharps and gave him a name. "I have nothing else to say."

Raif's jaw turned to granite. "Sharps, get outta here." His teeth were clenched, and Sharps figured he wouldn't argue. Attorneys took time. He put his notepad away and left the room.

"There are two people waiting to see you. They think you're their son. Any idea what you're going to tell them?"

"Nothing." He looked straight into Raif's eyes. "Keep them out of here, Raif. I can't see them, not now. Not until—"

"Until what?"

"Until this is finished."

"Finished! Does that mean until you blow up one of your targets, kill dozens, even hundreds of Americans?" Raif was practically shouting. "Is that what 'finished' means?"

Mustafa turned his head away. "Just keep them away from me, Raifim. I can't answer their questions, not now, maybe never. My family—"

"Family! We—"

"Not you, you fool! MY family! They are at risk! They'll be killed unless . . ."

Raif felt weak in the knees. He had never considered . . . never thought . . . He was stunned. He had to sit down.

"Unless? Unless you let them complete their murder?" Raif asked.

There was a long silence.

"Who knows I survived the mountains?" Mustafa asked.

"A few in the Sheriff's Office. Jess Farrell, Shad, and me. Mom and Dad and Terri Stevens."

"A man named Grant, does he know?"

"No. We found out he was a traitor. He's in the lockup."

"His attorney?"

"Not to my knowledge."

"Good. That gives me some time."

"Time for what?"

"Believe it or not, I want Beni stopped as badly as you do, and I'll deliver him to you on one condition."

"I don't believe it, but what's your condition?"

"In four days, Beni will hit his first target. If you want to stop him, you must ensure the safety of my family."

Raif didn't respond for a moment because he didn't know what to say. Then he said, "Getting someone into Iran would be a major feat, getting them out, especially when the government might not like it, seems monumental. But maybe you have an idea how we can pull off the impossible."

"In the first place, they're not in Iran, they're in Istanbul."

"Turkey?"

Hussa nodded. "I took precautions. A trusted friend, and brother to my wife, saw to their escape from Iran and is watching out for them."

"The FBI can—"

Hussa shook his head adamantly. "The FBI isn't to know anything!"

"Then we're done talking," Raif said just as firmly.

"The *Nizari* are no small time militia group with men like Hawkes running them. They don't lack funding, and they have eyes and ears in Interpol, the CIA, and the FBI, not to mention the Israeli *Mossad*. My guess is they already know I didn't die in that avalanche and have gone to my home only to find my family already one step ahead of them. It will take them two, maybe three days to find out where they are, then I will not be able to help you because to do so will risk the lives of Krisha and the children. You must outrun them, brother, and you cannot use the FBI because to do so will only cause both of us great loss."

"I don't believe you."

"Then we are defeated before we begin, and Beni wins."

Hussa pushed himself up in the bed. From the look on his face the pain the movement caused was extensive, and this was a man apparently not unfamiliar with pain.

"Before you say no, count the costs, Raifim. Beni has in mind to kill thousands and bring terrorism to your country beyond anything you think possible. You can stop him."

"No. You can do the stopping."

"But I won't—not until my family is safe."

"How do I know you'll keep your word?"

"My life depends on it as much as yours. Do you think Beni is going to let me live? He will come here, soon. The sheriff will need to move me to a safer place before another hour passes. Again, believe me when I tell you I want Beni and his *Nizari* friends dead or imprisoned just as much as you do, for this and other reasons, but I have no desire to be alive if my family is dead."

"And you would let innocent people die if I fail?"

"Yes and no. If you fail because you refuse or play silly games with me, yes, I will let them die. If you fail because they stop you, or because you die trying to save my family, I will find Beni and kill him myself." He laid his head back, tired. "I do not expect you to fail, Raifim. I know your skills. You have made Beni most unhappy by the use of them. That is why I trust you, and you alone, with my most precious possessions."

"Why not just have your friends bring them here?"

"Because they are wanted by your country as much as I am and because the real leader of the *Nizari* has as many friends in Turkey as he does here and would turn them over to the *Nizari* if they tried. There are a dozen reasons," he said, frustrated. "Enough questions. Will you do it or not?"

Raif paced, thinking. "I can't do it without FBI help."

"No, you—"

Raif lifted a hand. "Only Sharps then. He can be trusted."

Hussa thought a moment, his eyes searching those of

his younger brother. "You are willing to stake your life on it? That is what you will be doing, Raifim, I promise you."

"I have no choice. Passports, your safety, and the safety of Mom and Dad. Emergencies, contingencies, all that crap. I need his savvy."

Hussa couldn't hide the look of admiration. "You are beginning to think like them."

Raif stopped pacing. "Why do you say that?"

"You know they will try to get to your parents."

Raif found it interesting that Hussa did not claim kinship to the man and woman who had given him life. Had he rejected his American life so completely that he refused to admit even their paternity? Raif searched Hussa's eyes. Nothing had really changed. This man was someone else. Hussa had died, and this distorted man had taken up residence in his physical form. Raif had almost been taken in by the look. He was glad to be reminded.

"All right. You've got a deal, but when this is over, when Beni is dead or behind thick layers of concrete and steel and your family is safe, you go to jail, you stand trial, and you hang if that's the verdict." He said it out of spite, knowing the President's pardon meant Hussa would never see the inside of a jail.

Mustafa smiled but didn't reply.

Raif stepped forward, the cold knot of anger churning in his stomach. "You're thinking it'll never happen, that somehow I'll either let you walk away or you'll escape. Let's get something straight, Mustafa, or whatever your name is. I don't consider you kin, not anymore, and I'll shoot you down like the animal you are if you don't keep your end of this bargain, and I'll have Sharps do it if you try to run. Got it?"

The smile left Mustafa's face. "Well said, Deputy, but saying is only half the battle." The cold, empty blackness of his eyes gave Raif the intended chill. He must never let his brother's face deceive him again. It might get him killed.

He turned and went to the door, calling for Sharps to come in. When the door was shut again, he filled the FBI agent in on what was about to happen.

Sharps responded by grabbing Raif by the coat sleeve and dragging him from the room. Making sure no one was within earshot, he put his face an inch from Raif's before asking him if he had taken loss of his senses. Raif told him he didn't think so, then they argued until Raif pointed out what Hussa had said about traitors inside the Agency. That brought Sharps up short, and he chewed on his cigar until he bit it in half. He spat the remains on the ashtray near the elevator and then began to pace. Each time he came to Raif, he stopped, gave him a hard look, then kept pacing, mumbling something Raif thought it was just as well he couldn't hear.

Finally Sharps stopped in front of him, a deep scowl on his face. Removing a fresh cigar from his pocket he proceeded to light it. Raif was thankful he blew the smoke to one side instead of in his face and took it as a good sign.

"I got one Presidential pardon here, and it don't have my name or yours on it. Does that mean anything to you?"

"Yeah, if things go bad we'll need to get a couple of good forgeries."

Sharps smiled. "My exact sentiments. We'll move your brother within the hour. Moen's out. Who can you trust?"

Raif told him then pulled Terri's cell phone from his pocket and dialed the number of Ms. Legal in the internal directory. He had a plane to catch.

CHAPTER

22

The Lear was basic. No fancy living-dining area, no bedroom with full master bath. The leather seats were comfortable with plenty of leg space, the fridge was well-stocked with drinks suitable for both Mormons and Gentiles, and the dinner was as good as any he'd eaten, but other than that it wasn't much different than first class on Delta. Except the company.

He sat across from Terri, watching her down the last of her second dessert, and tried to decide what to do about his feelings for her.

Terri had flown the plane for the first couple hours, then her father had taken over until Minneapolis where they had refueled and prepared for the overseas journey to Istanbul. They had been in the air more than twelve hours, stopped in Paris for more fuel, then Frankfurt. Now they were on the last leg.

Raif was impressed to find that both Terri and her father had licenses for props and jets and both had extensive hours flying them.

It also reminded him how different their two worlds were. Not that he would ever expect her ever to live on his paycheck, just that being unable to provide fine things for her would grate on him, and he knew it.

She shoved her plate aside and glanced at her watch. "Another thirty minutes and we'll be in Istanbul."

All Raif had wanted was a ride to Minneapolis to catch a connecting flight. When he explained why, neither Terri nor Bob would hear of it, insisting they help shuttle Hussa's family back to Jackson. It would save a full day's time and be safer, Bob said. Having their own plane would be something Hussa's enemies wouldn't expect, Terri added. Besides, they could get in and out without waiting for flight schedules and long lines.

Raif had fought them until he saw that he couldn't win and figured he'd just as well make a deal while he could still control it. They were to fly to Istanbul, stay aboard the plane, wait for him to retrieve the family, then fly back. Nothing else. They had agreed, but when Raif saw a bunch of sealed containers being put aboard in Minneapolis and asked what they were, he got only evasive answers like "food for the natives" and "baksheesh." He figured he would have to nail Bob and Terri down to keep them from getting more fully involved.

"Is this going to cause the loss of your loan?" Raif asked.

"If it does, there are other banks, but it won't. Dad's got a positive cash flow, assets enough to buy a big chunk of Jackson, even as expensive as it has become, and he and the bank president play golf together."

"No pun intended, but the last will probably swing the vote."

"Most likely." She reached out and held his hand, concern in her eyes. "Are you sure about this?"

"I've always wanted to save the world, now's my chance," he said.

Terri pulled the hair on the back of his hand, forcing him to jerk it back.

"Ouch, knock it off, or I'll add dishes to your chores."

"Mucking out and dishes. I don't know which is worse." Their hands coupled again. "Dishes," Raif said sincerely.

After a moment's laughter Terri's face grew serious. "Do

you think Hussa was right about the FBI and all that? Will
his enemies know about you?"

"They don't need an insider. Not anymore." It was Bob,
who had just come out of the cockpit. He handed Raif a
fax. "It is a news story. Seems somebody leaked information
to the press."

Raif read the headlines out loud: "'Terrorist Caught in
the Tetons.' I hope the rest of the story is more accurate
than their selection of mountains." He read on.

"Do they give his real name?"

"Yes, and his past history." He thought about the impact
on his parents, the community. Though people kept their
noses out of each other's business as a whole, there were
gossips and judges in Jackson just like everywhere else. He
should be there.

Terri seemed to read his mind. "They'll be all right,
Raif. Anyone who knows your parents will keep their
heads."

He nodded. "It says the press wants answers but can't
find the sheriff, the agent over the case, and half of the
Sheriff's Department."

"Someone's trying to smoke them out! Get Hussa in the
open," Terri said.

"Hussa was right. The FBI has a serious leak, and
whether whoever it is knows it or not, he is aiding and
abetting the enemy."

"Anything about you, us, what we're doing?"

Raif shook his head in the negative. "Only that I'm not
available for comment." He smiled. "Shad and I are in the
hills bringing out stranded horses." It was obvious the
sheriff and Sharps had planned for this and left a good
cover story in place among the deputies and other personnel.

"The leak has to be someone in the FBI, maybe even
Sharps. If not him that weasel partner of his," Terri said.

Raif thought about it. It wasn't Sharps. He had bet his
life on it and still backed the wager. Moen was a candidate,

but so was the deputy director whom Sharps had been reporting to but was supposed to have been left out of the loop since Raif had made his deal with Sharps. Was he putting out this story because his feelings were hurt or was he the insider, ordered by the enemy to smoke Hussa out of hiding? They were in the dark, desperate to get at Husayn. Regardless, the word was out, the enemy informed, and they'd move. That probably meant he didn't have much time.

"How long will Sharps be able to resist the pressure?" Bob asked.

Raif didn't know and said so, but he figured it wouldn't be long before some senator looking to get in the news would start making demands and insisting Hussa be put in federal prison for safe keeping, that the sheriff and his office tell them what was happening, that the people have the right to know, and so on. The pressure would quickly mount. He folded the paper and shoved it in his back pants pocket. The plane was dipping, and they were losing altitude as the co-pilot prepared to land them in Turkey. For the first time, Raif was glad they had come by Lear. The extra day might make all the difference in the world.

He glanced at his watch and figured the time difference. It was 3:45 in the afternoon, Istanbul time. The commercial flight would still be seven hours out. There was something to be said for avoiding layovers and plane changes.

As he waited to disembark, he thought of Hussa's family, wondered what they were like. What would they think of him? How would they handle all this?

When the plane was on the ground, Raif stood and removed his revolver from his belt and handed it to Terri. He felt naked but knew he'd never get it through Customs without a lot of questions he didn't want to answer. Especially if Hussa was right and his enemies had associates in the Istanbul police force. As Bob lowered the door, Terri kissed Raif on the cheek. "You still have my cellular. It's hooked into this part of the world. Call if you need us. Oh, and take this, you might need a little extra." Terri put a small stack of money into Raif's hand. "Bahsheesh."

Raif hesitated, glancing up at her and then nodding.

"Thanks," he said. "You're a real wonder." Then he pulled away and left the plane.

He walked across the tarmac and entered the building where a couple of police sat in straight-backed chairs smoking cigarettes. They saw him and got to their feet to check his luggage.

He tossed his small carry-on on the counter. "This is all you wish to declare?" the one questioned.

"Business. I'll only be here a day or two."

The man nodded and motioned to the metal detector. "Go through, go through," he said, unzipping the carry-on and looking inside.

Raif stepped through the metal detector then responded to the other's request to show his passport and pay twenty dollars.

The first official looked him over, then asked, "What is your business?"

Raif hesitated, then figured Bob wouldn't mind if he hired himself to his company. "Printing. Books, magazines, just about anything."

"And the people you will meet with?"

Raif began to sweat and his mouth went dry. "Your government. We want to bid the printing of passports and other official materials."

The man nodded, his eyes still going through the passport like there was something there—which there was. Raif had been to Mexico once, a year before, to pick up a fugitive, but it wasn't enough to keep anyone's attention for more than a few seconds. This guy must be studying the watermarks in the paper itself! He finally stamped the passport and pointed to the door. "There is a shuttle car outside. It will take you to the main terminal. Present your passport and pay another twenty dollar visa tax and you will be let through."

Raif suspected there was only one visa tax but didn't argue. Not today. The first man handed him his carry-on and the two went back to their conversation and another cigarette.

He found the shuttle and took the ride, paying the driver five dollars for his efforts. Entering the terminal he found Customs, selected a line, and waited to go through. On the other side he paid the second twenty dollars, went through the luggage retrieval area, and walked outside. People lined the entrance around the door as if some important dignitary were arriving, but from the looks of the signs and families, it was just a normal reception on a normal day.

For this trip his attire did not include his usual western boots and Stetson. Instead he wore a beat-up pair of Nike's and no hat at all, but he felt out of place just the same. He seemed to garner more than his share of side glances, and paranoia set in, causing him to wonder which one of these hundreds would step forward and put a gun or a knife to his ribs.

He tried to concentrate, keep his focus, relax a little as he walked to the street and hailed a taxi. He felt better when he was inside. When asked where he wished to go, he used his smattering of Arabic to instruct the operator to just drive and he would give him an address shortly. As the cab pulled into traffic, Raif pulled out the cellular and dialed the number Hussa had given him. There had been no instructions accompanying the paper except that the people who would answer would tell him where to go and when.

The phone was picked up on the second ring. The young man who answered spoke in Arabic. He was apparently not interested in making small talk.

"Yes?"

"My name is Qanun. My brother Husayn sent—"

"We know no one by that name."

Click.

Raif looked at the phone. In a flash he realized he had misdialed and felt a wave of dread come over him. He would have to be more careful. He dialed again. When the phone was picked up he disregarded the usual amenities.

"Mustafa sends me from the United States. He is hurt. He has sent me to find his family and bring them to him." Then on a hunch, he added, "Beni has sent someone. Their lives depend on your cooperation."

There was a lengthy silence, then a voice said, "Go to the Obelisk Hotel. We will reserve a room for you."

Click.

Though it didn't give him much, Raif figured there wasn't any reason to try again. He leaned forward and gave the driver the name of the hotel. A nod told Raif he knew where it was, and he sat back to enjoy the scenery.

The highway to the old section of town bordered the Marmara Sea. From what Raif had heard, this piece of water was one of the most polluted in the world. Human, factory, and other wastes were dumped into it in such con-centrations that it was practically a dead sea. He could see areas of beach with groups of people scattered about. Though it was a fairly warm day, no one was even near the water, opting instead to play at kicking a soccer ball or just stroll about on the sand.

On the inland side of the road, large and small mosques dotted the skyline, and sections of the ancient city walls of the old Christian and Ottoman Turk periods could be seen in places.

The cab driver slowed, then darted across on-coming traffic onto a road that ran under a section of the old wall. Raif turned for the sixth time to see if they were being fol-lowed but saw nothing suspicious.

The street they entered was narrow and the buildings lining it old and worn. A few people were walking along a narrow walkway on one side and traffic vied for position coming and going. Horns blared constantly, and the cab driver kept up a profane battle between himself and other drivers as if they could actually hear him. They came into a wider and cleaner section of the city, and Raif saw ahead the minarets of a large mosque. He asked the cab driver which one it was. The answer was the Blue Mosque, one of the more famous in a city of hundreds.

They turned down a side street lined mostly with carpet shops and small hotels. The Obelisk was at the end, a light green building, well taken care of. He paid the driver with American money, for which he was thanked profusely, and took his bag into the hotel. At the door his paranoia insisted he glance over his shoulder and check the street. Several cars were parked next to the curb and traffic moved in both directions on the narrow road. One car pulled to the curb and a passenger rolled down a window to say something to a man sitting on the steps in front of one of the shops. They seemed to be friends, but Raif couldn't be sure. He went inside.

The lobby of the Obelisk Hotel was small and quaint and filled with sturdy antique furniture in good repair. He checked in and while the desk manager was doing the paperwork, Raif glanced at an advertisement about the hotel itself and noted that it was named after the Egyptian obelisk brought there when the city was Christian Constantinople. The obelisk was on display in a park near the Blue Mosque, not far from Hagia Sophia, one of the oldest and largest Christian churches of the Byzantine period. For just a moment, he allowed himself to fantasize about how pleasant it would be if he and Terri were just tourists, spending vacation time together in an exotic and foreign country.

He took the offered key and went upstairs to his room. His heart was beating at a runner's pace as he opened the door, unsure of what or who might be waiting. The room, however, was empty.

The bedroom had a double bed with clean sheets and blankets, along with a television sitting on a desk in the corner. The window was shuttered and the room semidark. He opened the shutters, then the window, slightly, for fresh air. His window looked out on the street. Down below, the car was gone, and he breathed easier.

Raif remembered reading somewhere that Istanbul was hot in the summer and cold in the winter. Though it occasionally snowed, the climate was moderate and snow seldom lasted very long. Being winter, he took it that this was not the peak tourist season. He estimated the temperature to be in the fifties. It was also humid, and he was glad he had brought a coat.

The phone rang.

"This is Raifim Qanun," he said in Arabic. There was no response. "I followed your instructions. Do you understand?"

A hesitant moment, then a voice responded. There was some sort of arguing in the background. "You must go to the Top Kapi Palace at seven o'clock tonight," the voice asserted in Arabic. "It is not open today, but someone will meet you near the front gate. Make sure you are not followed." He hung up.

Raif didn't like it. Too quick, the arguing. He swore under his breath, unsure of what to expect. But then, he had known there would be challenges. He'd be sure to stay public, give himself room to maneuver. Beyond that, he'd have to trust that Hussa's friends wanted to help him.

He undressed and took a shower, hot and steamy. When finished he dressed for cool weather and put on his jacket. Leaving the hotel, feeling anxious, he was relieved to find the car he had seen earlier hadn't reappeared, and no one seemed to be paying any particular attention to him. But he needed to be sure.

There was a small market on the corner, and he stepped inside and bought a couple of foreign candy bars and a container of yogurt with a plastic spoon attached. As he walked up the street, he ate the yogurt and fended off a succession of carpet salesmen who came out of the shops he passed, offering him an opportunity to drink strong Turkish coffee and discuss the wares in their shops. Raif used his Arabic to decline as kindly as he could. Seeing their work in the windows, however, he couldn't help but think how good some of the more modern designs would look and feel on the bare hardwood floors of his home.

Another time.

He noticed a man who seemed to be watching him from a chair near the door of a carpet shop on the corner. When their eyes met, the other man immediately looked away. Feeling conspicuous, Raif tried to play the part of a tourist, wandering casually along the street but at the same time watching closely, trying to spot anyone else who might be taking an unusual interest in him. His watch indicated he had an hour until seven o'clock.

Waiting for a cart being pulled by a burro to pass, he crossed the narrow street and entered a kind of courtyard lined with more shops, then climbed a flight of stone stairs. Reaching the top, he found himself in a dusty little park in front of the Blue Mosque. The man he thought might have been watching him was nowhere in sight.

Here park benches sat in rows, as if for an entertainment of some kind. To his right and further on, stood the old Christian church of Hagia Sophia, or Holy Wisdom. To his left was the Blue Mosque.

Walking across the park, Raif followed a sidewalk that led up a few stairs and through a wall to the entrance to the mosque. The architect had designed the place as a copy of Hagia Sophia's central domes, but with a typical mosque interior and more minarets. He gave a donation, then removed his shoes while looking at the people around him.

The man from the door of the carpet shop had reappeared and was standing next to a tree some fifty feet away reading a newspaper. Raif lifted the tarp hanging over the doorway and entered the building.

The inside of the place of worship was surprisingly large, with most of its walls and domed ceilings covered with ceramic tiles of different colors but mostly blues. Thus the mosque's nickname. The floors were covered with beautiful Turkish carpets and a dozen or so men were scattered around the open building, some praying, others reading the Koran. Toward the back of the building, near where he had entered, there were some women, wearing traditional black garb with their lower faces veiled. One of the women was struggling to control two young children who wanted to explore.

A railing separated the sightseers from the area designated for prayer, although the same carpet covered the entire floor. A number of large columns that Raif estimated to be at least twenty feet square held up the beautifully tiled central dome. Hanging from the dome was a ceiling of lights suspended perhaps eight feet off the floor.

Raif joined a group of tourists. A female guide was extolling the beauty of the building. Speaking English, she explained that the chandeliers were an example of early art of the metal worker and were designed to provide the interior of the mosque light during the night hours, particularly at the time of Ramadan. While keeping his eye on the door and looking for other exits, Raif heard her say:

"The fundamental requirement for a mosque is the consecrated space, there beyond the rail, in which worshipers, ranked in rows behind the prayer leader or *Imam*, perform actions of the required prayers—standing, bowing, and kneeling. No one is allowed in that space except in a state of ritual purity. You saw the wall of washing outside the building, and all worshipers must wash themselves there first."

The guide, a strikingly beautiful woman, moved a little closer to the railing and directed the group's attention to another part of the mosque.

"To indicate the direction of Mecca, which everyone must face during prayer, there is usually a closed arch, of different elaboration, called the *Mihrab*. You see it there. To its right is the *Minbar*, or pulpit, from which the Friday exhortation, or sermon, is delivered by an *Imam*."

As she moved the group further away, Raif noticed an opening to one side. He walked there and found himself at an entrance that led into a courtyard. As he tried to leave, a man blocked his way, telling him this wasn't an exit. Raif spoke to him in Arabic, while handing him a twenty dollar bill. He was then allowed to leave.

But without his shoes.

A young boy approached with postcards to sell. He asked in broken English if Raif was an American.

Raif said that he was, then asked in Arabic, "Are your postcards good postcards?"

The boy grinned broadly. "American cowboy who speaks Arabic. You have many dollars, yes?"

Raif smiled. "Not many, but enough to buy a postcard. How much?" He said it in English this time.

"For American cowboy, special deal. Only five dollars." The cards were linked together, and the boy dropped them accordion-style. There were ten.

Another boy stepped forward. "I have better deal. You crazy to buy for five dollars." The boys exchanged words in Turkish at fast forward, but Raif got the gist of it. Rival merchants.

"How much?" Raif said to the second boy.

"Four dollars," said the second.

"His pictures bad quality," said the first. Putting his packet forward again, he said, "Three dollars. Special deal."

"I thought five dollars was a special deal," Raif said.

"Supply and demand," the boy shrugged, looking at the

others. "They have supply, you demand good price," he grinned.

Raif began to walk away, feeling the cold of the stone pavers soaking through his wool socks. The boys kept pace, each bidding the other down. Raif could see he wasn't going to get away but thought one of them might be useful.

The first kid was down to ten for a buck. He had a sad look on his face and was complaining, "You steal from poor Turkish boy, but you get for one dollar."

Raif smiled and reached into his pocket. "Deal. I'll pay you one dollar for the cards, and give you ten more for a favor."

"Speak! For fifteen dollars, I'll steal for you!" He was grinning again.

"Ten, and no stealing. I left my shoes at the other entrance. I want you to get them and bring them here without being followed."

The boy was shaking his head in the negative even before Raif finished. "Not allowed! Not allowed! Man at the door give me to police for taking American's shoes. They cut off my hand and make me a beggar for the rest of my life. This not worth all of American's money!"

"Bring the man with you. I'll pay you both, but no one is to see what you're doing. No one is to see you bring me my shoes."

"Okay. Good deal." He got a funny look on his face. "What they look like?"

Raif laughed lightly as he described them in Arabic as best he could. When he said they were Nike's, the boy brightened.

"Ah, Nike's! Just do it!" he said, grinning, then scurried away. A few minutes later he returned with the beat-up shoes in hand, but a man had him by the ear. Raif quickly went to them.

"It's okay!" he said in Arabic, pulling money from his pocket. The boy was rubbing his ear and giving the old gentleman a piece of his mind as the keeper of the shoes took his money and went back into the mosque.

"I make him rich, and he pulls my ear. Not even a thank you!" He made some kind of hand gesture at the entrance, then turned to Raif with a smile. "I be your humble servant, show you our great city. Only fifty American dollars."

"Show me the back door to this place and I'll give you another five."

The boy grinned as if he'd struck gold and was already crossing the courtyard, motioning Raif to follow. They went out a side entrance, worked their way around the mosque, and were soon in a street. Raif saw no sign of his suspected tail. He paid the boy and asked for directions to Top Kapi Palace.

"Information for free, rich cowboy. Not far. Go up street until you come to Aya Sofya, old Christian church, now a museum. Turn right. Next street turn left. Can't miss it." He looked at him with a curious face. "Not open. Closed."

"Yeah, I know. I'm meeting someone at the gate. Thanks."

The boy bowed. "Okay, cowboy. I come to America and ride your horse someday."

"You do that." Raif waved and started down the walk, moving through a group of half a dozen other young street hawkers, profferring everything from Kodak disposable cameras to chewing gum to guide books. Holding up his hands and telling them a firm no, Raif turned the corner to the palace grounds and left them behind.

As he walked the couple of blocks to the palace, Raif tried to recall what his father had told him about it. The palace had once been a residence for a succession of *Caliphs*, but was now a museum. Royal jewels, some of them the most exquisite in the world, were housed there.

The most important exhibit in the museum, at least for Islamic believers, was the one honoring Mohammed. Here one could see the sword, bow, and cape of the prophet, along with the flag of Mohammed, now kept in a gold chest. According to Islamic tradition, in order to declare holy war, a leader had to have the flag, which was considered the military sign of right to call all of Islam together against her enemies, in his possession. Most outsiders didn't know this, and some leaders, like Sadaam Hussein, ignored the requirement. But then, most of Islam ignored him for the crackpot that he was. Many Islamic followers considered him and other fanatic leaders an embarrassment to Mohammed's religion.

With the Palace closed, the street in front of it was empty except for two uniformed, armed guards, who stood near the entrance, their weapons at rest near their sides. Approaching, Raif hesitated, wondering how he would know the person he was to meet. He paused, pretending to take an interest in a small mosque shrouded in scaffolding for repairs.

Minutes passed. It was almost seven o'clock. He felt as though he was being watched but did not know by whom. He checked the street. Parked cars, down at the corner, but all empty. He glanced at each of the few persons on the street. Nothing suspicious. The guards kept eyeing him, though, probably wondering what the devil he was up to.

Then a young man stepped from the small door in the gate of the palace and came toward Raif. He was wearing a white shirt, open at the collar, dark pants and shoes, and had his hand jammed into the pocket of the jacket he was wearing. Raif could see enough to know it was wrapped around the handle of some kind of handgun. He began to sweat.

"You are Mr. Qanun?" the man asked.

Raif nodded, trying his best to look confident while wondering how this was going to come down.

"Who sent you?" the man asked.

"My brother, Husayn. You know him as Mustafa."

"You do not look Persian, American. Do you have some proof you are brothers?"

Raif pulled out his wallet and removed a photograph. It was several years old. "That's our family before Husayn left for Iran."

The young man took Raif's picture, staring at it for long seconds, then smiled. "I never expected to see him as a child. He has changed very much."

"Yeah, we all have."

"What do you want?"

"Answers. Help. His family. More or less in that order. How do you know my name?"

"Your brother called, told us you were coming." He moved toward the gate. "Come with me." As they passed the guards, the man thanked them in Arabic and instructed them not to let anyone pass. Referring to the guards, the young man explained, "They are friends of ours."

Inside the palace complex, he escorted Raif along a road bordered by big trees in a large, enclosed, park-like area. They came eventually to another old wall and gate— the entrance to the inner palace. Before entering, the man motioned to a stone bench and the two of them sat down.

"What may I do for you, Mr. Qanun?" he asked.

"How much do you know about Hussa's past, before coming to Iran, I mean?" Raif asked his guide.

"I and his wife, Krisha, have been told most of it," the man said.

"Can you tell me what he has been doing since leaving home? Why haven't we heard from him? Why didn't he let us know where he was?" Raif asked.

"He had good reasons not to contact you."

"I don't suppose you'd care to elaborate."

"I think he will tell you when he is ready, but I will say this, in Iran Mustafa was never known to be an American. He had Turkish papers and was considered a Turk when he entered the country. Even then he was mistrusted for some time. In those days, if there had been even the slightest evidence he was an American, he would have been tortured and then killed. Would you or your parents have wanted him to take that chance?"

"Times change. He could have gotten word to us later."

"By then he was deeply involved in his work in the underground. The result would have been the same. Even now, many with whom he worked will think he was spying for your country, and if they could get to him they would kill him."

"What do you mean by the underground? The *Nizari?*"

The man looked surprised but quickly contained it. "No, he is not *Nizari.*" He paused. "Are you familiar with *Twelve Imam Shi ism?*"

"The basics."

"Then perhaps you know that ninety-eight percent of Iranians are *Shi ite*, while the largest majority of Muslims are *Sunni.* The meaning of the word *Shi ite* is 'party of Ali,' a group originally comprised of a small circle of Persians who advocated the candidacy of Ali ibn Abi Talib as successor to Mohammed. Ali was a cousin to the prophet as well as his son-in-law. He was also one of the first converts to Islam and gained fame as a defender of the faith, a warrior. The *Shi ites* believe that Ali, even though passed over as the first *Caliph*, was the first of twelve *Imams* with special spiritual powers. Whereas Mohammed was the last of the prophets that included such men as Abraham and Jesus, the *Imams* were the 'cycle of authority' after Mohammed, and they were known to have supernatural knowledge and authority, as well as a station of merit equal with that of Mohammed.

"The last of the twelve is known as the '*Hidden Imam*' and is thought to still be mysteriously alive. He will return as the *Mahdi*, the 'Guided One,' a figure who will appear at the end of time to restore righteousness briefly—before the final judgment. The reign of this *Mahdi* will be a respite in the darkening of the cosmic cycle and will unite all sects in Islam. This reign will be finished before the Antichrist appears to play his role and Jesus comes to destroy him."

Raif was listening closely. He knew there were schisms in the Islamic faith, but had never studied it in detail. Maybe this man could shed some light on his brother's bizarre behavior.

"There are many *Imams* in Islam," the man continued. "Anyone who leads prayer in a congregation is an *Imam*. But the *Shi ites* have made them more. So much more that it has caused a serious rift in Islam as a whole. Even within *Shi ism*, the interpretation of who has the divine power of this kind of exalted Imam, or who may be the *Mahdi*, has led to splintering. There are the 'Zaydis' at one end and the 'Ghulat' at the other, more fanatical end. In the middle are the 'Twelvers' who assert that the *Imam* holds both spiritual and political preeminence and possesses special graces, miraculous powers, secret knowledge, and favor, which God has bestowed on no one else.

"During the time Khomeini was in power, some considered him the *Twelfth Imam*. Your brother was fanatical in this belief. He was convinced that Khomeini was the *Mahdi*." He paused. "Try to understand, when Mustafa came to Iran, he was thoroughly schooled by extremists in extremist doctrine. He was no longer your brother, Raifim Qanun. He didn't contact you, or his parents, because, to him, he had no parents. He was *Shi ite*, celebrating the return of the *Twelfth Imam*. Khomeini was his father, his mother, his family. His very life. To admit that he had any kind of past outside that realm was not possible. He gave up the past to become a warrior of God and Khomeini was his prophet. There was no other life than this. By the time he came to his senses, he was in too deep. Not only was his life at risk, but that of his wife and first child."

Raif remembered how Hussa had declared Khomeini the *Mahdi* to their father. How their father had denounced

Hussa for it and told him if he ever spoke such a notion in his home again, Hussa would no longer be welcome. It was one of the main reasons Hussa had left them in the first place. Now all of that had changed? Why? What greater cause had come along than family that made him face the fact he had been wrong?

"It must have been a blow to Hussa when Khomeini up and died without accomplishing the *Mahdi's* charge," Raif said, bitterly.

"Mustafa had become disillusioned before Khomeini died, not just in the man but in the doctrine itself." He paused. "But, he had given up so much, committed himself so completely, that it took some time for him to let himself believe that the ideas professed in *Twelve Imam Shi ism* were nothing more than man's attempt to usurp power that neither Mohammed or the Koran gave them. By that time, Mustafa had become one of Khomeini's avowed assassins."

"That's when he went to Israel. Blew up innocent people," Raif said flatly. He didn't try to hide his disgust.

"Yes, and believe it or not, that is the part of his life he has been trying to undo for the past five years."

Raif didn't believe it. "You will have to give more convincing evidence than pretty speeches."

"This is not for me to do," the man said. His voice had a tinge of sadness in it.

His guide stood and motioned toward the second gate where a number of people busied themselves, raking up leaves and cleaning the area. There were also a number of small shops and a ticket office located there. As they approached the gate, Raif's guide spoke to the people and was greeted warmly in return.

Raif had noticed that the young man was young in body alone—that the eyes were those of an old man and showed years of wear. He wondered what these young eyes had seen, what the young soul behind them had gone through.

They were also honest eyes, and behind them was a soul who believed in whatever it was Hussa had become.

"May I know your name?" Raif asked.

"Yes, it is Abdul."

"Well, Abdul, it would help me to know what changed my brother's mind," Raif said.

Abdul smiled. "Many things, over time. The war with Iraq, one of the most bloody and unnecessary wars in our history, and, the fact that it was Muslim fighting Muslim made many reconsider.

"Another factor was that the promises being made by Khomeini about a new order, a new society, simply were not fulfilled. We would come home from the wars and find our families in poverty, starving because of the chaos or because they had followed a *Mulla* who had lost favor with Khomeini and his regime, they would be in prison. Ration cards were no longer available. In some instances we returned to find our families thrown out of their homes. Your brother was one of these. Something snapped inside him, and he became bitter." The man smiled. "That was when he organized the *al Muqanna.*"

"'The veiled ones?' And his purpose?"

"To fight the corruption and bring an end to the slaughter and the imprisonment of those who opposed fanatical religious leaders. Most important, to support Mohammad Khatami and his presidency." He smiled again. "Without his knowledge, of course, but we protect him just as the *Nizari* try to bring him down."

"By the same methods, I assume."

"When you swim with sharks, you had better be prepared to bite."

"Who is Beni?"

"A man by the name of Kalimah. Isdris Kalimah. He organized the *Nizari* during the time of Khomeini. Your brother used to be one of his lieutenants. They remained friends even after Mustafa retired from active duty due to his capture by the Israelis."

"How come the Israelis let Hussa go?"

"Beni has one endearing quality. He does not leave his men stranded. He kidnapped a member of the Israeli *Knesset*, and an exchange was made. But your brother was no longer able to function as an agent, though he still trained others, even after he organized *al Muqanna*."

"That's how he knew the *Nizari* were planning something in the United States?" Raif asked.

"Yes, but it is a bit more complicated than that. Shortly after your brother's release by the Israelis, there was a threat on Beni's life by that country's intelligence organization. Beni decided it was time to go into deep cover. He went to the *Mullas* who funded the *Nizari* and offered them a plan that, in their eyes, had great potential."

"Plant Beni and a woman in the United States and organize an underground there," Raif said.

"Yes. The organization is much more extensive than you can possibly imagine. When the *Mullas* decided to strike both at the United States and Khatami, Beni contacted several former members of the *Nizari*. Mustafa was one of them. Though it would be very dangerous for him, our counsel decided he must infiltrate the organization and stop the intended operation."

"Alone?"

"Yes, alone. There was no one else. It had to be someone with the respect and trust of the terrorist world, and Mustafa had that trust. In addition, although known only to a few of us in *al Muqanna*, he was a former American. His English and familiarity with the country would help."

"No offense, Abdul, but your organization is run by fools."

"On the surface it may seem so to an outsider, but trust me when I tell you, it is not. First, your brother is no ordinary agent, and second, you must remember, it was Beni who selected his training team, not us. We were lucky to have anyone at all. Third, if some fool American had not interrupted the transfer of the weapons, Mustafa would have removed them from Beni's possession and slipped away into the mountains." He smiled.

"Touché, but it wouldn't have been so easy. Duren was a professional tracker. Slipping away with half a dozen pack animals would not have been easy."

"Then Mustafa would have blown them up to prevent their use." He paused. "Mustafa had another role. He went to gather information. Names, mostly of those Beni had recruited in your country. He will deliver it to your agents when he is ready."

"And just how was he going to get it to us if they'd killed him out there?"

Abdul smiled. "Your mail service is vaunted for its ability to deliver anywhere, anytime. It would have come, Raifim. Somehow it would have come."

"He should have contacted us. To take those kind of chances—"

"Possibly. It is always easy to make judgments from the end of any operation. At the beginning the risks seemed minimal. Though it may seem wrong from your perspective, Raifim, from his, the decision to leave local law enforcement in the dark was correct."

"Did he know where Beni was planning this operation?"

"That he was going to Jackson? Not at first. It was well into the final planning stage before he learned the name of the man selected to operate Beni's training facility."

"Peter Hawkes."

"As you Americans say, a bad break. When we researched the name through a contact of ours in the American Embassy in Greece, Mustafa considered backing out, but there really wasn't any choice. He had the best chance of stopping Beni."

"But Hawkes knew Hussa was a former American," Raif said, frustrated.

"He and Hawkes were never to have met. Beni didn't want the locals interfering with his training teams and operatives."

"Our investigation shows their paths crossed several times. The training team lived at Jackson Village, and several of the locals met with them there."

"Mustafa did not stay there. As the on-site commander, he was to go directly into the mountains and remain there. As everything went smoothly for more than three months, I would say that he was successful in evading Hawkes."

"Something went wrong. Hawkes seems the most likely fly in the ointment."

"It is something Mustafa will have to tell us."

Raif figured there was no use dwelling on the past and let it go. "You said they intended to hit your country as well as mine. What did you mean?"

"At least one of those missiles is intended for Mohammad Khatami, our president. The religious fanatics want to get rid of him. How better than to blow up his car with an American-made missile?"

"Then blame us. Very neat."

"You see why we cooperate with you now, why I tell you all this. Those missiles must be found."

"All your illustrious leader has to do is point us in the right direction," Raif said, sarcastically.

There was no answer.

"Any chance they would have sent the missiles out of the United States already?" Raif asked.

"If Mustafa believed it to be so, even saving the lives of his family would not prevent him from stopping it. No, they are still in your country. I assume you have closed off all the exits from your valley."

"So tight even the wind is trapped."

"Then he will wait." He paused as they passed a small

group of workers and traded greetings. "There is a woman. She disappeared at the same time as Beni."

"Probably the one who played his wife. We think she and a child are in Paris."

"She is even more dangerous than Beni and would not leave his side, even for a child. Her name is Leina Khabur. Until she is dead, she will be your enemy, Raifim. When Beni started organizing his team, he passed over Mustafa. It was Leina who convinced him to change his mind. She will have her revenge. If not on Mustafa, then on you and your parents."

"You could have gone all day without telling me that."

"You have them under the protection of others, but watch this one. Do not let her escape, or you will never be able to sleep peacefully."

Raif felt the hair stand up on the back of his neck. "I'll remember."

They approached the ticket area outside the inner gate where there were rest rooms and a gift shop, all closed. They walked through the main gate and under the thick wall. A toll booth for ticket collection stood on the far side. Circumventing it, they began walking across the courtyard around which the palace buildings were erected.

Raif had a sudden desire to talk to Sharps and pulled out his cellular. "What do you dial to get out of this country?" he asked.

Abdul smiled bemusedly. "A wonderful tool in this business," he said. He told Raif what to dial. And while an international operator attempted to connect him to the United States, Raif spoke his mind.

"Even though it took Leina Khabur's help, Mustafa must have been well-respected to get inside such an operation."

"Yes. His arrest has been a great shock to a lot of people, on both sides."

"He can never return to your country, you know that," Raif said.

"Others will take his place. He has trained many."

Raif heard the phone click off, the line go dead. He looked at it, wondering what had happened.

"Sometimes it happens. This technology is still new in this part of the world. Try again." Raif did and got another operator. This time one who didn't speak English very well, and Raif had to use his rudimentary Arabic. That didn't work so well, either, and he handed the phone to Abdul, who quickly had her doing what was needed.

"Hello." The voice was sleepy, but it brought Raif out his thoughts.

"Sharps?"

"Qanun! Is that you?"

"Just checking in."

"You picked a great time," Sharps's voice oozed with sarcasm.

"Anything new?" Raif asked.

"Remember me asking you about a job? I'm going to need it."

"That bad, huh?"

"That bad."

"Talk to—" Raif almost said "Hussa," but remembering how notoriously insecure cell phone lines were, he thought better of it. "Talk to him," he said. "Tell him you want the names he's compiled of Beni's entire organization. Then fax a few of them to your boss. That'll keep him happy for a few days. When you give him the rest, he'll have to promote you."

"He has those kind of goods?" The voice was much more alert.

"Supposed to. Tell him I don't fly outta here until he's turned it over."

"Are you at the number you gave me?"

"Yup."

"I'll call back."

"And, Sharps?"

"Yeah?"

"We're up against some people that are even worse than we thought. I don't want my parents leaving that place until the enemy is either dead or behind bars. You understand?"

"Gotcha."

The line went dead, and Raif put the phone away.

They walked past a building on the west side of the complex that was heavily guarded. No one seemed to pay any attention to them except to give a friendly greeting to Abdul. "You must own this place."

"I was forced to leave my country a year ago. I live here now. I work in the restaurant we will pass through soon."

"Do any of these people know what you really do?"

"They know I fight Iran. For them, that is enough."

The phone rang. It was Sharps. From the sound of his voice, Raif figured he was doing a jig in the middle of the living area. He had the papers. "Get the guy's family here, Raif. He's on our side."

"Could be phony, a trap." The phone went silent. "Just kidding, but you might want to keep it under wraps until you verify. Just to be safe. Oh, and, Sharps?"

"Yeah."

"This can't get to the press," Raif said.

There was an audible grunt on the other side of the line. "This flat face may look stupid, Qanun, but the mind behind it still works. Moen's the problem, has been all along. That's why I left him outta this."

"Moen doesn't strike me as a man with enough brains to get entangled with Middle East power players."

"He's not. He's just stupid, easy to play. It's the guy who's playing him I'm after, and who I'll get, eventually. But for now, I've cut the traitor's lifeline, and that'll keep our 'mutual friend' alive. Look, we're closer than ever on this thing. We've nabbed all of Beni's leads. His operation is botched. Sooner or later he's got to make his move. Just do your part. And hurry!" He hung up.

They approached a set of steps and went down them into a restaurant. Skirting some outdoor tables and chairs, they exited the palace grounds and climbed down the side of a hill overlooking the Bosphorus Strait. After making their way to the shoreline, they boarded a small fishing boat. At Abdul's order, two of his friends removed the ropes tied to small trees and Abdul started the engine. Minutes later they were headed into deeper water and turned left toward the Galata Bridge, which spanned the Golden Horn. Abdul turned the wheel over to one of the hands and stepped outside the cabin where he stood next to Raif.

"It is time Mustafa's family left this country. They will be safer in America now."

Raif suspected that Abdul said it as much to convince himself as anyone.

"Mustafa's wife and children are being hunted. The *Mulla* who works most directly with Beni has his henchman here, looking for them. There has been a promise of a very high reward. Additionally, rumor tells us the *Mulla* himself comes. He wishes to emphasize the importance of capturing my sister and her children. Under these conditions, even the authorities cannot be trusted."

"Your sister! Hussa is married to your sister?" Raif said, understanding more clearly Abdul's willingness to help him.

"That is correct. Krisha is my sister, and her children my niece and nephew."

"How much is the reward?" Raif asked.

"A million of your American dollars."

"I've got a Lear jet at the airport. Help me get them there, Abdul, and they're home free."

"The one problem is passports. They have none."

"In a town like this there ought to be someone willing to create something."

"We made such arrangements. It was done through a man we have trusted and used for a long time, but he never arrived with them and is probably dead." Raif studied Abdul's face. He looked tired, a man whose life had been slowly sucked out of him by the death of friends and the killing of enemies.

"I'm sorry someone else had to die," Raif said.

"He didn't talk. We consider his resistance and death honorable. He will go to Allah." Abdul shrugged. "In the end, what else is there?"

"My government wants Hussa's cooperation. We'll see what they can do." Raif said it while masking his own apprehension. He wasn't sure who to approach or how. Not in this part of the world. He'd call Sharps once he had Hussa's family in hand.

The breeze off the water was cool, forcing Raif to pull his collar up around his ears. In the distance he could see traffic moving across the bridge and several ferries moving in either direction across the strait. The setting sun was was just dipping below the mountains surrounding the sea to the west. It was an idyllic evening, which made Raif wish he had both the time and peace to enjoy it, but his mind was numb and he hurt inside for all the grief, hate, anger, and death he had been forced to deal with over the last ten days.

Abdul brought him out of his thoughts. "I know much of you, Raifim Qanun. Your brother reveres you as an honorable man. If it were not so, this meeting would never have taken place."

Raif was a bit stunned. The idea that his brother considered him at all was new to Raif, let alone that he might revere him. But then, everything was a shock when a person you thought was dead came back to life.

"Where do we go to get your sister and the children?"

"They are in hiding at the business of a cousin, in the Grand Bazaar."

That explained the arguing in the background during his second phone call.

The boat was soon docking near the Galata Bridge. As the Raif and Abdul disembarked, Abdul spoke in Arabic to his two men. Raif understood enough to know they'd been instructed to bring the boat back at some later time. They shoved off and motored away in the growing dusk.

Abdul led Raif to a taxi stop near the front of a large mosque across from the docking area, and they caught a cab.

Winding their way through traffic, they reached Divan Yolu Street. At Abdul's direction, the cab pulled to the curb not far from a trolley platform, and Raif paid the driver. People milled about, shopping, talking, waiting for the trolley. The numbers increased the closer they got to the bazaar itself, setting Raif's nerves on edge. He kept his eyes panning the crowd, watching for some sudden movement, some unseen approach to them that could mean trouble, or worse. Abdul appeared relaxed, but a closer look showed eyes that took in all and the taut muscles of a man ready to do battle.

They passed through a large entrance into Istanbul's Grand Bazaar where there were row after row of small shops selling leather goods, Islamic art, Turkish carpets, souvenirs, clothes, jewelry and a thousand other items. The entire place was covered under one roof and loosely divided into sections for different kinds of wares. The aisles were for walking only, narrow, and in some instances no more than a trail between rows of goods spread out from shop to shop.

They worked their way through hoards of people into an area that sold leather goods, then turned right and headed down a long line of jewelry shops. The windows literally glistened with every size and shape of gold and silver jewelry and precious gems. Watches cluttered some windows and crystal dishes filled others. Turkish coffee pots with small cups sat in sets, their beautiful dark blues and reds enhanced with pictures and designs. Some of these were hand-painted, others of lesser quality done by machine for those tourists who didn't know the difference or wanted to save fifty percent on the price.

After wending their way through enough streets to get Raif thoroughly lost, Abdul ducked into a shop and said something in Turkish to the shopkeeper, who only motioned to a curtained door. They were through it quickly, and Abdul paused to peer through a small crack to see if they were being followed. Nothing.

"How far to your sister and the kids?" Raif asked.

"Not far. But, American, you stand out like a camel in a horse race. Do you have money?"

Raif opened his wallet and took out a hundred. "That enough?"

Abdul shook his head. "Another hundred for a coat."

Raif gave it to him.

"You wait here and I will get you suitable clothes." He was gone before Raif could protest. Instead he sat down on a stool to catch his breath. His body was still trying to catch up with the ten-hour difference in time, and he realized he was exhausted. Ten minutes later Abdul returned carrying some new clothes and a shoebox. Raif removed his coat and shirt and put on the ones provided. The shirt was a pullover with short sleeves, the coat of black leather with a nice lining but lacking the warmth of his lamb's wool. Abdul opened the box to reveal a pair of loafers.

"I hate loafers. What's the matter with the Nikes?" Raif said as he removed them.

"They are of a style sold only in the United States," Abdul said.

Abdul stuffed the American clothing in a large shopping sack and handed it to Raif. "Now you are Turkish. He plopped a skull cap on Raif's head. "Now Islamic, Turkish."

"I haven't seen that many blonds," Raif said.

"Turks come in many colors."

Raif wondered what Abdul's life had been like, why he had decided on joining *al Muqanna*. Was it Hussa's influence, or were there other things, more deeply seated, that made a young man into a killer without a future?

They left the store and weaved their way through half a dozen more alleys before Abdul stopped and looked both ways. He saw nothing to give him a reason to hesitate, and they entered another shop, one that sold jewelry and crystal.

Abdul nodded to the shopkeeper who was helping a customer, but continued to the back of the shop, where he and Raif ducked through a curtain covering a narrow opening. Beyond this darkened room there was a wooden door that opened into another, small, dimly lit room.

As they entered, a woman came quickly to her feet, looking first at Abdul, then at Raif. Two children, an older boy and a younger girl, sidled in behind her, each holding a leg and peering up at Raif. A man, carrying what looked like an Israeli made Uzi automatic pistol in his hand, stepped from a darkened corner. When Abdul said something to him in what Raif knew to be *Farsi*, the man put the weapon in the oversized pocket of an ankle-length leather coat and left the room without a word.

"Why did you send him away?" Raif asked.

"You will see few of us, Raifim. Our faces are not to be known."

"You will leave as well?"

"I remain until you are out of the country. I am family."

"And if we need them again . . . ?" Raif said, motioning to the closed door.

Abdul smiled. "They are nearby."

The woman seemed to relax. "You are Raifim. Yes, Mustafa has described you, but you are much older now."

Raif felt as though he was dreaming—a stranger in a foreign land, who suddenly meets a cousin or uncle he's never seen before. You stutter through introductions, feel unsure, out of place, and hope that somehow they won't

think you odd. He wiped his moist palms on the legs of his
Levi's and craved a Tylenol for his headache.

He looked away from his sister-in-law and at the little
girl. "Does she speak English?" he asked.

"Yes," the woman said.

"What is her name?"

"Tasli."

"'Peace be upon you,'" Raif said, translating the name.
It fit the round olive skin face and black curly hair. Her
dark eyes were like those of a small deer, shaped like
almonds.

"I am Krisha," the woman said. She was striking, a
grown-up version of her beautiful daughter, and was dressed
in Levi's, a cotton blouse, and a black leather coat. Raif
wondered at a thin scar that ran through the left side of
her lips.

"This is Hussa's son, Raoul. Tasli is three, Raoul is five."

"His grandfather's name," Raif said.

She nodded, a mystified look on her face. "Mustafa has
told you none of this?"

"We didn't have much time." He turned as the door
opened. A man came in and spoke hurried words to Abdul
then left.

"It seems we have been found. The closest exit is about
a hundred yards from here. It empties into the street at the
south end of the Bazaar," Abdul explained. "I will go there
and get us a cab. In five minutes Krisha will bring you and
the children, and we will leave immediately." Abdul left.

"My husband. Will he be all right?" She spoke English
with only a slight accent.

"He's in good hands, but he does have a broken arm."

"It has been much worse." She said it as if commenting
on the weather. Raif thought emotion for her must be a
dangerous thing.

"They won't stop until he is dead. You know that," she
said.

"They, as in the mysterious *Mullas* that Abdul tells me about?"

"One particular one. Abdul has not told you his name," she stated. Then smiling slightly, she said, "My brother is a man in many ways, but he tries very hard to make things more clandestine than they are. The *Mulla's* name is Maktub."

Raif had heard the name in the news—the force behind Islam in Iran.

"You can stop him," Raif said. "You and Hussa."

"Yes," she gave a wry smile. "I am aware of that. If it were not so, Maktub would not be trying to kill us."

"He'll try to take you hostage first, use you as leverage."

"It will end the same because I will fight him, and either I will die or he will." She said it without hesitation. But there was no anger in her voice, just a cold direct presentation of the facts. Raif realized that Krisha was as determined to change her country as his brother was, and were Raif an enemy, she would slit his throat to protect her husband and her children. For some reason he thought of Leina Khabur and wondered which of the two women was most deadly. It gave him goosebumps to think about, and he was thankful he had been quick to call Sharps.

"It's time to go," Raif urged. "I'll rely on your eyes. You know who to look for."

She nodded even as she picked up her daughter. Raif reached for Raoul who went to him only after his mother's glance of approval.

Raif removed a hundred dollar bill from Terri's gift, and as he stepped into the shop, he handed it to the cousin with a request stated in halting Arabic. The shopkeeper smiled, nodded, and bowed. Krisha thanked the man with a kiss on both cheeks. He hugged Tasli and ruffled Raoul's hair, wishing Allah's blessings upon them, then smiled at Raif, praising him for helping Krisha.

Raif cautiously stepped into the street, letting Krisha

pass as he did. In spite of her westernized clothing, she reminded Raif of an Arabic queen. She walked with a simple kind of elegance, brisk but seemingly unhurried. He glanced over his shoulder to see the shopkeeper talking with two other men. The three then followed them at a little distance. Still carrying the children, he and Krisha worked their way through the crowded aisles of the bazaar, coming at last to where they could see the exit. Krisha stopped as if noticing something in a shop window. She let Tasli to the ground and Raif did the same with Raoul.

"There are two men standing on the far side of the entrance," she said to Raif. "They wear leather coats with sweaters, one red and one brown. Do you see them?"

Looking over the people in the crowded aisle, Raif nodded.

"The taller of the two is Hakim. He works for Maktub. Once he was a friend, we vacationed together with our families two years ago. Mustafa wanted to recruit him, but he wasn't ready. He knows us very well." She had pulled a silky scarf from her pocket and draped it over her head and wrapped it around the bottom half of her face. Raif sensed that she was tense, but there was no panic. He figured she had done this before, perhaps many times.

Raif took a quick look and saw two others join these same men. They appeared to be arguing, while looking over the crowd of people. Raif was glad for his new set of clothes. Even the loafers.

"Go inside the shop and look at things," Raif said. He glanced back the way they had come. Catching the eye of the friendly shopkeeper who had been following them, Raif nodded toward the enemy, and the man disappeared. It was then he saw Abdul's man, the one with the Uzi. Most likely he wouldn't open fire now, not here, but if the shopkeeper did Raif's bidding, he wouldn't need to.

Raif kept Raoul at his side, grateful the boy wasn't spoiled and a crier when his mom stepped out of sight. He stooped down and spoke. "You're a brave boy, Raoul. In a minute I am going to pick you up and we are going to go through the gate to a car. Okay?"

Raoul nodded, his index finger in his mouth.

Standing straight, Raif watched Hakim and his companions from the corner of his eye. Abdul's man had disappeared. When enough time had passed for the cousin to be ready, he walked to a spot where he could see Krisha and signaled her to come. She was at his side when a handcart suddenly appeared out of nowhere. It was moving quickly toward the gate, fully loaded with boxes. Two men, one the shopkeeper, were pushing the cart and yelling obscenities at each other, oblivious of where they were going. The people in the path of the cart, darted out of the way, cursing the parentage of the quarreling men.

Suddenly the cousin jerked on his side of the push bar and the other lifted his high. The boxes spilled everywhere, creating chaos in the street. Hakim and his friend were momentarily distracted by the commotion of the spilled boxes. Then the cousin threw a punch, and a fight broke out.

Raif started to bolt for the door, but Krisha grabbed his hand and pulled him up short, moving them at an even pace through the gate and outside. Seeing the cab fifty feet in front of them, Raif wanted to increase his stride, but Krisha continued to hold him back. Twenty-five feet. He glanced over his shoulder as sweat gathered on his face. The melee still had the enemy occupied. The shopkeeper and his friends had earned every dollar of the hundred Raif had given them and had him wishing he'd given more.

They slipped into the open door of the cab and Abdul closed it behind them, then took his seat in front as the driver pulled from the curb.

"You are smart for an American," Krisha said smiling. "Your diversion was a good one."

"Thank your cousin next time you see him." He rested

his head against the back of the seat. He wondered how Krisha was able to cope with the constant fear. "You kept me from bolting. Thanks."

"Sudden movement draws the eye. We learn to fit in, that is all."

"I could never do it."

"Necessity gives the strength to do many things we never thought possible, Raifim. In your world, in your wilderness, you survive by obeying the rules of the hunt. It is really no different here except that we are the prey."

"How do you know about—?"

"Mustafa told me of your days in the mountains. They were wonderful memories for him."

That was news to Raif. He had assumed Hussa despised everything about his former life. He was beginning to see a different picture of his brother.

The taxi ride was fast and frantic but without calamity. The driver used the horn constantly, depending on that and a variety of hand gestures directed at other drivers to navigate through the traffic. Raif's heart was thumping, and in spite of the cool temperature in the taxi, sweat beaded up on his brow. He realized after a time that he was still grasping the shopping bag full of his clothes so tightly that his hand ached. As they careened along, Tasli sucked her thumb while Krisha clutched the little girl tightly to her chest. Raoul was on Raif's knee, his eyes pinned to the pulsating city that passed by outside the window. Raif wondered what kind of an effect a life of hiding, living in constant fear might have on a young boy of five. From what he had seen in Abdul's eyes, Raif thought it couldn't be favorable. In the United States, in the Hole, his life could only be better.

He sat back and closed his eyes. When they hit the highway that bordered the Marmara Sea, he knew they were headed in the direction of the airport.

They weren't home free. They'd have to hole up

somewhere until they could get passports, and he wouldn't feel safe until they were actually in the air. But they'd made a good start.

Question was, could it last?

23

Raif was calling the number of Sharps's cellular while staring out the window of the apartment building and across the dark face of the Sea of Marmara.

Sharps was wandering near the barn smoking a cigar when his phone jingled. "Where the devil are you, Qanun?" Sharps asked when Raif said hello.

Again fearful that someone might be listening, Raif was evasive. "We're halfway home." Cautiously he filled Sharps in on what he had been doing since his arrival.

"Maktub. Doctor Death if our intelligence community is even close to accurate," Sharps said.

Raif didn't comment. Maktub already had him spooked, and he didn't need more information that would make the condition worse. "I assume your end is still going smoothly?"

Sharps gave him a few generalities, no location, nothing critical. It was obvious he had the same concerns about secure phone lines. Sam, now returned from the wilderness, the sheriff, and Sharps himself were on duty. There were others, but numbers weren't mentioned.

"If anyone wants to rob a bank in Teton County, now is the time." Sharps paused, and Raif sensed the gloating even over the phone. "You might like to know, I handed those names over to my boss. It worked. He's handling the press and has the President helping him."

Now *that* was something Raif hoped the enemy would

overhear. He felt half a dozen knots releasing themselves inside his gut. Maktub's new American revolution had suffered a devastating setback. "That's great," he said.

"The master of understatement," Sharps said. There was a pause. "Do you know a place called Crystal Creek Ranch?" he asked.

Raif told him yes. It was a summer place belonging to some rich Californian, usually boarded up in the winter, located a few miles up Gros Ventre canyon. Sharps proceeded to explain that the place had caught fire but no fire trucks could get to it. By the time they got to the place it was nothing but ashes. "There musta been an explosion, probably the chopper."

"Chopper?"

"Yeah, it was burned to a crisp along with two men who were apparently working on it."

"Any survivors?"

"Tracks leading into the backcountry indicate at least one, maybe two. The sheriff is tracking 'em.

"Any sign of the missiles?"

"Just empty crates. No sign of Daniel Beni."

"Then the missiles were gone before the accident."

"Right. It looks like they're on the move." Another pause. "Get back here tonight, will you?" Sharps said, frustrated.

"Yeah, but I need passports."

There was a long silence. "You're kidding, right?"

"Nope."

Sharps sighed. "I'll need to call in some old debts. I'll get back to you."

"Make it quick, will you? I feel like a sitting duck."

Sharps laughed. "My pleasure. Getting you out of there will really tick them off. I can't think of anything I'd enjoy more, except busting Beni."

"Yeah, I know what you mean." Raif hung up then pushed the button again to make another call.

The phone on the other end rang only once before it was picked up.

"Hello."

"Hi."

"Raif! Where are you?" Terri asked. "Are you all right?" Her obvious concern felt good to Raif.

"I'm fine. Right now I'm in an apartment overlooking the beach." He looked out at the darkness. "I can see a club of some kind, with a swimming pool, bar, restaurant, most everything you would see at any such place." Beyond the beach, out on the water, he could see rows of lights. Ships backed up, waiting to go through the Bosporus Straits to the Black Sea.

"Regular Club Med. How about you?" he said.

"Well, let's see, I've counted 121 planes landing, nearly that many taking off. Two-thirds were commercial, most of the rest military, and half a dozen private."

"Nearly as much fun as hunting in Wyoming."

"Except that I don't have a klutz for a guide. Do you have his family?"

"Yeah, safe and sound, but they don't have passports. Sharps is taking care of it, but its going to be sometime tomorrow before we can move."

There was a long silence. "A lot can happen between now and morning."

"Sleep is all I want."

"I hope sleep is all you get. We could come—"

"As much as I'd like that, it's not needed. Is the Lear fueled?"

"To the brim."

"Great. I'll see you in the morning then."

Raif had taken the phone from his ear and was about to punch the end-call key when he heard a loud noise come from the phone.

"Terri?"

"Sorry, I just wanted to say one thing more."

"What?"

There was a pause. "Be careful, Raif . . . just . . . be care-ful, okay?"

"Right."

They hung up.

* * *

Terri looked out the window of the aircraft. The airport was taking fewer and fewer flights, and in the dim light she could see support personnel were dwindling in numbers. She and Bob had discovered that few flights came into Istanbul between the hours of midnight and six a.m. and that they'd need special permission to get out between those hours. Her father had gone to look into it.

She opened the small fridge and stared at the items there without really seeing them, thinking of Raif. She had finally admitted to herself that she was in love with him. At least, part of her was, and the other part was finding him hard to resist.

Rummaging through the galley, she found a Hershey's Almond Chocolate bar and tore open the wrapper. She wasn't really hungry—just bored, bored and anxious to see Raif and get underway. Taking a seat by the window, she nibbled on her bar and stared out at the airport landing lights. She had called her office in New York and instead of making excuses for being a day late getting back to work, she had turned in a verbal resignation. There was an imme-diate scramble by her partners, who all came on a confer-ence call and tried to get her to change her mind. It ended with her making a promise to think it over and at least return long enough to turn her cases over to others.

At the time she had wondered which had been more active in her decision to quit—her father's offer to come to work for his new subsidiary or her feelings for Raif. Now she knew the answer, and it frightened her. Was there a chance that Raif would ever join the Church? And if he did, would it be because he had become a believer or just because he thought it would make her happy or reduce the conflict that was sure to exist?

She looked out the window again. The two large crates they had brought with them stood near the door of the plane, still unopened. From Raif's last report they probably wouldn't be needed, even though both had cleared custom's inspection and been dutifully stamped as having their import tax paid.

She thought of his description of his surroundings. He was along the coast somewhere, probably not far from the airport, and there was a club of some kind. Couldn't be too many of those, could there? Her father had been here, done business, maybe he would know. Or know someone who did.

She set the half-eaten chocolate bar aside then removed the table and converted two of the large chairs into fold-down single beds.

Raif Qanun had caused her to consider something she hadn't previously thought possible—marrying outside the Church. The thought created all kinds of emotions, fears, internal conflicts, but it didn't go away—even when Raif did. As she smoothed out the sheets she realized one thing was sure, she was going to have to deal with those emotions soon, and it had better be before Raif walked through passport control and up the short steps of the Lear. After that it would simply be too late.

24

After eating something light, Raif and Krisha started getting the children ready for bed. Abdul went outside. Raif figured he had others watching the place and was checking in with them. The four-story apartment building was surrounded by a small yard with a vine covered fence that stood maybe ten feet tall, making it difficult to see into the first level of the building—the level they occupied. Access to the apartment building was via two gates, one at the back, one at the front, but any intruder would be confronted by an entrance guarded by a security system that would rival any used by banks and large corporations. The heavy doors were armor plated, electronically bolted, impervious to most weapons fire, and would stand against a fair-sized battering ram. But Raif suspected it would take more than electronically bolted doors to stop Maktub if he wanted to get in.

Krisha took Tasli into the bathroom.

"You are my daddy's brother?" Raoul asked, as Raif helped him remove his clothes and put on pajamas. The boy spoke English fairly well, even though he stuttered some.

Raif smiled and nodded. "Yes, we're brothers, why?"

Raoul's eyes were heavy, and he struggled to keep them open. "Because you don't look like him," the boy said.

"Do you know what *adopted* means, Raoul?"

Raoul nodded. "My friend from where we live, his father was killed in fighting somewhere. Then his mother left him at a school. He was adopted by the people he was living with, I think."

"Well, I was adopted by your father's parents—your grandmother and grandfather."

"Were you like me when they adopted you?"

"Your age? No, I was just a baby. Your grandparents have always been my parents. I don't look as much like them as your father does, but I feel just as much a part of them as if I did."

"Is Daddy with them now?"

"Yes, and we are going there tomorrow."

"Mommy says you have beautiful horses and that I can ride them." He smiled.

Raif took the blankets found in a nearby closet and made a bed on the thick rug while telling Raoul about the ranch, then the Shagya. "I will let you ride him if you like."

"Tomorrow!" he said excitedly. "Please, tomorrow!"

"Well, it is a long way to the ranch, so maybe the next day."

Krisha came in and was putting Tasli to bed on the floor as Raoul stepped to a section of the carpet and began his ritual prayer. Raif watched as the boy took the time to do all of it perfectly. By the time he was finished, Tasli was asleep and Krisha then tucked Raoul in next to her.

"Will you stay tonight?" Raoul asked Raif.

Raif nodded.

Raoul looked relieved. "I asked for Allah's blessing on your horses, Uncle Raifim."

"Thank you, Raoul."

Raoul turned on his side and stuck his thumb in his mouth. Krisha sat on the couch at the opposite end from Raif, both waiting for Raoul to fall asleep. It didn't take long. Krisha stood and snapped off the light. The rays of the moon came through the window and outlined the two children in a perfect square, as if protecting them.

"They are beautiful, Krisha."

She nodded her gratitude for the comment. "This is the first time Raoul has gone to sleep without complaint for many days." She looked at Raif, the moonlight casting a shadow across her large, dark eyes. "Thank you."

"My privilege." He had so many questions for her, like how she dealt with the constant danger, how she could love a country that took so much, or how she could love a man who killed the innocent. But now wasn't the time.

"Why haven't you married, Raifim?" she asked.

He shrugged. "The usual reasons. Too busy, too poor, too ugly."

She laughed lightly.

He told Krisha about Terri. Why, he didn't know, except that he wanted, needed, to talk about the future and avoid the past.

"She sounds very nice."

"It's nothing serious yet, mind you. At least, I don't think it is. There's another man she's on the rebound from. It's messy. But one thing is sure, she's tough. In Jackson Hole, that's a prerequisite if you intend to survive." He smiled. "After what you've been through, I'd say you would probably thrive there."

"Looks can be deceiving, Raifim. I wonder if I could live around beautiful things like your mountains anymore."

The answer caught Raif off guard, and it was a minute before he spoke. Maybe now was the time. "How do you survive living like this?"

"We don't usually live like this. At least the children and I don't. Until now, I never feared for our lives. Our identities were always unknown, as are the identities of the families of others. It is an essential when you do what Mustafa does."

"But the worry . . . the fear of his dying . . ."

"Yes, that is hard to live with, and if I did not believe as much in what Mustafa does as I do, I could not do it."

Raif took a deep breath. "And if he dies? If Beni or Maktub or someone else gets to him? Would you still believe?" He realized as it came out that it sounded harsh, but it was said, and he waited. Her face remained the same, almost passive. He didn't know what to think, what to say, so he let the silence remain. When she finally spoke, it took him aback.

"Allah will be pleased."

He knew what she meant. It was the standard holy war line. He should have expected it, but Hussa was more than Allah's warrior, he was Krisha's husband, the father of Tasli and Raoul! He felt anger build inside him.

"That's all? Allah is pleased?"

"Do you understand, Raifim, that Mustafa's whole existence is dedicated to saving lives?"

"I've never thought of terrorism as life-saving."

"He is not a terrorist," she said evenly. "Let me tell you something about your brother. When he was trained as an intelligence officer in the revolutionary guard, he was sent to the West Bank to help the Palestinians. Contrary to his instructions and at some risk, Mustafa tried to get them to hit only military targets. In their frustration and hate for what had been done to them, and because others like Mulla Maktub had greater influence than Mustafa, his philosophy was rejected and he was forced to back off. He continued as a believer, but I could see a few doubts were haunting his nights. When he was caught, tortured by the Israelis, then freed, he thought surely Maktub was right—the Israelis were the devil's advocates, but he also saw that we were no different, in fact worse, because we tortured not just the enemy but our own kind. It was then he began to take a careful look at what was being done." She sat back in the couch.

"If something is rotten, it isn't hard to become disillusioned once you look at it carefully. That is why men like Maktub hide the truth from people, keep them hating so that they are too busy to look at things, see them as they really are. When Mustafa and I looked past the facade, we discovered that the real enemies to peace were the ones claiming to fight for it with the last ounce of everyone else's blood. The Maktub's and Beni's, the men who lust for power and use the name of Allah to declare their butchery honorable and just—they are the ones who must die, and when a man kills them, is it far-fetched to believe that Allah is pleased?"

"But isn't that the same philosophy that Maktub uses, just on a different scale? He justifies killing Americans in the same way you and Hussa justify killing him. My entire country is considered by him a threat to religious progress, so we must be eliminated." He was shaking his head. "It's only a matter of numbers."

"And innocent lives," Krisha said.

"But who gives you or Maktub the right to judge who is innocent and who is not? Why have laws if we're all going to make ourselves judges anyway? A mass murderer of prostitutes in New York City judges them as a disease on the body of society—isn't he just as justified in his judgment as you or Maktub are in yours?"

"Moral agency, Raifim, the right to choose, is the greatest gift Allah has given mankind. When someone takes this from us, we must fight them, even to death, no matter what laws they may pass upon us. Surely we must try peaceful means first, but when you are dealing with the Maktub's of this world, this doesn't work. Death alone will stop them, and death alone will free the ones they wish to enslave. We must fight for the right to choose, and when some cannot fight for themselves, we must be their soldiers." Tasli tossed and threw off her blanket. Krisha leaned down and gently placed it back on her daughter.

"I know that your American army came to the Middle East to protect its oil interests when they put Sadaam

Hussein in his place and drove him out of Kuwait, but they also freed many people who would have been in bondage to this madman had they not come. This is the only justifiable reason for war, for killing. It is the reason you capture and imprison the mass murderer of prostitutes, and it is the reason we fight Maktub now, together." She smiled. "You and Mustafa are not so different, Raifim. You both fight injustice done to others, to bring violators of human rights to justice. The only difference is that you have a framework of just laws in which to do it. Mustafa does not. He fights an enemy who answers to no law but his own."

There was a noise at the door, and Abdul came in. "My men are in place." He seemed to sense that he was walking into the middle of something and excused himself before disappearing through the door of a small bedroom.

Krisha leaned forward and took Raif's hand. "Raifim, do not misunderstand my feelings for Mustafa. Should he die, a large part of me will die with him, but I am at peace knowing that he will have died for others, for the freedom of my children and the children of many who can't fight the Maktub's of this world themselves." She sat back and a long silence passed between them.

"We must get some rest," Krisha said. "I will sleep here, you—"

"No, you take the bedroom," Raif said.

She started to object.

"I'll call you if the children need something, but you need a good night's rest, Krisha. No argument."

She nodded, stood, and went through the hall door, turning back only to say good night.

Raif slipped off the loafers and stretched out on the couch. The wound in his leg ached a little. It seemed like something old, a nuisance, nothing more, and yet it had happened to him only days before. So much had happened, changed, in those days. It overwhelmed and depressed him, and he tossed and turned for another hour before he halfdozed into a sleep filled with strange and warped images of the last few days. The helicopter that had nearly killed him, the face of Hussa as Raif turned him over, the sound of automatic gunfire. . . . There was something about the gunfire that didn't fit the bizarreness of his dream, and it awakened him.

He sat up carefully and peered out the window. There had been gunfire outside. He was sure of it. Just then Abdul came out of his bedroom with an automatic pistol in hand. He removed a handgun from behind his belt and handed it to Raif as Krisha appeared.

"Take the children. A door in the kitchen leads to the basement. From there you can reach the alley beyond. Go to the docks half a mile down the street. The fishing boat we used to get you from the palace earlier is there, the keys to the ignition in the drawer. If I can I will follow," Abdul said.

Raif hesitated.

"Go!"

Raif scooped up Raoul as Krisha did Tasli.

"Watch the street, there are men in a car out front!" Abdul prompted in a loud whisper.

Gunfire broke out at the front door as they got to the kitchen. Raif turned to go back, but knew he couldn't leave Krisha. Abdul and his men would die to give them time. He had to use it.

They bolted down the stairs to the basement, and Raif was careful to close the door behind them. When they got to the door leading outside, Raif peered into the darkness through the small window in it, but could see no movement. He put Raoul on the floor and told Krisha to wait while he opened the door and stepped into the yard, his weapon ready. He crossed to the ironwork gate.

Gunfire from the front of the building rang loudly, mingling with the panic and confusion coming from outside the fence and on the upper floors of the apartment. While opening the gate and checking the alley, he prayed the innocent would keep their heads down. As he did so, a shadow moved into a thin stream of light from the street near a building across the alley. The man raised a weapon to fire. Raif beat him to it and the man slammed into the wall, his gun clattering to the stone pavement.

Raif quickly used the gun on the gate lock and it sprang open. He signaled Krisha and she came across the yard with Raoul in tow and Tasli in her arms. They were both breathing heavily, scared and unsure. Raif waited, listened. Krisha said something to Tasli in Farsi, put her down and was past Raif and into the alley before he could protest. She crossed to where the gunman lay dead, grabbed the weapon and returned. Pulling back on the lever she checked the chamber, then ejected the clip and made sure it was full before slamming it home.

"You've done this before," Raif said as he watched.

"You go to the corner," Krisha said. "I'll cover you. Take Raoul." She said it as a command, and Raif, trusting her experience, took Raoul and did as he was told. When he reached the corner, he took up a position behind a garbage dumpster and waited while she warily traversed the same ground.

"The dock is down there," Krisha said, pointing along the dark street. "About two hundred yards. Stay in the shadows." Raif picked up Raoul and began running, Krisha at his side with Tasli on her back. They had covered half the distance when Raif heard the screaming of tires and a car turned the corner into the street in front of them and bore down on them. Krisha ran for the sidewalk, keeping low behind the solid line of parked cars along the street. Raif followed her cue, but knew they'd never make it.

"Krisha!" he yelled. "Take Raoul! Get out of sight!" She started to protest.

"Now!" He was already moving back into the street. The car was thirty feet away, its lights blinding him when he raised his handgun and fired. The bullets penetrated the glass as he jumped to the left. His shoulder slammed into the pavement as the car zagged left then right before crashing into two vehicles parked at the curb.

Raif was struggling to his feet when he heard footsteps on the rock pavement and looked up to see another armed man running at him, cursing his parentage in Arabic. Raif had lost the pistol when he dove and had no choice but to find cover. He ran, threw himself over the trunk of the wrecked car and came to a crashing stop on the other side as bullets ripped into the car's gas tank. The explosion threw him away from the vehicle and against the solid rock wall of a fence, knocking him windless. He tried to get up, his ears ringing, head spinning, and lungs gasping for air. Still disoriented, he stood dazed as the man who had come down the street approached around the inferno and raised his black automatic pistol. Raif stood, wondering what it would be like to die, if life after death were really the paradise of Islam or the hell of Christianity.

Then he saw a light and heard an engine. A dark object flying at them from out of nowhere. The man with the gun just stood there a moment with a bewildered look on his face that was nearly comical. Then he acted to save himself and threw his body toward Raif, narrowly avoiding the path of a speeding motorcycle. Raif connected his fist to the man's chin and sent him sprawling against the wall, where he melted to the ground. He turned to see a second cycle pull up, even as the first came to a sliding halt next to Krisha and the kids.

"Get on!" A voice came from beneath the helmet. It was hard to hear over the engine noise, but it was definitely Terri's.

"What the—?"

"Never mind, Raif, just get on!" She shouted.

Raif looked at Krisha who seemed confused. "It's okay," he yelled. "They're friends." Krisha stuck the kids in the sidecar and jumped on behind the other cyclist as Raif looked back up the street where the sounds of gunshots continued to fill the night air.

"Get off," he said to Terri.

"What!"

"I left somebody back there. I have to go back. You aren't coming with me." He pulled on her arm and she got off. He grabbed the handlebars and was quickly aboard, then he saw the unconscious man's gun. He pointed at it. Terri understood and grabbed it for him. He stuck it behind his belt.

"If you get yourself killed down there, I'll never forgive you," she said.

"Me neither. Get aboard the other cycle. I'll meet you back at the gate to the private terminal." He used the gas and had the cycle spinning in a complete circle, then speeding down the street before she could even tell him she loved him.

Raif saw Abdul coming through the back gate. He braked to a halt in front of him and smiled. "Need a ride?"

Abdul's eyes grew wide, and Raif could see he was going to ask the expected question.

"Never mind, just get on." Abdul did. "Anyone else in there?"

"Two of my men. They're pinned down."

"You got any ammo in that weapon?"

"It has a full clip."

Raif handed Abdul his. "I'll drive, see what you can do with both of those."

He twisted the throttle and was at the corner in seconds. Peering around it he could see the enemy guns emitting strands of fire in the darkness from three different locations. "There are two on one side of the street, one on the other. You see 'em?" Raif said.

Abdul nodded, flipping off the safety and gripping the seat with his knees. "You are a friend, Raifim Qanun."

Raif nodded, then accelerated and headed down the center of the street. Abdul began firing.

25

Terri removed her helmet as Bob lifted the kids from the sidecar and Krisha joined Terri. "He is a survivor," Krisha said.

Terri forced a smile, her worried eyes scanning the street leading to the gate. "Yeah, I know, but his nine lives are just about used up."

The guard came through the gate and asked for ID. Bob and Terri presented theirs and Bob began to make excuses for Krisha and the kids.

"Do you want to keep the cycle?" Krisha asked.

Bob saw what she meant and offered it to the guard who glanced over his shoulder at his partner standing just outside the guard house on the inside of the double gate.

Krisha interpreted.

"You had two when you left," one man said.

"Both are yours if these people are allowed through," Bob said. Krisha gave the guard the word.

The man looked down the highway and shrugged. "One is not—" The sound of the cycle caught their ears and the guard grinned. "Two is enough." He opened the gates and Bob took Krisha, Terri, and the children through as Raif and Abdul drove up on the second cycle. Raif wasn't smiling, and as he came to a stop Krisha could see that he was hanging on to an unconscious Abdul's hands to keep him from falling off the machine. She started toward them when Raif waived her off and quickly drove through and went to the plane.

The guard yelled but Bob lifted a hand and told him as best he could that he'd get the cycle in a minute, that one of their group was drunk. Krisha was already running hard toward the plane, and Terri and Bob quickly followed, the two children in their arms.

Raif did the best he could to ease Abdul's fall to the tarmac and was kneeling beside him feeling for a pulse when Krisha joined him. She was the first face Abdul saw when his eyelids lifted. "The children, are they all right?" Abdul said it so softly Krisha had to bend down to hear. She nodded, wiping the tears from her cheeks.

Bob pushed a button on a device in his pocket, and the steps came down. He could see that the guards were getting nervous and starting this way. "Get him inside," he said. "Or we'll be leaving him behind."

Raif tried to pick him up and grimaced. Terri saw that he had been shot in the arm as well and told her father, who helped Krisha with Abdul. The children climbed up the steps after their mother.

"How bad?" Terri asked as she tried to get a look at the wound.

"It matches the one in my leg. Clean through."

The first guard had come up, and Terri pulled the keys from the new cycle and tossed them to him. Satisfied, he turned and said something to his friend, then backed away from the plane.

"He says this one's for his friend. He wants the one with the sidecar," Raif explained.

"That was easy," Bob said.

"Don't hold your breath, we've still got to get out of here. And it won't be any picnic finding someplace to land, even if we do," Raif said.

"You've got friends in high places, remember?" They were climbing the stairs and inside, Abdul was lying on one of the beds, blood already soaking the sheets. Bob retrieved the onboard first-aid kit and handed it to Krisha who had removed her brother's shirt and was using the contents of the kit expertly. Bob had moved the two children to the cockpit where a still sleepy co-pilot was preparing the plane for flight while also keeping them entertained.

Raif sat down, and Terri ripped his shirt away.

"How bad?" Raif asked Krisha.

"Not life-threatening, but he'll need a doctor very soon. There is one in Paris we can trust."

"Paris it is," Bob said.

"He saved my neck," Raif said. "Between us and his men, we'd cleaned them out but there was someone in the car. Someone we hadn't seen. We were just standing near the gate, exhausted, when the man decided to take a shot. Abdul threw himself in front of me and took the bullets."

"And the man in the car?" Krisha asked.

Raif hesitated. "He left me no choice."

C H A P T E R

26

Terri stopped her vehicle next to the barn and quickly buttoned her coat before pulling on leather work gloves. She had come to love this part of her life and was looking forward to getting horses of her own. She had already gone to an architect about building a barn on a piece of property she was looking at, and she had used Raif's as her model.

She pushed the doors open and let the fresh air in as she walked to the light switch and flipped it on. Several of the animals stuck their heads out of their stall doors to look at her. It gave her pleasure to imagine they were as happy to see her as she was to see them.

There were two new tenants in Raif's barn, and she went to them first. They belonged to Sam who had gone to Lander for a few days to see a sick brother.

The smell of horseflesh, mingled with manure, fresh straw, hay, and liniment filled her nostrils as she walked to the end stalls and gave Sam's two animals the once-over. They needed fresh straw, and she went to work.

A noise near the door startled her. "Who's there?"

No answer. Just nerves. They had been back from Turkey more than a week now, and Daniel Beni was still unaccounted for. The fear that he might suddenly show up had given her nightmares and left her jittery. She tried to shake it off. Glancing at her watch, she wondered why Raif wasn't there yet. She tried concentrating on her work.

The Lear had flown into Jackson after leaving Abdul in Paris. Hussa and Raif's parents were there to meet the plane. Terri had never seen a woman as delighted as Sarai Qanun had been when she took her grandchildren into her arms for the first time. The reunion between Krisha and Hussa had been anything but an example of typical Arabic restraint, and Raif had commented about the fact that his brother hadn't completely changed after all. They hugged and kissed like newlyweds, and Krisha had been unable to stop crying. Ray's heart was immediately captured by Raoul, his namesake, and by the time they were in the Suburban provided and protected by Sharps and his men, the little boy had been promised his own horse to ride anytime he wanted. Raif and Terri went with his family, while Terri's father had refueled and flown to Minneapolis to meet with their bankers about his new subsidiary.

Sharps had made immediate arrangements to take Hussa and his family to a safe house near Washington, D.C. for debriefing, and to wait for the mopping up of Beni's American terrorist group. It had been twenty-four hours now since Hussa and his family were whisked out of Raif's life as quickly as they had come.

Describing his conversation with Hussa, Raif had told Terri that they hadn't said much at first, but as they opened up, Hussa had made it clear he would try to return to Iran soon. Somehow, someway he would go back to help the *al Muqanna*. Though his identity was now known, though he would have to convince even his own people he hadn't been the enemy, nor had he sold them out, Mustafa would make no other choice. His life was in Iran. When Raif asked about Krisha and the children, the answer was simple. If he survived the return, they would follow. If he did not, there would be enough money to get them settled here or wherever Krisha wanted. When Raif told Terri that, they had both smiled. Krisha would follow, when she wanted, and whether her husband liked it or not. The hard decision would be whether or not the children would go or stay with their grandparents for a while.

The next day Sharps took them away to Washington, and Sarai and Ray went with them, to look after the children. Terri looked for and found a house to buy in Jackson, a comfortable home sitting on five acres of horse property. And Raif went back to work, hoping Beni would soon be captured and the whole mess could be put to rest. It was late in the game, and Raif was certain Beni would soon play his hand. Terri only hoped they would be ready for him when he did.

She and Raif had met a couple of times for dinner, and he had kept her informed on the happenings of each day as the rest of Beni's organization unraveled. Arrests began with a group of three, well-heeled Americans who had donated money and expertise to Beni's cause. An agent by the name of Simms was discovered to be the FBI insider who nearly got them all killed. He was head of the Middle East desk for the CIA and had made Moen all kinds of promises. Moen had gone along willingly. Both were in custody, Moen was cooperating, and Simms's sordid past was unfolding. He'd been taking money from Iranian *Mullas* since 1990, when he was the CIA's head man in Istanbul. Terri couldn't help but wonder how many Americans and others had died because of his betrayal.

She forced herself to think of other things as she led the first of the two animals back into the stall.

She heard the familiar sound of Raif's pickup outside the barn and after a minute turned to see him come through the doors. The doctor had put Raif's lower arm in a cast that extended to his palm but left the thumb and fingers on his right hand free. He would have to wear the cast for a few weeks.

Terri had determined that any relationship between them would be allowed to develop over time. She would buy her own home and build her own barn, providing them a little distance, but they had committed to study each other's religion, to discuss their questions, and to search together for answers. For her it had been a big victory. She had been through that process, and she had found Christ and his Church. She was hopeful Raif would do the same. But, she had her reservations. Raif was stubborn, which was good and bad, and since the trip to Turkey he had seemed to hold even more tenaciously to his own religion. Before becoming a committed Mormon, she had been stubborn, too, but she hadn't had roots in another faith like Raif did. With everything that needed to be worked out, it was likely to be a lengthy courtship at best.

"Hi," she said, her heart racing. He walked to her and they embraced, then kissed. As always she had to force herself away. However long the process took, it was not going to be easy to keep her heart in check.

"I see you're well on your way to getting the job done. Want me to leave you at it?" he asked.

"Less talk, more work, please," she said.

He went to the Shagya's stall and brought him out, then grabbed a pitchfork. After ten minutes of work, made awkward by his cast, he spoke. "They found Leina Khabur."

The woman terrorist had fled into the mountains. Sam had tried to track her, but another big storm had covered the tracks and forced Sam and his party out of the backcountry. When they went back they hadn't found any sign of her. Terri knew they were still trying.

"Where?"

"Half way the other side of the mountains. Nearly made it out before freezing up like a Popsicle." He shook some hay into the Shagya's manger. "She had a note in her pocket. She and Beni were supposed to lie low until two days ago, then meet in Alpine. He hasn't left the area, Terri, and he must be nervous as a cat on a hot grill."

They worked quickly, finishing the job in less than an

hour. As they left the barn Raif's department radio broke the stillness of the night air. He walked to it and responded. Terri listened.

A man by the name of Beatty had reported a stolen truck, a big diesel rig with a logging trailer behind it. At the time it was loaded with logs, but from what Terri gathered, whoever stole it was probably just after the rig. It was new, loaded, and worth a small fortune in faraway places like Los Angeles.

"Where was it?" Raif asked the dispatcher.

"At his place out south of town. He needs someone to take a report. Everyone else is, well, they're busy on the roadblocks. What with—"

"Let him know I am on my way," Raif said, then hung up the mike.

"You wanna come?"

She smiled. "Are you asking for a date?"

"Doesn't offer much in the way of entertainment, but . . ."

Terri laughed as he stepped aside and let her slide into the seat. "Just being with you is always entertaining, Officer Qanun. I know. I haven't had a single dull moment since we met."

They were quickly headed toward the south end of Jackson by backroads Terri hadn't traveled yet. A few Christmas lights were already hung, and it was a beautiful drive. Raif located Beatty's place and left Terri in the pickup while he went inside the large garage, left empty by the theft, to interview the angry owner. Fifteen minutes later he was back in the seat next to Terri, and they were headed toward the main highway.

"Hungry?" Raif asked.

"Starved."

"We haven't eaten out for nearly twenty-four hours. Wanna try it?"

"Believe it or not, I can cook."

"I believe it. Want to go to a grocery store, grab a few

things, go to your place . . ." His voice trailed off as they came to the stop sign. A large truck loaded with logs rumbled past them, headed south. A heavy, V-shaped snowplow blade decorated the front.

Raif swore as he picked up the mike. He craned his neck trying to get a look at the driver. "This is Qanun, anybody there?"

"We read you, Raif, what's up?" the dispatcher answered.

"I just got a visual on Beatty's truck. It passed me doing about seventy headed toward the Hoback. Better warn the boys down there it's coming. I couldn't make out who was behind the wheel, but I'm betting this is what we've been waiting for." Raif jammed the pickup into reverse, negotiating a three-point turn with reckless abandon. Terri grabbed the arm rest on her door to steady herself.

"Will do, Raif. Any turn-offs before Hoback we need to worry about?" the dispatcher asked.

"I'm in pursuit. I'll try to catch up to him and confirm his position."

The truck's tires spun out on the highway as Raif put the gas pedal down. He flashed a little grimace at Terri. "Hope you don't mind."

"Like I said, never a dull moment."

Another mile and a half and Raif could see the loaded logging truck up ahead. He switched on his flashing blue light. The truck only seemed to speed up. The same thought occurred to both of them. The man behind the wheel of the logging truck just might be Beni. Raif reached under the seat and pulled out his revolver, while Terri tugged her seat belt more tightly across her lap. She could only hope it would soon be over.

* * *

Shad Petersen and half a dozen deputies were making light conversation at the roadblock at Hoback Junction when the radio message came that Beatty's truck had been spotted and was headed in their direction. Traffic on this late December night had been light, and there had been plenty of interludes to sip hot chocolate from the convenience store across the road and swap tales.

One of the young deputies had just told about his first date when the radio crackled with news of the stolen truck. Shad immediately looked up the road toward Jackson and spotted a set of vehicle lights.

"Don't those lights seem high? I mean off the road, high up," the young officer asked.

Shad said, "Beatty's truck is a mean-looking machine. It's got that big, V-shaped snowplow on the front, and those lights are mounted in front of the sleeper cab, up above the blade. Beatty's always bragged he could move anything with that rig."

By then, the lights were only a quarter of a mile away and coming fast.

They reached for their weapons but stood mesmerized as the massive rig bore down on them, picking up even more speed, the blade a threatening menace before it. Just before chaos struck, all of them came to their senses and bolted. They dove over the snowbanks on either side of the road as Beatty's rig rammed the police vehicles with its massive plow, tossing them aside as if they were tin models.

The rig and trailer swerved with the impact, first left, then right, then left again. It began to skid sideways, sliding toward Shad's pickup, the convenience store, and its fuel pumps. By a miracle the driver redirected the heavily loaded logging truck just enough to miss the pumps, but it glanced off a pickup truck and side-swiped two empty vehicles parked in front of the store before coming to a halt in the parking lot. As Shad pulled himself out of the snowbank, Raif's truck, emergency light flashing, hurtled past him then skidded to a stop behind the large rig.

The driver of the logging truck was trying to get going again as Shad ran toward it, racking a shell into his shotgun. The wheels of the truck whined as they spun and the rig slowly nudged free, sliding right then left, jerking the load of logs behind it. By then Raif was out of his truck, holding his gun in his left hand and running alongside the load toward the truck's cab, then jumping aside to avoid being run over by the swerving vehicle. As the truck halted, Raif fired his gun, shattering the rearview mirror on the driver's side. His round was answered by a burst of shots from an automatic weapon directed out the window of the cab of the truck. Shad and Raif dove for cover behind the trailer as the truck's wheels caught hold of solid highway and the rig lurched ahead.

Refusing to let the maniac get away, Raif jumped, reaching for one of three or four logs that extended beyond the rear wheels of the trailer. With his cast impeding his mobility, he dropped his weapon and dragged himself up onto the load as the truck began picking up speed. Shad watched helplessly as the truck moved into the darkness, with Raif struggling to secure a hold.

* * *

Hanging on, Raif glanced back at the mayhem the rig had created. The road was cluttered with broken cars and twisted metal. His own vehicle was still operable, but it would take time to clear a path.

He grabbed another log and eased his way up the load, the highway passing below him more rapidly with each passing second. The wind from the speeding truck stung his face and small bits of bark blowing off the logs blurred his vision. Leaning to the right and squinting, he took a cautious peek at the rearview mirror to look inside the cab.

Though the cab of the truck was dimly lit, he was certain the driver was Daniel Beni, silver hair and all.

Even though Raif felt Beni had no idea he had a passenger, he knew trying to climb inside the cab would only get him shot. He ducked back, eyeing the huge chains holding the logs together and wondering what would happen if he loosened them, let the load go . . . but could he get off in time? One thing was sure, he had to stop the truck before Beni either got away or killed someone with that deadly blade on the front of the rig.

The load swayed and groaned as the logs grated together. Some of the logs were longer than others, and he was huddled in one of the gaps at the back of the load. Taking a deep breath and imagining himself being bucked off the speeding load or being crushed between the heavy logs, he climbed to the top. As he did, he saw a metal crate jammed between the logs. A missile. His jaw turned to granite. He would have to undo the back chain first.

He found the come-along holding the two ends of the chain together, and using the shift of the load to gain a little slack, Raif tried to open it. On the third effort it flipped open and the load shifted, the logs separating. He lunged forward, reaching with his good hand for the stump of a branch on one of the logs, struggling to keep from falling into the space between the logs. He knew that if he slipped, it meant certain death under the truck's back wheels. He grasped another branch, then another, pulling himself forward as the logs continued to strain against the holding power of the remaining forward chain and outside stiles.

Raif needed a safer position, but before he could move, the driver shifted down and the truck began to slow. Beni had felt the load shift, seen the break-away, and was probably cursing a weak link or a faulty latch. Knowing he didn't have much time, Raif struggled to the top of the shifting pile and grabbed the remaining latch. He lifted with all his strength. Nothing. Again. Nothing. The stress against the chain was too great. He would never get it to release, but it didn't matter. The load was going, slowly, but it was going! He knew he had to get off.

The truck veered left, then back. To keep from falling, Raif sprawled onto one of the logs, wrapping his arms and legs around it. The log shifted, jutting out at an angle from the rest of the failing load on the right side of the truck. His broken arm slammed against a log shooting an excruciating pain all the way to his shoulder.

He hung on to the underside of the log with his legs and one arm as the trucked veered further right, sending him dangerously close to the plowed embankment and nearly scraping him off.

Hanging on for his life, he glanced up toward the cab and found himself looking in the rearview mirror. Beni's eyes locked with his, and an evil grin creased Beni's lips. Raif braced himself as Beni jerked on the wheel, throwing the load right and hanging Raif even further out in space. Though dizzy with pain, Raif saw the icy bank coming at him and hung on grimly as the top of the bank of snow clipped at the log and his body.

The truck veered again; throwing the log back toward the load. Raif hung on with his legs and used his arm to grab for another in the pile, but missed. He could feel his log was about to go, and knew he had only seconds to live. Quickly he shinnied forward on the log and made a desperate grab at a vertical stile holding the front of the load. He missed the first time, but got a handhold the second. Using all his strength, he pulled himself onto the load just as the log slipped from beneath him and tumbled away.

It landed in the highway behind them, bounced crazily, then rolled and disappeared in the darkness. Then another left the load, and another. Holding his injured arm Raif scrambled up the remaining logs as the load unraveled beneath his feet. Holding onto the forward post, he swung around it, and threw himself on top of the truck's sleeper as the forward chain burst and the entire load bucked free and into the oncoming lane.

Raif felt the cab lurch as the trailer buckled out of control and began to spin on the snow-packed highway. He knew he had no choice but to get off. As the cab started to lift, Raif launched himself toward the snow piled along the road. He hit, felt the pain clear to his toes, bounced, rolled down the side of the embankment, and skidded for nearly fifty feet on the snow-covered road before coming to a halt against the cold embankment.

On the other side of the road, and a quarter mile farther on, the truck exploded and sent a fireball shooting into the sky. Metal and burning debris fell from the air and clattered around Raif's motionless body.

* * *

With Shad behind the wheel, Raif's truck weaved its way through the scattered logs, to a point where the road was entirely blocked a hundred yards away from the wreck. Her heart in her throat, Terri jumped out of the truck and ran forward.

She caught a glimpse of the driver first, but there was no help for him. His body was still sitting in the seat of the rig, now a part of a very large candle burning against a dark sky.

She found Raif with his back against a snowbank watching the flames, his right arm askew and sitting gingerly in his lap. Blood streaked his face and clothes from several cuts in his cheeks and scalp. She went quickly to his side, kneeling next to him, wanting to reach out and touch him but not daring, biting her lip against the tears.

He smiled tiredly at her and asked, "You wouldn't have a couple of Tylenol would you?"

Her tears gave way to a smile and she slumped down next to Raif on the snowy road. Together they stared at the melting rig. After a time, she remarked, "It would have been a better bonfire if you'd left the trees aboard."

Raif nodded, "I'll be more careful next time."

Shad joined them. Raif smiled up at him. "Get on the line and tell the sheriff. If I'm not mistaken, we'll find the missiles in the wreckage of those metal cases." He pointed to the logs strewn on the road. Several cases of high-impact metal could be seen among them.

Shad headed back to the pickup, and Terri laid her head on Raif's shoulder. After several moments of silence, she said, "Promise me something, Raif Qanun."

"Yeah, anything."

"Promise me it's over."

He laughed lightly as he put his good arm around her shoulder and pulled her close. "Yeah," he said. "Yeah, it's over. I promise."

Too tired to move, they sat quietly and waited for the ambulance. Terri didn't know what the future would hold, but for the first time since meeting Raif Qanun she figured it would be less perilous than their past.

She looked at the burning rig and shuddered. Dead as he was, Beni and his kind still had the world by the throat—forcing people to live in fear of terrorism. But at least Beni would give no one else that kind of pain, and if there was a hell that evened things out, that made a man or a woman pay for what they did to others, well . . . she hoped Beni would be there a long, long time.

She helped Raif to his feet and together they hobbled back toward the oncoming flashing lights. It was time to go home.